A DANGEROUS DESIRE

"God, but you're beautiful—you know that, don't you?" he asked huskily.

There was no mistaking the desire in his voice. She knew she ought to turn back while she could, and yet as his hands moved up her arms, her pulse pounded, drowning out reason.

Her eyes were large and luminous in the darkness, then they closed as his hand lifted her chin. "So beautiful," he whispered thickly.

As his head bent nearer, she could feel the caressing warmth of his breath on her skin. It was as though they were the only people in the world, as though time itself paused. She hesitated, then she slid her arms around his waist, returning his embrace.

It was all the encouragement he needed. She was soft, yielding, and so close he could feel the swell of her breasts pressed against his chest, her heartbeat through his shirt. And he forgot who she was and what she stood for. Tonight she was the woman of his vision, and that was all that mattered.

◆↑◆ TOPAZ

DANGEROUS DESIRE

☐ **FALLING STARS by Anita Mills.** In a game of danger and desire where the stakes are shockingly high, the key cards are hidden, and love holds the final startling trump, Kate Winstead must choose between a husband she does not trust and a libertine lord who makes her doubt herself.
(403657—$4.99)

☐ **SWEET AWAKENING by Marjorie Farrell.** Lord Justin Rainsborough dazzled lovely Lady Clare Dysart with his charm and intoxicated her with his passion. Only when she was bound to him in wedlock did she discover his violent side ... the side of him that led to his violent demise. Lord Giles Whitton, Clare's childhood friend, was the complete opposite of Justin. But it would take a miracle to make her feel anew the sweet heat of desire—a miracle called love. (404920—$4.99)

☐ **LORD HARRY by Catherine Coulter.** When Henrietta Rolland discovers that a notorious rake, Jason Cavander, is responsible for her brother's death at Waterloo, she sets out to avenge her dead brother. Henrietta disguises herself as the fictitious Lord Harry Monteith, hoping to fool Cavander and challenge him to a duel. But the time comes when all pretenses are stripped away, as Henrietta and Jason experience how powerful true love can be. (405919—$5.99)

Prices slightly higher in Canada

Buy them at your local bookstore or use this convenient coupon for ordering.

PENGUIN USA
P.O. Box 999 — Dept. #17109
Bergenfield, New Jersey 07621

Please send me the books I have checked above.
I am enclosing $_____ (please add $2.00 to cover postage and handling). Send check or money order (no cash or C.O.D.'s) or charge by Mastercard or VISA (with a $15.00 minimum). Prices and numbers are subject to change without notice.

Card #_____ Exp. Date _____
Signature_____
Name_____
Address_____
City _____ State _____ Zip Code _____

For faster service when ordering by credit card call **1-800-253-6476**

Allow a minimum of 4-6 weeks for delivery. This offer is subject to change without notice.

COMANCHE MOON

by

Anita Mills

A TOPAZ BOOK

TOPAZ
Published by the Penguin Group
Penguin Books USA Inc., 375 Hudson Street,
New York, New York 10014, U.S.A.
Penguin Books Ltd, 27 Wrights Lane,
London W8 5TZ, England
Penguin Books Australia Ltd, Ringwood,
Victoria, Australia
Penguin Books Canada Ltd, 10 Alcorn Avenue,
Toronto, Ontario, Canada M4V 3B2
Penguin Books (N.Z.) Ltd, 182–190 Wairau Road,
Auckland 10, New Zealand

Penguin Books Ltd, Registered Offices:
Harmondsworth, Middlesex, England

First published by Topaz, an imprint of Dutton Signet,
a division of Penguin Books USA Inc.

First Printing, July, 1995
10 9 8 7 6 5 4 3 2 1

This book is dedicated to my agent,
Denise Marcil,
who has always believed in me.
Thanks, Denise.

Boston: June, 1873

"I am sorry, Maria," the young man said softly as she reread her step-uncle's awkwardly phrased letter. "I did not wish you to be alone at such a time."

Guilt washed over Amanda Mary Ross, followed by an empty ache beneath her breastbone. Her aloof, aristocratic Spanish mother was dead. She closed her eyes and sat very still, recalling the bitterness between them, the bitterness that had kept them estranged for nearly ten years. If she lived to be a hundred years old, she did not think she would ever forget the day her mother had tried to explain why she was marrying Gregorio Sandoval. "He is like me—we are both of the old families—we are not Anglos, Maria," she'd said. "Please try to understand—as much as I loved your father, we were of different worlds. And I am not a young girl any longer."

The plea had fallen on the eleven-year-old girl's deaf ears, for she had idolized Big John Ross, and she bitterly resented the unctuous Señor Sandoval. But Gregorio and her mother never understood Amanda's bitter opposition. "Maria," Gregorio had assured her, "no matter what happens, the Ybarra-Ross will be yours. I have accepted that Doña Isabella can bear no more children."

In the end, the rancor between mother and daughter had been too much for either of them, and Amanda had been sent to live with her father's sister, Katherine Ross Ryan, in Boston, ostensibly for a good Catholic education, but after graduating she'd never returned.

She'd never wanted to. Without Big John, she told herself, the sprawling Ybarra-Ross was nothing to her.

She looked down at the letter again and shivered almost convulsively at Alessandro Sandoval's words. "Your mother and my brother had not the chance," he'd written. "They were discovered out alone by the Comanche devils. Gregorio we buried where we found him, but your mother was not so fortunate, and they took her captive. By God's mercy, she died before they reached the Pecos River, and we were able to bring her back to Ybarra for a proper Catholic burial. You will be pleased to know that we meted out God's punishment to the war party that took her, may they all rot in hell."

"I am so sorry, Maria," Ramon repeated, cutting into her thoughts. "My father had hoped to ransom Tía Isabella through the Comancheros, but it was too late. The Indians killed her when she could not keep up with them. But at least none of those savages got back across the Pecos alive."

"Yes, of course," she said tonelessly. She looked up, catching the sympathy in his dark eyes, and she blinked back tears. "Poor Mama. She was so afraid of Indians," she whispered. "So very afraid of them. God only knows what terror she must have felt."

"And with reason. For what it means to you, Gregorio fought to save her. He was tortured unspeakably before they killed him." Ramon shuddered visibly. "They are devils, Maria, devils. If it had not been for his boots, we could not have recognized my uncle."

Gregorio Sandoval was dead. A brief image of her handsome stepfather passed through her mind and was gone. While she had resented him, she had certainly never wished him to die. "I shall, of course, write my condolences to your father," she managed. "The loss of his brother must've been a terrible shock to him."

"Write to him?" For a moment Ramon stared blankly at her, then he recovered. "No, Maria, you do not understand. I am here to take you home to Texas.

The Ybarra is yours now. You must come home to it—you *must*. I have traveled all this way for that reason."

"The Ybarra-*Ross*, you mean," she reminded him. "It was my father who made it what it is. Without John Ross it would still be nothing but a desert full of rattlesnakes."

"Forgive me, Maria—it was not my intent to slight Señor Ross, I assure you," he said quickly. "If I have called it the Ybarra merely, it is that your mother's family held it long before Señor Ross was born," he added smoothly. "To us, it has always been the Ybarra."

The Ybarra-Ross. One hundred eighty-five thousand acres of rugged rock and treacherous desert claimed by ancestors too far away to realize the danger of Indians. It wasn't until after his marriage to Isabella de Bivar y Colona-Ybarra that Big John had made a vast but seemingly useless stretch of land into a prosperous cattle ranch right in the heart of a Comanche war trail.

While he'd lived, the Indians skirted it, never actually daring to attack the high adobe-walled fortress he'd built there. Instead, they'd contented themselves with butchering a few longhorns for food and continuing their raids farther south. And as for rustlers coming up from Mexico, most of them had wound up swinging from a stout rope. To Indian and Mexican alike, John Ross was the law on the Ybarra-Ross.

She swallowed, fighting the pain she still felt every time she thought of him. "My father loved Mama, you know," she said softly. "He wanted to give her everything. Aunt Kate told me he was smitten the first time he saw her." Her mouth twisted as she tried to smile at the memory. "They eloped, Mama said. She was so very beautiful then, and he would not wait long enough to persuade my grandfather that he was worthy of her. She was only sixteen then, and he was twenty-five."

His hand clasped her shoulder comfortingly. "Come back to Ybarra-Ross, Maria," he coaxed. "It is your home." When she did not answer, he looked directly into her eyes. "For Tía Isabella. For Señor Ross. For my father. For *me*, Maria." As her eyes widened at the intense warmth in his, he released her and stood back. "It is yours, and we wish to help you take your place there."

"There you are, Amanda," Aunt Kate murmured, coming into the formal parlor. Taking off her kid gloves, she began untying her fashionable bonnet. Setting the hat on a table, she smiled brightly. "You really should have gone with me, dearest. Mrs. Rush was quite right—there was imported lace to be had for four cents to the yard, and the best French velvet was selling for a dollar and a half. Oh, I know it is out of season, but it is never too early to think ahead. Who knows . . . ," she added slyly, "but what you might be making up your trousseau quite soon. All of the Donnellys are quite taken with you, you know—I had that from Margaret herself."

"Aunt Kate . . ."

It was then that Kate Ryan noticed Ramon Sandoval. For a moment she was at a loss, then she recovered enough to smile. "Well, gracious, what you must think, sir—Charles did not tell me we had company." Looking to Amanda, she chided, "You might have stopped me from rattling on long enough to present the gentleman."

"Aunt Kate, Mama is dead."

The older woman's smile froze, then faded. "Dead?" she echoed hollowly. "But she cannot be—I mean, she wasn't even forty. Surely—"

"She was murdered by Comanche devils," Ramon explained.

"Indians!" As the import of his words sank in, Kate Ryan collapsed into the nearest chair. "Oh no! Oh, my poor Isabella! She was such a lovely creature—so refined—so elegant—"

"And they killed Uncle Gregorio also, señora."

"Poor Isabella," she said again. "Of course I did not know him—Señor Sandoval, that is—but I would not wish—Comanches! How utterly awful!" She looked up at him. "You are one of the Sandovals, then?"

He bowed slightly. "Ramon Sandoval. My father has managed the Ybarra . . . the Ybarra-Ross," he corrected himself hastily, ". . . for the last five years, señora."

"But I thought Isabella's husband—"

"Uncle Gregorio did not have the heart or head for the cattle business, so Aunt Isabella engaged my father to help with everything. And he did very well for her, señora. Last year we shipped five thousand head of cattle to Chicago—and that did not include the beeves we sold by contract to the government," he added proudly.

"My brother always said there was a fortune to be made in Texas, but it seems as though the money is cursed," the older woman murmured, shaking her head. "Johnny did not live long enough to enjoy all that he worked for," she said sadly. "And now poor Bella." Turning her attention back to her niece, she clucked sympathetically. "Oh, my poor dear, I am so sorry."

"I know. It just doesn't seem possible, does it?"

"It is the God's truth, Maria," Ramon insisted. "I am saddened to be the bearer of the news, but my father did not want you to be alone when you read his letter."

"Well, we must not dwell on the circumstances, but rather on the fact that no matter what she endured, your mother is in God's care now. And we shall, of course, have a memorial Mass said for her," Kate decided.

"Yes, that would please Mama."

Her aunt rose and went to Amanda. Clasping the younger woman's hands, she squeezed her fingers reassuringly. "Would it help if Charles sent for Father Riley? Or for Mr. Donnelly?" she asked gently.

Again, Amanda felt empty and guilty. She shook her head. "No—now that I have been told, I should rather be alone."

Ramon Sandoval reluctantly reached for his hat. "You must think about Ybarra-Ross, Maria. I will call again tomorrow and we will plan the best way to get you home."

"Amanda, surely you aren't thinking of returning to Texas!" Kate gasped. "Not after this . . . this terrible thing!" But as she looked into her niece's eyes, she felt a certain foreboding. "Besides, what of Mr. Donnelly?" she argued. "After all, it is common knowledge that he expects to marry you and . . . and . . . well, it simply won't do to jilt him! Not when he has been *most* particular in his attentions, dearest. Why, there are girls all over Boston who would give their eyeteeth to snatch Patrick Donnelly. Charles says there is no other young man in Boston with half so much promise!"

"Please, Aunt Kate—I don't want to think about that just now."

"Señora, I will take care of Maria," Ramon promised. "She will be safe with me."

Kate Ryan's expression hardened. "Mr. Sandoval—"

"Please—not *now*. I have a headache, and I just want to go to my room."

"But—" Realizing that she risked setting Amanda's back up, Kate retreated. "Yes, of course, dearest." Turning to face Ramon, she extended her hand half-heartedly. "When you come tomorrow, you really must stay for dinner—provided there is no more talk of taking my niece to Texas, of course. Good day, Mr. Sandoval."

Having been so quickly dismissed, there was nothing he could do but bow over her hand. "Until then, señora." To Amanda, he nodded. "I shall count the hours," he declared, smiling warmly. "Despite the sadness of my mission, it has been a pleasure to discover my lovely cousin."

As the door closed behind him, Kate exhaled her relief. "Well, I must say he behaves rather familiarly, doesn't he? A cousin, he called you, when it is no such thing. Do you even remember him from Texas?"

"No. But perhaps he considered step-cousin a bit standoffish."

"Just the same, lest he gets any notions, I shall expect you to scotch them right in the bud. Oh, dear—I think Mr. Donnelly is to be dining with us tomorrow. And what he is to think of Mr. Sandoval—well, I am sure I don't know. Perhaps I ought to warn him, for I cannot think he knows any Mexicans."

"Why would he have to think anything?" Amanda asked, betraying a certain annoyance. "And the Sandovals are Spanish—like my mother."

"Well, I don't know, but I wouldn't want him to believe Mr. Sandoval any sort of rival."

"I have no interest in either of them, Aunt Kate," the younger woman responded tiredly. "Indeed, I find Patrick too full of conceit for bearing. I can scarce get my own opinion into any conversation. Not that he cares, of course, for he quite expects everyone to agree with him."

"Amanda Mary Ross, how dare you say such a thing? Why, he's going to have a brilliant career in politics! You ought to be on your knees before the Blessed Virgin, thanking her for his interest in you! Patrick Donnelly is everything I could wish for you—everything!"

"Aunt Kate—"

"And if you must know, I have prayed and lit two candles every evening for a twelvemonth, just hoping he would notice you," the older woman admitted. Seeing the mutinous set of Amanda's jaw, she added defensively, "Well, I had to do something—it is one and twenty you are already. In another year or two there'll be none eligible as will look at you, and you'll have to be settling for a widower like Mr. Kelly—and him with five children already."

"If Pat Donnelly is the best your prayers can get me, I'd as soon you spared the breath," Amanda muttered. "And I would never consider Mr. Kelly—with or without the children."

"Here—is that any way to be talking? If John Ross were alive, he'd already have attended to the business. Indeed, Isabella wasn't even seventeen when she caught his eye, and—"

"I don't want to hear about Mama just now. Or Papa either. Please—I do have a headache."

Kate's manner changed abruptly. "Oh, my poor child! What am I thinking of?—and at a time like this! Are you quite certain you don't want to have Father Riley come?"

"Yes." Rising, Amanda took a step toward the door. "I shall be in my room."

"Yes, of course. What you must be feeling . . . why, I—"

Amanda cut her off. "Right now, I feel nothing but sadness for Mama. She scarce wrote to me after she married Gregorio. Sometimes, I have thought she wanted to forget Papa so much that she forgot me."

"Now how can you be saying that, I ask you? Your Mama *loved* Johnny, and well you know it! And if she didn't mourn him the way you wanted, well, just perhaps she was like you and couldn't deal with her grief."

"I cried for Papa for a year, Aunt Kate. And if she loved him so much, she wouldn't have gotten herself another husband."

"Now there you are wrong. If anything, Isabella loved John too much. She was far too lonely after his death. I only wish she would have come back here for a while, for I am sure I could have helped her."

"She was so lonely that she could not wait a decent year after Papa died to marry again," Amanda muttered. "But I don't want to talk about it. If you don't mind, would you ask Molly to make me some willow bark tea for my headache?"

Making good her escape, she climbed the stairs to her room, where she sat facing the lace-curtained window, looking out over the garden below. The sun shone brightly, as though everything was right with the world, as though it didn't care that Isabella Sandoval had left it.

For a long time she did not move, telling herself that it didn't matter, that her mother had loved Gregorio more than her. She closed her eyes, trying to recall Isabella—her perfect profile, her shining black hair, her delicate olive skin, her petite, slender figure. The image of her mother came to her, and once again she felt the brief brush of Isabella's lips on her cheek, her last kiss before she left for Boston.

When she'd been small, when Big John had still been alive, she'd wanted to be just like her mother. But it hadn't happened. No, she was tall, and instead of black hair, hers was auburn like Big John's. Instead of her mother's perfect complexion, she'd inherited her father's fairness down to the smattering of freckles across her nose. All she'd gotten of the Ybarras were her brown eyes, and even those weren't nearly so dark as she remembered her mother's.

What a pair they'd made—the beautiful Isabella and the big, handsome Irishman. Even after more than ten years Amanda still couldn't think of him without wanting to cry. While her mother had given birth to her, it had been Big John who'd given her life, who'd cherished her, who'd shared his great, grand plans for Ybarra-Ross with his daughter.

And he'd made Ybarra-Ross, like everything about him, seem bigger and better than anything else. There were three things in this world he'd found worth loving, he'd told her—his wife, his daughter, and his land.

Tears welled in her eyes, spilling over—tears not only for him, but now also for her mother. Leaning forward, she rested her head against the windowsill and finally let a dam of ten years' making break. And once it happened, she cried and cried, sobbing until her breath came in gasps. Big John was gone forever. And she'd never see her mother again, not even to make peace with her. All that was left of them was the Ybarra-Ross they'd both loved.

"Amanda?" Her aunt followed with a rap on the door. "Amanda, Mr. Donnelly has come to see you," she called through the door. "He wishes to express his condolences to you."

"How does he know?" Amanda sat up and wiped at her wet face with the back of her hand.

"Well, I thought—" As she came into the room, Kate's words died on her lips. "Oh, Amanda, love—"

But the younger woman pushed her away. "Aunt Kate, I *told* you—"

"Yes, but I was sure he would want to know. And he came right over, just as I knew he would. When a man cares for a woman, he wants to ease her sorrows."

Sucking in a deep breath, Amanda regained control of herself. "I should rather keep my cares to myself," she declared, sniffing back the last of her tears.

"If John were alive today, he could not have found a better man. And—"

"I know," the girl cut in wearily. "I'm not getting any younger, and as you have pointed out, pretty soon there will only be Mr. Kelly."

"Exactly."

But as she said it, Amanda could almost see the portrait of her and Patrick Donnelly surrounded by well-scrubbed children, the perfect Irish Catholic family sitting in the pews every Sunday, and she shuddered. If she married the dominating Mr. Donnelly, she'd never be allowed another original thought. No, there was too much of Big John in her for that.

"Tell him . . ." She hesitated for a moment, then decided. "No, I shall tell him myself and be done with it." Clasping her hands together for courage, she dared to meet her aunt's gaze. "I hope Patrick Donnelly becomes mayor of Boston one day, but I'm afraid I won't be here to see it happen." As she heard her own words, she drew a certain courage from them. "I own the Ybarra-Ross, Aunt Kate, and I think now that Mama is dead, Big John would wish me to go home. One of us ought to be there, and I'm the only one left."

"But—"

"Oh, I know I must sound ungrateful, but I cannot quite see Mr. Donnelly riding a horse across West Texas. He would have to sweat, you see, and I am not at all sure he is capable of doing it."

"Amanda Mary Ross, you cannot be serious!"

"I'm going back to Texas, Aunt Kate."

"To a place where only heathen Comanches and wild animals can live!"

"I know. But it is mine," Amanda answered simply.

"Whatever are you going to tell Mr. Donnelly?" her aunt wailed.

"That I'm going home."

"Maria." Ramon shook her shoulder gently, trying to wake her. "Maria, we are nearly to the station."

At first, she'd been so lost in her dreams that she didn't respond to the name. Maria was someone else. She was Amanda Mary—even the sisters at school had called her that. Not Amanda. Amanda Mary, for her second name was for the Virgin. She turned her head against the hard leather of the stagecoach seat and tried to remember, but the dream did not return.

"Maria, you need to eat."

"Not Maria," she mumbled sleepily. "Amanda."

"Tía Isabella called you Maria," he insisted. "Always Maria."

Reluctantly, she sat up and leaned forward, stretching an arm still numbed by sleep, clasping her hands in an effort to ease her cramped shoulders. Yawning, she asked, "Where are we, anyway?"

"We are stopping to eat and change horses." He looked out the window briefly, then added, "Please do not be too friendly to anyone here, Maria. Only very rough people run stagecoach stations in this part of Texas."

"I don't suppose it matters where we are," she decided wearily.

"If nothing happens to slow us down, we will be sleeping at Fort Stockton tonight," he promised.

If nothing happens. It seemed like nearly everything that could possibly happen had already befallen them.

The only other misery she could think of just now would be Indians attacking the coach. And with only a driver, one lone guard, and Ramon left to defend it, that prospect was altogether daunting.

She closed her eyes for a moment, thinking she felt as though she'd been traveling for months rather than weeks. Oh, how she wished she'd never consented to taking the old Panhandle Route, or whatever it was called, no matter how much Ramon had insisted it was safer for a "lady of means." Given what she'd encountered since leaving the comforts of her aunt's house, she had to wonder now how those possessed of less fortune managed the journey at all.

After the six days by train from Boston through Ohio, Kentucky, Tennessee, and Mississippi to New Orleans, there had been the steamer crossing to Galveston, then the eighteen-dollar-a-head ride in a hot, airless railroad car crowded with sweat-soaked cowboys playing California Jack with packs of dirty, greasy cards. The only thing worse than their disgraceful cursing had been their tendency to spit tobacco juice onto the floor until she'd had to lift her full skirt and petticoats to walk down the narrow aisle lest she soil her clothes with the nasty stuff. Finally, she'd complained to the conductor, who declared stoutly that he was not about to take his life in his hands by confronting them over so minor a matter.

The final straw on that leg of the journey had been a break in the tracks near someplace called Eagle Lake, where they'd all been emptied out to spend the night in makeshift tents. The punchers, as the cowboys were called, had drunk heavily, sang loudly, and punctuated their verses with gunfire until every last one of them finally sank into a snoring stupor. When at last dawn broke, she wandered outside to discover that the place had neither eagles nor a lake to recommend it.

Taken by wagons into Columbus, Texas, they'd spent the next night in a ramshackle place where the only thing worse than the mosquitoes was the bedbugs.

There, seeing the light beneath her door, Ramon had mistakenly thought her frightened and had wanted to share the room with her—"for your protection, Maria." Of course, she'd declined, snapping that if she couldn't have any comfort, she still preferred to have a decent reputation.

By the time the rails were repaired, she was tired, cranky, and completely disgusted with her overly attentive step-cousin. And she had still faced that final leg of public conveyance, a cramped stagecoach with yet another ugly assortment of men of low degree. And now, even though the last unkempt fellow had gotten off one stop earlier, the air within the passenger compartment smelled of stale smoke, whiskey, and the lingering odor of male sweat. Everything combined, it was enough to make her think longingly of Boston— and almost fondly of the conceited Patrick Donnelly. At least he neither swore nor spat, and he was far too fastidious to allow himself to perspire.

Thinking she suffered excessively from the heat, Ramon picked up his folded newspaper and fanned her, cooling the damp tendrils of hair that clung to her forehead. "You are all right, Maria?" he asked solicitously.

"I had forgotten how big Texas is—and how hot it is in July," she muttered. "I don't remember it being this unbearable at Ybarra-Ross."

He shrugged. "Ah, Maria, there are days when food can be cooked on rocks without a fire. But once you become used to it again, you will not mind the weather, I swear it." He dropped the paper and reached to possess her hands, saying earnestly, "It will be different now, for you are the mistress of Ybarra, Maria, and everyone will take care of you. You will have nothing to do but be the beautiful señora, while Papa and I tend to the *ranchero*."

She pulled her hands away. "I just want to get there," she said shortly. But she wanted to scream at him that it was the Ybarra-*Ross*, that her name was Amanda, not Maria. But it would do no good. She'd already said it a hundred times and more, and still he persisted. "I have no interest in being a beautiful señora, Ramon," she added tersely. "I am more like Big John than like my mother, I assure you."

He looked hurt. "I have offended you, Maria," he said softly.

She was hot, tired, and cross, and she knew it. "No," she said, "It is the heat more than anything."

"Maria . . ." He leaned forward, and as his dark eyes met hers, he took her hands again. "I know you will say it is too soon, but perhaps I too am like Big John Ross was with Tía Isabella." He placed one of her hands against his chest. "I look at you, and I feel something here."

"You are hungry," she muttered, once again retrieving her fingers from his damp clasp.

"No . . . no, you mistake me. I am full with—"

She cut him off quickly. "Perhaps a bromide might settle your stomach. I am sure if you asked the proprietor here—"

For a moment he was perplexed, then he reddened. "It is not that," he said quickly. "Ever since my eyes have seen you, I—"

Deciding he was beyond being deterred, she leaned across the seat and wrenched the door open. "Well, whatever ails you, I expect you will feel better when you are out in the air," she declared briskly.

"You are not like your mother at all," he said, sighing. "She had the Spanish soul."

"I'm afraid I don't remember that either, but then I was still a child when last I saw her." As the station attendant placed the small step on the ground, she took advantage of it. Looking back at the chagrined Ramon, she gave him a thin smile. "Since you will wish to walk about to settle your stomach, I shall go on inside and order something to eat. I hope they will have something better than beans and a fried tortilla, for I am sick of them."

With that she twitched her blue twilled silk walking

skirt into place, smoothed the frilled jabot at the neck of her white cotton waist, and readjusted the basque points of her perfectly tailored jacket, pulling them down at her hips. Tucking a loose tendril of auburn hair behind her ear, she started toward the door of the bullet-pocked station.

"Well, I'll be goddamned!" the station man said loudly. "Now if that ain't a sight—whoooeee!" His words ended in a whistle.

"I'd very much prefer that you keep your profane language to yourself," she retorted, turning around. Realizing suddenly that he wasn't looking at her at all, she bit back the rest of the acid setdown she'd been about to give him. Shading her eyes against the blazing sun, she followed his gaze curiously until she saw what he saw. Momentarily forgetting her own manners, she stared.

Crossing the dusty desert toward them, a solitary man rode, his shoulders hunched over his pommel, his right arm cradling a double-barreled shotgun. His face was as dark as the so-called tame Indians she'd encountered near Columbus, but the hair that fell over his shoulders had been bleached white–blond by the sun. Her gaze moved from a black frock coat to buckskin leggings and fringed moccasins. And if his dress were not ludicrous enough, he was too tall for the spotted pony he rode, so much so that his legs dangled within a foot of the ground. Behind him, led by a rope tied to the saddlehorn, a mule followed doggedly, bearing a man's body tied over the packs with a rope.

"Good God, that's McAlester, ain't it, Sam?" someone said.

"Yeah, it's him all right."

One of the men unharnessing the tired team stopped to look, then shook his head. "Poor bastard must've been worth a lot," he decided. "He usually don't bother bringin' 'em in."

"Yeah." The man called Sam straightened his shoulders. "Guess we ought to go inside—he ain't a man as likes to be watched none." But even as he said it, he didn't move.

The rider stopped a scant ten feet from Amanda, and as he dismounted, shotgun in hand, she got a good look at him, and it was enough to give her heart pause. He had the strong, well-chiseled features of a Greco-Roman god, and a build that would have done an ancient sculptor proud. He was facing her, his coat open, showing two gunbelts crossed over a collarless white shirt unbuttoned several inches at the neck. But it was the eyes that sent a shiver through her. They were an icy blue, and they were utterly devoid of emotion. It was as though he didn't know they all watched him.

Apparently, Sam shared her thoughts, for he muttered under his breath, "Damn, but he's got them killer eyes."

Without speaking to anybody, McAlester turned back to the mule and loosened the ropes. The macabre load slid to the ground like a sack of sand to lay facedown in the dirt. To her disgust, he turned it over with his foot.

"Get up," he ordered curtly. When the body did not move, he kicked it in the ribs so hard that she could hear the air whoosh from a man's lungs and she saw manacled hands come up defensively. What she'd first thought to be a dead man was in fact a prisoner. When the man in the frock coat kicked him again, she felt compelled to intervene.

"*Mister* McAlester," she called out clearly, drawing herself up to her full five feet five inches, "it ought to be obvious to you that he cannot stand."

Ignoring her, McAlester continued to regard his prisoner contemptuously while the fellow rolled over and retched. Finally, he reached down, grasped the man's filthy shirt, and pulled him up by the back of it. When it appeared that the man couldn't or wouldn't walk, he gave him a shove toward the adobe building.

Amanda turned to the station man. "Did you see that?" she demanded indignantly.

"Yeah," he grunted.

She stared incredulously. "Well, aren't you doing to *do* something?"

"I ain't no fool—no, ma'am."

"But this is your station, isn't it?"

"It ain't none of my affair, and I ain't about to make it any," he said, spitting tobacco juice at her feet. "And if I was you, I'd just get myself something to eat, and I'd keep real quiet while I was eating it."

His condescending tone angered her even more. "You, sir, may be a coward, but I assure you I am not."

Ramon caught her by the arm. "You don't know what you are doing, Maria—you must not say anything to him!"

Shaking her step-cousin off, she continued to face Sam. "If you stand here and let him continue to offer violence to one of God's creatures again, I shall report you to your superiors," she told him furiously.

He shrugged. "You do that, ma'am—they ain't going to fault me none for it. That's McAlester," he added, as though that ought to explain everything. "You don't want to make him mad, I can tell you."

"It doesn't make any difference who he is," she retorted. "And I don't care how angry I make him."

"Maria!"

Sam looked her up and down, and a wide grin split his face. "You go right at it, little lady."

"I'm not a little lady," she snapped. "I am Amanda Ross—of the Ybarra-Ross."

"Yeah? Well, that there's one hell of a Texas Ranger," he countered.

"Surely not," she muttered.

As she turned to look again, the prisoner staggered, then fell to his knees. He raised his shackled hands in supplication when he saw her. *"Por favor, señora,"* he croaked through cracked, bleeding lips. When no one moved, he cried out in broken English, "In name of God—mercy, señora! *Agua*—"

The ranger pointed the shotgun barrel against the

back of his prisoner's neck, prodding him with it. This time the squat Mexican struggled to his feet unaided, and, with the ranger's hand pushing him forward, he managed to stumble past her.

"Very well, I guess I'll have to attend to the matter," she declared purposefully.

"Don't, Maria!" Grasping her shoulder, Ramon stopped her, then leaned to whisper, "That is the most feared man in all of Texas."

"I don't care what he did—he shouldn't be beaten while in the state's custody," she retorted.

"Not the prisoner—the *ranger,* Maria. *McAlester.*" As though he thought he might still be overheard, he whispered still lower, "After the war, he was with the State Police, and now he is one of the rangers. He is afraid of nothing—nothing, I tell you. He is a killer."

"Ramon, I can scarce hear you," she complained peevishly. "And I don't care so much as a snap of your fingers who he is. He has no right—"

"You must *listen* to me, Maria!"

"Oh, for heaven's sake," she retorted, "get some gumption, Ramon!"

"I tell you he is a very bad man, Maria—many times, he just kills the prisoners. But when reports are written, he always says they died while trying to escape. We have a name for it—*la ley de fuga.*"

Shaking free, she lifted her skirt hem out of the dust and started for the adobe building, but Ramon still tried to stop her. "Wait—promise me you will say nothing to make him angry," he pleaded.

"Are you afraid for you or for me?" she gibed.

"You wound me, Maria."

"Well, if you are so afraid of this McAlester, you stay out here, but I'm getting something to eat. *After* I give this McAlester a good piece of my mind," she added.

"Maria!"

Ignoring her step-cousin, she went inside, then stood just past the open door as her eyes adjusted to the dim-

ness. The ranger sat at a table, his back against the
wall, his feet crossed out in front of him. The shotgun
lay across his lap. His prisoner faced him, his head
resting on his hands. An ugly bruise covered half the
man's swollen face, and congealed blood oozed thickly
from a long gash down his cheek. Behind swollen slits,
bloodshot eyes made a mute appeal to her.

She hesitated, then walked directly to where they
sat. "It *is* Mr. McAlester, is it not?" she inquired
coldly. Without waiting for him to acknowledge it, she
plunged ahead. "I just want you to know that never before have I ever witnessed such a despicable display of
brutality, and—"

"No!" Ramon shouted at her.

"And I will report—" He looked up, and his cold
eyes nearly unnerved her. "Well, I just do not want you
to think you can get away with this sort of thing," she
finished somewhat lamely. "It bespeaks of the barbar-
ian rather than the peace officer, and certainly any *gentleman* of the least refinement would never
condone—"

"You aren't from Texas, are you?" he asked, abruptly interrupting her.

"I was born here, sir," she answered stiffly. "But I
cannot think that has anything to do with this. I know
what I saw out there, and I shall, of course, inform the
proper authority."

His mouth curved slightly, but his eyes never
warmed. "I guess that'd be me," he said. "Unless you
aim to write to Captain Walker—Hap Walker, that is—
then you have to send it in care of the postmaster at
San Angelo."

"Was you wanting to eat, miss? Stage leaves in
twenty minutes, and they ain't waiting for nobody,"
Sam reminded her somewhat hastily.

Glancing around her, she saw that everyone there
watched her, and she knew if anyone was losing any
face in the exchange between her and the ranger, it was
she. Trying not to show her chagrin, she straightened

her shoulders. "I'm afraid you have not heard the last of this, sir," she informed McAlester haughtily. Turning away from him, she stalked toward another table.

Behind her the prisoner called out plaintively, *"Por favor, señora—agua—*a drink for a poor man. *Por favor, señora."*

As much as she wanted to help him, she forced herself to sit down. Nearly as angry with herself as with the ranger, she felt as though she'd backed down, making her almost as much a coward as the rest of them. But, she consoled herself, when she got to the Ybarra-Ross, she wasn't going to bother with Captain Walker. No, she was going to demand the governor take action against Mr. McAlester.

Ramon gave the ranger and his prisoner a wide berth, circling halfway around the room to avoid them. As he sank into his seat, he said low, "I try to tell you—that man, he is more Indian than the worst Comanche, Maria."

"I don't want to discuss him any further," she retorted. "I've nearly lost my appetite."

"No—no. You listen to me now." He leaned closer, so much so that his nose nearly touched hers. "Ask the station manager here, and he will tell you how McAlester was sent to guard a stagecoach through Wild Rose Pass because of the Comanche raids."

"Look, Ramon—"

"No, no—this time you *listen* to me. The passengers, when they saw him, they were more afraid of him than an Indian war party. So help me God, Maria, they chose to go without him, saying they would feel safer taking care of themselves."

"Oh, for—" She glanced to where the ranger sat, one hand on the shotgun, the other on a tin coffee cup. "He's just a bully—an uncivilized bully."

"No, it is more than that, Maria. You look at him and see an Anglo, but he isn't. When he was very young, he was adopted by the Comanches, and he thinks like them. Even the Apache scouts are afraid of him—they say he knows how to torture a man to death, and that is why there are no prisoners." He shuddered visibly. "Myself—I have watched him walk into a cantina, and everything stops—the music—the voices—everything. This I have seen with my own eyes."

"I don't want to talk about him," she declared with finality.

Abruptly, Ramon's manner changed, and his hand closed over hers. "But I am here to protect you, Maria."

"Ramon—*please*," she hissed. "Not now." Then, realizing it took nothing to encourage him, she added, "I don't need protecting from anyone." Uncomfortable, she tried to draw away, but his fingers tightened on hers.

"Maria—yes, we have not known each other very long, but I *love* you, Maria. You have had my heart since first I saw you, I swear it." His voice rose earnestly. "I would cherish you, *querida*—I swear it. I will build the Ybarra for our children. Maria—"

"Amanda," she corrected him crossly. "Or Amanda Mary, but never Maria—I have told you before that I don't like being called Maria. And I just don't feel—"

"Maria—Amanda—you must listen to me! I offer you my heart and my name! Surely you—"

"Ramon, this is not the place to—" She looked up nervously and saw that nearly everyone watched curiously. "For heaven's sake," she muttered under her breath, "let go of my hand."

Ramon finally turned her loose, then sprawled in his seat, his expression petulant. "I do not offer my name lightly, Maria," he told her. "If the Sandovals were good enough for Doña Isabella—"

"Oh, for pity's sake!" Irritated, she exhaled audibly, then declared flatly, "Look—it has nothing to do with your name, nothing at all. I scarce know you."

"Then I may hope?" He brightened slightly.

"Ramon, it is far too soon for this. And if you do not mind, I'd rather not discuss it further."

"But I *love* you, Maria! I want to marry you!"

Exasperated by his unwillingness to listen, she finally snapped, "But I don't want to marry anyone—at least not yet, anyway. So if you wish to maintain any sort of friendship between us, you will cease this nonsense right now."

"Maria, you wound me—here," he said, covering his breast with his hand. "But Ramon Sandoval does not accept defeat easily, Maria. One day you will be persuaded."

It was obvious that nothing less than brutal honesty was going to deter him. "Look—in the plainest English possible, I am telling you I don't want to marry anyone. Must I say it in Spanish for you? What is there about the word *no* that you cannot understand? It's about as short and to the point as I can get. No. N.O."

At that moment the station keeper interrupted them to set before her an unappetizing bowl of stringy meat and potato chunks floating in what looked to be more like brown water than gravy.

"Bowl of buffalo stew before the stage leaves?" he asked Amanda.

"I . . . uh . . . I'm not particularly hungry," she lied, pushing the bowl toward her step-cousin. "He is welcome to have mine."

"Ain't much else to be had, ma'am."

"Perhaps some tea?" she ventured hopefully.

"Nope—just coffee and rotgut. Beer's been out since Tuesday, and m'order's late coming out of San Antone."

"Rotgut?"

"Nickel-a-shot whiskey. Nothing a female'd want," he assured her. "Got to have a stomach for it."

"Then I shall just have water from the pump and bread and butter. You do have bread and butter, don't you?"

"Water's brackish," he maintained obstinately. "Ought to take the coffee."

"If the horses can drink the water, then so can I," she countered.

He shrugged and turned to Ramon. "What's it to be for you?"

"Whiskey," her step-cousin muttered.

"I dislike drunks," Amanda reminded him.

He regarded her balefully before looking up at the other man. "Two shots—no water," he declared defiantly.

As the station keeper passed the other table, the prisoner renewed his plea for water, only to be ignored. McAlester finished his coffee and held out his cup without speaking. The man took it and hurried to refill it. Bringing it back, he carefully set it beyond the prisoner's reach.

Amanda had seen more than enough. Rising from her seat, she walked purposefully, her skirt swishing against her petticoats, to the bucket behind the counter. She put a dipperful of the tepid water into a battered tin cup, then carried it across the room. Her back to the ranger, she held it out to the Mexican.

He leaned forward as though he meant to take it, then lunged for the ranger's shotgun instead, grasping the stock with both hands. Before she could react, McAlester shoved her aside and wrenched the gun free. Using the barrel like a club, he slammed it against the prisoner's head, knocking him off the chair with such force that dust rose from the floor. Standing, he jabbed the weapon into the Mexican's stomach and cocked it. He stood there, looking down, his finger hooked over one of the triggers.

The room went deadly quiet, the silence broken only by the sound of the prisoner's gasps for breath. Finally, Amanda could stand it no longer.

"If you fire that shotgun now, Mr. McAlester, it will be murder," she said evenly. "In front of witnesses."

It was as though time stood still, but finally the

ranger carefully uncocked the shotgun. As Amanda breathed her relief, he swung the butt around and hit the Mexican hard in the face. The fellow howled and rolled onto his side, his manacled hands covering what had been his nose. He choked, then spat blood and a couple of teeth onto the floor.

Still holding the shotgun with one hand, McAlester reached for the cup she'd brought and tossed the water into his prisoner's face. Turning those cold blue eyes on Amanda, he demanded, "Just what the hell did you think you were doing?"

Stung, she stiffened. "Obviously I was trying to give him the drink he asked for."

His eyes traveled over her, contemptuously taking in her expensive clothes, then returned to her face. "You're damned lucky you didn't get everybody killed."

Furious at his manner, she fought to maintain her dignity. "You are no better than an animal, Mr. McAlester, and when I am through with you, you will be fortunate if you stay out of jail," she promised him, her voice tight.

He didn't bother to respond. Leaning down, he grasped the chain that joined the Mexican's hands and dragged him across the floor toward the door. At the framed threshold, he fairly flung the man through it, then he disappeared outside.

Aware that the stagecoach driver, the guard, and the station keeper all stared at her as though she were some sort of lunatic, she felt the heat in her cheeks. Rather than be outfaced, she picked up the empty cup, carried it to the bucket, refilled it, and went after him, her back stiff, the hem of her skirt brushing the dusty floor like a broom.

When she crossed the wood-framed threshold, McAlester had already shackled his prisoner to the spokes of one of the stagecoach's wheels. As he straightened his tall frame, he saw her. He turned away.

"You could give this to your prisoner," she said.

He didn't answer. Without so much as another

glance at her, he started back inside. She hesitated, then blurted out, "When I write my complaint, it won't be to Captain Walker, I'm afraid. I think Governor Davis ought to hear of this."

"Maria!" Ramon screeched from the doorway.

"And before you think he will not listen to me, I happen to own the Ybarra-Ross. People like me pay your wages, Mr. McAlester."

He stopped, turned around, and walked back to face her. For all her words otherwise, she suppressed involuntary fear. For a long moment his eyes met hers. Then, very deliberately, he tucked his shotgun under his arm and dug in a coat pocket. Retrieving a worn leather coin purse, he opened it. Before she knew what he meant to do, he gripped her waist and forced her clenched fingers open to receive a coin. As he closed her hand again, he murmured, "That ought to more than cover your share."

She waited to look down until he walked off. He'd given her a penny. "My share of what?" she demanded.

At the doorway he paused to answer, "The thirty-three dollars you and the rest of Texas pay me every month." Lifting his hand in a mock salute, he added, "And when you write to him, be sure to tell Davis I'm bringing him Juan Garcia, and he owes me two hundred dollars."

He went inside, leaving her to stare after him. Never in all of her life had she encountered anyone quite as insufferable, she was sure of that. He was cold, brutal, utterly arrogant—and he didn't give a damn what she thought of him. She caught herself, realizing she'd actually thought the d— word. She'd only been in Texas for a few days, and already the roughness of the place was corrupting her, she decided wearily.

Sitting beside a decidedly sullen Ramon, Amanda fanned herself, trying to stir the stale, hot air, wishing she'd waited for another stage rather than sharing it with the grim, forbidding ranger and his prisoner. Yet for all her disdain, she could not quite help casting surreptitious glances at the two men opposite, wondering how even a man like McAlester could be so inured to such misery.

Juan Garcia lay against the side of the passenger compartment, his bruised, bloody head supported by the wall, his arm twisted behind him by the manacle that secured his wrist to McAlester's. No matter what he'd done, he could not have deserved such a beating. No one could have. But she'd been entirely alone in her opinion, and that still irritated her.

They were all afraid of McAlester, and they didn't mind admitting it. But even worse than that, they all seemed to take for granted his brutality. He'd lived among the Indians, Ramon said, as though that were some sort of excuse. But to her way of thinking, that was no reason for decent people to give him a badge and condone what he did. Torn between indignation and curiosity, she dared to watch him from beneath discreetly lowered lashes.

He was asleep, his tanned fingers laced together over his crossed gunbelts. Were it not for the frock coat, the white cambric shirt, and that pale hair, he would have looked every inch the savage he was, she decided. When he opened his eyes, he did, anyway.

No, even if he visited a barber and dressed like Patrick Donnelly, no one would mistake him for a gentleman. Not with those merciless eyes.

She studied him openly now, scrutinizing his face, wondering how God could have made someone like him so handsome, yet so violent. But she had to wonder also if the Comanches hadn't taken him, if he hadn't been raised like them, would he have been different? Or had he been born the killer Ramon called him? Her gaze rested on his closed eyes, and she gave a start. Behind the narrowest of slits, dark pupils glinted. He wasn't asleep at all. He was watching her.

Unnerved, she raised her fan, plying it faster in the hope he wouldn't see her hot face. When she dared to look again, he hadn't moved a muscle, and yet now it seemed there was the faintest of derisive smiles on his lips. And the awful notion took hold that he was amusing himself at her expense.

He'd been studying her for the better part of an hour, wondering how a girl like her was going to survive in West Texas. She was too pretty, and she had too much spunk, things life on the Texas frontier tended to take out of a woman. Given a few years, the heat and sun would tan that porcelain-perfect skin like leather and fade that dark red hair. He'd seen a lot of women who'd been pretty once, and most of them had either dried up from the relentless weather or gotten fat on too many fried tortillas. But none of them had owned the Ybarra-Ross, he reminded himself. Armed with expensive lotions and creams and a houseful of servants, Amanda Ross might beat the odds.

It didn't matter, he decided. He wasn't fool enough to think she was watching him because she had any real interest in him. He was a curiosity, that was all. By now, he ought to be used to that, and most of the time he was. But somehow that look coming from the self-righteous Miss Ross pricked his pride. As she fanned herself, he opened his eyes.

"Anybody ever tell you that ladies don't stare?" he gibed.

Her flush deepened, almost burning her face. "No gentlemen, anyway," she shot back.

She had a quick wit, he'd give her that. He leaned back, regarding her lazily, smiling faintly, trying to get her goat. It didn't take long for him to succeed.

"I wish you wouldn't do that," she snapped.

"What?"

"Look at me like that."

"How was I looking?"

He had her there. She wanted to reach out and wipe that derisive half smile off his chiseled face. Instead, she nearly strangled saying, "You know very well, sir."

"Sir?" One eyebrow lifted slightly. "Why, Miss Ross," he drawled, "I was only trying to return your obvious interest."

As several shots rang out, her caustic setdown died on her lips. The coach gave a lurch, nearly unseating her, then picked up speed. From the top of the box the guard shouted his alarm, but she could not make out the words. She half turned to Ramon and saw that he had a sick, pale look on his face.

McAlester leaned forward to look past his prisoner. "Damn," he muttered under his breath. Bending so close that his hair fell over her skirt, he quickly retrieved his shotgun from beneath his feet. As he straightened, his gaze met hers. "Get down," he ordered brusquely, "and keep that red head out of my way."

"Is it—?" Her mouth was suddenly too dry to finish the words. Her heart paused, and her stomach sank within her. Dear God, she thought, it must be Indians. A quick glance at Ramon seemed to confirm her worst fear. He'd drawn a small derringer from beneath his coat, but rather than looking out the window, he was cringing against the back of his seat.

McAlester eyed him contemptuously, then unholstered a polished Colt revolver and handed it across without a word. Breaking his shotgun open, he checked his load, and closed it again. Taking a key from a coat pocket, he unlocked the handcuffs, freeing his arm. He warned his prisoner, "You move, *amigo,* and the lady'll be wiping your brains off that silk dress—savvy?"

The Mexican's eyes flashed malevolently, but as the ranger cocked the shotgun, he cowered against the side wall, his hands protecting his face.

More shots rang out, and the guard toppled from the box, falling past Amanda's window. She closed her eyes and swallowed, fighting nausea. Ramon leaned away from his side of the compartment, pressing his body against her shoulder, as he spun the magazine of the gun McAlester had given him.

The ranger looked her way. "Comancheros," he explained tersely. Seeing the relief wash over her, he added grimly, "With or without your hair, you're just as dead."

Above them the driver was trying frantically to outrun his pursuers, and the coach careened wildly as he cracked his whip over the horses. A bullet hit the window next to Ramon, breaking it. He dived to the floor and covered his head with his arms. McAlester pushed her out of the way, then swung across to where her step-cousin had been. Putting the shotgun to the broken window, he aimed and fired, shattering what was left of it. The discharge reverberated through the passenger compartment, momentarily deafening her, while the acrid smell of burnt gunpowder filled her lungs. She coughed until her eyes streamed tears.

There must have been eight or nine Comancheros, and as the smoke cleared, they could be seen on both sides. As the ranger reloaded, one of them drew close and raised his arm to fire. McAlester cocked the hammer again and pulled the trigger. The Comanchero screamed as the buckshot tore through his body, knocking him off his horse. The animal reared, then bolted, dragging the dead man by a foot still caught in the stirrup. His body bounced over the dry earth, raising dust.

Ramon huddled against Amanda's feet, his shoulders shaking convulsively as he wept like a baby. At first she thought he'd been shot, but then she realized he was too terrified to be of any use. Wrenching McAlester's revolver from him, she drew her knees up onto the seat, crouching to face the opposite window. As another Comanchero closed in, she held the gun with both hands, cocked it, and fired, missing him. The smoke burned her eyes and throat. Blinking to clear her vision, she pulled back the hammer again, then squeezed the trigger. As the recoil jerked her wrist, the fellow fell from sight.

From above the driver howled, "I'm hit!", but mercifully he managed to keep his seat. McAlester yelled up through his open window, "Pull up!"

"No!" she screamed at him. "Are you insane? They'll kill us!"

But the coach slowed. Despite his battered face, Garcia managed a triumphant grin that faded as the ranger caught him by the neck, thrusting him into the shattered window, where he rested the barrel of the shotgun across the back of the man's neck. A Comanchero rose in his stirrups to shoot, then saw Garcia.

"You want him? Come and get him!" McAlester called out.

As the man hesitated, McAlester fired. Blood trickled from a wide hole in the man's chest. For an awful moment he looked bewildered, then he toppled forward. From the back it looked as though his whole left shoulder had exploded.

Someone shot from the other side, narrowly missing her. Without thinking, she fired again. Almost before she heard the report, her attacker's head snapped back, and then his body slumped over his saddlehorn.

More shots peppered the walls of the coach, splintering the wood. Garcia jerked like a fish on a line, and blood spattered Amanda's dress. McAlester grabbed the back of the Mexican's hair, lifting his head into the window, letting his rescuers see that they'd killed him. When he let go, the body fell on Ramon, who screamed as though he'd been the one hit.

As quickly as the attack began, it was over. Having failed to rescue Garcia, the Comancheros still living fled, spurring their horses viciously in their haste to be gone. As the ranger withdrew from the window, Ramon crawled from beneath the dead man and pulled himself up onto his seat. Embarrassed now, he couldn't meet Amanda's eyes.

She continued to grip the gun tightly until the stagecoach rolled to a complete stop. McAlester reached out to pry open her nearly nerveless fingers, then repossessed the weapon. Returning it to his holster, he leaned back.

"Thanks."

That was all he said. It was as though she'd passed him the potatoes at dinner.

She stared at her hands for a moment, then looked across at him. "I . . . I've never killed anyone before, Mr. McAlester," she choked out.

"It's war, ma'am," he said sympathetically. "That's the way you've got to look at it. If they'd have managed to stop this coach, we'd all be dead right now."

"Yes. I guess we owe you our lives, don't we?" she managed.

"You did a damned good job of helping yourself." He regarded her soberly for a moment. "Surely they didn't teach you that back East?"

"No. But I was afraid they were going to shoot us," she murmured, looking down at Garcia's blood on her dress. She shuddered visibly. "I've always believed that every death in this world diminishes us," she said, her voice low. Her gaze strayed to the dead man lying between them. "Poor Mr. Garcia."

"Don't waste any sympathy on him," he said curtly. "Last year he ambushed two state policemen over by El Paso."

"Still—"

"He cut Billy Jackson's throat and left Romero Rios to bleed to death out in the desert. Rios had to crawl onto the Overland Road where the stage picked him up. Took him months to recover from it. Damned near kept him from becoming a ranger."

"Well, I couldn't know that, of course."

"You don't know much about Comancheros either, do you?"

"They are usually half-breeds who trade with the Indians, I believe," she answered, lifting her chin.

"They are the lowest form of life, Miss Ross—lower than a rattlesnake. They sell death."

"Like your Indians?" she retorted. Almost as soon as the words left her lips, she wished them back. But she was too late. His blue eyes had already turned to ice. "I'm sorry—I shouldn't have said that to you."

"My Indians, as you call them, are fighting to survive," he said tightly.

"And to do it, they torture and kill innocent people—people who have done nothing to them," she reminded him. "Why don't they fight the cavalry instead of settlers and ranchers? It's going to come to that, anyway, isn't it? How do they think they can commit horrible atrocities without punishment?"

Not wanting to answer, he stared out his broken window for a moment.

"You cannot deny what they've done, Mr. McAlester."

"No." The memory of Sees the Sun lying in a pool of her own blood came unbidden to his mind. "There's been a lot of killing on both sides." With that he opened his door and jumped down. Shading his eyes, he looked up at the driver. "How bad is it?" he asked.

"Clipped m'wing, that's all," the fellow answered. "Ain't no use going back for Joe—they drilled 'im in the head."

"Can you make it to Fort Stockton?"

"If they ain't coming back."

McAlester turned and reached for the body, jerking it out of the coach by the feet. "Garcia's dead, and they know it."

"You gonna ride shotgun for me?" the driver asked hopefully. "I sure could use you."

"No. I'm not letting them get away."

Bending down, the ranger began going through the dead man's pockets, taking out everything of value. Then he pulled off the man's shirt, boots, and pants. Walking around to the back of the coach, he disappeared from Amanda's sight.

Ramon collected himself, and when he turned back to her, he was apologetic. "I should not have brought you on the stage, Maria. I should have asked my father to send an armed escort for us. It is not safe for you here."

She bit back a retort, then said, "I suppose we were fortunate to have had Mr. McAlester, weren't we?"

"I hold him responsible for this, Maria. He should not have brought Juan Garcia with us. He invited the attack."

As irritated as she'd been earlier by the ranger's manner, she nonetheless felt obligated to defend him now. "Without Mr. McAlester, I expect we should all be dead."

"I would have defended you with my life, Maria," he declared.

"From the floor?" she demanded sarcastically.

He flushed. "I lost my balance, and then Garcia fell on me. I could not get up," he said stiffly.

She forbore pointing out that he'd telescoped the events to suit himself. Instead, she looked out the window at the dead Comanchero, stripped of everything but his long, dirty underwear.

The ranger came back into view, leading the paint pony and the mule. Both were lathered from the run behind the stage. Dropping the reins, he bent over Juan Garcia again, then straightened. Walking to the broken window, he drew out a folded paper and a pencil, and, holding the paper against the side of the coach, he wrote quickly. When done, he read it, then handed it up to her, forcing her to look into his face. This time, while his expression was sober, the coldness was gone from his blue eyes.

"I'd be obliged if when you reach Fort Stockton you'll see this gets to Captain Hap Walker. He ought to be there before me." With that he started toward the pony.

"Wait." As he turned back briefly, she passed her tongue over dry lips. "The danger is not entirely past, is it?"

He considered her for a moment, then removed one of the Colts from its holster. Counting out a handful of bullets, he walked back and handed them through the broken window.

"Here. That little thing your friend's got won't hit much." He smiled faintly. "Just have Hap keep the gun for me at Stockton, will you? Tell him it's brand new, and it cost me a month's salary."

Ramon reached for it. "You may give the revolver to me, Maria."

McAlester shook his head. "*You* keep it," he advised her. "At least you've got enough grit to use it."

This time he went to his mule and removed a black, silver-trimmed felt hat from where it was tied to the butt of a rifle. Putting it on his head, he looked back at her, touched the brim lightly, then mounted the odd little paint pony. Leading the mule, he struck out across the baked Texas desert, riding as slowly as he'd come into the Overland station.

The stagecoach began to move. "Wait!" she called out again. "You cannot leave Mr. Garcia unburied!"

It was the stage driver who shouted an answer. "Buzzards'll get him soon enough—this way they ain't got to wait for nothing to dig 'im up!"

As they picked up speed, Amanda counted the bullets into her drawstring purse, then placed it and the gun on the seat beside her. Curious, she opened the note McAlester had entrusted to her and began to read it.

Arrested Juan Garcia June 19. Ambushed by Little Pedro, Javier, and their band June 24. Am going after them. See you at Stockton within week or I'll write again. P.S. Prisoner killed during attempted escape, but I have proof of capture. Please apply for reward for me.

The thought crossed her mind that he wrote nearly as tersely as he spoke.

"Maria, are you all right? You do not listen to me."

"Huh?" Aware now that Ramon watched her intently, she collected herself and straightened in her seat. "Yes, of course—as well as I can be under the circumstances, anyway."

His hands covered hers. "When we are at Ybarra-Ross, I will keep you safe."

She pulled free. "Mama died there."

"My uncle was a fool, Maria. Ramon Sandoval does not make such mistakes, I promise you. No, once we reach the *ranchero,* we will not travel again without my men to guard us."

"*My* men," she reminded him evenly. "And I am *not* Maria."

From a distance there came the report of gunfire. Without thinking, she closed her eyes and said a quick prayer for the ranger's safety. Whether she liked him or not, she didn't want him to die, she told herself.

Carrying his shotgun in one hand, Clay McAlester crawled on his stomach, silently cursing the rising moon that vied with the setting sun to light the sparse scrub on the rocky hillside. He stopped to listen, hearing the murmured Spanish on the other side of the hill, and he felt a grim satisfaction. Now he could wait until they were settled in to surprise them.

The gang that had tried to spring free had split to throw him off their trail, but it hadn't worked. Once he'd discovered the missing nail in a horseshoe, and the odd gait of an animal going lame, he'd tracked two of them for a day and a half—until he'd gotten close enough to identify Little Pedro and Julio Javier through his spyglass. Now he was in luck, and he was going to bag both in a matter of minutes. Then he'd go after the others, even if it meant going into the Comancheria.

They were looking for Quanah Parker and his Quahadi Comanches—Garcia had told him that during interrogation. It seemed like every Comanchero coming in from New Mexico was looking for Quanah these days. And with good reason—Ishatai, the band's medicine man, had called the Cheyennes and the Kiowa to join the Comanches in a Sun Dance, promising to make medicine powerful enough to drive the whites from the plains, to stop the slaughter of the buffalo.

Army scouts had carried the tale back—and by fall Colonel Ranald S. Mackenzie and his Negro cavalry would be ready to punish every Comanche who failed to move onto the reservation north of the Canadian River. Whether Quanah knew it or not, his band faced that grimmest of choices—civilization or destruction. Clay had no illusions about which path the half-breed war chief would take. With rifles provided by men like Garcia, Javier, and the rest of the Comancheros, Quanah would go down fighting.

Clay crawled closer, gaining the top of the hill just as they were making camp. While Little Pedro tended the mesquite fire, Julio Javier unsaddled the half-lame mare. The other horse, still saddled, threw back its head and caught Clay's scent. It whinnied, making the jumpy Javier reach for his gun. Little Pedro ridiculed him, saying that "el Diablo McAlester" was probably already in Fort Stockton, claiming his reward for Garcia's capture, while the foolish Javier saw him in every bush.

In turn, Javier roundly cursed Clay's name, wishing the Comanches would rid Texas of him. Instead, he complained indignantly, they let the hated *tejano* cross the Comancheria unmolested. Surely they could not still consider such a traitor one of them, not after McAlester had become a ranger.

In the distance a coyote howled, and the hairs on Clay's neck prickled. He knew that sound well. With the enthusiasm of youth, he'd practiced it, perfecting it before Many Feathers had taken him down his first war trail. He listened, hearing the eerie, lonesome sound again, and his heart raced, blood pounding through his veins. He waited, and when another howl cut through the air, he used it to cover the noise of loading both barrels of his shotgun. At the third call, he locked the lever and cocked one hammer.

He crouched, ready to move in an instant, watching Little Pedro pour whiskey from a bottle into a cup and offer it to the jumpy Javier. As the larger Comanchero reached to take it, McAlester stood and threw down on them.

"Put up your hands!" he shouted.

Javier dropped the cup and went for the pistol in his belt, while Little Pedro made a run for his horse. Without hesitation, Clay pulled the trigger. The first shotgun blast shattered the air, blowing Javier backward, where he fell into the campfire. Turning, the ranger cocked the other hammer and pulled the trigger, firing the other barrel, striking the second Comanchero as he swung into his saddle. Little Pedro's horse reared, dislodging the Mexican as it fled in terror.

Javier was dead—there was no doubt about that. But Little Pedro was still kicking and writhing in the dirt, screaming that he'd been hit, that he was dying. Before he approached either of them, Clay cupped his mouth and gave his own coyote call, followed by two hoots of a desert owl. From a distance there came an answer, then only silence. At least now they knew he was there.

Clay walked to the fire and pulled Julio Javier out of it, turning him over with his foot. The man's shirt was singed, but the blood spilling from the chest wound had soaked it too much to burn. If he'd been ten feet closer, the blast would have cut him in half. Turning his attention to the other Comanchero, he could see where he'd caught Little Pedro's lungs from the back. Pink froth foamed from his mouth, and there was a distinctive death rattle coming from his chest.

Clay rested the shotgun beneath Little Pedro's chin. The man's eyes cast about wildly, as though he looked for help, as though he didn't know that in a few moments he wouldn't need any. But his words gave the lie to that. "A *padre*," he gasped.

"Where are the others?"

"A *padre, por favor*—"

Clay jammed the shotgun harder, pushing the Mexican's head back. "The others—where are they?" he asked harshly. "If you don't answer, I'll send you the rest of the way to hell."

Little Pedro coughed, spitting more blood. "A *padre*," he repeated desperately.

"Who was with you? If you want any prayers, you'll tell me now."

The Mexican closed his eyes and tried to swallow the foam. "Mendoza . . . Velez . . ."

"Hernan Mendoza?"

"Sí."

There was no use asking about the others. By the looks of it, Little Pedro was checking out. Clay laid down the shotgun and knelt beside him. He wasn't a Catholic, so he knew he couldn't say the right words, but he felt he'd made some kind of bargain with the Mexican.

"Saint Mary, pray for God's mercy on Pedro. He was a sinner, but so are we all." He looked up at the darkening sky. "Lord, this man is in your hands now—do with him what you will." With that, he stood up and brushed the dust from his worn buckskin leggings.

It probably wasn't going to make any difference. He doubted that Little Pedro was going to make it through any pearly gates. If there was in truth a heaven and hell, the Mexican was probably on his way down rather than up. He leaned over, listening to the man's chest. The rale he'd heard was gone, and so was Pedro.

I've always believed that every death in this world diminishes it. Amanda Ross's words echoed in his mind, seeming to condemn him as he looked down at the dead man. She might believe it, but he didn't. She just didn't know any men like Garcia, Javier, and Little Pedro. No, the world was a better place without them.

Straightening up, Clay whistled, and within seconds his paint pony came over the hill, his mule following by a lead tied to the pony's saddle horn. Both animals passed the dead men and came to a stop beside him.

Briefly, he considered loading the two bodies onto the mule, then decided against it. Given the heat, by the time he reached Fort Stockton, the flies and the stench would be overwhelming. Besides, if it didn't take too long, he'd like to find Hernan Mendoza. Having made up his mind, he rummaged through Javier's and Pedro's pockets for some identification he could use to prove he'd gotten the two Comancheros. When he found what he wanted, he dragged both bodies about fifteen feet away from the campsite.

That done, he removed his saddle bags, loosened the cinch, then pulled his saddle and blanket off the paint. Slinging the bags over his shoulder, he dragged the rest closer to the campfire, where he folded the blanket for a bed, then placed the saddle at the end.

Picking up the shotgun again, he listened for another coyote howl, but all was quiet. He flipped the locking lever, broke open the barrels, and shook out the spent shells into his hand. Tossing them away, he reloaded, then locked the barrels in place again. While he expected no trouble, he couldn't afford to make any mistakes in a place where the nearest help was a hundred miles away.

Tired from nearly twenty hours in the saddle, he dropped down to sit on the blanket. Reaching into his frock coat pocket, he drew out a worn, leather-covered book, a stubby pencil, and his knife. Leaning against the saddle, he sharpened the pencil point, then he began writing his report to Hap Walker.

Night of June 25, 1873. Found Little Pedro and Julio Javier. Both resisted arrest. Bringing in personal effects without bodies. Please apply for one hundred dollar bounty on Javier. See if anything posted on other one. Am going to look for Hernan Mendoza now. If I find him, I'll bring him in, one way or the other.

That just about said it. Hap would write it up, no doubt embellishing it suitably before sending it on with his own recommendation for payment. And hopefully the editor of the *Daily Austin Republican* wouldn't make too much of the incident, at least not the way he'd done with the State Police.

The trouble with newspapers, he reflected bitterly, was that while they cried for protection of the Texas frontier, they refused to sanction the necessary means of achieving it. And he was tired of listening to them whine that too few outlaws lived long enough to make it to the hangman's noose. The fools writing their articles never seemed to understand the problem of transporting hostile thieves and murderers hundreds of miles across a barren, waterless land.

On the Comanche war trail, the Indians killed Anglo men for just such a reason, taking mostly women and children too young to pose a threat. An occasional Mexican they'd keep for a slave, but the captor was responsible for seeing that his prisoner behaved and kept up. That made a lot of sense to Clay.

He put his report book back into his pocket and lay down. Rolling into the blanket, he pulled it up over his shoulder and stared into the coals of the campfire, listening to the seemingly empty desert, knowing that he was not alone. Out there somewhere there was a Comanche war party.

He turned onto his back and stared up at the bright, almost orange moon. A Comanche Moon, the settlers called it, saying whenever it was full like this, a man could always bet the Indians were going to raid. And they'd be right. Even as he thought it, Clay could feel the tug of another lifetime and remember the excitement of a warrior's first war trail.

The sky itself was so clear that it looked as though a man could reach up and touch the stars. On nights like this, when he lay in the silence and closed his eyes, he could still remember Sees the Sun's face, and he could still feel the comfort of her arms about a young white boy's slender shoulders.

They were all there, permanently etched in his memory. The father who'd taught him to ride with the skill and grace of a Comanche, who'd taken such pride in teaching an adopted son the ways of The People. The round-faced little Cries Too Much, who'd gotten her name by wailing when brought to the medicine woman. Walking Woman, the wrinkled grandmother who'd had the patience to teach a frightened boy sign language, then how to speak her tongue. The fierce Buffalo Horn, who'd valued bravery over everything else, who'd honored a thirteen-year-old Stands Alone for carrying not one but two wounded warriors home. The old chief had even reported Clay's first coup, making sure that his parents held a giveaway dance for it.

And poor old Mexican Pete. The image of Pete lying on the cold ground, his body still shielding Cries Too Much, came vividly to mind. And with it came the others—Sees the Sun, her eyes glazed, her life's blood spilling from her neck. Walking Woman dead in his arms. He'd never forget the horror of that day. Never.

The Texans had nearly killed him with the Comanches, but a young ranger had stopped them, saying he was white. Some had wanted to shoot him, anyway, arguing he had been with the Indians too long to ever be civilized. But in the end, Hap Walker won, and he took the half-savage boy to San Angelo with him.

For months after he'd been captured and returned to so-called civilization, Clay'd tried to go back, to find what was left of his Comanche family. But each time he ran away, either soldiers or rangers caught him, until finally they managed to discover another, earlier life for him. He was Clayton Michael McAlester, they said, named for his mother, Ellen Louise Clayton, and his father, Michael James McAlester, both killed during an 1850 Indian raid near Gainsville, Texas. His unlucky parents had been on the southern trail bound for California, lured by stories of fortunes made there in gold, his aunt had later told him.

For a time he'd refused to believe any of it, but at night, tossing fitfully on a hard army cot, he began to remember a pretty blond woman who'd sung to him, and a tall, stern man who'd seldom smiled. But for whatever reason, he never had any memory of the raid that killed them. All he remembered was a long, cold ride, and a full moon's light on frosted mesquite limbs. And finally the welcoming arms of Sees the Sun, who laughed and cried as she held him.

In the end it had been Hap Walker who located an aunt in Chicago willing to take a rebellious fourteen-year-old boy. A tall, determined woman, Jane McAlester had done her best to civilize her brother's only son, hiring tutors rather than risking his ridicule in a public school, seeing he not only learned to read, but that he read what she considered to be the classics, sending him to a Presbyterian Sunday School, where he heard of a heaven whose streets were paved with gold and a hell where the ungodly burned forever. It was the predestination that bothered him. He figured if God already knew what was going to happen, then a man was doomed before he got started.

Aunt Jane had done her best for him, he knew and appreciated that. But despite all her efforts, there was still that within him that refused to be tamed, that refused to accept anything more than the thinest veneer of civilization. The result was decidedly mixed, he had to admit—what she'd made of him was a reasonably literate rebel, one able to quote Shakespeare, Homer, and the Bible, who still believed more in himself than in any higher power.

Six months past his eighteenth birthday, by mutual agreement, Jane reluctantly gave up the struggle for his soul, and he left for Texas with her tearful blessing and twenty-five dollars in his pockets. He still had ten of it left when he reached New Orleans and enlisted in the Confederate army, becoming a soldier in that hopeless cause. And with the separation of time and distance, he and his aunt came to the understanding they'd lacked when he lived with her. In her loneliness she wrote often, and no matter where her letters found him, he took the time to answer as soon as he received them. She was, after all, his only living relation.

By the summer of 1865, he'd found Hap Walker again, and together they'd bummed around Texas until the carpetbag government organized the State Police, where he'd served, often with such ferocity that his superiors were appalled. But with the reinstatement of the Texas Rangers, Hap Walker had gotten himself commissioned a captain, then hired Clay, saying he needed "a man as tough and ornery as a Mexican, a Comanche, and an outlaw combined."

So for thirty-three dollars a month and all the ammunition he could use, Clay'd signed on with the understanding that he could bring in horse thieves, rustlers, Comancheros, and any other desperadoes he found plying their trades in sparsely populated West Texas, dead or alive. All he'd had to do was furnish his horse, his mule, his guns, and his traveling gear. In the absence of any sort of ranger uniform, he'd kept the three-dollar badge from his state police days, wearing it when it suited him, which wasn't very often. He'd never actually needed it. Most folks on the western Texas frontier knew who he was, anyway, and more than half of them were afraid of him.

His paint pony lifted its nose, then moved restlessly, breaking into his reverie. He sat up, his hand on the shotgun, listening intently. Not that he expected to hear or see anyone, not when a lone Indian could steal a regiment's horses without so much as a sound. As the paint settled down, Clay lay back, his hands laced behind his head, staring up at the still-rising Comanche moon.

His thoughts turned to the young woman on the stage. John Ross's daughter, all dressed up in silk, come to claim a piece of Texas someone else had fought and died for. But for all her fancy airs and high temper, she'd taken that Colt and and fired it, hitting not one but two Comancheros, while the dandified Spaniard with her had quailed at her feet.

But the way she'd looked at him still irritated him. As though he were the savage, Garcia the victim. Still, she was about as pretty a girl as he'd ever seen, he'd give her that. Tall, slender, with a delicate face framed with that dark red hair, and expressive brown eyes that betrayed her thoughts. A man might not like it, but he'd know where he stood with her. If he didn't, she wasn't afraid to tell him.

He turned on his side again and closed his eyes. He was too tired to think anymore, and tomorrow he had a long ride back beneath a broiling sun. He just hoped she remembered to give his report to Hap. And leave his gun at the fort. He'd paid too damned much for the newest and finest pair of revolvers to lose one of them.

When he finally slept, there were no dreams, no nightmares to break his peace. But he woke up suddenly, thinking he'd heard something. Alert on the instant, he realized he'd be seen reaching for the shotgun. His body tensed, and beneath his blanket, his hand crept to the butt of his Colt. Slowly, he eased it out, and as he rotated the cylinder one chamber, he threw back the blanket, rolled away, and came up on his knees with the gun ready to fire.

A rider bolted past him, but before he could take aim, a shadowy figure jumped on Little Pedro's nervous horse, reached down, and grabbed the half-lame mare's bridle. Whirling, as if for a show of horsemanship, the first rider came back at full gallop, then reined in. And by the light of the moon, there was no mistaking the dark paint on his face nor the pale stripe that parted his hair. He was Comanche. And he was on the war trail.

Keeping his eyes on both Indians, McAlester laid aside his Colt and stood up, showing himself. The man on Little Pedro's horse leaned down quickly, dropping something, then applied his rawhide thong to the animal's rump, and raced off. His companion wheeled again, dug his moccasined foot into his pony's sides, and disappeared into the night.

Sliding his gun back into its holster, Clay looked first to where the sturdy paint stood grazing on scrub next to the imperturbable mule. Turning around, he saw that the two Comancheros' bodies lay where he'd left them. He walked over to where their horses had been and bent down to retrieve the broken arrow the brave had dropped.

His hand ran the length of the split mulberry shaft to the turkey feathers, and he knew why they'd given it to him. He was still one of The People, and no matter why he was there, he was safe among them.

He stood for a time, staring first at the arrow, then up at the full moon, and he felt an intense yearning for the years of his youth, a desire to belong somewhere again. Finally, he shrugged it off and lay down. But this time, as his fanciful mind wandered toward the valley of sleep, he could hear the distant, rhythmic beat of Comanche war drums calling him.

By the time she'd arrived at Fort Stockton, Amanda was more than half-sick, suffering what the post surgeon called exhaustion and heat prostration. She'd intended to stay only overnight, but one of the officers' wives had joined the doctor in insisting she remain, saying the weather must surely improve. It had to—the surgeon said the thermometer in the infirmary had read one hundred ten degrees by noon every day for the past week. A drop to one hundred would seem like a cool spell, he'd joked.

Not that she'd required much persuading. The prospect of another two or three days of bone-jarring travel, added to her step-cousin's determined declarations of affection, was daunting. Unfortunately, her Alabama-bred hostess, Louise Baxter, thought Amanda utterly foolish for discouraging him.

As they crossed the dusty parade ground toward the officers' mess, the silly creature persisted, declaring, "Why, it's plain as the nose on your face that he adores you, you lucky creature. Such a courtly manner—ah swear, if ah weren't a married lady, ah should encourage him myself."

Fed up, her husband snapped, "He's a damned Mexican, Louise!"

"Why, Charles, ah do believe you are jealous! It's no such thing—is it, Miss Ross?" Before Amanda could answer, Louise Baxter had turned back to her mate. "He's Spanish, Charles—just like Miss Ross."

"No, he isn't," he retorted. "She's half-Anglo." Coloring, he stammered an apology to Amanda. "Pardon, ma'am—the Ybarras were fine folk, I'm told."

"I quite understand," Amanda cut in quickly, seeing Ramon. "Really, I . . . uh . . . I ought to get inside—the heat, you know." But even as she said it, she was too late. He'd found her, and there was no way to avoid him.

"Mr. Sandoval!" Louise waved her handkerchief. "Why, what a pleasant circumstance—isn't it, Charles? Mr. Sandoval, ah was telling Miss Ross—"

The lieutenant laid a restraining hand on her arm, growling, "Don't make a spectacle of yourself, Louise."

Unperturbed by Baxter's scowl and Amanda's chagrin, Ramon bowed. "Señora Baxter, you are so lovely." Grasping Amanda's fingers familiarly before she could draw away, he murmured softly, "Ah, Maria mia, you are recovered of the heat, no?" As he spoke, he turned her hand over and pressed his lips to the inside of her wrist. Coloring uncomfortably, she quickly disengaged her hand.

"Señora," he said to Louise, "see how she blushes? The nuns have taught her well, no? Such modesty and such beauty," he added warmly.

But the lieutenant's wife had her eyes on him rather than Amanda. "Why, suh, how you do go on—doesn't he, Miss Ross?" she said, simpering.

"Yes," Amanda muttered, "he does go on."

"Tell me, suh," the blond woman asked, fluttering her lashes, "are all Spaniards as flatterin' as you are?"

Amanda eyed the simpleton balefully, and Lt. Baxter appeared ready to strangle her, but Ramon flashed a grateful smile.

"Most of 'em are thieves and Comancheros," her husband muttered under his breath.

"Oh, if ah didn't know better, ah'd think you meant such a thing," his wife teased. She half turned to address Amanda, and stared over the younger woman's shoulder instead. "Well, ah do declare—now where in the world did *he* come from?" Wrinkling her nose in distaste, she added with considerable feeling, "Really, Charles, but there ought to be a law protecting decent folk from that man."

Her husband followed her gaze. "He *is* the law, Louise."

She sniffed. "Even the newspapers say he's a cold-blooded killer."

"Editors and reporters don't fight the wars," he retorted. "If it weren't for men like him, the only people in this half of Texas would be soldiers living in forts."

"The man is a savage," Ramon declared.

"Well, ah just hope he doesn't expect to dine with us. Ah swear ah couldn't eat a morsel with him at the table. He *will* eat with the nigras, won't he?"

Somehow, Amanda knew it was Clay McAlester. Turning to look, she confirmed it. She felt a stab of guilt that she hadn't been able to deliver his report or the Colt revolver to his captain. She shaded her eyes, thinking her eyes hadn't deceived her before—he was still the wildest-looking man she'd ever seen. And the best-looking.

That blond hair streamed from beneath the broad-brimmed black felt hat that shadowed those eyes, obscuring their coldness. This time, he wasn't wearing the frock coat, and his sweat-soaked shirt clung to his shoulders and back, giving him a raw masculinity far different from the men Amanda had known in Boston. Momentarily, she thought of the immaculate Patrick Donnelly.

As she watched, the ranger reined in and swung down about twenty feet from where she stood. Without so much as a nod to anyone, he headed for the colonel's house, leading his odd little pony and the pack mule. At the rail he dropped the reins, and both animals stood. Moving to the mule, he untied what looked like a blood-stained cloth sack from his packs. He dropped it on the ground.

Coming out onto the porch, Col. Hardison saw

McAlester, and his expression froze. "I heard you'd gone to Mexico," was all he said.

"Last month."

"More rustlers?"

"Uh-huh."

"One of these days you won't get back," Hardison warned him. "One of these days they're going to hang you down there."

The ranger shrugged. "Maybe. Maybe not."

It was then that the colonel noticed the sack. "What's that?"

"What's left of Hernan Mendoza. I was wondering if there was a price on him."

Hardison flinched. "Hernan Mendoza," he repeated. "A Comanchero?"

"Yeah. He and some others tried to get Garcia from me. When I went after them, he split from Pedro and Javier." Clay smiled faintly. "He thought he'd made it, but when I was finished with them, I tracked him down."

"Garcia's dead," the colonel said matter-of-factly.

McAlester nodded. "His compadres killed him by mistake."

"I see. And the other two—or should I ask?"

"They resisted arrest."

"Before long you're going to run out of Comancheros," Hardison observed dryly, his eyes still on the sack.

"Not as long as they can make money trading with Indians. Well, let me know if you find out anything on Mendoza, will you?" With that the ranger turned and walked toward the post store.

Hardison looked to where several Apache scouts lounged along hitching rails. Motioning them over, he gestured toward the bloody bag. "Bury this."

One of the Apaches picked it up. "Where you want?" he asked.

"I don't care. Somewhere outside of the fort." The

colonel took a deep breath, then let it out. "I don't want to know anything about what's in there."

"My God," Baxter murmured. "He took McAlester's word for it."

"That man tortured Mr. Mendoza to death," Louise declared. "Ah just know it."

"Don't be ridiculous," Amanda snapped. "There isn't room for a body in that sack. I don't know what it is, but it's not a body."

"It's probably Mendoza's head," Baxter guessed.

"That man is an animal, Maria," Ramon whispered. "You must promise me you will stay away from him until we leave here."

His manner irritated her, prompting defiance. "I hardly think even a man of Mr. McAlester's reputation could get away with bringing in someone's head," she muttered. Starting after the ranger, she called out loudly, "Mr. McAlester!"

"Miss Ross!" Louise Baxter gasped.

Clay stopped and swung around, his hand resting easily on his remaining Colt. For the briefest moment his eyes flicked from her to Ramon, then back, and he relaxed enough to give her that hint of a smile.

"Miss Ross," he acknowledged politely.

Embarrassed by her own boldness, she passed her tongue over suddenly dry lips. "I . . . uh . . . still have your gun. And Captain Walker isn't here, so I couldn't give him your letter."

That surprised him. "Hap's not come in?"

"No one's seen him."

Clay frowned. "He must've run into something." His expression lightened abruptly, and he shrugged. Taking off the black felt hat, he wiped his soaked hair back with his arm. "Thanks for the reminder—I'll be sure to get it before I leave again."

As he walked on, the Baxters caught up to her, and Louise was fuming. "Of all the uncivil—Charles, did you see that? Not so much as a word to me!" she sputtered indignantly.

"You wouldn't have spoken to him," her husband reminded her. "You despise him."

"Ah know, but one would have thought he'd have at least tried. After all, ah am your wife, Charles." She looked to Amanda. "And ah'm shocked to find you know him, Miss Ross. Why, he's downright evil."

"Well, I wouldn't precisely say we are well acquainted," Amanda protested. "We were on the Overland stagecoach when it came under attack, and he merely loaned me his gun for the rest of the journey here."

"I would have protected you, Maria," Ramon declared glumly.

"Yes, I saw that," she reminded him.

"You cannot know how depraved he is," Louise insisted. "Why, Charles was at Fort Concho when—"

"That's enough," her husband said, cutting her off. "It doesn't do you any credit to repeat tales, Louise." He took his wife's elbow, steering her toward the officers' mess. "Come, my dear—it grows late, and Col. Hardison doesn't like to wait for his dinner."

"As if he could eat after this," she complained. "Ah know I cannot."

As Amanda started to follow them, Ramon reached to stay her, whispering, "She is nothing to me, Maria." When she didn't respond, he insisted, "It is she who flirts with me."

"Charles Baxter probably deserves a great deal better," she muttered. "The woman's too silly for words."

"*Sí*. You do not need to be jealous, *querida*. I would not give her the second look, I swear it. You are a jewel, and she is a common stone."

"I'm *not* jealous, I assure you."

He moved closer. "Maria, how can I convince you I love you?" As she backed away, he said earnestly, "You have become everything to me."

She looked about her for the means of escape, but aside from the staring Apaches, there was no one. "Ramon, you've got to stop this." She took another step backward. "I like you quite well as a cousin," she lied.

"I want more than that, Maria."

"Ramon, I have no romantic attachment to anyone."

"Then I will hope."

"Nor do I want one," she declared flatly.

"You see a desperate man, Maria. What must I do to win your heart?"

"*Would* you listen to me?" As he came still closer, she lost her temper. "Ramon, is something wrong with your ears? How many ways do I have to say it? I have tried to spare your feelings, but you won't let me!" As his face darkened, she gave vent to her feelings. "Look—you were Mama's nephew by marriage, and while I am prepared to tolerate you for that I don't feel anything more—and I don't think I ever will."

"Maria—"

Checking her anger, she said more gently, "You must not think I am ungrateful for all you have done for me—for all your family did for my mother and the ranch—but I . . . well, I wouldn't make a very good wife for you. You deserve a woman who wants to marry you, and I am sure there must be dozens of them."

"There is another man in your heart."

"Of course there isn't!" she snapped. "I don't even know anybody out here!"

He reached out to her. "I can make you happy, Maria. Let me show you—let me prove to you that—"

"Ramon, you've got to stop this! And you've got to stop it now! I've no wish to travel all the rest of the way to Ybarra-Ross like this! Do you hear me? I'd rather go on alone than listen to any more of this!"

His hands dropped, and he stepped back. For a moment his liquid brown eyes flashed anger. He drew a deep breath, then let it out. "I see that you spurn me, Maria."

"Oh, for pity's sake!"

"It is not necessary to say anything more."

She exhaled heavily, then shook her head. "I'm sorry—truly sorry. Now, if you will pardon me, I think I will go in to dinner."

She walked about five feet before he spoke again. "I treat you like the Spanish queen, Maria. The blood of Andalusian princes flows through these veins, and I would have given it to our sons."

She spun around to face him again. "Look, I said I was sorry—what more can I do? I'm not ready to marry anyone, Ramon. Right now, I'm going home to run a ranch."

"You will be sorry, Maria."

Coming back outside, Clay saw that the girl was still having trouble with her unwanted suitor, and he made a spur-of-the-moment decision to intervene. Before he reached them, he rested his hand lightly on the butt of his revolver. "Sandoval," he said softly, "you're bothering the lady."

Turning around, Ramon gave a start, then his dark skin paled. "Señor, I assure you it is no such thing," he said stiffly.

Clay looked to Amanda. "Miss Ross, I'll take my other gun now."

"Yes, of course—it's in my room. If you'll wait here, I'll bring it right out," she murmured gratefully.

Without so much as a glance at Ramon, she hurried toward the officers' quarters where she'd been staying with the Baxters. Once inside, she closed the door and leaned against it for a moment. She'd not wanted to hurt anyone, not even Ramon, and she felt more than a little guilty. Surely there must have been a better way to deter him, but for the life of her, she hadn't been able to think of one.

Maybe she should have held her tongue until she got home, but the oppressive heat had made her irritable enough to forget her proper upbringing. Now she faced at least two and maybe three more days with her step-cousin. And that brief glimpse at the anger in his eyes was unsettling. It was, she reflected wearily, going to be a miserable journey, even if the heat broke.

She went to her traveling trunk and opened it. There, on top of her folded clothes, was Clay McAlester's revolver. Picking it up, she handled it gingerly, then took out the small bag where she'd put the bullets he'd given her. She'd not needed them, but they'd provided a sense of security she was going to miss. Maybe she ought to buy a gun of her own before she left Fort Stockton. At least then she wouldn't be wholly dependent on Ramon for protection.

Returning to where she'd left the two men, she found McAlester alone. As she handed the weapon back to him barrel first, she said simply, "Thank you for letting me carry it." There was an awkward pause as her words just seemed to hang in the air. "And thank you for dealing with my step-cousin," she added sincerely.

A faint, somewhat sardonic smile curved the corners of his mouth, and for the briefest moment, it seemed to melt the ice in his eyes. "Mighty wearying having men throw themselves at your feet, huh?"

"I beg your pardon?"

"It's a pretty girl's burden. The ugly ones don't have the problem."

"Is that supposed to be a compliment, Mr. McAlester?"

"You could take it that way."

"I don't think I will," she decided. "It lacked something."

"Yeah—well, I don't pass out too many."

"Somehow that doesn't surprise me," she murmured.

He held up the Colt, inspecting it, then rotated the cylinders, loading five. While returning the gun to his empty holster, he met her gaze again. "Out here, you'd better get used to being pestered. If this wasn't a Negro post, you'd have had a dozen offers in the first fifteen minutes."

"Probably because there aren't any women," she murmured.

"Not too many," he admitted. He hesitated, then tipped his hat. "Thanks for keeping my gun."

With that he walked off. She thought of Louise Baxter, and some imp prompted her to call out, "Wait!" When the ranger paused, she dared to ask, "Aren't you going to eat dinner?"

"I'm going to wash up first."

That meant he wouldn't be in the officers' mess, and that stood to reason—he probably knew he wasn't wanted there. She watched as he crossed the parade ground, and she wondered how he could endure being such an outcast among his own people.

The Baxter woman had chattered incessantly, making supper a tedious affair. Pleading a headache, Amanda managed to escape as a fiddler struck up a reel. Afraid Ramon might follow her, she hesitated, then walked purposefully not to her hot, stuffy room, but rather the short distance to Comanche Springs.

By day the place had been impressive, but with the light of a three-quarter moon reflecting off the water, it was truly beautiful. She sat down at the edge of the spring pool and drew up her legs, covering them with the skirt of her green muslin gown. Even though the sun had long since gone down, the night air was warm, and her clothes too hot, too confining for comfort.

Certain she was alone, she unbuttoned her bodice, exposing the top of her lace-edged cambric corset cover, and sat there, fanning her bosom, trying to cool the elastic that stuck to her damp skin. She'd have liked to loosen her stays and the horsehair pad that itched her backside through her drawers, but it was too much trouble.

She resented the wire and bone cages a fashionable female had to wear, and when she got home, the first things she'd dispense with would be those devices designed to shape her body into something it wasn't. If

God had intended woman to look like a bottom-heavy hourglass, He would surely have created her that way. No, corsets and bustles had to be the Devil's invention.

A slight breeze stirred over the water, blowing strands of hair away from her face, cooling her. She took a deep breath, smelling the scent of wild roses in the air. There was a serenity, a comforting solitude that lulled the senses. Even though she could still hear the fiddle music coming from the officers' dining room, she felt as though she were in a different world.

Emboldened by the darkness, she reached beneath the cambric to unhook the front closure of her corset. As it came loose, pulling apart over her breasts, she breathed deeply, savoring the release, feeling the cooler night air in the depths of her lungs. Leaning forward, she undid her thick hair, letting it fall forward until it almost touched the ground. Her fingertips massaged her damp scalp, relieving the itch from more than a dozen pins. Straightening up, she pushed her hair back from her face, combing it with her fingers.

She removed her shoes and rolled down her stockings. Taking them off, she edged closer to the spring pool to dangle her feet in the water. It was so cold that she had to wiggle her toes to keep them from going numb.

She sat there for a long time, enjoying this moment of freedom, this brief respite from the oppressive heat, knowing that she still faced the long ride home under the burning sun. She leaned back, and her long hair slid down her back. It was so utterly, completely peaceful that she could almost hear her own thoughts.

Across the pool, shielded by shadows, Clay lay stretched out, his head propped on an elbow, watching her, wondering if he ought to let her know he was there. He puffed on one of Little Pedro's cigarillos, thinking the Mexican had liked strong tobacco. Exhaling fully, his gaze strayed again to Amanda Ross, and his pulse raced. She was one fine-looking woman, he'd give her that. But there was more to her than that—as rich as she was, she didn't turn her head and pretend she didn't see the ugliness around her. No, she wasn't afraid to confront it. A man had to admire a woman like that, even if he didn't much agree with her.

He took another drag off the cigarillo and grimaced. It was funny how he'd never acquired a taste for tobacco, given how much the Comanches prized it. He guessed he just didn't like the way it smelled on his hands and his clothes.

Amanda knew she oughtn't to be out alone, but it felt so good to be away from Ramon's sulks and Louise Baxter's mush-mouthed chatter. The woman couldn't know how she sounded, she just couldn't. Every sentence she uttered seemed to begin with "ah," as though hers were the only opinions that counted. It might have been sufferable if she'd cared about anything, but as far as Amanda could see, she was totally absorbed in herself.

She looked out across the water, then froze. A small red glow brightened, then faded in the darkness. She remained very still, almost afraid to breathe, her gaze fixed on that speck of light. Every story she'd ever heard about the stealth of Comanches sped through her mind, sending a shiver of fear down her spine, followed by the rational thought that no hostile Indian could have ventured this close to an army fort, particularly not one where sentries could see for miles across the West Texas desert.

The glow brightened, then faded again, as it moved closer. Hampered by the bulk of drawers, petticoats, bustle, and full skirt, she knew it would be futile to run. No, if she had to, she was going to scream her lungs out and hope she could get the top of her corset fastened before help came.

"Who . . . who's out there?" she asked nervously.

Clay flicked the tobacco-wrapped cigar into the water, where it hissed and disappeared. "Just me," he said. "Clay McAlester."

Relief washed over her, followed by chagrin. "How long have you been here?" she demanded.

"Long enough, I guess," he admitted. "I was beginning to think you were going to shed all your clothes and jump in."

"Well, I wasn't." She could feel the color rise in her face, and she was grateful it was too dark for him to see it. "Besides, I thought I was alone." She rose quickly, gathering her skirts about her wet legs. "Don't come any closer," she warned him.

"Why not?" He took another step.

"Stay where you are," she protested, backing away from him. Her hands crept to where her breasts pressed against the top of her corset cover.

"Nice night out," he observed laconically.

"You know, most gentlemen wouldn't intrude on a lady—you do know that, don't you?"

He bent over to pick up her stockings and shoes. Straightening, he held them out to her. The moonlight reflected eerily in his eyes.

"Not too many gentlemen around these parts." When she made no move to take the clothing, he shrugged, then dropped his tall frame to the ground at her feet. Looking up at her, he said, "Actually, I was here first, and if you'd have come just a mite earlier, you'd have caught me buck-naked in the water." Reaching into a pocket, he drew out another cigarillo and studied it for a moment, frowning. "Care for one?"

"No, of course not."

He tossed the little cigar away. "Amazes me what people do for pleasure," he murmured. "Little Pedro had a real liking for the things." Looking up again, he actually smiled, revealing fine white teeth. "You going to sit down or run like a scared jackrabbit?"

"I haven't made up my mind."

"You don't have to leave on my account, Amanda."

"What happened to Miss Ross?" she asked peevishly.

"I don't know—I guess it didn't sound right." His

smile broadened. "At least I'm not like Sandoval, calling you Maria."

"I know," she said tiredly. "There's nothing wrong with Maria, but I was named for my father's mother."

"Yeah, Big John liked to put his brand on everything."

"You knew him?" As soon as she asked, she knew it was a stupid question.

"No, but I heard a lot about him."

She stood there, looking down on the ranger, feeling awkward. "He died while I was a child," she said finally.

"Indians or rustlers?"

"Neither. Big John stood six feet five inches tall—almost as tall as Sam Houston himself—and he was killed by falling off a horse." Her hands smoothed her skirt. "It has been nearly ten years, and it still seems such an impossible way to die."

"Sometimes a man can be pumped full of lead and live to tell about it," he observed. "Other times, all it takes is a tap on his head to break his neck."

"Yes. Everything about him was bigger than life—everything. The way he built the Ybarra-Ross—the way he thought—even the way he practically stole my mother from beneath her family's noses. He never thought there was anything he couldn't do, Mama said."

He held a far different view of what John Ross had done. As far as he was concerned, the Ybarra heiress wasn't the only thing Ross had stolen.

"Mama came from one of the original families that settled Texas—before the Anglos came, she liked to tell me. And my grandfather, Don Leandro Ybarra, didn't like the Texans—he'd have fought against them, but he hated Santa Ana. He just stayed home and waited for the war to end." She took a deep breath, then exhaled fully. "You don't want to hear about people you didn't know, do you?"

"It's better than sitting out here alone. So, have you

decided to stay—or are you afraid of what I might do to you?"

She still hesitated. "Well, before I sit down, will you tell me what was in that bag?"

"What bag?"

"The one you gave Colonel Hardison."

"Oh, *that* bag."

She felt utterly foolish, but she wanted to know. "Lieutenant Baxter said it was probably Señor Mendoza's head. And Louise thinks that it was what was left after you were done torturing him. I guess you heard Colonel Hardison tell the Apaches to bury it," she added.

"But what do you think?"

"Did you torture him—Mendoza, I mean?"

"No."

"Did you cut off his head?"

"No."

"I didn't think so."

Sitting there, his wet hair clinging to a water-spotted white shirt, he didn't seem such a dangerous man. Gone were the crossed holsters and the pair of six-shooters. As she stared into it, even his face seemed unguarded. She hesitated, more fascinated than afraid, then she sank down beside him and gathered her skirt around her legs with one hand. She would have tried to fasten her bodice, but she'd draw more attention by fiddling with the buttons than by leaving them alone. Besides, she was covered, if only just barely.

"You can't want to hear about my family," she insisted.

"Go on—I don't have anything better to do."

"Well, after the war, Big John came to see Don Leandro about buying cattle, and he saw Isabella Ybarra. He was a red-haired Scots–Irishman, with bright blue eyes, and she was this small, dark-haired, dark-eyed Spanish girl with a black lace mantilla on her head. They eloped within the month." She hesitated, then sighed. "I always thought she was happy, but if she was, she forgot him soon enough. Whenever I think of him, it still hurts almost as much as it did the day he died. I don't know why we can't keep the memories without the pain."

He sat there, his arms around his knees, looking across the water. "I don't know why either," he said finally. "But we can't."

"And you—do you have any family left?"

"Here?"

"Anywhere."

"Well, the only one I know of is an aunt."

"Have you met her?"

"Yeah. I lived with her for a while, and she deserved a lot better than I gave her. If I had it to do over again, I wouldn't raise half as much hell. But it never daunted her, and in four and a half years, she almost managed to civilize me." He picked up a stone and skipped it over the water. "I've got a lot of respect for her."

"Ramon said you were raised by the Comanches."

There it was, the thing that kept him apart from nearly everybody, the thing that made him a curiosity. He drew a deep breath and expelled it slowly. "Yeah," he said finally.

"It must have been awful for you," she murmured sympathetically. "Awful," she repeated. Without thinking, she reached out to touch his arm. "You must have felt so very alone and afraid."

He drew away. "Save your pity for somebody else," he said harshly. He looked across the spring, his jaw tightening visibly. "Those were some of the best years of my life."

"I guess I just cannot imagine how anyone—"

"No, you can't—nobody can."

"I'm sorry," she said simply.

Abruptly, he heaved himself up, towering over her. "You'd better put yourself together before somebody thinks you've been tumbling in the grass with me. I don't care, but a lady like yourself might not want the gossip."

"Look—"

"Go sleep on your fancy featherbed, Amanda."

With that he disappeared into the darkness as silently as he'd come out of it. She waited, hearing nothing but the sound of the water. Even though she couldn't see him, she knew he was still out there, and she turned away to rehook her corset before buttoning up her bodice. Pulling her hair back, she attempted to give it a semblance of order, pinning it together by feel.

She crept back, hoping no one besides the bemused Negro sentinel she'd passed had seen her. She stopped to look back, but there was no sign of McAlester.

As she entered the Baxters' quarters, she was nearly overwhelmed by the stifling heat. Finding her way to her bed in the darkened house, she undressed completely, wishing she could sleep naked. But her aunt had always said one ought to be decently covered in case there should be a fire. With that reluctant thought, she put on her nightgown, pried open a window, and lay on top of the covers, knowing she'd not sleep in the heat.

Her thoughts turned to McAlester. Aside from surprising her, he'd been pleasant until she'd brought up the Comanches. *Those were some of the best years of my life.* She could hear him say it.

Well, it didn't really matter if she'd somehow angered him, she decided. As soon as the heat broke, she was going to Ybarra-Ross. And after that she'd probably never cross his path again. Oddly enough, she didn't feel good about that either.

While she lay awake inside, Clay McAlester stared at the stars from his bedroll. Beside him the reflection of the moon shone on the mirror of water. Usually he reveled in the beauty of a place like this, but not tonight. Tonight he just felt alone.

He closed his eyes and listened to the night sounds, and for a moment he relived the pain of a fourteen-year-old boy on the cold November morning when the soldiers and rangers raided Buffalo Hump's small camp, killing almost everybody but him. But when he turned to rest his head against his saddle, it was the pity in Amanda Ross's voice that echoed in his ears. And pity was the last thing he wanted from her.

Amanda sat on the Baxters' porch, fanning herself determinedly, keeping time with the creaking rocking chair. It was too hot to stay inside, but as she looked at the bright, cloudless sky, she had to admit there was little relief anywhere.

It was as though everything was brown and dead, and only an occasional Negro soldier or an Apache scout dared to stir beneath the blazing sun. The hottest day of his memory, the post surgeon had called it, reporting at noon that the thermometer in his infirmary had registered one hundred and eleven degrees.

Moved as much by boredom as by pity, she'd gone there to do what she could for the five men unlucky enough to be sick on such a day. One of them, Trooper Hill, had been half out of his head with a fever brought on by an infected wound. Dr. Abbott, the surgeon, said he needed to take the leg, but Hill didn't want to give it up without a fight. The world had little enough use for a Negro, let alone one with one leg, and once he let them cut it off, the army wouldn't have him either. Buffalo soldiers, the Indians called men like Trooper Hill, comparing their wooly hair to that on a buffalo head. But whatever the name, they were still outcasts. Mostly former slaves, they fought the white man's implacable Comanche, Kiowa, and Cheyenne enemies. Yet she'd heard Louise Baxter complain, "Poor Charles will never get a promotion until he commands soldiers rather than nigras." As though these men who fought and died to make Texas safe weren't people.

"Howdy, ma'am."

Startled, Amanda came down hard on the runners of the rocker. She'd been so lost in thought she hadn't noticed the rider approaching.

"Sorry," he said. "Reckon I shouldn't have surprised you like that."

"No, no," she murmured, recovering. "Not at all—I was daydreaming."

His blue eyes were warm and friendly within his tanned face, and his smile lifted a full mustache. He removed his hat, revealing thick, curling brown hair.

"You aren't from around here," he decided.

"No—well, I was born at the Ybarra-Ross, but I've been away for years," she admitted.

"Mighty big place, the Ybarra."

"Yes—yes, it is."

"I knew the fella that owned it."

"John Ross?"

"Yep."

"He was my father."

"Well, I'll be—" His smile broadened. "Yeah, me and him fought Comanches way back. 'Course I wasn't dry behind the ears back then, you understand." He dropped his reins and swung down in front of her. Stepping onto the porch, he wiped his hand on dust-caked pants before holding it out. "Name's Walker—Hap Walker, ma'am."

"Amanda Ross." As she shook his callused hand, she instinctively liked him. "It is a pleasure to meet you."

"You wouldn't know if Clay McAlester's made it in yet, by any chance?" he asked. "Big fellow on a little pony," he added for description. "Can't miss him—looks like a cross between a mountain man and an Indian—got yaller hair halfway down his back."

"He arrived yesterday."

He appeared relieved. "I was kinda worried about the boy. Well, he ain't really a boy—must be twenty-eight or twenty-nine by now. Yeah, that'd be about right. Damn, but I'm getting old." Catching himself, he apologized, "Sorry, ma'am—didn't mean to cuss. Out here, a man don't meet too many ladies."

"Hap! Hap Walker!"

He spun around, his hand on his gun, much as Clay McAlester had done, then he relaxed. "Well, if it ain't Billy Samson! Haven't been running any wagons in from the territory, have you?"

"Cap'n, you know better'n that! No sir, them red-skins ain't gettin' no mo' chances at this ole wooly head. I'm bringing supplies over from Griffin now."

A grizzled Negro carter crossed the grounds toward them. As he drew closer, Amanda could not help notic-ing the awful scar that ran from his forehead halfway up to his bald crown. Hap Walker reached out to pump the old man's hand, then turned back to her.

"Comanches caught him out," the ranger explained. "Only man I know of that survived a scalping—'course they botched it and only got half his hair."

"So I see."

"Everything going good for you now—what with the government contract, I mean?" he asked Billy.

"Yeah, I been hauling for the army since last win-ter." The old man shook his head. "But did you hear about Nate Hill, Cap'n? He's down—real bad."

"What happened?"

"Outfit ran into a war party up by the Pecos, and a bullet plumb shattered when it hit Nate's thigh bone. Guess they didn't get all of it out. I dunno—maybe you might talk sense to Nate—tell 'im he's got to let go of that leg afore it kills him."

"Mr. Hill is refusing the amputation," Amanda cut in. As they both turned to her, she took a quick breath, then let it out. "I've seen it myself, and there's no hope of saving the limb. I . . . I could smell it, I'm afraid."

"Jesus." Recalling himself again, Hap Walker looked sheepish for a moment. "Sorry, ma'am, but he was in the State Police with me, and like most of the coloreds, he had a hard time getting much respect for it."

"Told me he nearly got lynched over in Walker County," Billy recalled. "Would have, he said, if it hadn't been for that McAlester." His face broke into a wide grin. "Fired a load of buckshot out of that double-barreled shotgun right over that mob. Took the vinegar right out of 'em, Nate said. Faced 'em down, telling 'em he'd take the first man that moved with the other load. Nate said he had the coolest head he'd ever seen. No sir, they wasn't wantin' t' tangle with 'im, not a-tall. That boy's a rough 'un, Cap'n."

"Clay's not afraid of much," Walker agreed.

"Much? He ain't afraid of nuthin'!"

"And you think I can change Nate's mind?"

"Well, he always said you was the finest white man he ever met—best officer in the State Police. Maybe if you was to tell him to let go of that leg, he'd mind you. He's got a woman and a boy in San Antone, Cap'n."

Hap squinted up at the relentless sun, then looked down at his boots. "I guess it wouldn't hurt none to talk to him, but I don't know about asking a man to give up his leg, Billy—mighty hard thing to do." Abruptly, he jammed his wide-brimmed felt hat back on his head. "Yeah, I'll give it a try," he decided. With that he jumped down from the porch and started across the dusty ground.

Billy Samson turned back to Amanda. "Thank you, ma'am, for looking in on Nate." Glancing at the door behind her, he added significantly, "There's them here that don't care if a colored man's going to die. I ain't namin' names, you understand, but that's just the way it is."

"I just hope it isn't too late."

"Well, if the cap'n tells 'im, he'll listen. Hap Walker don't tell no lies—no, ma'am, he don't. Ain't a finer man a-livin' nowhere. Ain't another man I'd want beside me in a fight neither," he declared.

"Not even Mr. McAlester?"

"Lordy, but that'd be a choice, wouldn't it?" he said, rolling his eyes.

Shading her face with her hand, she watched Hap Walker. He walked with a slight limp, but there was a determined set to his shoulders. It occurred to her that if he'd fought the Indians with her father, he was worth knowing. She rose and smoothed her skirt over her petticoats.

"Excuse me, Mr. Samson, but I think I'll go with him."

The old Negro moved back diffidently. "Tell the cap'n I've gone to fetch Mr. McAlester—he'll be sure enough glad to see him. It was him that brought the boy back from them thieving Indians."

Gathering her skirt with her hands, she stepped off the porch and hurried across the yard. When she reached the infirmary, the ranger captain seemed surprised she'd followed him. He'd paused to take off his hat again, and as he smoothed his sweat-soaked hair back from his forehead, his smile crinkled the skin around his bright blue eyes.

"No need to come on my account, ma'am. I kinda know my way around this place."

"I came for Mr. Hill," she said simply. "Perhaps if he agrees to the surgery, I can be of help." She hesitated for a moment, then met his gaze soberly. "I was nearly thirteen when my cousin Joe came back from the rebellion, Captain Walker. He was with the second Massachusetts, and at Gettysburg he took five Confederate bullets. He lost an arm, and his leg was shattered, and there were two balls that they couldn't remove because they were too near his spine. We tried to nurse him, but he died from the infection," she recalled bitterly. "So I assure you that I am not likely to swoon at the sight of blood—or of the surgeon's saw."

"Whew—I guess not." Shaking his head, he exhaled fully, then reached for the door. Standing back to let her pass, he waited until she was inside before he spoke again. "A lot of men died then, and a lot who came back were never the same," he said quietly. "I guess folks here in Texas don't stop to think what the war did to the Yankees."

"You fought in the rebellion?"

"I fought for the Confederacy, ma'am—under John Bell Hood. But in the end, there were just too many goddamned Yankees for us. We killed a lot of 'em, but they just kept on coming, until they even overwhelmed the likes of Bobby Lee."

"Slavery was wrong."

"Texas joined the Union in 1836 by choice," he countered. "In 1861 we chose to get out of it, and that damned Yankee Lincoln had no right to stop us."

"You sound just like Mr. McAlester."

"I reckon he got it from me." Looking past her, he saw the post surgeon directing the application of wet cooling sheets over his patients. "Jesus God—it's hotter'n hell in here," he muttered. "Sorry, ma'am."

"I'll probably hear worse before I die."

Leading the way between the rows of cots, she found Nate Hill's bed. His eyes were closed, his teeth clenched, and his breathing shallow. She reached out to touch his forehead. It was hot and dry.

"He ain't no better'n he was," a soldier in the next cot told her. "Been out of his head since you left."

"He's worse," she observed. Leaning over Nate Hill, she tried to rouse him. "Can you drink some water?" she asked loudly. "I'll get you cold spring water."

He opened eyes that seemed yellow against his gray–brown face. "Help me," he rasped. "Help me, Sergeant."

"Captain Walker is here," she told him.

"Don't leave me . . . can't ride . . ."

Reaching past her, Hap shook the trooper's shoulder. "Nate, it's me—Hap Walker."

"Don't let 'em have m'hair, Sarge . . . don't . . ." The eyes closed.

"Mr. Hill, you've got to let the doctor operate," Amanda pleaded, taking his hand.

"He doesn't know what you're saying, Miss Ross," Abbott, the post surgeon, said behind her. "He's beyond consent now. We're going to put him on the table."

"This should have been done yesterday—or the day before."

Ignoring that, the physician walked to the other side of the cot and lifted Nate Hill's big hand. "Uneven pulse," he muttered. "Fever's high."

"I can try to bring it down. I can bathe him with cold water," she offered. "I've seen it done."

He looked up, his expression pained. "Miss Ross, I know what I'm doing, I assure you." Letting his patient's hand fall back to the cot, he wiped perspiration from his own face. "I know it's too damned hot for this." Turning to two soldiers waiting behind him, he ordered, "Heave him up, boys and make it quick. Thompson, you're going to have to fan me while I do the cutting." Turning to Hap Walker, he said, "Guess you saw your share of this in the war, Captain."

The ranger nodded. "Can he make it?"

"Chancy—real chancy." Twitching the sheet back, the surgeon exposed Nate Hill's leg. As Amanda looked away, he told Walker, "Feel that."

Hap stepped to the bottom of the cot and grasped Nate Hill's toes, then he shook his head. "Cold," he said quietly. "Dead cold. How much, do you think?"

"The whole thing," the doctor answered grimly. "At this stage I can't risk anything less." Nodding curtly to one of his aides, he ordered, "All right, let's go, boys. Thompson, fetch the chloroform while we put him up. Best get on before we start, Miss Ross—it's not going to be pretty."

But as the men lifted Trooper Hill, his eyes opened, and he blinked in bewilderment. Then it was as if the confusion lifted, and he realized what they were going to do to him. "Cap'n," he begged desperately, "don't let 'em—eeeeowwwwwwwww!"

"Nate, listen to me," Hap said, leaning over him.

"You're going to lose that leg. It's dead—it's poison now."

"No—no—" Hill bucked between those who held him and turned his head from side to side. "No! Ain't no use for—"

"Thompson!" the surgeon barked.

The man stepped forward with a pad soaked in the chloroform. As he slapped it over Nate Hill's nose and mouth, he advised Hap Walker, "Better step back, Cap'n—you too, ma'am. Stuff's powerful strong."

Hill twisted his head, trying to escape the fumes, then choked. His body fell limp. Amanda moved away, hesitated, then walked purposefully toward the water bucket. No one even noticed when she carried it outside.

Her petticoats stuck to her damp legs, and sweat ran down her neck, trickling between her breasts. It was too hot for anything—too hot for what they were going to do to that poor man inside. Pushing back wet tendrils of hair from her forehead, she stumbled toward the springs, where she splashed her face and arms with the cold water. She dipped the bucket, half filling it, and hurried back toward the infirmary.

The bandage over Nate Hill's gangrenous leg was gone, and the wound that had not healed gaped. As the post surgeon pressed the skin above it, it oozed. She forced herself to walk to the trooper's head. Taking a cloth from the instrument table, she dipped it into the cold water and began wiping his dark, ashy face.

"Miss Ross, get the hell out of here!" Abbott barked.

"I'm all right," she insisted.

"Devil take you, then," he muttered. "If you faint, I'm going to leave you where you fall." With that he went to work. "Got to close off the artery above—just about here—yeah, ought to be it," he said, talking to himself.

He sliced into the swollen limb, and the foul odor gagged Amanda. She kept her eyes on Nate Hill's face as she washed his forehead. Turning away, she wrung the cloth out again, then made a compress. When she dared to look up, her eyes met Hap Walker's, and his were red.

"Got to go up further—can't save any of it. It's going to have to be the hip joint. Damn."

The air in the room was hot and heavy as the stench of dead flesh mingled with the smells of chloroform and male sweat. As the surgical saw bit into the bone, Nate Hill's body jerked. "More chloroform, but not much," Abbott ordered, adding, "and will someone take over the fan? I can't see for the sweat in my eyes."

A slender Negro, a youth scarce out of his teens, picked up the piece of cardboard, and looking away, he began waving it vigorously.

"That's better. Well, there won't be any wooden leg for him, that's for sure." A stream of blood spurted into the air, spattering him. "Got to close that off—" Wiping his face with the sleeve of his shirt, Abbott turned around to take something from the enameled tray. "Yeah," he said, returning to his work, "I think that'll hold for a few minutes."

He kept up a steady stream of conversation with himself, while Amanda continued reapplying the cold compresses to Nate Hill's head. Suddenly, the surgeon's shoulders jerked.

"Jesus—he's going. Back off with that chloroform!" he barked. "He's got too much of it, and we're sending him into shock! Give me that fan, soldier!" Jerking it from the man's hands, he waved it in Nate Hill's face. Then he dropped it and began beating the trooper's breastbone. "Come on, Hill!" he shouted, "get that ticker going!"

"It ain't no use, Doc," Thompson said after several minutes.

For a moment Amanda didn't want to believe it. Abbott leaned over and delivered one last blow as though he could somehow wake the dead. Nate Hill's arm jerked by reflex.

The surgeon looked up at Hap Walker. "If we'd had a little ether, he might have stood a chance. No, I'd be lying if I said I believed that. He was too far gone to take the shock of the saw," he said finally. Turning away, he began washing his hands in Amanda's bucket of water.

"No!" As the cry escaped her, she caught his arm. "You cannot let a man die just like this! You've got to do something!" When he shook her off, she mistook the reason. Returning her attention to Nate Hill, she began pounding on his breast, trying to rouse him. It seemed as though he sighed. She looked up and saw Hap Walker shaking his head.

"But he just took a breath—you heard him take a breath!"

"Miss Ross—" Abbott's voice was pained. "You expelled the last air from his lungs." Nonetheless, he lifted the closed eyelids and studied them. There was no question now—the blank stare told it all. "I'm sorry," he said simply.

"Sorry?" she shrieked. "*Sorry?* He's dead!"

His shoulders slumped, then he straightened up. Looking her in the eye, he told her, "No physician wants to lose a patient, Miss Ross. Yesterday he might have made it—or he might not have. I'm not God, so I can't answer that."

Hap Walker's hand closed over her shoulder. "Come on, Miss Ross. You did what you could."

She wanted to cry, but she managed to nod.

He led her outside, where she leaned against the adobe brick wall. For a time she couldn't speak, then finally she choked out, "Will they bury his leg with him, do you think?"

"I don't know. I guess they will. Does it matter?"

"Yes. Otherwise, he won't be whole in Heaven."

He eyed her curiously, then he understood. "Guess you must be a Catholic, ma'am—stands to reason, anyway, what with your ma being an Ybarra."

"Yes."

"Nate won't mind," he said gently. "Unless I miss my guess, he was a Baptist. Come on—I'll get you a cup of coffee."

"I made a fool of myself in there."

"No, you didn't. You've got a real kindness to you." He paused to squint up at the blazing sun. "My ma was like you, you know. She knew how to comfort a body when he was hurt. It's a real gift—there's only few that's got it, and the rest don't even have a notion. Now, how about that coffee?"

"No, but I thank you." She forced a twisted smile and held out her hand. "Most people wouldn't agree with you, you know. I'm accounted rather headstrong."

"Then any as would say that just don't know you."

"Why, theah you are, Miss Ross!" Louise Baxter, parasol in hand, headed toward them. "If you aren't careful, you'll be as brown as a walnut, deah." She stopped. "Now don't you just look like you ate a lemon—doesn't she, Captain Walker?"

"I watched a man die, Louise."

The woman stopped, staring blankly. "But . . . who?"

"Trooper Hill."

Obvious relief washed over Louise Baxter. "Oh, thank goodness—for a moment ah was afraid it might be someone." Seeing that Amanda's head snapped up, she compounded the mistake. "Well, ah meant it was one of the nigras—that is, well, it isn't as though he was an officer."

"He was a man, Mrs. Baxter," Amanda responded evenly.

"Well, yes, but—"

"Now if you will excuse me . . ." Turning to Hap Walker, Amanda held out her hand. "You have been most kind, sir."

"Well," Louise observed huffily as her houseguest walked away, "now that is downright uncivil, ah must say."

But Hap was watching Amanda. "No," he said softly, "that is one hell of a woman." Tipping his hat to excuse himself, he headed toward the small drinking establishment just outside the post ground. Clay was waiting for him.

"You ever going to get a haircut, boy?" he asked.

"Billy told me you'd come in," Clay responded, ignoring the question.

Hap sucked in his breath, then let it out. "Nate didn't make it."

"I knew he wouldn't. I saw him last night."

"Yeah." Shading his eyes, Hap looked to where Amanda stood on the Baxters' porch. "A real fine-looking woman," he murmured. When Clay said nothing, Hap pressed him. "Ever meet her?"

"On the stage."

"Well? What do you think of her?"

"I try not to pine for things I can't have," Clay lied.

"Damned if I know what ails you, son," Hap complained. "Sometimes I wonder if you got blood in those veins. I was going to ask if you thought I'd have a chance at courting her, but I guess you ain't talking enough to tell me."

"Hap—"

"So, what do you think?"

Clay shrugged. "You asked for it. I think she's too young and too rich for an old forty-dollar-a-month ranger."

"Old?" Hap fairly howled. "I'm not out of my thirties yet. How old do you think she is?"

"Maybe twenty—maybe twenty-one."

"Well, there ain't anything that says a man can't look, is there? Just because he can't afford a diamond don't mean he can't appreciate it. And I'll tell you one thing, boy—she may be rich, but she's got something worth a helluva lot more than money. She wasn't too fine to go over there and help with Nate. No, she's got a caring nature."

"Yeah, I've seen it. She cares about everything but Indians."

"What's that supposed to mean? Hell, nobody but you likes 'em, anyway." The older man peered more closely at Clay. "Say—you ain't trying to throw me off the trail, are you? You ain't taking a shine to her yourself?"

Clay studied her for a long moment, then looked away. "You ever know me to make a fool of myself for a woman, Hap?"

"Hell, I haven't even seen you look twice at one." Hap draped one arm around Clay's shoulder and pushed open the door with another. "I don't know about you, but I'm not going to stand out here all day. I think I'm going to get me a good belt of whiskey, and then I'm going to jump into that spring water with my clothes on. Come on—the first drink's on me."

"I was getting worried about you when I got here and Baxter said you hadn't come in."

"Romero Rios and I went to El Paso to quiet things down over there."

"El Paso's a hell of a long way from here."

"Yeah. But they're still fighting over the goddamned salt. Wouldn't surprise me if it didn't turn into an outright war one of these days." As Hap dropped his spare frame into a chair, he sobered visibly. "While we were there, Rios got wind of something—looks like Comancheros are getting up a big shipment of guns for Quanah Parker."

Clay nodded. "I've already run into some of them."

"Not like this. If the load's half as much as Rios was told, we're in for hell in Texas—real hell. I sent Buck Evans to tell Mackenzie they're coming in from New Mexico. Way I hear it, it'll be real soon. And," he added significantly, "if the Mexicans can be believed, it's going to be old Sanchez-Torres himself trading the guns."

"That'd mean a whole wagon train."

"Yep."

"You drinking today, Cap'n?" the barkeep interrupted them.

"Whiskey—straight."

"Nothing for me," Clay decided.

As the man left, Hap leaned back in his chair and regarded his protege soberly. "Damned if I understand you—you don't get drunk, and you don't chase women. Hell, you don't even really *smile*. A man's got to loosen up sometime or he'll bust."

"I'm loose enough." Clay looked down at the table for a moment. "You can tell Rios I got even with Juan Garcia for him. I reckon he'd like to hear that."

"Yeah. You bring Garcia here?"

"No. I had him on the stage, but Little Pedro and Javier tried to spring him, and I guess you could say he got in the way. I've got some of his personal effects, but I couldn't bring in the body—it was too hot, and I was going after his friends."

"Any witnesses this time?"

"Miss Ross and Sandoval."

Hap appeared relieved. "I'll put in for the reward."

"Inquire about Little Pedro and Javier while you're at it. Hernan Mendoza, too."

"Jesus—all of them?"

"Yeah. I wrote it up for you, but you'll probably want to make it sound better. There was another one, a fellow by the name of Velez, but I couldn't find him."

"Where in the hell are they all coming from? The whole Chihuahua Desert must be crawling with damned Comancheros."

"It is."

Hap leaned forward and lowered his voice. "See anything I ought to know about?"

"Two Comanches. It may be that I missed the rest—or it may be that they aren't out there this year. But it could make sense of what you found out about the gun-running. Maybe they're with Quanah and they're all coming down in the fall."

"God, I hope not. I guess you heard that the state of Texas in its infinite wisdom bowed to Washington and released the Kiowa chiefs," Hap said sarcastically.

"Kinda makes you want to puke, doesn't it? Those damned Quakers in the Indian Agency are hell-bent on coddling the murdering sons of bitches. They're so goddamned stupid they really think all it takes is handing out coffee and beef to civilize Kiowas and Comanches! And what they're doing is keeping 'em fat enough in winter, so's they can raid come summer!"

Clay let him vent his frustration, then interrupted him abruptly. "It's too late for the army to stop Sanchez-Torres, Hap. There are too many places for a Comanchero to slip past the regulars."

"Well, I don't know how the hell we're supposed to cover every trail coming up from Old Mexico, across from New Mexico, and down from the Indian Territory. You tell me how, and I'll listen."

"I can make the circuit between here and Fort Davis, then on up and cut back toward the Staked Plains. If I see anything, we'll at least know where they're going. I can probably find Quanah's camp."

"Would you turn him over to the army?"

"No, but if I know where he is, we can cut his supply route."

"Be like looking for the needle in the haystack," Hap muttered glumly. "Quanah's got a hundred places to hole up."

"I know my way around the Llano, Hap. I've been in every canyon up there. I know where they can hide."

"But you've been away from 'em for a long time, Clay. What's to say it won't be your hair on Quanah's scalp pole? He's not apt to take it kindly when he discovers what you're up to."

"I'm *Nermernuh,* Hap—no matter what happens, I'm *Nermernuh.* If I rode into Quanah's camp tomorrow, I'd be welcomed."

"Even he was to know you were coming to betray him?"

"I'm not betraying him. You don't see me scouting for the cavalry, do you?" Clay countered. "But if those guns get through—if they make it possible for him to raid—he's done. It'll take a while, but Mackenzie will scour those canyons until there isn't a Comanche left alive. I don't want to see that." He looked across the table, meeting Walker's eyes. "Come on, Hap—what have we got to lose?"

The older ranger was silent for a moment, then he sighed. "Just you," he answered finally. "When do you want to leave?"

"Tomorrow night. I'd rather travel at night—unless you want me to go earlier."

"You never get rid of those Indian ways, do you?"

"How's that?" Clay asked.

"You're still following that Comanche Moon."

"There's something to be said for traveling when it's cooler. It takes less water."

"When do you ride in winter?" Hap countered.

Clay's faint smile didn't reach his eyes. "At night whenever I can."

"I rest my case. You still think you're a damned Comanche. You've got to get over that, Clay, or you'll never have anything. A man's supposed to find a good woman and put down roots before he dies."

"Like you, Hap?"

"Who says I'm what you want to be?" The image of Amanda Ross flashed through Walker's mind. "And if I found the right woman, I'd settle down, you damn well better believe it. I could see myself with a piece of land, maybe doing a little farming. I wouldn't mind having a couple of kids. At least then I'd be leaving something behind that says I've been here. You ought to think about that before you get your fool head blown off."

"Maybe I will someday. Yeah," Clay murmured, "I'd sure like to get a look at the woman who'd have me." He pushed back from the table and rose from his chair. "Maybe I'll advertise back East for a bride."

"Yeah—you could write it up real nice, and—" Hap looked up and caught the twitch of a suppressed smile.

"Oh, get on with you! Here I am all serious, and you—"

"And I'm smiling, Hap." Clay laid a quarter on the table.

"What's that for?"

"I'm buying."

"Damned if I won't have another whiskey, then."

The sun was blinding as Clay emerged. He stood there for a moment, letting his eyes adjust to the brightness, then he stepped off the boardwalk and headed toward the post store. Before he left, he was putting some ammunition on the state of Texas's account. Where he was going, he expected to need a lot of it.

He started across the open yard and saw Amanda Ross. She was again sitting on the Baxters' porch, fanning herself. His first impulse was to keep going, then he changed his mind. She smiled when she saw him coming.

"Well, I see you met Hap," he said. "He was pretty taken with you."

"Oh?"

"Yeah. I was sorry to hear Nate died."

"Yes."

"I tried to talk to him yesterday."

"So did I. It was just too late by the time Dr. Abbott decided to do it."

He squinted up at the sun, then took a deep breath. "Yeah, I know. It's funny how it happens sometimes—death, I mean."

"Yes—yes, it is," she agreed. She laid aside her fan and sighed. "Well, since it doesn't look like there's going to be any break in the heat, I've decided to leave in the morning for home."

"You'd better take plenty of water with you."

"We are. And you—where will you go now?"

"Back out. So I guess it's adios, amiga."

She stood up and held out her hand. "If you get near Ybarra-Ross, I hope you'll stop in."

Her fingers seemed small within his. "Maybe I will," he said, dropping his hand.

She waited until he was several feet away, then she called out, "Be careful."

He swung around, and this time he actually smiled. "I always try to."

He knew what Hap Walker had seen in her, and it was more than beauty. She didn't have to like a man to care what happened to him. When she told him to be careful, she'd actually meant it.

The high, hot sun sun bore down without mercy, soaking nearly everything about her with sweat. Amanda refolded the nearly dry handkerchief she'd dampened less than an hour before and mopped her brow, her cheeks, and her neck with it, trying to cool her hot skin. It was no use. The still, arid air made the whole desert feel like an endless oven. Determined to gain some relief, she reached to draw the canteen from beneath the wagon seat. Unscrewing the lid, she poured more of the tepid water onto the cloth and repeated her effort. Replacing the canteen, she tried again to shade her face with her parasol.

Beside her, Ramon sat, his face stony beneath his dusty sombrero. In the hours since they'd left Fort Stockton, he'd said little beyond grunting answers to direct questions. Clearly, he was pouting, but she no longer cared. All she wanted now was to get home and take a long, soaking bath.

She shifted uncomfortably on the hard, wooden seat and tried to adjust her horsehair petticoat. If she'd had any sense at all, she'd have dispensed with everything but her dress and a minimum of underwear. But she hadn't, and now the elastic between her corset stays stuck to her sweaty skin, adding to her misery.

Eighty-eight degrees at seven o'clock, with one hundred by early afternoon a near certainty, Hap Walker had observed at breakfast in the officers' mess. But she was tired of waiting, and since the fort's scouts had reported no Indian parties, she'd been determined to leave. Now she wasn't quite so sure it had been a good idea. At least there she'd had cold water from the springs.

To take her mind from the oppressive heat, she turned her thoughts to Hap Walker and Clay McAlester. They were an unusual pair, the one sociable and likable, the other solitary, at times almost hostile. And yet there seemed to be a mutual bond between them. Like blood, Lt. Baxter said.

Her last conversation with McAlester had been a strange one, as though he'd wanted to say something, but hadn't. But then she supposed after the life he'd had, words just didn't come easily. As his image came into focus, she thought of his aunt in Chicago. Lord, if McAlester the man was the product of twelve years away from the Comanches, McAlester the boy must have been quite a handful for the poor woman. It was a wonder they'd managed four and one-half years together.

Not that her opinion of either man mattered. Somehow she couldn't see Walker or McAlester paying a social visit to the Ybarra-Ross. No, it wasn't at all likely that she'd encounter them again. And it was just as well—for as much as she'd been drawn to Hap Walker, she was even more fascinated by the dark-natured McAlester. As cold and violent as she knew he could be, she still felt a certain attraction for him. She guessed it was the wildness, the danger that she could see in his eyes. He wasn't the sort of man a lady ought to know.

She squinted against the brightness, studying the dry earth dotted with squawbush and tumbleweeds snared by a stunted stand of mesquite. As far as she could see, there was no life, only the bleached skull of a long-dead longhorn, but then she supposed that unlike her and Ramon, most creatures were possessed of enough sense not to venture out in such heat.

Her gaze dropped to the Spencer rifle Ramon had bought at the post store the day before. Not wishing to rely solely on him, she'd taken the precaution of purchasing her own short-barreled revolver, something called a pocket pistol, and the single box of cartridges someone had traded in with it. Despite the scouts' reports, she was determined to take no chances. She'd already decided that she wasn't going to share her mother's fate. Rather than be subjected to the terror and indignity of capture, she'd save the last bullet for herself. Her hand crept to her drawstring purse, and her fingers touched the outline of the gun, reassuring her.

She wanted a drink, but Ramon was worried they'd empty all five canteens of water long before they reached Ybarra-Ross, so except for what she'd used to cool herself, she'd tried to conserve as much as possible. How had Hap Walker said it at dinner the night before? *In the best of times, summer in West Texas tries a man. In the worst, it kills him.*

Finally, unable to stand it, she retrieved the container from beneath the seat and unscrewed the cap. Tipping it up, she drank greedily for a moment, wishing there were enough of it to splash over her hot face.

"Maria, you waste too much water."

She recapped the bottle. "You cannot tell me you aren't as hot as I am," she muttered.

"You have been gone too long, while I have lived here most of my life." He smiled grimly. "I am used to it."

At least he was speaking, affording her an opening. "I don't remember the heat, but I suppose it was always like this. Only then I was a child, and I daresay the clothes were considerably more comfortable."

He fell silent again, leaving her to her own thoughts. She sighed, then tried to remember the ranch, wondering if it were as vast as she recalled, or if its size had been magnified in the eyes of a small girl. Anymore she didn't know how big an acre was, not after years of living in Boston, where land was measured in narrow lots, where houses were set close together or attached in rows.

She ran her tongue over dry, cracked lips. "I don't remember Mama very well, you know," she said, assaulting the barrier between them once more. "I wish you would tell me about her—not about how she died, but what she was like while she lived."

"Tía Isabella?" He shrugged indifferently. "I don't know what you would wish to hear."

"I remember she was quite pretty," she ventured.

"She had the beauty of ice, even Tío Gregorio came to admit that. He'd wanted fire, and got ice. He said it was as though nothing touched her heart. She was like you, Maria."

"I must say you were more charitable about her when you spoke of her before," she retorted.

"Perhaps I wished you to think better of her."

"You make it sound as though they were unhappy."

"Perhaps they were pleased enough in the beginning, but after a while she did not even care when he left her bed for Rosanna."

"Rosanna?"

"One of the serving girls."

"Oh. Mama was such a lady—maybe she did not want anyone to know she knew about it."

"When Rosanna grew big with his child, Tía Isabella sent her away. But there was no quarrel. No, Maria, she was ice."

"She wanted to marry Gregorio. She told me she wanted to marry her own kind."

"If she did, she changed her mind. Maria, it was always 'My Johnny did this,' or 'John always said,' until we were all sick of it. A man does not wish to hear everything was better with someone else. And it was her money, her house, her land—everything."

"I guess she never got over losing Papa," Amanda murmured.

He half turned to look at her. "She was like you, Maria. She was a cold woman."

"What an awful thing to say."

"It is the truth."

"No, it's not. It's just ... well, I want to be on my own ... to feel out how things are at Ybarra-Ross. And when I marry, I want what Mama had with my father. I want . . ." She paused, searching for the words to explain. "I guess I want someone like him," she said finally. "It has nothing to do with you—or with who you are."

His jaw tightened. "You flaunt yourself before that savage, and turn up your nose at me," he declared bitterly. "To me, Ramon Sandoval, who can trace his ancestors to Spanish princes, you are cold and heartless. You grind my pride under your feet as though it is nothing."

"Oh, for—Is that what bothers you?" she asked incredulously. "If you are speaking of Mr. McAlester, I scarce know him."

"No, Maria, I know you are lying to me. Do you think I am blind—do you think I am too stupid to see? I see you that night with him—I see you buttoning your dress afterward, Maria—and it makes me sick inside. You are no better than Rosanna."

She gaped at him for a minute, then found her tongue. "Now you have gone too far—way too far, Ramon Sandoval! If you are speaking of night before last, I went to the springs to cool off. I didn't even know he was there until after I had loosened my corset hooks enough to breathe! I was trying to brazen it out until he left. I was quite mortified, I assure you."

"There is no need to shout at me, Maria," he said stiffly. "I am neither deaf nor a fool."

"You had no right to spy on me—no right at all," she snapped. "And let me repeat myself—I *didn't* know he was there! What would you have had me do? Look him in the face and button up my bodice while he watched? If you think that, you *are* a fool!"

"I know what I see."

"No, you are blind! You cannot be persuaded with reason or logic! If you could, you would know I don't

care a button for you or Mr. McAlester! He's nigh to
a stranger to me!"

"I don't want to hear your lies, Maria."

She took a deep breath and tried to control her anger. "Well, maybe I think there is a loose telegraph
wire somewhere between your ears and your brain,"
she said evenly. "If you cannot learn to say Amanda,
maybe you cannot learn anything."

"I offered you my heart and my name, and you—"

"And you scarce know me," she cut in. "You don't
know me now. But I can assure you that once we get
home, whatever degree of acquaintance we have will
be at an end."

"You have scorned me, Maria."

"For the last time, my name is Amanda, not Maria,"
she gritted out.

He turned away and flicked the reins hard, making
the mules run, nearly oversetting her. As she caught at
the seat to keep her balance, she turned loose of her
umbrella. "Stop it!" she shouted at him. But he paid no
attention. She looked back into the dusty wake of the
wagon. "What do you think you are doing? You've lost
my sunshade!" Reaching in front of him, she tried to
take the reins, but he held them tightly. "Did you hear
me? I said stop the wagon!"

"I am taking you home, Maria!" he yelled at her. "I
am doing what you ask!"

"If you turn us over, I'll never forgive you!"

"Hah! I am not so weak as Gregorio, Maria! I give
you what you deserve!"

The wagon bounced over the rough trail, its wheels
rattling. Flecks of foam from the mules flew back,
spotting her dress. Finally, he seemed to regain control
of his temper, and he reined in. His face set, he slowed
the team to a walk.

"I should like to go back for my umbrella now, if
you please," she said coldly.

"We cannot afford the time," he answered tersely.

Reaching to his neck, he slid the button that tightened the sombrero cord beneath his chin. "Here."

She took it and pushed the damp inner rim down over her crown, flattening her hair. Maybe she would care about how she looked once she got to the ranch, but not now. There was no use carrying the argument further.

He'd spied on her. He'd accused her of the basest behavior. Still seething, she stole a glance at Ramon's grim face, and she knew she'd meant what she'd said. She didn't want him at Ybarra-Ross. And when she got there, she was going to send him packing.

She refolded her handkerchief and ran it over her hot cheeks. When she looked at it, it was streaked with dirt. Reaching under the seat, she retrieved the canteen again. Unscrewing the lid, she gulped a drink, then wet the handkerchief. This time, Ramon said nothing.

He turned off, leaving the rutted road. She looked up at the sun, then toward the distant purple–gray hills, thinking it had been so long since she'd been home that she no longer remembered the way. But it was south toward Fort Davis, she knew that. And unless she was confused, they were heading north.

"What direction is this?" she asked finally.

"West."

"Are you sure? Ramon, that cannot be right—the sun is over there. It looks as though we are turned north."

"You think Ramon Sandoval does not know Texas well enough not to get himself lost?"

"No, of course not," she lied. "There must be landmarks to follow."

"I do not need anything to tell me where I am, Maria. I have lived here the whole of my life. But if you do not believe me, what can I say?"

"Ramon, look at the sun. Something's not right."

"I am taking you where you belong," he responded tersely.

"Isn't Ybarra-Ross south of here?" she persisted.

"A little, yes. But we will get there. I don't want to cross a war trail."

"I thought the scouts said they hadn't seen any Indians."

"The army never finds any Comanches until it is too late. There weren't supposed to be any when the devils caught my uncle and Tía Isabella. You don't want to end up like that, do you?"

"No, of course not."

He lapsed into silence again, but she was still uneasy. She pulled his sombrero forward to shade most of her face, telling herself that he must surely know what he was doing. If they would just make good time, she wouldn't even complain of the heat. If they would just get there.

The wagon bounced and jarred her for several more hours, while her shaded eyes scanned the dry, desolate land, watching distant hills that never seemed to get any closer. That was what Big John liked about Texas, she reflected. He'd said one could ride for days and get nowhere, that unlike Boston, Texas provided a man with all the room to roam he could want. She shifted the sombrero back to check the sky. The sun was nearly three-quarters down, making it about five o'clock. And it was on the left. They had to be going north.

Hungry now, she unbent enough to ask, "Are we making good time, do you think?"

"Very good." He actually smiled, making his teeth a flash of white against his dust-darkened skin. "Do you wish to stop?"

Actually, she did, for more than one reason, but she forbore saying it. "I can wait until you find a place," she murmured.

"Are you hungry?"

"Yes."

"Well, I think it is too early to camp, but I too must stop." He reined in, halting the wagon, then jumped down. "Wait here, Maria, and I will be back."

Her gaze followed him to a stand of scrub oak, and she realized he meant to relieve himself there. She looked away, embarrassed. Surely there must be a better place, but no matter which direction she surveyed, it all looked about the same. Still buttoning his pants, he walked back.

"At least I didn't see any snakes," he told her. Seeing that she picked up the canteen, he frowned. "What are you doing with that?"

"I'd thought to wash some of the dust off. There are four other bottles of water," she reminded him.

"You are wasting too much. There is no more water between here and Ybarra."

"I'm only using enough to wet this cloth." She could scarce see beneath the sombrero brim. But she wasn't about to give it back to him.

He shrugged as she picked up her black knitted purse and climbed down. Her cramped legs felt stiff and unsteady. And her back ached from sitting too long on the hard wooden seat.

"You need to walk, or you will be sore."

"I am sore," she muttered.

She walked toward where he'd been, and turning her back behind the scraggly screen, she began unbuttoning her bodice and loosening her corset. If she'd have had more privacy, she'd have liked to take her stays and her petticoats off entirely and leave only her undershift beneath her gown. She quickly opened the canteen and poured a trickle of water directly on her sweaty skin. Taking the handkerchief, she wiped it up. Her sunburned neck stung at the touch of the cloth. There was no doubt about it, she mused wearily—Hap Walker was right. Texas was hell in summer.

As she reached beneath her skirt to ease her drawers down, she heard him walk the mules. She squatted indecorously, praying he had enough decency not to watch. The iron-clad wagon wheels rattled as they picked up speed. Dropping her skirt, she hurried out. For a moment she stared, wondering what he was doing. Then her heart sank with the realization that he was driving off without her.

"Ramon! Ramon!" she shouted. "Ramon, come back!"

Choking on the cloud of dust, she dropped the canteen and ran after him, but the gap was widening between them. She wrenched her pocket pistol from her purse and fired it into the air. He didn't even look over his shoulder. Breathless from the heat, she stopped and shaded her eyes, watching as the wagon grew smaller and smaller.

She stood there, first shocked, than furious. He was trying to frighten her, punishing her for rejecting him. He was going to let her scream herself hoarse, then he would come back for her. Once he'd satisfied his Spanish pride, he would come back. He couldn't leave her there.

But at least she'd managed to keep his hat. Her head pounding now, she turned and walked back to the canteen. Bending down, she picked it up and shook it. At least she still had water.

At the scrub oaks, she sank down to wait. Her eyes traveled over the vast, empty land, seeing an endless sameness all the way to the horizon. No, there was not even a road to follow across the desert. There was nothing.

She looked down at the gun in her hand, thinking she'd wasted a bullet. Resolutely, she opened her purse and retrieved another bullet to replace it. When he did come back, it was going to take a great deal of discipline not to shoot him with it. A very great deal. He had no right to frighten her like that, no right at all.

She raised her eyes skyward, guessing there were possibly four hours of light left, knowing that if he didn't return, she was going to spend the night alone. And she remembered her father telling her once that "snakes and every other varmint come out at night in Texas." It wasn't a comforting thought.

And what if Ramon didn't come back? She couldn't

just sit there—not once the water was gone. She'd die, and once the coyotes and God only knew what else was done with her, she'd be nothing but bleached bones lying in the desert. No one would even know what happened to her.

No, if she could just follow the wagon's dusty tracks back to the road they'd left about noon, the Overland Stage or even someone traveling between Fort Stockton and Fort Davis might find her. Only this morning, Hap Walker had said that McAlester would be going to Davis, and if Ramon had wanted to wait until late afternoon, the ranger could accompany them that far. Of course her step-cousin had declined, saying he didn't want to travel at night.

She sat there for a few minutes, mustering her strength, telling herself she would survive. Even if Ramon didn't come back, she would survive. God in Heaven would not let her die alone in such a place. Picking up her purse and the canteen, she began the long walk toward the Overland Road.

Despite the lowering sun, it seemed that heat came up in waves from the baked ground, reaching beneath her skirt. And now even the sweat on her limbs seemed precious, for she had no water to lose.

She plodded along, trying to keep a steady pace, trying not to think of the distance. Finally, after about fifteen minutes, she stopped to unbutton her bodice and loosen the corset hooks. She had to get out of the corset. Reaching around to her back, she felt the wet laces and untied them. Then, throwing all modesty to the wind, she pulled off her gown and peeled down the horsehair bustle pad and damp petticoats. Stepping out of them, she undid her corset cover and took it off. Standing there in nothing but the corset, she patiently worked the back laces all the way down, then loosened the wet elastic. Stripping it away, she breathed a sigh of freedom.

For a moment, she let the hot, dry air absorb the perspiration, then she pulled on her gown. But she was dizzy from the heat. She glanced down at the dirty handkerchief for a moment, then picked it up. Soaking it again with the now precious water, she folded it crosswise, pushed the sombrero back, and tied the cloth over her hair. Leaving her discarded garments behind, she told herself that she felt cooler, better. As she walked, she allowed herself one sip of water. She was rationing it now.

She heard the faint sound of wheels, and she looked up, her heart in her throat. The wagon was headed toward her, a cloud of dust behind it. And she didn't know whether to laugh or cry with relief. Ramon had come back for her. She waved her arms wildly, shouting, "Over here! Over here!" And she began running toward him.

He slowed, then stood up from the wagon seat, his rifle in his hands. Raising it, he took aim and fired. It sounded as though a bee buzzed past her. She dived and rolled on the hard earth, then lay very still, her heart thudding. Not daring to raise her head, she heard him drive away again.

It wasn't until she could no longer hear distant rattle of wagon wheels that she twisted her head to look around her. There in the dust she could see the faint, undulating sworls, a reminder that she wasn't quite alone. Somewhere nearby there was a sidewinder. Probably more than one.

Her hands and knees hurt from the force of her fall, but she managed to sit up gingerly and look about her, first at the ground, then into the distance. Ramon had disappeared again, this time apparently satisfied he'd killed her. With an effort she picked up the hat, the canteen and her purse. Twisting the purse strings around her wrist, she began walking once more. The wagon tracks were so fragile that even a light wind could blow them away.

She was frightened now. And tired. And already thirsty almost beyond bearing. She wanted to sit down and cry, but she couldn't waste the tears. She was her father's daughter, she reminded herself fiercely, and he had despised cowards. He would expect her to put up a fight to survive. Anything less would be unworthy of his only child.

She wiped her stinging eyes with the back of her dirty hand and plodded ahead. To take her mind from her fears, she began praying. *Hail Mary, full of grace, the Lord is with thee. Blessed art thou amongst women, and blessed is the fruit of thy womb, Jesus. Holy Mary, Mother of God, pray for us sinners now and at the hour of our death. Amen. Our Father who art in Heaven, hallowed be thy name . . .*

Clay McAlester crested the hill and surveyed the desert beneath, his weary eyes squinting to focus, searching for some sign of life, of movement. From above, the blistering sun beat down, burning his head through the black felt hat, and below, undulating waves of heat came up from the land.

He'd been in the saddle all night, and he was tired. He'd planned to go on to Davis, but while cutting for sign, he'd come across enough broken brush to know that a large war party had recently passed within a few miles of the fort. And judging by the width of the path, they were returning from a horse raid, probably in Old Mexico.

It was enough to make him follow them north, hopefully to Quanah Parker's summer camp. If he found Quanah, he'd know where the Comancheros were coming. The trick would be to get between them before a deal could be made, and he had no illusions as to the difficulty of that. Sanchez-Torres was wily, enough so that he'd never actually been caught with anything more than a few empty wagons. He was, he always protested vigorously, merely in the salt business. Never mind that he was miles away from the El Paso flats or that there was never any trace of salt in the wagons.

But now the sun played tricks on his eyes, making halos when he blinked. If he had any sense, he'd just make a cold camp for the day and wait for nightfall. A little water, some buffalo jerky, and pinon nuts, and he'd probably feel a whole lot better. He half turned in the saddle, looking back toward his mule. The animal regarded him balefully from beneath his trail packs.

"All right, Hannibal," he murmured. "I guess this is about as good a place as any to stop."

At least it provided a good view all around, making an ambush impossible. He shrugged his aching shoulders, then swung out of his worn saddle and pulled off his bedroll. Using rocks to prop up his rifle and shotgun for posts, he draped the blanket between them, affording him shelter from the high sun. Uncinching his saddle, he dragged it and his saddle bags off, and carried them to his makeshift tent. Then he unloaded the mule. While the two animals drifted a few yards away to nibble on mesquite, he settled in.

Opening a saddle bag, he pulled out a cloth-wrapped package and took a day's ration of what Hap called "damned Injun food." Leaning back against his saddle, he began chewing thoughtfully, his mind on the job ahead of him.

As much as he wanted to stop the Comanchero trade, he didn't really want to set himself against Quanah—or any other Comanche, for that matter. So far, he'd avoided testing his own loyalties, mostly because he and Hap had a private understanding that he wouldn't be asked to hunt Comanches. He'd move to the border to fight Mexican rustlers, or to Ysleta to track unfriendly Apaches, but he still had a great deal of respect for the Indians who'd raised him.

But as he'd told Amanda Ross, Comancheros were another matter. With their guns and whiskey they were hastening the end of the People. Allies now, Texas and the U.S. Army stood ready to kill every Comanche, if that's what it would take to stop the raiding. And Mackenzie had proven last August that he could take the fight to the Comanche when he'd struck at them in the canyons that laced the Llano Estacado, deep in the heart of Comancheria.

But it would be hard, if not impossible, to look Quanah Parker in the face and tell the half-breed war chief he couldn't have the guns. Not when Quanah believed the war trail was the only path left to survival. Not when he believed life on a reservation would mean the death of the People.

It was coming, whether Quanah wanted to accept it or not. But Clay didn't want to be there when Colonel Mackenzie and his cavalry herded them across the Red River into the Indian Territories. Sometimes he still thought if they had any chance of surviving, of keeping the land, he'd want to stand with them. But as his Aunt Jane had once said, if wishes were pigs, he'd have pork chops every day. And it was too late to go back. He'd never be fourteen again.

He finished his food and reached for his hat. Lying down, he started to put it over his face when something caught his attention. In the distance dark specks circled in the sky. He watched them for a few minutes before he rolled over, reached into his saddlebags, and drew out his glass. Squinting again, he looked through it.

Buzzards. Four of them.

Adjusting the glass, he looked to the dry earth below, expecting to see the rotting carcass of a wild longhorn or a javelina. As he drew the lens back toward his position, he saw something else. Two thin ribbons cut into the dust. Wagon tracks. He felt the prickle of excitement just looking at them.

Alert now, he stood up, debating whether to leave his gear in his camp, or whether to saddle up and follow the trail at high sun. Another look at the wagon tracks decided him. Sometimes, to fool Texas authorities, a line of wagons would keep to the same tracks, making it look as though only one had come through. He dragged his saddle from beneath his makeshift tent and threw it on his paint mare, cinching it beneath her belly. "Come on, Sarah," he murmured, running his hand along her neck. "We've got to get a move on."

Walking to where the blanket still shaded the small spot of ground, he rolled it up, draped the saddlebags over his shoulder, picked up his Whitney and the

Henry rifle, and reset the hat on his head. The guns
were almost too hot to hold. Carrying them back, he
fastened the bedroll and checked the rifle before
sheathing it in the saddle scabbard. As he secured the
packs on the mule, the animal threw back its head and
bared its teeth in protest.

"Sorry, Hannibal," he murmured sympathetically.
"But it looks like it's going to be a workday."

The mule's ears flattened and its nostrils flared, then
as the paint nudged it with her nose, it accepted the inevitable. Clay mounted the mare, settled the shotgun in
front of him, and dug his moccasins into the animal's
side.

As Sarah moved down the hill, he almost forgot his
earlier fatigue. No, there was nothing quite like the satisfaction of finding a trail early on. He might just get
lucky. Maybe the rumors were wrong—maybe Sanchez-Torres was coming from farther south. If he was,
it would sure save Clay some unpleasant choices.

Distances were deceiving—it took him nearly three-
quarters of an hour to reach the wagon tracks, and then
he was disappointed. While a quick study of the
ground told him they were fresh, probably not much
more than a day old, if that, it also told him that the
wagon was too light to be carrying a full load of guns.
And instead of heading northward, it had made a turn
and gone back.

He squinted up at the sky and saw that the buzzards
were still hovering, waiting almost lazily for whatever
it was to die. He took out his glass, rubbed the eye-
piece on his shirt sleeve, then took a quick visual
sweep of the area.

There, lying next to a gnarled mesquite, was a dead
animal. No, it was a brown hump. Refocusing the
glass, he narrowed his vision. It was an article of
clothing—some sort of bustle. And just beyond it lay a
crinoline snagged on a clump of prickly pear.

He rode down for a closer look. It was a bustle all
right. Dismounting, he went for the other undergar-

ment. Tangled with it was a fancy lace-trimmed chemise. The hem, scalloped to show small embroidered roses and tiny pink bows, tore as he freed it. It was dainty, fragile, as though it had been possessed by a lady of wealth rather than by a homesteader's wife.

Carrying the clothing, he caught a glimpse of corset some twenty-five feet away, probably dragged there by a nocturnal animal who'd abandoned it upon the discovery that elastic and whalebone made poor eating. He retrieved that also. As he held it up, he could see the fancy frill above the front hooks, reminding him of the lace he'd seen across Amanda Ross's cleavage. It was far finer than anything he'd seen in bordellos and border cantinas. He stuffed the crinoline and chemise into his bedroll and tied the bustle and corset on by their laces.

The most obvious answer was that part of the Comanche war party had passed this way with a female captive. And unless he missed his guess, when he found the body, it wasn't going to be a pretty sight. The last one he'd found had been scalped, skewered on a lance, and hung on a tree, still alive when he found her—Jacob Misner's widow. The only help he'd been able to give the woman was a burial, followed by the few remembered words of a hymn spoken rather than sung. It had seemed woefully inadequate even then.

He considered going on. It wouldn't make much difference, anyway, and he was short on time. But the buzzards were still there. Reluctantly, he remounted and headed toward them again. Judging from the fact that they were south and the Indians had been going north, the captive could have been killed or left to die anywhere along the trail, and the clothes could have been thrown away as the war party lost interest in them. But that didn't explain the wagon. Nor did it explain the cleanly swept path that ran along side the faint tracks—a path that looked like cloth had been dragged over it.

He thought of Amanda Ross. She and Sandoval had

left Stockton early yesterday, and by now they ought to be almost to the Ybarra. At least they'd been on the Overland Road most of the way to Davis, and they probably wouldn't have encountered a war party on that route.

Looking down, he saw the imprint of small square heels that went on for several steps, then they disappeared. Now he understood—a woman had been walking across the desert, and her skirts had brushed her footprints from the dust. But what the hell was she doing alone in the middle of the west Texas desert? Had she somehow managed to escape from her captors? While it wasn't likely, it was possible. While he'd been with the State Police, a naked woman had stumbled into his camp, bloodied, bruised, and in one hell of a shape. She'd crawled out on her hands and knees while the Comanches slept, and by some quirk of fate, she'd found him.

No, he had to look for this one. As hard and disciplined as he considered himself, he couldn't leave a woman to die out there. He hadn't been able to do anything to save her, but he'd been there to hold Mrs. Misner when she died. He straightened in his saddle and nudged Sarah with his knees, turning her back onto the faint wagon trail.

It was probably another half hour before he found where she'd stopped. Dropping down to study the dusty earth more carefully, he discovered a threaded cap. And a few feet away, there was was the empty canteen, along with a pair of women's shoes. He picked them up, then stood. Looking upward, he checked the location of the buzzards again.

Damn, but it was hot. Hot enough to boil water on a rock, Hap would say. He took off his hat and wiped the sweat that ran down his forehead with his shirtsleeve. He'd lost so much sweat that he felt dizzy, and he was used to being out like this. But somewhere out there, there was a woman with no water, few clothes, and no shoes.

He climbed into the saddle again and rode slowly now, fixing his gaze on the ground, making sure he did not miss her trail. And with each plodding step, his appreciation of how far she'd managed to come grew. He was following one hell of a woman. She was doing her damnest not to die.

Ahead, one of the buzzards swooped low, testing its target. Clay raised the shotgun and fired, killing it and scattering the others. They rose higher, but did not leave. For good measure, he fired again, taking down another.

And then he saw a bare, bloodied foot extending from behind a stunted stand of scrub oak. But any exhilaration he'd felt at the discovery was soon dispelled by the realization that the body was prone and unmoving. Afraid he was too late, he reined in and swung down. Taking his canteen, he walked toward her.

What he saw stunned him. It was Amanda Ross. She lay there, her head cradled by one of her arms, her other hand holding a purse with a short-barreled revolver half out of it. She wasn't moving.

Her closed eyes were sunk in the sockets, and a small trickle of blood had dried on her cracked lips. He knelt and turned her over gently, then probed along her neck for a pulse. It was faint and uneven, but it was there. His hand moved lower, slipping under the unbuttoned waist of her dress. Her ribs rose and fell rapidly, shallowly, beneath his touch. And her skin was as hot and dry as if she ran a high fever. But at least she'd used her hat and handkerchief to shade her face, so that the worst of her sunburn was on her cheeks and throat.

"Miss Ross—Amanda—can you hear me?" he asked gently. "It's me—Clay McAlester."

She didn't respond. Lifting one of her lids, he saw the pupil narrow. He pried open her jaw and checked her tongue. It was nearly black from the lack of water. Another hour or so and she'd have been dead when he found her. But right now she was alive, and he was going to do his damnedest to keep her that way.

The trick was going to be getting enough water in her quickly enough to do any good. And if he managed that, then he could turn his attention to the rest of her. Lifting her, he balanced her shoulders with his knee while he unscrewed the cap of his canteen.

"Come on, girl—you've made it this far. Don't give up now," he coaxed, holding the bottle's lip to hers. Her hand came up weakly, brushing at his wrist, then fell limply to her side. "Amanda, it's McAlester," he told her. "Come on—just a sip for now. You're alive, and that's all that matters."

Dazed eyes fluttered but did not fully open. "Papa," she croaked.

She was hallucinating, but that was to be expected. He slid an arm beneath her shoulder, taking care to touch the cloth as much as possible. Thankfully, she hadn't discarded her dress, or she'd have been sun-poisoned from the burn.

"It's all right, Amanda—all you've got to do is drink, and I'll take care of the rest." He held the canteen to her lips. "Come on—drink." He tipped it slightly, allowing a small trickle. As he watched, her throat constricted, telling him she swallowed. "That's good. Just a little more—not too much." But even as he said it, the water hit her stomach, and she began to retch. He shifted her against his leg and watched helplessly as the water came up.

"Come on—not so much next time. We can't afford to waste it." Trying again, he kept his grip on the canteen, giving her only enough to wet her dark tongue. "That's better."

"Papa—"

"Don't try to talk. Just take it easy."

"He threw me Papa . . . I hurt . . . ," she mumbled incoherently.

"One more sip, then I've got to get you out of the sun," he said, tipping the canteen again. "That's enough for now."

It wasn't nearly enough, and he knew it, but it was

a start. Now if he could keep her alive until nightfall, if he could keep her drinking, he thought she could make it. All he had to do was figure out how to cool her off before her body temperature affected her brain. Maybe it already had, but he hoped not.

Easing her to the ground, he stood up and looked around before retrieving his bedroll. Undoing it, he spread it between two mesquite bushes for a shade. Then he laid his saddle beneath it and covered that with his coat. It wasn't much of a shelter, but it would have to do. It felt like she didn't weigh much more than her bones when he lifted her, then eased her body down under the makeshift shelter.

"I'm giving you one more drink," he told her, "then I'm going to try to make you feel better. You've got to keep this down, Amanda." This time he did not raise her to drink. Instead, he pulled out a corner of her cracked lower lip and let a small amount of the warm water trickle in. He watched her swallow. "No more," he said, taking the bottle away.

Her lip trembled. "He threw me, Papa . . . I didn't mean . . ."

"It's McAlester," he said again. "Clay McAlester. And you're going to be all right. You're going to be all right."

"No . . . no . . ." She blinked, clearly uncomprehending. "Don't kill him, Papa," she whispered.

She'd had a heatstroke, he was sure of that. But he hoped her mind would come back when he got enough water into her. He stood up again and dusted his hands on his leggings.

"Mama, tell him . . ." She turned her head as though she could see someone. "Tell him . . . he didn't mean . . ."

Going to his saddlebags, he took out his Bowie knife, then stood there, looking for something useful. He settled on a clump of prickly pear. But he'd need a fire to burn off the needles, and he wasn't sure he had the time to make one. No, he'd just have to cut them off.

He went to work harvesting the flat, round leaves, sawing off the spines. As dry as it was, he wasn't going to get much out of them, but it would be better than nothing, he told himself. And whatever he could get would help save his water.

As he straightened up, his eyes caught the dust clouds in the distance, then the riders. A straggling war party, he guessed, and by the time he identified himself, it just might be too late. He grabbed the Henry rifle and cocked the hammer, thinking it was a hell of a place to make a stand. Out in the open with nothing close but buckbrush and mesquite for cover. Edging behind the paint, he dropped the Bowie knife and leaned down for the shotgun. Now he could count six of them.

They spied him, and sped toward him, raising a high-pitched war cry. It was a choice between trying to take all of them or brazening it out. But there was Amanda Ross to consider, and if he took a bullet in the exchange, he had a fair notion of what they'd do to her before she died. In a split second he made up his mind to gamble.

He held both guns up in full view and shouted *"Nermernuh!"* then threw them down as the war party closed in on him. Walking with a confidence he did not feel, he went to meet them.

A tall, barrel-chested Indian separated from the others, riding hell for leather, whooping for show, making a wide circle around Clay. He waved a war lance, shaking the scalps that hung from it. Coming around again, he made another circle, this one much closer. When McAlester did not flinch, he reined in, his painted face scowling as though he were trying to stare the white man down. The crow feathers in his scalplock indicated he was Kiowa, rather than Comanche. He poised his lance as though he would strike.

Another Kiowa rode up and, leaning from his saddle, pushed the lance down with his hand. *"No Te-jano,"* he said, using Spanish. Looking to Clay, he gestured, asking, *"Nermernuh?"*

"Nokoni," Clay answered.

Seemingly satisfied, the apparent leader turned back, addressing the others, saying that the Kiowas and Comanches were brothers who hunted and made war together. As a murmur of agreement passed between them, Clay exhaled his relief. He'd done it. Even to a Kiowa, a Nerm was a Nerm, whether Quahadi, Nokoni, Penateka or any of the other bands.

The barrel-chested one began to sign, asking how his Comanche brother was called. Clay hesitated, then swept the air with his hand before answering. Raising his hand at a right angle from his elbow, he indicated Stands. His eyes on the war leader, he added the sign of Alone.

"Nahakoah," he said aloud.

The Kiowa repeated the Comanche name. Clay nodded. It was out in the open, lying between them, either a bridge or a chasm. The warrior rode in a slow circle around him, then reined in, a smile splitting his wide face. His hands talked, giving his name, then he said it.

"Wabetai." Two Owls.

The others followed suit. Fast Wolf. Big Head. Bent Tree. A youth called Little Eagle. And the war leader of the party was Stone Hand. They were on their way back from Mexico, Two Owls said, headed toward the Llano, and they'd been guarding the rear of the larger Comanche war party. Now they were trying to catch up to it so they could make their triumphant entrance into Ketanah's camp together.

Ketanah. Clay recognized the name of his mother's cousin, and his heart beat faster as a certain exhilaration coursed through him. Ketanah was alive, and he had a band of his own.

Two Owls saw Amanda and asked, "Who?"

"My woman," Clay told him. "She's sick."

"What ails here?"

"The sun. She needs water."

"Bad time. No water."

"Yes."

The Indian grunted sympathetically. His curiosity aroused, he dismounted to take a closer look. Bending over, he reached a dirty hand to touch Amanda's hair, then her face. "Ummmh," he said, straightening up. Looking back to Clay, he noted, "Very bad."

"Yes."

The Indian rose and untied a bloated buffalo paunch from behind his saddle. "For your woman," the big Kiowa's hands spoke. "No water, woman will die. You take. Ketanah's camp at spring beyond gap."

Given the heat and the fact that the closest water was a good ride away, it was a generous gift. Clay nodded, then went to his own packs, where he found the rest of the cigarillos he'd taken from Javier and Little Pedro. He gave them to the Kiowa, who bobbed his head, grinning broadly.

Stone Hand called out, saying they had to leave if they were to catch up to the others. Two Owls nodded, then signed hurriedly for Clay. Ketanah's band was Noconi, and there was a good medicine woman there. Nahakoah ought to take his woman to Nahdehwah, who could cure everything, even ghost sickness. With that the big Kiowa remounted, and the small party took off. About a hundred yards out, Two Owls held up the fistful of little cigars, then kicked his horse. The party disappeared in a cloud of choking dust.

Clay took his washpan from his packs and went back to work on Amanda. Using water from the buffalo paunch, he began wetting her face and neck to cool her down. Then he splashed her from her neck downward. The wet cloth clung to her breasts, revealing the nipples, but that hardly mattered now. All he knew was that if he didn't get her fever down, he'd be riding to Davis with her body tied over Hannibal's packs. And then all hell would break loose in Austin.

"Amanda, can you understand me?" he asked, shaking her.

Her eyes opened and her tongue worked to make words in her dry mouth. "I ... saw ... Indians," she whispered. "Thirsty ... so thirsty."

"They're gone, but they left you some water."

Her head was pounding, and dizziness again threatened to overwhelm her. "My head ..."

"I know." He held the canteen for her, and she took a couple of swallows before pushing it away.

"So sick ... so sick ..."

"Yeah. You're way too hot, and if we don't get you cooled off, you're going to be in one hell of a fix."

"I am."

"You can't drink much, but you've got to drink often. Otherwise, you're going to lose it as fast as I get it into you. You understand that, don't you?"

"Yes."

He felt her forehead, then her cheeks with the back of his hand. Her face was like fire. He knew what he had to do, and he knew she wasn't going to like it. He took a deep breath, then reached for the front of her gown.

"Amanda, I don't want you to think I've got any wrong notions or that I'm going to take advantage of you, but the only way I know to do this is to get you wet all over. I've done it before on overheated horses," he added conversationally as he began working on her buttons. Her hands caught his, but he brushed them aside. "Don't. You can make this a whole lot easier on both of us if you don't fight me."

She didn't have enough strength to stop him, and she knew it. As he pushed the bodice down from her shoulders, baring her breasts, she closed her eyes. Leaning her over his arm, he pushed the sleeves down over her hands. As he laid her back again, he grasped the hem of her skirt and yanked it off, leaving only her frilled drawers.

He poured water from the paunch into the pan, then took the dirty handkerchief she'd had on her head and wrung it out in the water. Using it for a rag, he began washing her hot skin from her forehead to her chin, her neck to her breasts, her arms, her legs below the drawers. He repeated the process several times until it seemed as though she was cooler to his touch. Then he picked up his hat and fanned her damp skin vigorously.

"Feel better?"

"No," she choked out.

As sick as she was, he knew she was mortified. "Hey, don't you know you don't have anything I haven't seen somewhere else?"

She swallowed visibly, but didn't open her eyes. "No."

He felt her forehead. "Yeah, Amanda, I think we did some good with that bath. Now if you can just drink enough, pretty soon you're going to feel a whole lot better."

"Please . . ." Her hand reached toward her dress.

He shook his head. "You need to let the water dry on you—that's what cools you down." Instead of the dress, he shook out the wet handkerchief and laid it across her breasts. It didn't cover much, but maybe she wouldn't know it.

"One more drink," he decided, lifting her against his knee. She was greedy now, and her hands held his wrist, pulling the canteen closer. Now he was afraid she was getting too much. "Whoa—that's enough."

She lay back. "Ramon—"

"I know."

"I have to tell—he—"

"It's all right. We'll take care of him later."

But she wanted him to know. "He left me . . . he left . . . I walked . . . I walked . . ."

"You don't have to say anything—I followed your trail for miles."

"I couldn't ..." She licked her cracked lips. ". . . walk anymore."

"I saw that."

"He tried to kill me," she whispered. "He shot at me, but he missed. I fell, and—"

"It's over. In a few days, you'll be all right."

"But ... he tried to ... kill me."

He had to keep her calm. Reaching over, he smoothed her tangled auburn hair back from her temples. "He won't get away with it, not now. I reckon you and the state of Texas are going to have one hell of a surprise for him. What you need to do now is get some rest."

She was still dizzy, and her eyes were so sore it hurt to blink, but she felt a certain satisfaction just knowing she'd survived. That she was going to live to see Ramon Sandoval hanged. That God was going to let her get even.

"Thanks," she murmured, closing her eyes again.

Clay heaved his tired body up and went to get the prickly pear he'd cut for her. Returning, he sank down and began slitting each piece open. When he was finished, he rubbed the wet insides over her face, her burnt forearms, and her swollen, blistered feet. It wasn't agave, but it was better than nothing.

Crawling under the makeshift tent, he lay down and set his hat over his face, covering his eyes against the light. The day was more than half over, and he still had a long way to ride after sundown. Only now he wasn't going to be alone, he reflected grimly, and that was a big complication he didn't need. Now he'd made himself responsible for the woman lying beside him.

If he tried to take her to Davis or Stockton, he risked missing the gun wagon. And the stakes were too high for that. No, he was going to have to take her with him. His thoughts turned to Ketanah and the medicine woman he could still see in his mind. He wondered if just once he dared go back. If he dared take Amanda there. And somewhere in the depths of his mind, he heard the answer—he had to. Nahdehwah would take care of her.

He turned over, his body touching hers, and he wakened with a start. Amanda lay there, her eyes closed, her breathing shallow. He reached out and felt along her jaw. She stirred, but did not rouse. It didn't matter—her skin was warm, slightly moist even, and beneath his fingertips, her pulse was thin but steady. She was better.

He rolled from beneath the makeshift shelter and sat up to flex his shoulders. It was still almost unbearably hot, and his clothes were soaked with his sweat. Yawning, he ran his hand over the stubble on his face and looked around.

In the west, the setting sun was blood red, and the dead mesquite branches stood like stunted black skeletons with arms outstretched, reaching for the orange sky. He sat there, taking in the barren beauty of a desert about to come to life. It was a place where a man was limited only by his own ability to survive. Maybe he felt that way because he was damned good at surviving, but to him, this place was as much his home as any.

As he stared across to distant hills, he thought of Ten Bears speech to the peace commissioners at Medicine Lodge in what seemed another age. He'd been moved enough when he read them to commit the old chief's words to memory.

I was born upon the prairie, where the wind blew free and there was nothing to break the light of the sun. I

was born where there were no enclosures and where
everything drew a free breath. I want to die there and
not remain within walls. I know every stream and every wood between the Rio Grande and the Arkansas. I
have hunted and lived over that country. I live like my
fathers before me and like them I have lived happily.

He understood what the old man meant. Even now,
whenever he was alone in the vast open spaces of
western Texas, he could feel it. And he could still feel
the tug of the powerful images those words gave him.
It was something that defied explanation, something he
couldn't even share with Hap, who was as close to him
as anyone. If Hap knew the land, it was as a means of
getting from one place to another. No, Hap preferred
the warmth of a woman, the softness of a good featherbed, to this.

In another year or two at most, the Nermernuh
would be gone from the hills, canyons, plains, and desert of Texas, herded like cattle onto reservations. And
Stands Alone, son of Many Feathers In His Hair,
would exist only in his own memory. Then there could
be no returning to The People.

For him, the dream was already fading. The language didn't come easily anymore, and he could even
foresee the day when he would understand Comanche
little better than he'd understood English that day Hap
Walker had caught him. It was inevitable, and he knew
it.

But not yet. Tonight he was going to ride north toward the Pecos, where with any luck at all, he would
find Ketanah and a Nokoni band. And if he asked
around a bit, he could probably discover where Quanah
Parker was waiting for his wagons loaded with guns.
It'd make his job a whole lot easier if he just knew
that. If only he could do it without feeling guilty, without feeling as though he was there for all the wrong
reasons.

He was going to do all he could to persuade Ketanah

against following Quanah's war trail. He'd tell him that no matter how many Comanches, no matter how many allies Quanah could command, they could not win, and in the end, Ranald Mackenzie and his buffalo soldiers would prevail. The Nokoni chief wouldn't want to hear it, but he might recognize the truth, sparing his people the suffering and hardship of defeat.

His thoughts turned to Amanda, wondering what she was going to think when she found herself among Comanches. Once she saw that the Nokonis wouldn't harm her, he hoped she'd settle down. He'd have to say she belonged to him, but there was no help for that. In a way, the notion was actually appealing. But he'd have to tell her that, after he'd dealt with Sanchez-Torres or whoever was running the guns, he'd take her to the Ybarra. He'd be going there, anyway, to arrest Ramon Sandoval for attempted murder.

If he didn't come back, if he got himself killed ... He'd always been more or less fatalistic—he knew it was bound to happen someday. Men in his business didn't grow old, not often anyway. This time, he'd have to be careful. With Amanda waiting for him, he'd have to survive.

He reached for the buffalo paunch, checking to see how much water was left in it. Untying it, he drank deeply, and the tepid liquid overflowed, dribbling down his chin. But it was wet going down, and that was all that mattered. His thirst somewhat slaked, he looked at the bag, and he knew she wouldn't want to drink out of it. For a moment, he considered filling his canteens from it, then decided she'd probably know anyway. There was something about the skin that changed the taste of water.

Paunch in hand, he walked to where Sarah and Hannibal stood chewing on branches of stunted mesquite. Taking out a chunk of lye soap, his razor, and the pan that served for everything from a coffee pot to a wash basin, he poured himself some water, stripped himself naked, and washed the sweat and dust from his body. Using the dirty water, he shaved by feel. Like the Comanches, he couldn't stand letting hair grow on his face.

A horsefly buzzed her face, wakening Amanda, and for a moment, she stared in bewilderment at the old blanket above her. She'd been dreaming, she knew that—no, it had been one nightmare after another. There'd even been a hideously painted savage leering at her, touching her hair. And she'd been so dizzy, so thirsty, so very, very thirsty. It was as though she'd been to hell.

Then she remembered—Ramon Sandoval had abandoned her, and she'd walked until her strength was gone. Finally, when there was nothing left to draw on, she'd lain down, too weak, too exhausted to think. And all the while, those birds had watched, mocking her attempts to rise, waiting for her to die.

Even now, her mouth was too dry to swallow, and nearly everything between her pounding head and her feet throbbed, telling her she had to be alive. She moved, then realized that she was only wearing her drawers. For some reason, her dress was lying on the ground beside her. Clutching it to cover her breasts, she turned her head, seeing the horse and mule, and finally Clay McAlester. He stood, his back to her, his body bare below the pale hair that hung over his shoulders. It was the first time she'd ever seen a man's naked backside, and she knew she ought not look at him.

He leaned to rinse his razor, then wiped the straight blade clean before wrapping it to put away. Going to his packs, he got a shirt, shook it out, and shrugged it over his head. It reached nearly to his knees. As he was buttoning the neck placket, he turned around and saw her.

He regarded her warily, taking in the tangled mass of auburn hair half perched atop her head, the red, puffy eyes. Right now, she didn't look much like the woman he'd encountered at the stagecoach station. Nor did she look like the one he'd caught unhooking her corset top beside the water. It was just as well. He was distracted enough as it was.

"Good—you're awake," was about all he could think of to say.

"Yes." It was more a croak than an answer.

There was another moment of awkwardness, then he added, "I . . . uh, I was sort of taking a bath and shaving."

When she said nothing, he knew she was embarrassed. "Still thirsty?" he asked.

"Yes."

He picked up one of his canteens and tossed it to her. "Don't drink too much at once—it'll make you sick, and if it comes up, you'll just waste it."

Removing the lid, she took a mouthful of the warm water, then held it, savoring its wetness before swallowing. She could have drunk the whole thing, but she forced herself to recap it. She was sick enough already.

"Thank you," she managed.

"You look like hell," he muttered.

"I feel like I've been there."

Moving again to where Hannibal stood, he retrieved a worn pair of buckskin breeches. Keeping his back to her, he balanced himself against the mule and pulled them on. Still barefooted, he picked up the tin pan, tossed the now-brown water, and refilled it. Carrying it and the soap, he walked to stand over Amanda.

"I don't know if you feel like washing up, but it'll cool you off. Uh—if you can't do it, I'll try to help you."

She was looking up at him, her dress bunched in her hands, pressed tightly against the crevice between her breasts. Unlike her red face and forearms, the skin on her shoulders was pale, almost as delicate, as luminous as satin. He sucked in his breath, then let it out. "I reckon you want to try it yourself, huh? And you'll probably want to be alone."

"Yes."

It occurred to him then that there was nowhere to

go, that as far as he looked, the land was flat and almost barren. "Tell you what—you get on the other side
of that blanket, and I'll fix supper," he decided finally.

She eyed the pan, then him, and the lure of soap and
water won. But as she tried to rise, her legs buckled,
and her feet were so sore she couldn't stand. She stumbled, tangling the dress between her legs. He lunged,
catching her, but not before the garment fell completely. Standing there in naught but her drawers, she
felt her face go hot. She couldn't look at him.

"My feet wouldn't hold me," she choked out.

He stepped back and she sank to the ground, where
she sat hunched over her knees, nearly too dizzy to
think, fighting an inexplicable urge to cry. Hot tears
stung her sore eyes and threatened to spill onto her
face.

He picked up the canteen and unscrewed the cap for
her. "Here," he said gruffly. "Take another drink and
sit there." This time, her stomach fought back. She
closed her eyes and swallowed, trying to calm rising
nausea. Resting her head on her knees, she waited until
it was safe to speak. "I'm all right," she mumbled. But
she wasn't. She felt awful.

She was still suffering from too much heat and too
much sun, but there wasn't much more he could do
about it. "For what it's worth, you'll get better," he
told her. "You have to."

"I know." She wiped her eyes with the back of her
hand. "I despise weeping females, but just now I cannot help it. All I want to do is get home."

"And see Ramon Sandoval hang," he reminded her.
"You managed to tell me that when I found you. You
were more than half dead, but you got that out."

"Yes," she admitted, her voice still little more than a
whisper. "How far is it—to Ybarra-Ross, I mean?"

Rather than answer her, he went back to his packs
and found the lace-edged cambric chemise she'd discarded. With some regret, he unrolled his last clean
shirt. He returned to thrust the clothes at her.

"If you get washed up, you can put this on. With your chemise, it'll more than cover you." When she didn't take it, he added, "It's clean—I washed it with lye soap before I left Stockton. But if you don't want it, I guess you can suit yourself."

"I can't go home in my underwear," she said tiredly.

He guessed he might as well get it out now, and he knew she wasn't going to like it. He sucked in his breath, then exhaled fully. "I wouldn't worry about that. I'm going north—up toward the Pecos."

It sank into her numb mind slowly. He wasn't going to take her home. For an awful moment she thought he was going to leave her alone there. Then reason reasserted itself.

"I can pay . . . I can pay . . ." She wet her raw lips, then blurted out, "Two hundred dollars—two hundred dollars to get me to Ybarra-Ross. I'll pay you when I get there."

"No."

"That's a lot of money."

What she meant was it was a lot of money for a man like him, and he knew it. His jaw tightened visibly, and his eyes went cold, but he didn't answer.

"Five hundred, then," she said. "For saving my life and getting me home. Well?"

"No."

"No?" Her voice cracked on the word. "Do you want more?"

The look he gave her would have wilted a flower.

"All right," she decided wearily. "Just tell me what it takes."

She was offering him more than he could make in a year, and yet he was disappointed in her. He shook his head.

"Please."

"Look, if I try to take you back—say as far as Davis, even—I run the risk of missing a shipment of guns coming across from New Mexico." He looked straight into her eyes. "Tell me you're worth more than a hundred families living out here," he said evenly. "Because if Quanah Parker gets those guns, that's what it's going to cost. Maybe more. He's not going to go onto the reservation without one hell of a fight."

She was nearly too sick to think. "I didn't know—but surely the army—"

"The regular army couldn't find a Comanchero if he had the word painted on his back, and by the time Mackenzie's ready to take to the field, it'll just be to get even with the Comanches. And then it's too late." Rather than argue with her, he turned and walked off.

"Wait—" She licked her raw, cracked lips again. "Where are you going?" Then, as she considered the possibilities, she wished she hadn't asked. "That is . . ."

"To get firewood."

He knew he was being hard on her, but he resented her thinking he could be bought. As if she didn't know what she was costing him already. Now he had to be careful, now he had to think of getting both of them back alive. And if he'd been alone, he'd have eaten his usual handful of berries and a couple of pieces of jerky and been on his way before now. As it was, he'd only brought food and water for himself. And with everything dried out between here and the Pecos, it was going to be a hard trip. Since it hadn't rained in weeks, he knew there'd be so much gypsum in the river that she wouldn't want to drink the water.

He picked up his Bowie knife and walked about fifty feet, where he began hacking dead twigs and branches off the sparse mesquite and greasewood. He worked the knife with a vengeance, giving release to his anger. Gradually it dissipated, and he had to own that none of this was really her fault. She hadn't asked to be abandoned, but she'd done one hell of a job of trying to survive. And why wouldn't she think he'd want money? He'd already told her that he only made thirty-three dollars a month, and to her that wasn't very damned much.

She watched his back for several minutes, feeling utterly helpless. Then she remembered how hard she'd worked to live, and she wasn't going to quit now. If she couldn't stand, she could surely crawl. With an effort, she dragged her clothes and the washpan with her, spilling some of the precious water. Exhausted, she lay there for a moment, then carefully sat up. Her head pounded. She was too weak for anything.

There wasn't very much water left, but she leaned over the pan and dipped both her hands into it, splashing her face, getting what relief she could. She rubbed the hard, strong soap between her palms, trying to make some sort of suds, then washed her face, her neck, her shoulders, and her arms. It didn't even matter that she had to rinse with the same water. Finally, she pushed down her drawers and washed herself there also. Much good that was going to do her, she thought wryly—she was just going to have to put them back on again.

She considered her dirty dress for a moment, then pushed it aside and reached for the chemise. It was too thin, but she didn't care anymore. She pulled it over her head and down over the top of her drawers. And then she tried the shirt. As it enveloped her, it smelled of sunlight and strong soap. Concentrating with an effort, she managed to button it almost to her neck. Leaving the pan, she crawled back and lay down again.

"Well, you look better," he observed as he dropped his armful of sticks.

"I feel like I could die," she said dully.

"The worst is over, so you'll make it. But you're probably hungry."

She hadn't had anything since breakfast the day before, but she felt too weak to eat. "No."

"Ever eat any jerky?"

"No."

"Hackberries?"

"No."

"That's about all I've got with me, and we've got to

get something in you before we ride. You need your strength."

Kneeling, he began arranging the sticks, putting the mesquite over the greasewood. It wouldn't burn long, but it'd burn hot enough to make coffee. He struck a match against his thumbnail, then touched it to the greasewood. There was a flare as it caught. He stood and wiped his hands.

"Done with this?" he asked, retrieving the pan.

"Yes." Despite her throbbing head and queasy stomach, she knew she'd insulted him with her offer of money. But while his head was inches from hers, she couldn't quite get up the nerve to apologize. Instead, she waited until he straightened, then said low, "You saved my life, and I'm grateful—truly grateful."

He didn't answer.

"I didn't mean to offend you about the money. I just thought you could use it." That hadn't come out quite right. "I mean, well, I wanted to go home and . . ."

"I understood you the first time. You thought you could buy me."

"No."

"Save your breath until you have something to say worth saying," he muttered.

While she watched, he filled the pan again, then placed it in front of his horse. The animal drank noisily until it was empty. He repeated the process, this time giving it to the mule. When Hannibal lifted his head, McAlester rinsed the pan out, added more water, and carried it to his packs, where he found his food bag.

Returning to his small fire, he opened a small, stained cotton sack and took out a handful of coffee, which he dropped into the pan. He set it in the fire, then turned his attention to the larger bag. He pulled out what looked to be some sort of dark balls. He skewered them on the ends of two green sticks and propped them next to the pan so that they didn't drip into the coffee. Almost immediately they began smoking and sizzling.

Her stomach rebelled at the smell of them. "What's that?"

"Hackberry."

"Are you sure they aren't grease," she managed, swallowing the gorge that rose in her throat.

"That's the buffalo tallow." Without looking up, he explained, "Comanche women pound the berries into a paste, then mix them with melted tallow, and as the fat cools, they roll it into balls, and store them in parfleches. When I was a boy, I thought they were the best thing I'd ever eaten."

"Ugh."

"Don't turn up your nose until you try them."

"I don't think I can eat."

"There's Indian bread—at least that's what Texans call it. You probably ate it at the Ybarra."

"My father didn't like Indians."

"But he liked their land well enough," he retorted.

She didn't want to dispute anything. She just wanted to lie there, but she couldn't let it pass. "The Ybarra-Ross came from Mama," she said tiredly. "Her family held the grant for a century before he was born."

"Maybe it wasn't theirs to give him." He got up to fetch a battered tin cup, a tin plate, and a piece of cloth. Using a stick, he pulled the pan from the smoldering coals, and one of the hackberry balls fell into what was left of the fire. He jabbed it, dragging it out, and dumped it, ashes and all, onto the plate. Then he turned his attention back to the coffee. Putting the cloth over the cup, he picked up the hot pan and sloshed its contents through the cloth, straining it.

"I don't have any sugar," he said, handing the cup to her.

She eyed it dubiously, but said nothing. The remaining hackberry ball joined the blackened mess in the plate. Clay McAlester dropped down beside her and speared the first ball with his knife. Holding it up, he waited for the ashes and grit to drip off.

"Go on—try it," he urged, gesturing to the other

one. When she didn't move, he sighed. "Look, it may not compare with anything you ate in Boston, but you've got to eat. I don't mean to stop again to rest before morning." She watched as he bit into his with the stick. Grease ran down his chin. "Try it," he urged her.

"I can't . . . I just can't."

He speared the hackberry ball on her plate and held it to her mouth. Rather than fight, she took the smallest nibble possible. Before her stomach could rebel, she swallowed, then took a gulp of hot coffee. She choked on it.

"Careful—Hap says I make that too strong."

Not trusting herself to speak, she nodded.

"Come on," he coaxed, "the more you eat, the better you'll feel."

This time, she forced herself to take a sizable bite. As soon as it hit, the grease was churning in her stomach. She swallowed more of the awful coffee, forcing it down.

He reached into his bag and took out what appeared to be a block sealed in paraffin. Cutting off several slices with the knife, he handed one to her. Then he opened a small sealed jar, and set it between them. As she hesitated, he dipped one of the slices into it, then carried it to his mouth.

She looked at it doubtfully.

"It's dried venison, pecans, and wild plums. You pound them together until the flavors mix, then you dip the whole in tallow. Air doesn't get in, so it'll keep for years." He smiled faintly. "It's one of the few Comanche foods white people like."

It couldn't be worse than the hackberry balls, she was sure of that. She took a breath, then broke off a piece of it between her teeth. As she was chewing, he took her wrist and made her dip the rest of it in the jar.

"Honey," he explained succinctly.

She managed to get several bites down, then shook her head. "I can't eat any more—truly I cannot."

"Then drink your coffee."

Her stomach knotted at the thought, and rather than answer, she shook her head. He regarded her soberly, thinking she was being difficult. Finally, he took the cup and drained it.

"All right," he said, standing up. "Just don't be telling me how hungry you are come midnight."

"I won't."

"It's getting late, so I'm going to pack up. If you need to take care of nature, you can take that blanket and hang it over a mesquite tree for privacy. Otherwise, I'm going to put it into my bedroll now." He studied her again for a moment, then asked bluntly, "Do you want me to go with you?"

"No."

"Just don't go far, and watch where you are. Things come out once the sun's down."

She tried to rise to her feet, but she couldn't make it. She lay back and rolled into a ball. Wave after wave of nausea washed over her as she desperately tried to hold the little she'd eaten down. "I can't," she whispered. "I just can't."

His anger gone, he felt sorry for her now. "I wish we could stay, but we can't. Come morning, it'll be hotter than hell again, and we don't have all that much water." He leaned down and grasped her arm, trying to help her up.

She fought back tears. "I can't stand up."

"I'll hold you."

"No."

"Because you're embarrassed?"

"Yes."

"Amanda, I've seen a lot of Comanche woman squatting along the trail. It doesn't make any difference to me."

She swallowed. "I'm not a Comanche woman," she managed through gritted teeth.

"Come on—I'll turn my head." He lifted her, then put an arm beneath hers, taking most of her weight off her sore feet. "You can do your business here, if you want. We're moving on, anyway."

In the distance a coyote howled, its chilling cry piercing the darkening desert. She shuddered, then tried to take a step, stumbling against him.

"I don't know how the hell you thought I could get you all the way to the Ybarra like this," he muttered.

"If I didn't want to see Ramon hang, I'd gladly die," she said wearily. "I'm so sick . . . so sick . . ."

She got no further. Her stomach convulsed, sending her food back up. He barely had time to lean her over his other arm before she vomited. As he held her helplessly, she retched and retched until there was nothing left to come up. And still she heaved. He dragged her to where he'd already packed the canteens. Opening one, he dashed a little of the water into her face.

"Better?" he asked hopefully.

"No. I can still taste the coffee."

"Poor Amanda," he murmured soothingly, turning her against his chest. Resting her head on his shoulder, she clung to him as though he were life itself. "It's all right," he whispered over and over. "You're going to get better—you have to."

"I know."

"Come one—let's take care of nature now." Easing her back onto his arm, he tried to walk her. This time, she didn't stumble, but she was mostly dead weight. "That's the girl," he encouraged her. "We'll stop anywhere you want."

"I don't care."

"How about here?"

"No."

"Amanda, you're damned contrary—you know that, don't you?"

"All right—here then."

She was too dizzy, too sick to care anymore. She reached out, gripping his hand. Holding her, he managed to get her drawers down, then he fixed his gaze on a stand of mesquite as she sank to a squat. It wasn't until she announced, "I'm done," that he looked down. The puddle was small and as dark as his coffee. She wasn't getting enough water.

"See—you didn't die, did you?"

"I thought about it."

He pulled her up and yanked up her drawers, catching her chemise under them. "Damn, but you're helpless as a baby, aren't you?" he said, straightening it out.

"Yes."

"I'm going to tie you onto Hannibal," he decided.

"I'm too dizzy to think."

"I know." She looked more like a lost waif than the Ybarra heiress. "But I'm going to have to try it."

"I'm telling you I'm sick."

He regarded her soberly. "Are you telling me you can't sit a mule if you're tied on?" he asked finally.

"I don't know."

"Amanda, I've got to get you somewhere where you can drink. Otherwise, you'll lose ground, and I'll have it all to do over again."

"But I'm sick—truly sick." Even as she said it, she swayed, and for a moment, the world went black. "Please—"

"Look, we've got to travel in the cool of the night. If you don't want to ride with the packs, you can ride with me." Seeing that she just stood there, he added brusquely, "It doesn't make any difference to me."

"I don't want to be tied down."

"Fine. Here—lean against this tree." Releasing her, he finished packing, then he swung his saddle over the paint mare's back, tightened the cinch, and checked it. He added the blanket to his bedroll and tied it behind. When he turned around, he was basically ready. "I guess that's it," he said. "How do you feel now?"

"I can make it."

"How about a drink before we go?"

"I don't think it would stay down.

No matter how she felt, he couldn't afford to wait

much longer. "All right. I'm going to put you up in the saddle, and you can hang onto the horn. I'll ride behind and hold you on. Think you can ride like that?"

She closed her eyes for a moment, then nodded. "Yes."

He lifted her up, pushing her into the worn leather saddle, and as her leg went over, her chemise rode up. Before she had time to pull the ruffled hem of her drawers down to cover her bare legs, he swung up behind her. Reaching around her for the reins, his arm brushed against her breast. There was a momentary pause in his breath, then he recovered.

"Ready?"

"Yes." Too sick to worry about propriety, she leaned back, resting her head on his shoulder. "I'll be all right—I've got to be."

Clay reached for the lead rope with his free hand, then nudged the paint mare with his knee. The horse started forward, but as the rope tautened, the mule threw its head back, baring its teeth. He jerked the rope, pulling the animal up short, and it sullenly fell in behind them.

"Keep this up, Hannibal, and one of these days you're going to be supper," Clay warned the mule.

His arm tightened around Amanda, holding her. It was nearly dark, and he could hear a whole pack of coyotes howling at the moon. He looked down at the shadowed head against his breast and felt an odd tenderness. Tomorrow she'd probably be the greatest nuisance of his life, but tonight she seemed frail and vulnerable in his arms, and he wanted to protect her. For a foolish moment he even dared to wonder what it would be like to have her, then he caught himself. As his Aunt Jane often said, that would happen when pigs flew.

Ahead he saw the eerie silhouette of two Indians against the brightening sky. Shifting Amanda's weight to his other arm, Clay reached for his spyglass. As he focused on them, he was relieved. Both wore the long, unbraided hair of Comanches, and it looked as though they might be waiting for him. He cupped his mouth with his free hand and gave his long, lonesome coyote howl. Almost before it ended, they answered. Amanda roused slightly and turned her head into his shoulder. It wasn't a very satisfactory position, but she'd been so dizzy when he'd stopped that he had to turn her sideways and hold her. Now his arm and back ached like the devil.

She seemed to be getting worse instead of better, and every drop of water he'd tried to put in her was coming back up. But he had to admire her—as sick as she was, she'd hung on. He brushed his hand against her temple, discovering it was hotter, dryer then before. Before the sun rose much higher, he was going to have to get something into her, and she was going to have to keep it down.

He shouldn't have made her eat the hackberry ball, he knew that now. The tallow had been too heavy for her stomach—that and the strong boiled coffee. He could still taste the bitterness himself, and he could drink damned near anything.

He was thirsty, terribly thirsty, but he didn't want to stop. Not yet. If he did, he'd have to get her down and then back up. And he was tired, nearly too tired to think. Days of unrelenting heat and his own lack of sleep were telling on him, and his nerves were strung as taut as bowstrings.

He closed his burning eyes, squeezing tears into them, then straightened up, shifting her again. Slowed by the weight of two people, the paint mare walked doggedly, and he knew she was as tired as he was. Before the sun got much higher, he was going to have to change mounts, which would necessitate changing packs between her and Hannibal. The temperamental mule tolerated him, but it would probably balk when he put Amanda on.

When he looked up again, the Indians were gone. He blinked, and they reappeared, two riders with a horse between them, coming down the gentle slope toward him. They closed the gap, then pulled up less than a hundred feet away, and Clay could see yellow warpaint in their hair. One of them called out, asking his name. It was as though there was a momentary pause in his heartbeat, as though time waited for the answer he would give them.

"Nahakoah!" he shouted. *"Nermernuh!"*

Awakened, Amanda tried to sit up, but his arm tightened around her. "It's all right—just stay still," he told her. Raising his free arm, he pointed his hand at them, asking "Nokoni?"

"Nokoni!" one of them responded.

Hearing the foreign words, Amanda looked up at him in bewilderment. He didn't know whether she could understand or not, but he tried to reassure her. "They're friendly," he said under his breath. "They won't hurt you."

"No," she croaked.

"These are my people, Amanda—because they think you belong to me, they welcome you."

She turned her face into his shoulder and held on. "I'm sick . . . so sick," she whispered.

"I know," he consoled her. "But once I get you to Nahdehwah, you'll get better."

The one leading the horse rode closer and struck his breast. "Tshantai," he announced. Bear Claw. And the painting on his shield indicated he belonged to the Crow Warriors. Turning in his saddle, Bear Claw gestured to his companion. "Asenakei." Waits for Deer.

Waits for Deer raised a lance high at the introduction, then grinned as he lowered it. Half a dozen fresh scalps swung below its sharpened point. By the looks of him, he was a Crow Warrior also. The war party had sent two members of the highest Comanche military society to guide him to Ketanah's camp.

"I am honored," he said, acknowledging their worth.

Bear Claw looked Clay up and down, then nodded. "We have heard of you, Stands Alone. You are brother to my brother."

It was an acknowledgment of kinship between The People that even Hap couldn't understand—a bond of belonging rather than one of blood. Clay nodded. "Brother," he said solemnly.

Glancing to Amanda's still form, Waits for Deer clucked sympathetically. "The Kiowas told of your sick woman. Like you, we have little water, but you are welcome to it."

"She can't keep it down."

"If she can live until we reach Ketanah's camp, Nehdehwah will cure her."

"She'll make it—she has to." But as Clay looked down, seeing Amanda's head against his shoulder, he wasn't as sure as he sounded.

"You have other wives, Stands Alone?" Bear Claw asked.

"No—only this one." Seeing that they regarded him with pity, he added, "She has no sisters."

"But you gained her brothers," the Indian murmured, trying to put the best face on what he perceived to be Clay's unfortunate predicament. "They hunt with you."

"She doesn't have any brothers," he admitted. "She has no one."

Bear Claw digested that, then decided, "You are a good man to take a girl without family, Stands Alone. I married a woman with two sisters, so now I have three wives who help each other." He gestured to Waits for Deer. "His wives are not sisters, and they quarrel too much."

Not wanting to discuss his situation, the other Indian changed the subject abruptly. "We brought a horse for your woman, but I can see she cannot sit alone," he said. "Two Owls did not tell us she would need a travois, and we have no poles to make one," he added apologetically.

"I can hold her until we stop." As he spoke, Clay flexed his tingling fingers, trying to increase his circulation. When he did stop, he was going to have to try tying her onto Hannibal. By now, the mule ought to have lost enough of his vinegar to stand for it, he reasoned.

Bear Claw turned in his saddle to survey the flat terrain, then shook his head. "Not here," he decided. "There is no place to hide."

"But soon there will be a small hill," Waits for Deer promised. "Then if she cannot ride, I will take Stands Alone's woman on my horse."

It was a generous offer, but if Amanda awakened in the Indian's arms, she'd be terrified. As sick as she was, Clay still more than half expected her to cut a real dido when she found herself in a Comanche camp. And if she did, he was going to suffer a real loss of face.

As the two warriors fell in beside him, they told of raiding deep into Mexico, all the way to Durango, and bringing back "many horses, many captives." They also said that while the main band was encamped near the big spring on Sulphur Draw, there were a number of Nokoni Comanches who'd come down as far as this side of Castle Gap, where the weeping springs still gave water. By Clay's reckoning, that put the camp twelve miles beyond Horsehead Crossing.

He didn't even want to think of Horsehead Crossing. That was the big test—he was going to have to get across the Pecos with her, and even in dry times, the river was treacherous and unforgiving of mistakes. There'd been a lot of folks who'd learned that lesson the hard way, and whole cattle herds had been known to perish there. As much as he disliked ranchers, he felt almost sorry for Rube Grey, whose thirst-mad herd had plunged over the river banks to drink, then died bawling in the quicksand below. It didn't matter—to get where he needed to go he was going to have to get across the Pecos. Resolutely, he turned his attention to the woman in his arms.

He couldn't see her face, so he didn't know if she slept, or if she was hiding from the two Comanches. All he knew was that he could feel her breath on his arm.

"Amanda?" he asked softly. "Can you hear me?"

"Yes." Her answer was barely a whisper.

"You're going to be all right—you know that, don't you?"

She didn't answer.

He slowed the paint to a walk. Transferring the reins to the hand that held her, he reached for his nearly empty canteen, twisted the lid off with his teeth, and caught it with his hand. Tipping the container, he drank enough to wet his mouth, hoping to slake his own awful thirst. He leaned forward, laying Amanda in the crook of his arm, then held the canteen to her mouth.

"Here," he urged her, "take a little of this. Come on—you've got to be thirsty—you've got to."

She pushed it away.

Bear Claw leaned out to touch her dry skin, then shook his head. "Bad," he grunted. He reached down and untied his food sack from his saddle. Dipping his fingers into it, he drew out several peyote buttons and gave them to Clay. "When I had fire in the gut and could not eat, they cured me," he offered in testimony.

"Thanks." Clay shifted Amanda again. "Try to eat these," he coaxed.

She turned her head and closed her eyes.

"You're making this hard—you know that, don't you?"

"No," she whispered.

"All right." His hand forced her mouth open and he pushed the peyote buttons between her teeth. "All you've got to do is chew these." She gagged, then recovered, but he held his hand over her mouth just in case. "Keep trying, and you can do it," he encouraged her. As he watched, she worked her jaws, then swallowed. "Keep going," he urged. She swallowed again. "That's good, *amiga*—get it all down."

As he looked into her face, seeing her sunburned cheeks, her cracked, blackened lips, part of him told him it would have been easier and kinder to have let her die. Instead he'd made himself responsible for her. And right now he was too tired to even ponder why he'd done it. But as her image that night at Comanche Springs appeared in his mind, the dryness in his mouth came from more than a lack of water.

It seemed as though an eternity passed before Waits for Deer observed, "Your mare is tired," breaking into Clay's thoughts. "And there is a hill behind us now."

Clay noticed he'd said mare rather than horse. But left unsaid was that a man should ride a gelding rather than a mare, that a mare was for a child, a woman, or an old man, not a warrior. "She's got more heart than any other horse I've ever owned," Clay declared. "There hasn't been a place I needed to go where she wasn't willing to carry me. We've crossed desert, mountain, canyon, and river together. But I probably ought to rest her and ride the spare horse for a while," he conceded, reining in.

The Indian dismounted. Walking to the paint mare, he reached up for Amanda, steadying her while Clay gingerly eased his aching body from the saddle. She swayed, nearly falling, then grasped the saddlehorn.

Her glazed eyes blinked, trying to focus on the hideously painted face. As a scream fought against her seemingly paralyzed throat, he smiled at her, then said something to McAlester.

Clay reached for her, lifting her, then carrying her to where Bear Claw had already laid a brightly colored Mexican blanket on the ground. As he placed her on it, she rolled to her side, drawing her knees to her chest. Nearly too dizzy to think, she curled up like a small child. Her mouth was so dry she couldn't swallow.

"Thirsty . . . so thirsty," she whispered.

As if he understood what she said, Waits for Deer untied an almost empty water bag and brought it over. "For your woman," he said. "We can get more at the river."

This time, when Clay propped her against his knee and held the mouth of the container to her lips, she drank noisily, guzzling it, spilling it onto his shirt, until he pulled it away from her. When he laid her back, he felt considerable relief. The peyote had worked, and once she kept the water in her stomach, she was going to feel a whole lot better. He took a big swig himself, and as it went down his parched throat, it was brackish, heavy with gypsum. If he hadn't been so thirsty, he'd have spit it out. But she hadn't noticed.

He walked, stretching his legs, swinging his arms to ease his aching shoulders. A big, thick-bodied diamondback buzzed in warning, but instead of killing it, he went the other way. He was just too hot and too tired to care right now. Leaning against the skeletal branches of a dead mesquite, he squinted up at the cloudless sky.

The sun would be high enough to blister the ground with its heat in another couple of hours, but there was no sense making camp. Not now, not when they were within a couple of hours of Horsehead Crossing. No, as hot as it was, it was better to get the treacherous Pecos behind them in full daylight.

He walked back and found that they'd already

moved his packs from Hannibal to Sarah and had saddled the other horse they'd brought. Waits for Deer had folded Clay's frayed government-issue blanket and placed it on the mule, tying it in place with a long piece of rawhide.

As much as they tried to hide it, there was no mistaking the eagerness of the two Indians. Having delayed long enough to make a triumphant entrance, the Crow Warriors were now hoping to reach Ketanah's camp before the scalp dance began. Clay would have told them to go on, but right now he couldn't afford to lose them.

When he approached Amanda, she sat up, still obviously dazed by the peyote, but there was no sign she'd vomited up the foul water. "Can you stand?" he asked her.

"No." Her voice was drowsy, thick like a drunk's. "Sleepy," she mumbled, falling back to the blanket.

He leaned down, braced her body with his, then shouldered her. Her arms hung loosely against his back. Steadying her with a hand on her rump, he carried her to where the two Indians waited. She was so drugged she didn't even protest when they lifted her onto Hannibal's back, laid her forward over the mule's shoulders, and secured her wrists around its neck with a braided hide rope. For good measure, they tied her ankles loosely beneath the animal's belly.

While Clay checked the knots, Waits for Deer gave what little water was left to the animals in the hope that they wouldn't stampede when they smelled the river. Finally ready, Clay swung into his saddle and took Hannibal's lead rope. Without a word, both Comanches moved ahead, leading the way.

Two hours proved to be an ambitious estimate. By the time the sun was straight overhead, the heat was too intense to expect anything more than a walk from the animals. The pace grew slower and slower until they had to dismount and lead the overheated horses. But they had to go on now. They couldn't afford to stop, not since they'd finished off their water and what little they'd drunk was coming back out of their skin.

Sweat ran from Clay's hatband down his forehead and neck, soaking his hair, and his wet shirt clung to his shoulders and back. In contrast, his mouth was so dry that his tongue felt thick. Yet he could still taste the gypsum, even more so than when he'd tried to slake his thirst with it. And he was so dizzy from the heat and loss of water that it was affecting his ability to think.

They ought to be nearly to the river by now. He looked to where Bear Claw walked stoically beside him, the paint on his face streaked with his sweat. His Comanche father had been like that, strong, disciplined, inured to pain. There'd been a time when water was so scarce that he'd threatened to kill any man who would drink before the children. Then he'd given the last few drops in his own buffalo paunch to Clay. Finally, when every bag was empty, he'd slaughtered his horse, and they'd drunk its blood. Clay could still remember the taste of it.

Two big black birds circled overhead—buzzards waiting for them to die. Clay drew his gun, took aim, and fired. One of them plummeted, leaving a few feathers to float after. The other one climbed higher. His second shot hit it. Without a word, Waits for Deer gathered both birds and tied the carcasses to his saddle, where they dripped, spotting the hard, dusty ground with blood. That was another thing to admire—unlike the rapacious white hunter, who left carcasses to rot, the Comanche never wasted anything.

Hannibal's head came up, jerking on his lead rope, and his nostrils flared. The animal smelled water. Shading his eyes against the blinding sun, Clay looked to the northwest, and sure enough, in the distance he could see the mesa split and the rimrock of the Castle Mountains dip low where the ancient Comanche war trail passed through them. Holding the lead rope taut, he swung back into the saddle. Both Indians mounted up, and Waits for Deer slipped a rawhide noose over the mule's neck from the other side to keep it from bolting. Herding Hannibal between them, they headed for the river.

Hap Walker likened the Pecos to a rattlesnake, saying it was mean, twisted, and downright deadly. Often, by the time anything stumbled upon the first water to be had in days, it was like one of Rube Grey's cows, so thirsty it plunged in, drank too much, and died. And it was easy to plunge in—unlike most rivers, the Pecos lacked a navigable bank. It was just there, a serpent lying in wait below a straight drop to water's edge, ready to swallow cattle, horses, men, and wagons. Dozens of bleached horse skulls, put there to mark the crossing, testified to its treachery, giving the place its name.

The horses caught the scent of water and went from a lethargic walk to a full trot. Between Clay and Waits for Deer, Hannibal tried to break loose. As the Comanche tightened the noose, the animal sidestepped, then lunged, stumbling into the Indian's pony. The rawhide slackened momentarily, and the mule bolted, tearing the lead rope from Clay's hand. Bear Claw took off in pursuit as Amanda bounced like a rag doll.

Cursing, Clay kicked his borrowed horse and raced for the river, hoping to head the mule off before it went into the water. The Indian dropped low beneath his mount's belly, trying to catch the trailing rope, but the mule eluded his grasp by inches. Flailing his rawhide thong against his pony's rump, Waits for Deer came from the other side, trying to sandwich the runaway mule between them.

Jolted half awake, Amanda locked her hands beneath Hannibal's neck and desperately hung on. As the animal went off the nearly ten-foot bank, she lost her grip and slipped to the side, falling almost beneath the mule's belly, hanging by the rawhide ropes that held her wrists and ankles. She screamed as she went under, and the swift, murky water closed around her. She fought frantically to free herself, while the mule thrashed and floundered in the ten-foot-deep water, struggling against the swift current.

Unless he got to her, she was going to drown before Clay's eyes. He kicked his horse harder, and as it plunged from the bank into the water, Clay dropped low, leaning to rip at the twisted rawhide with his Bowie knife, freeing her. But as he lunged to catch her arm, she slipped from his grasp, disappearing. He leaned lower, sweeping through the water with his hands, finding nothing. Cursing, he urged his horse downriver.

Amanda broke the surface ahead of him, then went under again. He slid into the water and swam toward where he'd seen her, letting the river's current carry him. Finally, in desperation, he dived several times, feeling along the bottom until his hand caught cloth. His eyes burning from mud, gypsum, and brine, he groped for Amanda's arms, then, with nearly bursting lungs, he managed to pull her up. Gasping, he started for the nearest bank.

Bear Claw threw him a rope, and as he held on, the Indian pulled him out and up the steep river bank. Exhausted, Clay crawled on his belly, dragging Amanda after him. Taking a deep breath, he dared to look at her. She wasn't moving. An impotent fury washed over him—after all he'd tried to do, it hadn't been enough. He rolled over and slapped her across the back. His wet, muddy shirt resounded like a sail hit by a stiff wind.

She retched, then choked. Heaving his body over hers, he leaned on her back, pressing the water from her lungs. Her breath caught, then she sighed. When Clay looked up, Bear Claw was grinning. Amanda was breathing. Clay sat back on his haunches, just looking at her, and despite the sunburn, despite the mud, despite the wet, bedraggled hair, in that moment, she was just about the best sight he'd ever seen.

Her brown eyes opened as he lifted her, holding her close, smoothing her tangled, dirty hair. She clung to him, shaking uncontrollably. His body was hard, strong, his embrace secure and comforting. She fought the urge to cry against his shoulder.

"Well, that's one way to get water, I guess," he said finally. "God, Amanda, but you gave me a fright," he added, his voice low, almost soft.

"I couldn't get loose . . . I couldn't get loose," she choked out.

"Shhhh. Don't think about it." His hand brushed her wet hair back from her temples. "There's a lot of life left in you yet. A few days with Nahdehwah and you'll be as good as new."

"I feel so sick," she managed, swallowing back the gorge that rose in her throat.

"It's the salt and the gypsum in the water. You've got to keep it down, Amanda—you've got to. There's nothing else between here and Castle Gap." When she didn't speak, he added, "I can get you some more peyote, if you'll eat it for me."

Clenching her teeth against the nausea, she shook her head.

Releasing her, Clay struggled to stand as his wet clothes bagged against him. Out of the corner of his eye, he saw Waits for Deer raise his rifle and take aim. Almost twenty yards downstream, Hannibal twisted and brayed as he sank deeper into the quicksand where he'd stopped to drink. Before the Comanche could pull the trigger, Clay shouted, stopping him. As Waits for Deer lowered the gun, the other Indian grasped a braided rawhide reata and edged along the high bank to where the mule struggled. Jerking a pack rope from Sarah, Clay followed.

They got two lassos on him, but Hannibal was too frightened now to help himself. But, slipping and sliding themselves, they somehow managed to pull the animal at an angle to the bank, until he gained a footing. From there, they led him to where the ground was just over five feet above the water. Eyes wide, nostrils flaring, the animal pawed and lunged straight up, stumbling onto the bank.

While the two Indians filled bags with the nasty water, Clay walked back to Amanda. She was muddy or bruised, maybe both, but she was alive, and she hadn't vomited. Her eyes opened again as he dropped down on his haunches beside her. He touched her cheek, with his raw knuckles.

"You're a hard woman to kill—you've got more lives than a cat, Amanda—you know that, don't you?"

"No." She swallowed. "I owe you my life again," she said, her voice so low he could scarce hear it.

"I don't want gratitude," he answered harshly. She didn't deserve anger now, not after what she'd been through, and he knew it, yet he couldn't help himself. "Look—all I want is for both of us to survive," he said finally. "You're going to get better, and as soon as I can, I'll take you home. That's what you want to hear, isn't it?"

She'd closed her eyes again. "How far is it?" she whispered. "The Ybarra-Ross, I mean."

"A long way—one helluva long way."

He heard it then—the faint but steady beat of distant drums. Comanche drums. Exhilaration coursed through him, like fire in his veins, nearly overwhelming him. After fourteen long years, he was going home. He might not be able to stay there, and probably the only person who'd even actually remember him from before would be Nahdehwah, but it didn't matter—for a few days he could be Nahakoah again.

The beat of drums grew steadily louder as they picked their way through the narrow, rocky gap that formed part of the Comanche war trail. And while it seemed to call to his soul, Clay was aware that the sound meant something far different to Amanda. He shortened the lead rope, bringing the mule closer, then leaned to reassure her.

"I guess you could call it a matter of honor," he said, "but if a Comanche's worst enemy came to him, he'd be expected to share what he had and send that enemy on his way with gifts rather than arrows. To harm a guest is forbidden." When she didn't respond, he went on, explaining, "And once they adopt someone, they honor that bond forever. To their way of thinking, I'll always be a *Nerm,* no matter where I go, no matter what I do. And right now I'm coming home, bringing you with me, so you have nothing to fear from any of them."

Too weary to wonder what a *Nerm* was, she didn't respond to that either. She understood she was going to have to put her trust in him, but that trust didn't extend to Indians. She still flinched whenever one of the two Comanche warriors came close to her, even when she knew they were only offering her more of the awful-tasting river water.

He fell silent, and his thoughts turned to what lay ahead. He'd see Nahdehwah again, but would she recognize her niece's son in the grown man who'd come back? It had been fourteen years, time enough for her to grow old, time enough for her to become a medicine woman. When he'd last seen her, she was still young enough that such powers were forbidden her. He closed his eyes momentarily and tried to recall what she looked like, but all he saw was a wide, flat face, and two long, greased braids that could have belonged to any Indian woman. The irony wasn't lost on him—she and Ketanah were the last of his mother's family, and he could scarce remember her.

Ketanah he'd seen only once. He'd been a young war chief then—short, squat, with the bowlegged build of a Comanche—but there'd been a fire in his voice and in his eyes that burned with a bitter hatred for every living Texan. He never once bothered to take captives himself, preferring instead to kill them. "A dead boy does not come back to harm The People," he had said. Now, after years of particularly vicious raiding, Ketanah was a peace chief, left behind when younger men followed the war trail. It didn't seem possible.

Fourteen years was a long time in an Indian's life. Even if he could remember them, even if they'd managed to survive that awful November morning still vivid in his mind, most of the men of his father's generation would be gone by now. To be an old man meant a decline of power, a life of reliving one's youth in stories told in the smoke lodge. Glory was today and tomorrow, not yesterday. It was in making war, counting coups, not in living long.

He could smell the smoke of cooking fires now. Drawn from his thoughts by it, he looked ahead, seeing the village, and his pulse quickened at the sight. Reaching out, he tried to rouse Amanda.

"We've arrived," he said, shaking her shoulder.

The loud, steady beat of the drums reverberated in her aching head. With an effort she managed to lift her head, and her heart and breath paused. She saw tipis, dozens of Indian tipis lined up along a dusty trail. And as the mule wended its way between the hide tents, the drums stopped, creating a sudden, ominous stillness.

There must have been a hundred or more Comanches, all watching her, their expressions inscrutable, their black eyes sober.

McAlester leaned toward her, murmuring, "Smile. They admire courage."

"Right now I don't feel very brave," she said, her voice scarce above a whisper.

Even as she spoke, a naked boy ran up, reaching out to touch her tangled, matted hair, then held up his hand as she recoiled. A group of equally naked children broke the silence with laughter.

"It's all right," Clay told her. "He was just proving he could touch you—counting coup, I guess you could say."

Dizzy and weary almost beyond bearing, she lay her head against the mule's neck again. "I thought coup meant scalp," she muttered.

"No, not always."

McAlester reined in before a group of men and dismounted. As he spoke quick, alien words to them, Amanda closed her eyes, hiding her fright from those who pressed around her. If McAlester hadn't been there, she could easily have thought she'd gone to hell. As it was, she had only his protection, and no matter what he said, that was an uneasy thought.

These were the savages who'd already brutally murdered her mother and stepfather, and given half a chance, they'd probably try to do the same to her. To bolster her courage, she tried to pray, but her tired mind kept straying, losing track of the words. All she could think of was *Holy Mary, Mother of God, pray for us sinners now and at the hour of our death,* which she found herself repeating over and over.

Clay came back to tell her, "Everything's settled, and Nahdehwah is expecting you." He patted her rump encouragingly, as though she were a dog or a horse. "As aunt to my mother, she'll welcome you," he added. "But I'm going to ask you not to insult her, no matter what she does. There's a lot of superstition and ceremony in Comanche medicine, and it takes years to learn it." When she didn't say anything, he tried to reassure her. "Look—all you've got to do is keep your temper and go along with her."

"She speaks English?"

"Not much—maybe a little she's learned from captives. But she's got sharp eyes."

"I'll try to keep mine closed," she responded dryly.

"Show a little spirit—she'll like that."

"Won't that insult her?"

"You must be getting better," he muttered. "Just don't act afraid, or you'll lose her respect. No matter what happens, don't show fear."

Taking the reins, he began walking, leading her through what seemed to be the entire length of the camp. Once Amanda dared to open her eyes enough to see that the same naked boy who'd touched her now trotted beside her, as did three others. One reached out to poke at her with a stick, trying to frighten her, but McAlester did nothing. To Amanda it was as though she were awake in a nightmare.

More Indians began following them until he finally stopped at the last tipi. A fat, elderly woman waited outside, knife in hand. Without hesitation, the white ranger enveloped her in his arms, hugging her. Feeling his face and arms with her gnarled hands, the old woman wept and grinned at the same time. When he released her, he gestured to Amanda, obviously explaining what had happened. An animated conversation followed, then Nahdehwah came over to look at her.

Saying nothing, she bent her head to cut the white girl loose, her greased gray braids falling forward, brushing against Amanda's leg. When she finished, she straightened, looking directly into Amanda's eyes. Her expression was closed, unrevealing, until she turned to address McAlester again. As she spoke to him, her flat, wrinkled face softened visibly.

So this was the medicine woman. Her manner toward McAlester should have eased Amanda's nerves, but it didn't. Too many stories of how Comanche women tortured and maimed white captives, cutting off or slicing open their noses, slashing ankle tendons so they could not flee, came to mind. With those small, deep-set hawk eyes, the old woman looked like she'd probably done all those things and worse.

As Amanda held her breath, Nahdehwah touched her face, pinching the skin of her cheeks. Her callused, leathery hands cupped Amanda's chin, then pried open her mouth. The black eyes peered inside for a moment, then she nodded gravely. Her gaze met Amanda's for a moment. Touching her sagging breast, she said, "Me—*pukahut*."

It was as though she'd given everyone permission to speak at once. Young men with painted faces pressed around McAlester, embracing him. Somewhere within the camp, the drummers began anew, and the crowd engulfed him, pulling him away, leaving Amanda alone with three Comanche women and an old man. She wanted to cry out to him but she dared not.

They pulled her down from the mule, then carried her into the tipi and laid her on a pile of hairy buffalo hides. When Nahdehwah shooed them out, one of the women reached out to jab at Amanda. The others laughed, then Nahdehwah spoke sharply, sobering them. It wasn't until they left that she turned her full attention again to Amanda.

The hot, airless room was dim, its only light coming from the smoke flap above. The odor of rancid fat was overpowering, and several feet away flies swarmed around drying strips of meat. Amanda turned on her side and drew up her knees, trying to hide her fear.

As if it weren't stifling enough already, Nahdehwah immediately busied herself replenishing the fire in a center pit. She nursed it carefully, adding bits of dried moss, dead leaves, and once it flared, she tossed in several buffalo chips. Rocking her squat, round body back on her heels, she loosened a drawstring bag and took out a handful of leaves, which she sprinkled over the fire. The pungent odor of burning creosote vied with that of the fat. If Amanda could have sweated, she'd have been soaking wet. As it was, she felt hot enough to die.

Rising with an effort, the old woman moved to stand over her. Putting a hand over her chest, she gave her name slowly, distinctly, "Na-deh-wah." Then she pointed to Amanda. "You Man-duh?"

Amanda nodded.

"Man-duh," the old woman repeated with satisfaction. She grinned widely, displaying toothless gums under thin, dark purple lips. Taking a stick, she drew the crude picture of a bird in the dirt floor, as though that ought to mean something. Then she reached back to her braids and pulled out one of the decorative feathers and carefully drew it from Amanda's forehead, down her nose, to her mouth. Amanda lay still as stone, afraid to move.

"It go now." Nahdehwah opened her hand, revealing several rounded seeds or nuts. "You eat," she said, poking them into Amanda's mouth. When her patient didn't comply, she ordered again, "You eat."

"I can't."

The old woman's bright, birdlike eyes bore into hers. "You eat," she repeated a third time. "No eat—bad." To demonstrate, she put one in her own mouth, then chewed. Nodding, she spit it out. Apparently, she thought Amanda was afraid they were poison. "Eat," she insisted doggedly.

There was no way out of it. As Amanda began to chew them, she realized they were the same thing McAlester had given her. Relieved, she managed to get all of them down.

"Good," Nahdehwah said, bobbing her head approvingly. She picked up a large-bladed Bowie knife and brandished it high.

As weak and sick as she was, Amanda rolled away and came up crouched, ready to fight. Forgetting McAlester's advice, she screamed for help. The old woman shrugged, then returned to the fire. Squatting down, she used the knife to cut six green sticks and put them over the firehole in a pattern of wagon spokes. Like everything else, they began to smoke. Opening a bag, she carefully selected a number of large, smooth stones from it and placed them inside the spokes.

The tent flap opened, and Clay McAlester stepped inside. He looked from Nahdehwah to Amanda. "What's the matter?"

"She's got a knife," Amanda croaked.

"It's part of her medicine. She won't cut you with it." Leaning over, he pressed her back against the pile of buffalo robes. "I told you—there's a lot of ceremony to what she does." Sitting down next to her, he combed Amanda's tangled hair with his fingers, soothing her as though she were an agitated child. "You've been through hell," he murmured.

"Yes," she said simply.

Without looking up, Nahdehwah said, *"Pulke."*

Clay looked around him, saw the paunch, then leaned to get it. "You're in luck—she's got some Mexican *pulke* for you. It's just a drink made from cactus." As he spoke, he tipped the neck to her mouth.

The liquid ran down her chin, but after the bitter brine of the Pecos, it actually tasted good. Nahdehwah snapped a word at him, and he lowered the bag, making it easier for Amanda to drink. She got down quite a bit of it.

"What did she say?" Amanda asked.

"That I was clumsy."

"Oh."

The old woman spoke again, gesturing with her hands, then went back to turning the stones in the fire.

"What did she say then?"

"She said you have to drink enough to sweat—that your tongue is black, which is a bad sign."

"Is that why she's got it so hot in here?"

"No. She is heating medicine stones." Looking

across the tipi, he addressed Nahdehwah, then rose to leave.

"Please . . . don't go." When he hesitated, Amanda pleaded her case. "She frightens me, McAlester—she could be saying she's going to cut out my tongue, for all I can tell." Afraid he wouldn't listen, she grasped his hand and held it tightly. "If you were sick, I wouldn't leave you."

He pulled free, but he didn't go. Instead, he conferred with the old woman for a moment, then came back. "All right—she'll let me stay until she gets everything ready, but her medicine doesn't work when she's watched. Her power comes from the eagle, and the eagle won't answer her if I'm here."

She stared at him, then finally found her voice again. "Surely you don't believe that." When he didn't say anything, she looked up at him. "You don't, do you?"

"I've seen Indian medicine work. Oh, I'm not saying that everything she does is a cure, but it's part of the whole process. If she didn't make a ritual out of her medicine, no one would pay her. You just have to go along with what she does."

"I'm a Catholic—I believe in angels, not eagles," she muttered. Satisfied that he was staying, she lay back on the buffalo robes, closed her eyes, and told herself she felt too awful to die. The *pulke* rolled in her stomach, and the tipi spun around her.

"It's going to come up," she gritted out between clenched teeth.

"Just hang on—the longer you can keep it down, the better chance it'll have of staying there. It won't be long before the peyote helps."

"No," she whispered, swallowing.

He stroked her hair back from her temples. As dark as it was in the tipi, he couldn't see the mud and dirt, but he could remember she had the prettiest auburn hair he'd ever seen. And he could recall how she looked that day in the stagecoach station. She'd been fired up then, and with that hair, those flashing dark eyes, and that indignant posture, she'd been something to behold. All he had to do was close his eyes to see her like that again. He found himself doing it often.

"You're going to get well," he said softly. "You'll go to sleep, and when you wake up, you'll feel a whole lot better."

"You won't leave?"

"No. Not for a while."

His touch was gentle, soothing. But then she hardly knew what to expect of him anymore. Almost every opinion she'd formed from his brutal treatment of Juan Garcia had changed. It was as though there were two sides to him, one terribly cruel, the other surprisingly kind.

"Stomach settling down?" he asked.

"Yes."

"If you can, you'd better drink a little more *pulke*."

She was so tired, so very tired, but she knew she had to help herself get better. "All right."

He lifted her against his knee and reached for the container. He let her drink her fill, then he retied it. Laying it aside, he slid his arm around her, holding her. She leaned back against him. As long as he was there, she could suppress her fear.

He sat for a time, silently watching Nahdehwah work her medicine with the green sticks and the stones, feeling very much as though he'd come home. He glanced down at the woman in his arms, and he could see the drug taking effect. Reluctantly, he eased her back onto the buffalo robes. Nahdehwah nodded, telling him it was time for him to go. He rose and stretched, then ran his hand over his face. He'd been up too long, and he was going to have to find a place to put his bedroll before he fell asleep standing up.

Unaware he left, Amanda sank into a deep netherworld of vivid dreams. She was running from Ramon Sandoval, going from house to house in Boston, pounding on closed doors, while he was getting closer and closer. He raised a gun and took aim. As the shot was fired, she fell. But he hadn't hit her. She looked back, and he was lying in the street, his eyes open. She stumbled away, screaming, and Clay McAlester caught her from behind, holding her. "Sandoval's dead," he said. "Now you can go home to Ybarra."

She was shivering and sweating at the same time. And somewhere in the distance, the old woman chanted rhythmically, tunelessly, seemingly in time with the steady beat of drums. Amanda managed to open heavy lids, but the tipi was dark except for the fire. The eerie light of flickering flames caught the beading that outlined a painted sun on a buckskin dress. She was alone with the medicine woman.

Nahdehwah was rocking back and forth, her hands outstretched, palms up. Above, the smoke flap slapped in the wind like beating wings. Abruptly, she stopped and opened a bag, taking out some berries, which she sprinkled over the flames. The hot tipi filled with cedar smoke. *"Ekapokowaipi,"* she said when Amanda began to cough. Rising, she dipped her hand into the ashes, then came around the pile of buffalo robes to touch Amanda's forehead, drawing across it with her thumb, making a sign almost as a priest did on Ash Wednesday. The opposite fire cast an orange glow, illuminating the deep wrinkles creasing the medicine woman's flat face.

"McAlester ... I want McAlester," Amanda whispered through lips nearly too parched for speech. "Please."

Instead of answering, the old woman went back to the firepit, where she removed the hot stones and dropped them into a kettle. They sizzled, and steam rose, adding water to the hot, stifling air. Carrying the pot, she returned to Amanda and sank her ample body down. Dipping the hot water with her hands, she dribbled it over Amanda's face and neck, repeating the process three times. It felt good.

The feeling was short-lived. Nahdehwah dried her

hands on her buckskin dress, working the buttons on the man's shirt Amanda was wearing with gnarled fingers. Afraid to protest, and not knowing what to expect next, Amanda lay there, letting the old woman pull off the dirty shirt, the chemise, and the muddy drawers. Apparently satisfied by what she saw, the old medicine woman nodded, then picked up a square of cloth and began washing Amanda as though she were a baby. When she was finished, she opened the drawstring of a small, dirty leather bag and dipped her fingers into a thick black grease. She smeared the odiferous stuff on Amanda's sunburned cheeks and lower arms. The rest of Amanda's body she powdered with something that smelled like sage.

Nahdehwah rocked back on her heels and held up her hands toward the smoke hole above, chanting, "Aiee—aiee—yi—yi," over and over again.

When she finally stopped, she offered Amanda more of the *pulke,* urging her to drink. Amanda drained the bag and would have liked more. The nausea that had been with her since McAlester found her in the desert was gone. And she was clear-headed, able to think.

The medicine woman covered her with a ragged blanket, then rose and carried the dirty clothes from the tipi. Alone now, Amanda stared at the smoke hole, seeing a lone star in the night sky. She'd slept for hours. Twisting her neck, she looked around the room curiously, but it was too dark to recognize anything beyond the glow of coals left from the fire. It was some time before the old woman came back. When she did, she sat again by the firepit. She crumbled leaves onto the coals, filling the tipi with smoke. As Amanda coughed, she heard a loud flapping above, and then there was nothing but the drums. Nahdehwah opened the doorflap and fanned it, drawing the smoke out, letting the night air in. When she turned back, she was grinning broadly, pointing up to the smoke hole.

"Eagle come," the old woman declared. "Make better."

"I hope so."

"Many better."

"Where's Mr. McAlester?" Amanda asked suddenly. When Nahdehwah's face went blank, she tried again. "Where's Clay? Clay McAlester? The *Tejano*?"

There was no recognition. Instead of answering, the old woman unrolled what looked to be a large piece of calico. When she shook it out, Amanda's skin almost crawled. It was a dress—a white woman's dress. Nahdehwah handed it to her, grinning again. The gray braids bobbed as she nodded.

"You take."

Amanda nearly recoiled. "Oh, but I—"

"You take,"

"Yes, well—"

"You take." The old woman's hand smoothed the wrinkled calico almost lovingly. "You *paraibo*—you take."

She wasn't going to accept no for an answer, that much was certain. Amanda held the dress up, trying to see it in the semidarkness. As far as she could tell there were no holes or bloodstains on it. And right now, with nothing to cover her, she supposed her fear of Indians was making her silly.

"Thank you. Uh ... I suppose McAlester's asleep, isn't he?" No reaction. She tried to remember what he'd called himself to the two Indians who'd led them there. Nahoka? Hahako? No, she'd been closer with the first one. "Nahoka—where is he?"

For a moment the old woman's brow furrowed, then she seemed to understand. "Nahakoah. You Nahakoah *paraibo*," she said, smiling again.

"Nahakoah," Amanda repeated, trying to get it right. "Where is Nahakoah?" Seeing that Nahdehwah still didn't get the question, she repeated it loudly and slowly. "Nahakoah—where—is—he?"

A spate of Comanche words followed. Amanda shook her head. "No speak ... uh ... no speak *Nerm* ... is that it ... *Nerm*, I mean?"

"Nermernuh?"

"I don't know."

Another volume of Comanche.

It was hopeless. Resigned, Amanda lay down again. But Nahdehwah wasn't about to be denied. She grasped Amanda's shoulder, pulling her up, then shoved the dress into her lap.

"You want me to put it on now?"

More alien words, but the gist of them indicated that was exactly what the old woman wanted.

"All right."

Telling herself that they could have traded for the dress, or else they could have stolen it without killing anyone, Amanda thrust her arms into the sleeves and drew it over her head. It was too big, but it covered her.

"My drawers—where are they?"

A blank stare.

"The clothes you took—what did you do with them?"

Another blank stare.

"All right, then—where's Nahakoah?" she asked again.

"Nahakoah." The old woman's head bobbed.

There was no sense in going through it all another time. Amanda buttoned the front of the calico dress. Apparently satisfied that she was going to wear it, Nahdehwah went back to her place by the firepit.

For a long time neither of them said anything more. Finally, the old woman stood up again. "Nahakoah," she said, her thin, dark lips curving in that toothless smile.

Apparently, Amanda had gotten his name wrong, for all the old woman wanted to do was repeat the word, not go get him. Rather than continue a conversation going nowhere, she turned her back and curled up on the hide bed, determined to go back to sleep.

For a few minutes she allowed herself to wallow in a surfeit of self-pity. She was in a tent with an evil-looking, toothless old Comanche woman, who not only could not speak English, but who also looked as though she could kill without compunction. Never in all of her life had she felt quite so helpless, so alone. The only one in the whole camp capable of understanding her was Clay McAlester, and she couldn't even communicate enough with the old woman to find out where he was or to send word that she wanted to see him.

But she was alive, she reminded herself. In spite of Ramon, in spite of too much sun and too little water, she was alive, and no matter what he said, she owed her life to McAlester. He could have left her where he found her, and there'd have been none the wiser, but instead he'd kept her alive through sweltering heat and thirst and swift, swirling water. If she lived to be a hundred, she'd never forget the terror of walking for miles alone across the desert, or of coming awake underwater. No, she owed him everything—every breath she'd ever take, everything she'd ever do or see, every tomorrow she had left on this earth.

She closed her eyes and remembered the strength of his arms, the solid hardness of his body, the gentleness of his hands washing her. What had the old Negro carter said of him? That there wasn't anyone he'd rather have on his side in a fight—or something like that, anyway. Well, now she understood what he'd meant. Clay McAlester knew how to survive in this godforsaken land, and he wasn't afraid of anything. She just wished he was here with her, that was all.

Nahakoah, or something very like it, the Indians called him. She had no idea what it meant, or if he'd told her, she'd been too sick to remember. He'd been sure enough of himself to lead her into a Comanche camp, where the same heathen, ruthless savages who gleefully tortured and murdered men, women, and children greeted him like a brother.

She was hot and sweaty. Rolling over, she looked to where coals still glowed in the firepit. On the other side of it the old woman snored, punctuating each rumble with a wheezy whistle.

Where was McAlester? she wondered. What was he doing? She lay there, looking upward at the small piece of night sky, listening, hearing the steady beat of drums, wondering how in the name of God Nahdehwah could sleep. What were they doing out there, anyway? Was McAlester with them?

Amanda sat up, and the snoring stopped midwhistle. The old medicine woman roused to peer across the darkness toward her, then rose and padded barefooted to touch Amanda's forehead. Her leathery hand plunged beneath the neck of the dress, finding wet skin. She mumbled something, then puttered among a pile of assorted bags and pots. Coming back, she held out a gourd dipper and gestured for Amanda to drink.

It wasn't *pulke,* and it had bits of something floating in it. If it hadn't been for that, she'd have thought it was warm water. But she had no way of asking, and truth to tell, she probably wouldn't want to know.

"Thank you," she murmured.

Nahdehwah grunted.

"Where's Nahakoah? Where's Clay McAlester?" Amanda tried again.

"Nahakoah—yes," the old woman said, nodding.

"Yes—where is he?"

"Nahakoah."

There had to be someone somewhere who spoke English, but she had no way to find out. Instead, she reached out and touched the medicine woman's shoulder. "You," she said.

"Me. Nahdehwah," the woman acknowledged.

Laying a hand on her own breast, Amanda said distinctly, "Me. Amanda."

"You Uh-manduh."

"Yes." Pointing to the tipi flap, Amanda tried to build on the small start. "Nahakoah?"

"Yes."

"Where?"

Instead of answering, Nahdehwah refilled the dipper and brought it back. "You take."

As she tipped the gourd, Amanda looked over the rim at the woman's black birdlike eyes. They were fixed on her.

"I suppose you could tell me a lot about him, if I could understand you," Amanda murmured, sighing. "What was he like as a boy? Was he always so sober?"

"Yes."

It wasn't really an answer, for the old woman had no idea what she was asking. "I'm sorry," she said finally. "You might as well get some sleep."

But Nahdehwah didn't budge. Instead, she kept those bright little black eyes on Amanda. "You— Nahakoah *paraibo*."

When she saw McAlester, she was going to have to ask what a *paraibo* was, but right now she couldn't make much sense of anything.

"You *paraibo*," she said more insistently.

Now she was confused. "No, me Amanda." Lord, but she was beginning to sound like the old woman. Somewhat unnerved by the piercing stare, she decided the sound of her own voice was better than nothing. "I don't suppose you want to hear about about Boston, do you? No, I don't guess so," she answered herself. "All right, then—how about my father? His name was John Ross—John P. Ross. The P was for Patrick. The Rosses came from Scotland, which is a long way from here. Some of the Presbyterian ones were sent to Ireland in hopes of countering the Catholic population there, but Papa was descended from those who favored Mary, Queen of Scots, and when she was captured in England, they went to France, so they were Catholic."

The old woman didn't even blink.

"I don't suppose Catholics and Protestants mean much to you, do they?"

Nothing.

"Half of Boston is Catholic." Seeing that Nahdehwah's expression didn't change so much as a flick of an eyelash, Amanda went on conversationally, "My mother was Spanish—her family came from Spain more than a hundred and fifty years ago. Her father held a land grant in Texas, and—"

The old woman interrupted her. "No *Tejanos!*" she spat out angrily.

"You don't like Texans?"

"No *Tejanos!*"

"All right—we won't talk about them. You don't know anything about Boston, but it is one of the oldest cities on the East coast, and—"

Apparently, Nahdehwah had heard more than enough. She walked to the firepit, where she stirred the coals, then went back to her bed. Within minutes, she slept.

The drums had stopped. Amanda lay down, listening for them, hearing nothing beyond Nahdehwah's snores. McAlester was out there somewhere, but she had no way of knowing what he did or where he was. The stillness outside was more deafening than the drums.

Turning her back to the firepit, she crossed her arms over her breasts, clasping her arms, embracing herself. And in her loneliness, she realized what she really wanted was for Clay McAlester to hold her, to keep her safe.

Clay had come outside to escape the heat and smoke of Ketanah's tipi for a few minutes, excusing himself for a call of nature. What he really needed was a full night's sleep, but the old peace chief had put on quite a feast for him. So while the Crow Warriors held their scalp dance at the other side of the Indian camp, he'd been feted with such delicacies as the bloody milk in a fresh-slain cow's udder and the animal's warm, raw liver. Somewhere in the past fourteen years, he'd lost his taste for both, and now they sat uneasily in his stomach.

Ketanah was expecting him back, but he needed to stretch his legs and clear his mind first. So he wandered aimlessly between tipis, listening to the night sounds. The sky above him was black, cloudless, and dotted with stars. Overhead, the moon's profile smiled.

He was at Nahdehwah's before he realized where he'd been going. He paused there, wondering if Amanda slept. Probably. He turned back, thinking he ought to get back before Ketanah thought he'd left the village. But he wasn't really in the mood to listen to every buck and old man spin stories. He was almost too tired to think.

Behind him there was the light scuffing of moccasins on hard earth, the hushed, furtive giggle of a girl sneaking beneath a tipi skin to lie with a young buck. He remembered that well, for by the time he'd turned fourteen, there'd been half a dozen girls coming to him, each hoping he'd offer horses to her father. Once he'd come close, when White Blossom's belly had grown round, but a man with the unlikely name of Buffalo Belly had come forward to claim her and the child. And everyone was too polite to notice that the son she bore him had golden skin and eyes.

That was the way of the Comanche—it was the girls who were supposed to start things, the boys who were supposed to be bashful. It saved a man a lot of face— before he took horses to her parent's tipi, he knew she was going to accept his proposal. In the civilized world of the white man, everything was reversed. A man took the risk of making a fool of himself, and if the woman accepted, he still didn't know what he was getting until it was too late. By the time he got to bed her, he was already married to her.

He stood there a moment, then retraced his steps back to Nahdehwah's tipi. Because of the heat, she'd left the door flap open.

"Grandmother?" he said softly, giving her the respect due her age.

It was pitch-black within, but he could hear her stir. Her flat, callused feet shuffled across the hard-packed dirt floor, then she peered outside. Her black eyes reflected the moon.

"Can it not wait for morning?" she asked sourly. Then she recognized him, and her scowl softened. "Nahakoah," she murmured, touching his face.

"How is she?"

"Nearly well."

"Already?"

The old woman nodded. "You tell no one, but it was the *pulke* and the water. When she drank enough, her mind came back. Now her body will follow."

"What do you think of her?" he wanted to know.

"She talks too much."

"About what?"

Nahdehwah shrugged again, then her wrinkled face broke into a wide smile. "Nahakoah."

"Old Woman, you don't speak English," he reminded her.

"She knows your Comanche name. Nahakoah, she says many times." She looked up slyly. "I am old, but I can sleep outside," she offered.

He could just see a lucid Amanda Ross waking up beside him. No, he had no illusions about that, and it was probably just as well. He didn't need anyone complicating his life any more than she already had.

"No. I just want to look at her."

She stepped back from the flap to let him inside. The only things he could actually see were a few live coals. He looked around, waiting for his eyes to adjust to the darkness.

"Over there," Nahdehwah said. As she spoke, she thew a handful of dry grass into the firepit. It flared, casting a flickering orange light. "Behind you."

He took a step backward and nearly stumbled. Turning around, he saw her. She was lying on her side, her face turned into the crook of her arm, her hair spilling over it. He reached out almost gingerly, lifting it. Where his fingertips brushed her skin, she was cool. He felt an overwhelming relief. She stirred, changing positions, and he could see the black salve smeared on her cheeks. It didn't make any difference—she still looked a lot better than he'd expected.

His gaze moved lower, taking in the curve of a breast, the roundness of a hip covered with calico cloth, and he had to remind himself she wasn't meant for him. Reluctantly, he tore himself away and retreated outside.

Nahdehwah followed him. "Two days, then you take her to your lodge."

He hadn't expected it to happen so quickly. He shook his head. "I've got to leave soon—and she can't go with me." Seeing her frown, he hastened to add, "I'd hoped to come back for her."

The old woman's lips pursed as though she'd eaten

a persimmon, then she turned away. "You did not come to stay," she said sadly.

"No, but I'd have you keep Amanda until I return."

"Without you, she does not belong here. I had hoped—" She caught herself and sighed. "But it does not matter. All my sons are dead, Nahakoah."

"I know."

"It is hard to be an old woman, even an old medicine woman," she went on, her voice low. "The sons of others must bring me food. It is left to those who share no blood of mine to call me grandmother. But you, Nahakoah, were son to Ekatonah, my sister's daughter."

"Yes." He knew what she wanted—she wanted him to stay and provide for her, and he couldn't. "When I come back, I'll hunt a deer for you," he promised her.

"She cannot live in my tipi—when she is well, her presence will take my power. The eagle will not come when I call him."

He couldn't argue, for medicine was a sacred thing. "All right," he said finally, "I'll ask someone else to take her."

Feeling beleaguered within and without, he made his way back to Ketanah's lodge. He hadn't missed much. Two Owls was recounting his successful raid "beyond the *Tejanos*." He had, he declared with sweeping gestures, "counted coup by taking enemy scalps and stealing many horses."

Apparent jealousy prompted a Comanche to scoff, "Where are these horses now? And why do you not feast with the Crow Warriors?"

The Kiowa regarded him balefully for a moment, then answered. "We had to eat two of them, but the rest I sent with One Hand to Quanah Parker to be traded when the Comancheros come." He drew himself up proudly, adding, "If you had chosen to follow the war trail, you would have seen me steal them."

"You pass wind with your mouth," his tormentor said, sneering. "Why would a great war chief like

Quanah do such business for you?" he demanded sarcastically.

"He is related to one of my wives," Two Owls declared haughtily. "His father was her uncle, and that is enough for him to call me brother."

To stop the dispute, Ketanah raised his hand. "There is no room for angry words in my lodge." Turning to the Kiowa, he said, "I'd hear more of these Comancheros, brother. When do they come?"

"Very soon. They wait for a *Tejano* to bring the wagons across the border, then they will have many guns to trade for good horses and fat cattle." Looking past the chief to the Comanche who'd started the argument, he gibed, "When Holds His Tongue sees that Two Owls has a gun that shoots a bullet for every finger, he will know he is a fool."

"A bullet for every finger!" Holds His Tongue snorted.

But Ketanah was suitably impressed. "I have many horses myself," he murmured thoughtfully. "I might want some of these guns."

Another of the Indians who'd followed the war trail with Two Owls spoke up. "I heard that when Quahadis join with the Cheyenne and the Kiowa for the Sun Dance, they will share these guns with those who smoke the war pipe with them."

Two Owls nodded smugly. "It is so."

"Comancheros wait for a *Tejano* to give them guns to sell Comanches. And Comanches and their Cheyenne enemies smoking a war pipe together. Never in nearly forty winters have I heard such a thing," Ketanah said, shaking his head.

"It is time the Comanche must join his Kiowa and Cheyenne brothers to drive the Anglos from this land. If we do not stand together, soon there will be no buffalo anywhere and we will become women waiting to be fed what we would not eat. Already too many of our people have gone tamely from places we lived long before the whites came. If we do not fight them now, they will take everything we have from us and leave us only what they do not want!" Two Owls declared, shaking his fist emphatically.

A murmur of agreement passed around the fire. Clay sat there, his face betraying nothing, listening. Already he'd learned enough to know why the rangers' planned ambush had failed. Without any telltale wagons, Sanchez-Torres had probably hidden in plain sight in border cantinas, waiting for a Texan to betray his own people.

"You know this *Tejano* who sells these guns?" Ketanah asked, turning to him. "You have heard of him, Nahakoah?"

Clay shrugged. "Maybe. Maybe not. I'd have to hear his name to know."

"The Comancheros do not even tell Quanah that," Two Owls said smugly. "The *Tejano* will not be with them when they come."

Ketanah puffed thoughtfully on the long pipe, then passed it to his left. As Clay took it, the chief decided, "Let us speak no more of guns and Quanah tonight. Tomorrow I will send someone to the Quahadis to hear more of this Sun Dance. To rid our lands of *Tejanos,* I myself am willing to follow the war trail. Though I have grown old, and my own time to lead Nokonis in battle has passed, I will gladly follow the Crow Warriors. Let them choose a war chief among them, and I will join him in this just cause." As a murmur of assent spread around the circle, he raised his hand, silencing it. "Tomorrow," he said. "Tonight we smoke and listen to each other, for Nahakoah has come home."

The mood mellowed as the pipe went around the circle, and the usual storytelling continued until the discussion turned to a man's medicine. At that, Ketanah turned to Clay again. "And you, Nahakoah, how did you receive your power?"

It would be impolite to refuse, no matter how little Clay wanted to speak of himself. He stood up, aware that every eye in the lodge was on him. "My father was Sansoneah, my mother Ekatonah, daughter to a war chief," he began.

Ketanah nodded. "I remember both of them. But go on, Nahakoah, that all may know from where your power comes."

"I was brought to the Nokonis when I was a small child, and as Ekatonah and Sansoneah had lost their only son, I was bought from my captor and adopted by them. This I know because my mother told me when she took me to be named."

"You were fortunate, for Sansoneah was a wise and brave man, and Ekatonah was a good woman," the old chief murmured. "But go on—we'd hear of your medicine."

Clay cleared his throat. "Well, when she decided it was time, my mother and I went to Toweaha, who practiced coyote medicine, and when I was in his tipi, I sat beside his fire. Without speaking, he watched me for a long time, until the fire went out, and then he blew on the ashes. 'Go,' he told me. 'The ashes have blown only toward the tipi door, and my medicine is not for you.' "

"That was too bad," Two Owls said. "He should have given freely of his power."

"When he heard what Toweaha had said, my father took his best horse, trying to change his mind, but the old man refused it. My mother went back with two horses, then three, then four, and every time it was the same. 'My medicine is not for your son,' he said. Finally, my mother threatened to take me to the medicine man of the Penetakas, so Toweaha promised to pray over it."

"It would have been a loss of face for him," Ketanah agreed. "Your mother was clever."

"My father thought it was because I was not born Comanche, and Toweaha did not want me to have any power. But this was the same *pukahut* who had given me my name."

"Did she take you to the Penetakas?" someone asked.

"No. The next morning, the old man came to our tipi, saying that he had heard a wolf howl in the night, that it was calling to me, wanting to give me its power. But I had to go out and sleep under the stars alone until the wolf came to me."

"Wolf medicine is very strong," Two Owls observed, suitably impressed. "Very strong. You went, didn't you?"

"Yes. I was not to take any food or weapon with me, nor was I to make a fire. The old man gave me only three peyote buttons," Clay recalled. "I was to fast, except for eating one button each night at sunset."

"Did you see the wolf?"

"It came on the third night. I heard it howl, and I sat up, too frightened to move. It came into the clearing and stared at me, making no sound, but when I spoke to it, the wolf seemed more afraid of me than I was of him. For a long time we faced each other, then it just turned and ran away. As soon as it was gone, I picked up my blanket and returned to my father, telling him what had happened."

"Ummm."

"The next morning, the medicine man said I had the power over all things that were afraid of wolves," Clay recalled. "My mother was so pleased that she held a gift dance, and my father gave away fifty horses." Clay looked around his audience, then exhaled. "So I have wolf medicine."

There was an appreciative silence. Finally, Ketanah spoke. "It was good that Sansoneah and Ekatonah kept going back to that old man, for you have been greatly honored. While the coyote is treacherous, the wolf has the greater strength."

One of the younger men, who'd been quiet most of the evening, looked at Clay. "If you have wolf medicine, how is it that you could not heal your woman?"

It was the chief who answered him. "Because," he

declared sternly, "wolf medicine is for the destruction of a man's enemies and must be used wisely." He reached to touch Clay's shoulder. "And can any doubt Nahakoah has used his medicine well?"

Coming from Ketanah, scourge of all whites, that was high praise. As a murmur of agreement spread, the brash fellow retreated into silence until it was his turn to tell his own story. By the time all had finished, the old chief's head was down, his eyes closed in sleep. Rather than wake him, they left quietly, stealing out as one of his wives held the tipi flap back for them.

His eyes burning from the smoke, Clay started walking toward the place where he'd left his bedroll. Beside him, one of the younger men cleared his throat, then spoke. "We are honored that Nahakoah has shared his story with us."

"Ketanah asked it of me."

"How long do you stay here?"

"I don't know," Clay answered evasively.

"It is too bad about your woman," the Indian murmured. "I am fortunate enough to have three wives, and you are welcome to one of them while you are here. I would be proud to count you as my brother."

It was a generous offer, one that could not easily be refused without offending a Comanche. "I would gladly accept your wife," Clay responded carefully, "but my heart is with mine. I do not feel like another woman tonight."

The other man clucked sympathetically. "Well, if you have the need, I do not mind." His hand came up to grip Clay's shoulder. "You are welcome in my tipi, Nahakoah."

Clay shook his head. "I thank you, but it is warm enough to sleep outside, so there is no need to crowd your family."

The Indian nodded. "There is peace beneath the stars tonight." With that, he left, fading into the shadows as he slipped between tipis.

Clay stood there, staring after him, feeling only

guilty. He was there for all the wrong reasons, and he knew it. He'd come to see Nahdehwah, hoping she'd help Amanda, then provide a place for her while he left for a few days, maybe even a couple of weeks. Now the whole band had welcomed him, not knowing he'd come to stop their trade with the Comancheros. If he were successful, he would be putting an end to their way of life, pushing them onto a reservation in the Indian Territory, where none of them wanted to go. But it was better than their certain destruction, he told himself. There were just too many Texans who truly believed the only answer to the problem was to kill every Comanche—man, woman, and child.

But right now, Clay's more immediate problem lay asleep in Nahdehwah's tipi. Even if he wanted to do it, he couldn't risk taking her with him. Hell, if he couldn't work with another ranger, what in God's name was he going to do with a lady from Boston? With her along, he'd have to change everything—the way he traveled, the risks he usually took—everything. And he'd have a witness who didn't understand it was a war he was fighting. If he didn't kill them outright, she'd be wanting him to bring them in for a damned trial. It wouldn't matter to her that they faced hanging, anyway. Expedience would offend her sense of justice, and she'd be writing letters condemning him to everyone fool enough to listen. Maybe. Maybe not. She owed him something now.

No, she'd slow him down, make him lose his edge. Alone, he had only his own survival to worry about; with her, he might get careless and cost both of them their lives. No two ways about it, he was going to have to impose on someone else to take care of her until he could get back. Maybe he ought to have left when Amanda was still too confused to know he'd gone. Nahdehwah might not have liked it, but she wouldn't have thrown the white girl out of her tipi. Not as long as she believed Amanda was his wife.

A faint warm breeze carried the scent of burnt cedar

on it. He glanced up and noticed he'd walked all the way to Nahdehwah's tipi again. He stood there, listening to the steady rumble and wheeze of the old woman's snoring. For a long moment he actually considered taking her offer, then he moved on. If he didn't quit thinking about Amanda Ross, he was going to make a fool of himself.

Too tired to sleep, he walked on to the spring. The water welled up, wetting the rocks, making them slick. He sat down and gathered his knees while he stared pensively at the reflection of half a moon in the pool. He'd wanted to come back this once, hoping he would find The People as he remembered them, but it was too late. Already their power was on the decline, already too many young men were gone. And soon so would the buffalo that provided everything for them.

He'd grown up believing in a man's medicine, in the spirits of sun, moon, and earth. He'd exulted in the hunt, in following the war trail, in being one of The People. He could remember playing naked on the Staked Plains, riding with the wind in his face. He could remember thinking himself invincible once he'd received his medicine. Now the only power he believed in was that provided by two Colts, a Whitney shotgun, and a Henry rifle. If his aunt's God was up there, He'd never felt inclined to let Clay McAlester know it.

Reaching to pick up a small stone, he skipped it across the water, listening to the ripples, feeling dissatisfied. It was, he supposed, that now he looked at The People through the eyes of a white man. Now bloody milk and raw liver held no appeal for a man who'd spent four years in Chicago eating off Jane McAlester's china plates, listening to her say grace before every meal, learning the proper use of forks and spoons, sitting on a hard pew every Sunday morning.

Oh, she hadn't really taken the wildness from him, and they both realized that. Now he picked and chose what memories and habits he wanted to keep. He ate jerky and pinon nuts, mesquite and juniper beans, Indian potatoes, prickly pear, and hackberry balls. He hunted best with rifle, shotgun, but could still bring down a twelve-point buck with bow and arrow. And when food was short, he could travel nearly a week on an empty stomach. But when he got to San Antonio or Austin, he knew enough to put on a coat and tie, slick back his hair, and wash down a steak with good whiskey, surprising men like Governor Davis, who wanted to believe he was a half-savage, half-literate heathen.

It was times like this, he reflected soberly, that made him wish he still believed in something. But if he did, he wasn't aware of it.

"Nahakoah?"

Nahakoah. Stands Alone. Sometimes he wondered if old Toweaha had somehow looked into the future when he'd given Clay that name. He hunched his shoulders as the other man joined him.

It was Two Owls. The barrel-chested Kiowa stood over him, chewing something. He spit part of it into the water, then leaned against a twisted tree, his black eyes glittering in the moonlight.

Clay skipped another stone across the water, then rose. Brushing the dust from his buckskin pants, he nodded, acknowledging the Indian's presence.

"Warm night," he observed laconically.

Two Owls breathed deeply, then let the air out slowly as though he savored it. Finally, he spoke again. "My power is great, Stands Alone, but not so great as that of the wolf. I would share your wolf medicine with you." Before Clay could respond, the big Kiowa added, "I would give you the choice of all my horses for it. You may have the best that I own."

"Ask of Nadehwah, not me."

"And what would she know of it? It is the eagle that beats at her tipi. No, the wolf calls to me, Nahakoah," Two Owls persisted. "I have heard it."

Clay considered for a moment, then relented. "All I can tell you is what Toweah told me—go alone beneath the full moon and stay until you hear and see a lone wolf. If it looks into your face, it has given its medicine to you. Upon returning, plunge three times into water, then dry yourself."

"You are a generous man, Nahakoah. To me, you are as a brother. All I have is yours—my horses, my tipi, my wives—you are welcome to what you would take."

"I am a man of few needs." Yet as he said it, Clay saw an opportunity in the offer. "But I may have to leave my wife here for a while if she is unable to ride any distance," he said casually.

Two Owls was ahead of him. Eager to please, the Kiowa assured him, "I would protect her with my life, and I will still give you two horses for what you have told me."

"She is unused to the way of The People. It will be hard for her to understand."

"Tell her she will be safe in my tipi, and my wives will treat her well. Tell her I will expect nothing of her."

"She will be honored," Clay said solemnly. He started to walk away, but the Kiowa caught up.

"Your wife—how is she called?"

"Amanda."

"Amanda," Two Owls repeated, turning the word over on his tongue. As they walked, he wondered, "Why did you sign to me when we found you—why did you not speak as you do now?"

"I had been away too long—I had to hear the words again before I could say them easily." A wry smile twisted Clay's mouth. "Under the circumstances, I didn't want to make any mistakes."

"But you have come back," the Indian said.

"For a time."

At Clay's mule and horse, they parted company. Someone had already fed both animals earlier, and they stood quietly, silhouetted by the moonlight. Un-rolling his blanket, Clay spread it against his saddle, making his bed on the ground. He lay down and turned

over to reach into his saddlebags, searching for what
was left of the peyote Bear Claw had given him. Taking the last two buttons out, he considered them for a
long moment before he chewed them. Raising his eyes
to the moon, he tried to remember the words the old
medicine man had given him.

"Brother moon," he said under his breath, "give me
wisdom, courage, and endurance that I may prevail.
Light my path in the cool of the night, and watch over
me when I follow the war trail. Give me the strength of
ten against my enemies and lead me to victory against
those who would dare to challenge my power." He fal-
tered, unable to go any further.

What he needed was enough luck to intercept
Sanchez-Torres, preferably by ambush. And to reason
with Quanah Parker before Texas soil was soaked with
blood. He had to make him understand that no matter
how many guns the Comanches had, it was all but over
for them. Ranald S. Mackenzie and his cavalry would
retaliate brutally and efficiently, killing every Indian
who resisted the reservation.

Holding his hands behind his head, he waited for the
peyote to take effect. If ever he needed a vision, something to tell him he was right, it was now. He fixed his
eyes on the moon, staring into the shadows on it until
they moved, taking the shape of a veiled face. And
somewhere he heard an echo of his own voice asking
his destiny.

Ghosts stood around him, beckoning, speaking to
him. He could see Sansoneah, his long hair flowing
past his shoulders, the dozen colored feathers still
twined in his scalplock. Beside him, Sees the Sun
smiled and Cries Too Much held out small hands, beg-
ging to be lifted. Many Feathers in His Hair swung her
up to ride on his shoulder, then he looked to Stands
Alone, saying, "Follow." With no further words, they
turned and walked away.

Clay looked down, seeing not the shirt of a white
man, but the bare arms of a boy warrior, feeling not the

weight of ammunition belts and Colt revolvers, only the freedom of a breechclout above his leggings. And suddenly he was running after them, trying to catch up as they walked the worn path toward tipis clustered near the pool of shining water.

His father stopped at the great lodge of Buffalo Horn, Nokoni war chief. Singing Dove, the war chief's favorite wife, held the tipi flap open. His mother nodded, then reached for his younger sister, carrying her away. As Nahakoah stood beside his father, he heard tuneless battle chants, then saw the painted warriors approaching in single file, their shields marking them as brothers of the Crow society. It wasn't until they had all entered Buffalo Horn's lodge that his father gestured for him to follow them.

He went in, going left, moving all the way around the big tipi until he found an empty place to the right of Buffalo Horn himself. He hesitated, looking to his father, then he sat down among the fiercest warriors of his band. Each man stood and recited the story of his greatest coup, then sat down, until all but the war chief and his father had spoken. Buffalo Horn rose, gesturing to the one closest to the tipi door. It was Broken Hand, a man who had counted more coup than any other.

The warrior rose, majestic in his full-feathered bonnet. Approaching Stands Alone, he removed it and held it out without a word. "Take it," the old war chief ordered. "If you would be of the Crows, it is yours."

His father stared straight ahead, offering no guidance. Raising his eyes to Broken Hand, he saw sadness in the other man's face. "I am not worthy," Stands Alone said finally. "It is yours."

"The People will need a leader greater than I," Buffalo Horn said.

"It is not in my blood."

"Quanah Parker will lead Quahadis down the warpath, and none will remember he is half white."

His father stood then, turning to Buffalo Horn. "My

son has given his answer. I have spoken to my father the Sun, and this is not to be my son's path." Looking to Stands Alone, he said, "You have seen what might have been, but will not be. Your destiny is not with us, Stands Alone."

"Show me my destiny, Father! Tell me where I can find Quanah!"

But even as he cried out, the tipi lifted, carrying all of them with it into the clouds, leaving Stands Alone staring upward from the ground. Weeping, his mother gave him one last look, then disappeared into a soft mist.

Suddenly, he was lying abed between soft, white sheets. A woman was bending over him, her rich auburn hair falling like silk against his chest, her mouth curved in a smile. Her skin was warm against his, her dark eyes inviting him to touch more of her. Resisting her, he called out, "Father, where are you?"

"No," came an answer from the darkness. "Toweaha was right, my son. You were meant to stand alone, apart from The People."

The woman was pressed against him, stealing his will with her body. Her skin was pale, soft, and she smelled of wild roses. "I am your destiny," she whispered against his ear. "I am forever."

"No!" But even as he denied her, his body would not listen and his pulse raced with desire. His arms closed around her bare body, and the curtain of rose-scented auburn hair enveloped him like a cloud of silk. He could feel his body join with hers, slaking his need deep within her, and his ears heard a crescendo of cries as he came. When he opened his eyes, hers were like dark pools reflecting the half moon. He was looking into the face of Amanda Ross.

"I heard you cry out in thirst," Nahdehwah said, shaking him awake. Lifting his head, she held a horn dipper to his lips and waited for him to swallow. As the water trickled down his throat, he realized she was not part of his vision, she was real. He'd called out loudly enough to waken her.

"Bathe in the water, and you will sleep well," she advised him. "And day after tomorrow you will take her from my tipi."

As he sat up groggily, she walked back to her lodge. He passed a hand over his eyes as though he could pull the cobwebs from his mind. He was sweaty, dizzy from the effects of the peyote. He staggered to stand, then weaved unsteadily to the spring, where he peeled off his clothes. Looking up, he saw a thin cloud crossing the profile of the moon. As the breeze touched his skin, he waded into the cold water, washing the peyote from his pores. He hadn't really had a vision—the drug had tricked him, that was all.

But as he stood there naked as the day he was born, it came to him with lightning clarity, the place where Quanah Parker and his Quahadis waited for Sanchez-Torres. They'd left their big camp in the Palo Duro, and in his mind he could see them moving southward toward Big Spring. He didn't know how he knew it now—he just *knew* it. It made sense, absolute sense. There was almost nothing between the eastern border of New Mexico and Big Spring to stop them. Only him.

As he drove the wagon down the narrow dirt road leading to the sprawling adobe hacienda, Ramon could see his father watching from the front veranda. While he could not make out Alessandro Sandoval's face, he did not doubt he was scowling. Ramon considered a number of excuses to offer, not that it mattered, he thought resentfully. No matter what he did, it was never good enough.

And he wasn't a boy to be bullied anymore. Reaching beneath the seat, he found the canteen. Slowing to a near halt, he unscrewed the lid and drank deeply of the tequila he'd bought in the cantina. It would have served the old man just as well if he'd not come home at all, if the Comanches he'd seen had killed him. But luckily their mounts had been too spent, and they'd been herding too many horses to bother with him. He just wished he still had his black sombrero. Fifty dollars he'd paid for the engraved silver conchos on it, and he'd left it with Amanda.

He'd almost realized his own mortality when he'd seen the Indians, and the experience had shaken him enough that it had taken him nearly a dozen bottles of tequila and a couple of days in the arms of a generous señorita to recover from it. If his money hadn't run out, he'd still be there, but both the cantina owner and the girl had refused his credit, he recalled bitterly. But one day he would get even. One day when he owned the Ybarra-Ross, he'd hire someone to take care of them. If Alessandro could be found in a generous mood, he might not even have to wait that long. And why shouldn't his father be generous? Had not his only legitimate son gained the Ybarra for him?

By the time he actually drove up to the house, the tequila had fortified him enough to think he could brazen out his absence—until Alessandro Sandoval actually stepped off the long porch to greet him. Then his stomach knotted, nearly forcing the liquor up. There was no generosity in his father's face.

"She's dead, Papa," he said, not daring to meet Alessandro's eyes.

"Where in God's name have you been?" the old man demanded through clenched teeth.

"Boston."

"But you wired almost a month ago that she decided to come." Glancing at those who lounged in the yard, he waited until they were inside to say anything more. Then, closing the door to his office after them, he confronted his son angrily. "Look at you!" he said, his voice dripping disgust. "What a fine *caballero* you are!" Reaching out, he slapped Ramon across the face, leaving a stinging mark. "You were supposed to be bringing her here, you fool! And now you haven't even the decency to mourn her, you drunken idiot—you sot," he sneered contemptuously.

"I did what you told me, Papa!"

"You stink of sweat and tequila! You cannot even act the part I give you!"

"I tried—I swear I tried!"

Alessandro threw up his hands. "Tried! I don't know why I have bothered, Ramon! You are not fit to wear my shoes, do you hear that? You are not fit to have the Ybarra!"

"Papa, they will hear you," Ramon protested weakly.

The old man lowered his voice. "She's dead, you say?"

"Yes."

"Where?"

"Half a day's ride north of the Overland Road, Papa. I did not think anyone would find her there."

Alessandro groaned. "Someone must find her body, or we cannot claim the *ranchero*. Otherwise, she must be declared dead, and that takes too much time."

"We do what we did with Tía Isabella," Ramon reasoned. "We send out the searchers, and when they find Maria, they will believe the Comanches killed her there."

Sinking into his leather chair, Alessandro put his fingers together and looked up at Ramon. "And how"—he bit the words off evenly—"do you explain that she is north of the road, my son?"

"But I have thought of that, Papa. Don't you see? The Comanches have carried her that way. And when she became a burden to them, they killed her and left her."

His father regarded him wearily. "To my knowledge there have been no war parties in the area. At least with Isabella, the time was right. Now we must create suspicion by sending a search party north."

"But there *were* Comanches there—I myself saw them." Wanting to impress Alessandro, he blurted out, "They would have captured me, but I fought them off, Papa. You nearly lost your son, much you care for that." When the old man's expression did not change, he added resentfully, "Only my wits and my new rifle saved me."

"If you had told me you ran, I might have believed you. It is not in you to stand like a man, Ramon." Sighing, the elder Sandoval shook his head. "Why could you not have gotten my spine? Why is it that all you had of me was your looks? No, you are Ramona's son more than mine. You deserve the name she gave you."

"There is no need to quarrel at me, Papa. It is done."

"You were supposed to court her—you were supposed to bring her back a bride. The other we could arrange later."

"You did not know her." Taking the chair opposite his father, Ramon tried to plead his case. He leaned forward, his voice earnest. "Maria Ross was not the sheltered señorita eager to fall into my arms, Papa. I did everything, I swear to you—I did everything to make her wish to marry me. She refused me—*me,* your son, Papa! I even thought if I kept playing the courtly gentleman, she would soften, but she did not. No, she was too good for me, yet she could expose her breasts to Señor McAlester!" he recalled indignantly.

"McAlester?" There was a pregant pause. "Which McAlester, Ramon?"

"The Texas Ranger—she preferred that savage to me!"

But Alessandro was ahead of him. "I don't like this. The rangers must suspect nothing. They must blame the Indians."

"How can they suspect anything? He left the same day we did—I heard he was going to El Paso. No, it would not even surprise me if he went across into New Mexico. He has a great hatred for the Comancheros, which I have seen with my own eyes." Noting that his father's expression had not lightened at all, he added defensively, "Papa, I did everything to win her, but I could see my suit was hopeless."

"Are you certain she is dead?"

Ramon nodded. "At first I just left her there, but then when I thought about how she had refused me, I got angry, and I went back and shot her. I saw her fall. And even if she did not die of the bullet, she had no water. She could not have survived even one day out there—you don't know how hot it was, Papa. And I know I did not miss when I shot her."

"I have but to look at the ground here to tell there has been heat," Alessandro responded dryly. "Well, it is done," he decided, his voice suddenly tired.

"You told me if she would not marry me, she would have to die," Ramon reminded him.

"I know." The old man sighed. "But it would have

looked better if you had scalped her like Paulo did with Isabella. Then there was no question. Everybody believed she was taken with my poor brother." Thinking of Gregorio, he whispered a quick prayer, then made the sign of the Cross over his breast. Recovering, he repeated himself. "You should have scalped her."

"Me?" Horrified, his son exclaimed, "Papa, I cannot stand the sight of blood!"

"Yes, I know that also," Alessandro said grimly. "You are like poor Ramona, may God rest her soul," he added, looking heavenward. "Why I do not know, but it has been my lot to be surrounded by imbeciles. At least your Mother had the excuse of being female."

"Papa—"

But Alessandro wasn't finished. "Even Gregorio was a fool, for he did not hide the other women from Isabella. Had the Indians not gotten him first, she would surely have divorced him. Padre Luis told me that over too much tequila—did you know that? She went to him, saying Gregorio had betrayed her too many times. And when he told her it was a sin to end a marriage, she said there was no Texas law against it. And I had warned my brother—I said the Ybarra is worth sleeping with ice, with stone even."

"Papa, I am telling you I *tried.*"

Alessandro favored his son with a look of utter disgust. "You are like him also—you do not know when to stay away from the wrong woman. Look at you! You have looks and grace, and yet you could not even make a grieving Maria Ross turn to you! Was it because you went at her like a rutting pig?"

"No!"

"No, do not lie to me! You have not the will of a rabbit! All you want is any place to put it, Ramon. By the time you are my age, you will be raddled with the French sickness!"

"I cannot help it if the women like me," Ramon protested.

"Like you? It is the money they like, you fool!"

Alessandro threw up his hands. "What are you to do when I am gone? Well, it cannot be thought. But I know this—if you do not stiffen your spine, you will lose the Ybarra from beneath your nose!" Catching himself, he lowered his voice. "But you cannot help it, I suppose."

"Papa, I did what you asked! She would not have me!"

"Then you should have brought her here and let me take care of it. There could have been a riding accident—or something could have fallen on her. As it is now, what is everyone to think? First Gregorio, then Isabella, and now Maria—all taken by the Indians?" Again, he shook his head. "Now I will have to press Governor Davis to do something about them, I suppose. I will have to take myself off to Austin and appear before the legislature, demanding more protection for the *rancheros*. And there will be rangers everywhere, which we do not want."

"I am sorry, Papa. I tried—truly I tried."

"Yes, you are always sorry." Alessandro's expression softened, and he leaned to cup his son's face with his hands. "But you are my son—everything I do is for you. More than anything I have dreamed of leaving the Ybarra to you." Releasing Ramon, he heaved himself from the chair. "So now we must send out the search parties, eh? But first, I will go to the kitchen and find an onion to rub into your eyes. You, my son, will drink no more tequila—no, you will stay in your room and weep for poor Maria until we are ready to leave."

"You did not know her," Ramon muttered sullenly.

"It does not matter. And when we bring her back to be buried here, you will sleep alone for a decent time. Whether you want to do it or not, you will mourn Maria Ross properly. You will not dance nor show any gaiety for a twelvemonth, my son. And you will lead the search party yourself, but I intend to send Paulo also to remind you of your grief should it wane."

"Papa, it is too hot to ride—and I just got home. I am tired. The heat has made me sick."

Alessandro gave him a withering look. "And who else is there who can help us to stumble onto poor Maria's body, I ask you? No, my son, you will swear vengeance on the Comanches—you will be too distraught to eat, to sleep, to think about anything but finding Maria. Do you understand me, Ramon?"

"Yes, Papa," his son said wearily. "You are making me weep for a woman who would not have me."

"You are inconsolable over a woman who promised to be your wife before she was so cruelly captured by the Indians. Repeat it—repeat it now for me."

"I am weeping for Maria." Seeing that his father still looked down his hawk nose at him, he capitulated. "All right—it has been a great sadness to me. We had come to love each other and were making plans to marry here at the Ybarra. Does that satisfy you?"

"Barely. I hope you show more emotion when you tell that to the authorities. Now, how is it that you have lived and she did not?" Alessandro persisted.

"I don't know."

"You must know, Ramon, you *must* know!"

"All I know is I lost a good sombrero."

"Imbecile!" The old man struck him across the cheek again, cutting it with his heavy ring. "Tell me how you survived!"

"What do you want me to say?" Ramon cried. "Tell me, and I will say it!"

"You were running to make a stand behind the rocks. She slipped, and before you could stop to save her, one of the savages pulled her onto his horse. You exchanged gunfire with them, wounding one, and they retreated, taking her with them." Alessandro's black eyes stared into his. "At least that way none will know you for the coward you are." When Ramon said nothing, he demanded, "Surely that isn't too much to remember, is it?"

"No, Papa," Ramon whispered. "No," he managed louder. "To please you, I will do it."

"See that you do," was the grim reply. "Now I will get that onion. And while I am gone, you will sit here, and you will drink nothing, my son. Nothing."

"Yes, Papa."

But as soon as Alessandro closed the door behind him, Ramon reached for his father's decanter. Removing the glass stopper, he took a long pull from the bottle. The old man had no right to treat him as though he were nothing, he told himself resentfully. After all, no matter what Alessandro said to him, it was Ramona Olivera de Behar, not Alessandro, who'd given him the blood of Andalusian princes. For all that the old man lorded it over everyone, he was actually almost common. And the only ones he truly fooled were the Anglos, who were too stupid to tell one Spaniard from another.

Clay entered Nahdehwah's tipi and saw Amanda. She was sitting up, looking alert, but it was a good thing she didn't have a mirror. Her thick auburn hair was plastered against her head, falling like string ropes over her shoulders. To compound the sight, the black grease still covered the sunburned portion of her face and neck. While he groped for something to say, she was truly relieved to see him.

She looked up, and as he stood over her, he seemed to fill the whole lodge. Acutely conscious of how dirty she was, she couldn't meet his gaze. When he didn't say anything, she sighed. "I'm quite a sight, aren't I?"

"How do you feel?"

"Better." She pulled the calico dress over her knees, trying to cover her lower legs. "I thought Indians only wore buckskin," she said.

"Not if they can get cloth from traders. They like the bright colors."

"You don't really expect me to believe that, do you? About traders, I mean?"

"Does it make any difference?" he countered.

"Well, I'd hate to think I'm wearing a dead woman's dress."

"Do you want me to ask her?"

"No, of course not."

"It's a little bit big on you, but you look pretty good in it," he offered.

She made a face at him. "Now *that's* a lie, and I know it."

"Well, you'd look even better if you washed your face," he admitted. "Then every *tuibitsi* in camp would be bringing horses to Nahdehwah's door."

"I don't think I want to ask what a two-bitsy is," she muttered.

"You haven't got the sound right on your tongue. A *tuibitsi* is a handsome man riding a fine pony." He dropped down to sit cross-legged beside her. "Fixed up properly, with a clean face and with silver and beads in your braids, you'd be worth four or five horses, maybe more."

"How awful." She thought he was teasing her, but she couldn't be certain. "Is that a good price?" she asked curiously.

"Fair to middling." He cocked his head slightly to study her fine-boned profile. "If your family wanted more, and if your *tuibitsi* could afford it, he'd probably come up with whatever they asked. But," he added, smiling now, "he'd want to know that you could butcher a buffalo, make his clothes, set up his tipi, make all his food, and carry his children on a cradle board hitched to your back. Otherwise, you'd be pretty useless to him."

"How primitive."

"Oh, I don't know that it's any more primitive than the way the Spanish go about it."

"Well, it is." Ill at ease, she studied the dress, pleating the cotton skirt with her fingers, then smoothing it out again. "Whoever wore this was a lot shorter and wider than I am. When I stand up, it doesn't come to my ankles."

"I wouldn't worry about that—I've seen a whole lot more than an ankle."

Her face flushed. "Well, I must say it isn't very gentlemanly to mention that," she muttered.

"What?" Then it dawned on him what she thought he meant. "Oh. Well, I wasn't expecting you to take it personally," he assured her. "To tell the truth, I was so busy trying to cool you down that I wasn't paying much attention. And I kind of figured you'd rather be alive than proper then, anyway."

"Well, I would, of course, but—"

"But you don't want to be reminded."

"No."

A strained silence hung like a curtain between them. He ought to have just asked her how she felt, then left. Instead, he was sitting there, as nervous as the first time a girl had promised to slip into his tipi after dark, trying to think of something properly impersonal to say, sinking deeper into the quicksand of last night's dream.

But he wasn't a complete fool. No matter what the peyote vision told him, he knew she couldn't be any part of his destiny. For one thing, she owned a big chunk of West Texas, for another, she was too damned civilized to look twice at a man like him. Yet as he clasped his arms around his knees and stared into the cold firehole, he was acutely aware of her.

"Nahdehwah says you are nearly well," he said finally. "She says you are drinking, and you ate this morning."

Relieved by the turn in conversation, she nodded. "Yes, but only God knows what I've been given, and I don't think I want Him to tell me. I don't even know what *pulke* is, only that I have drunk gallons of it."

"They didn't make any at the Ybarra?"

"No—or if they did, I didn't know about it. I'm sure we never had it in the house. I don't think Mama would have drunk anything like that."

"It comes from the maguey, the same cactus Mexicans use for making mescal and tequila. They get everything from soap to rope to paper from it."

"Oh."

It was the damned dream, and he knew it, but he couldn't shake it. Trying to find a safe ground between them, he told her, "You know, I didn't think you were going to make it out there. I thought by this time today I'd be digging a grave."

She clasped her arms around her knees also and leaned forward. When she spoke, her voice was distant. "There was a time . . . when I was alone . . . when the water was gone . . . that I was afraid," she admitted haltingly. "But I had to keep trying to walk back . . . . it was the only chance I had of being found. Besides, I didn't want Ramon to get away with leaving me there. I didn't want to die and have no one know what happened to me."

"I'm not sure I could walk that far myself. It took a lot of guts to try it."

"There wasn't anything else I could do," she said simply. "He left me out there."

"Was it a quarrel?"

"No. At least I don't think so." But even as she said it, she recalled how Ramon had accused her of behaving improperly with McAlester. Her chin came up. "What difference does it make why he did it? He left me, and then he came back to kill me," she said evenly. "Did I tell you that? Like a fool, I ran out when I saw him returning, and he shot at me. I fell when I heard the bullet pass, and I guess he thought he'd succeeded, because he drove off again."

"Do you think he wanted the Ybarra?"

"He tried to make me believe he wanted me," she responded tiredly. "But he's not getting Ybarra-Ross. If it's the last thing I do, I'm going to see him hanged." When he said nothing, she went on with feeling, "While I have lain here in this hot tipi, I have thought of little beyond revenge, I assure you. I don't care *why* he did what he did, but as soon as I get back to some sort of civilization, I'm going to demand his arrest. And then I'm going to watch him hang."

"He probably won't hang." As she turned incredulous eyes to him, he nodded. "You survived."

"What?" she choked out. "Oh, now that's too much!" But as she stared at him, she realized he was

serious. "Do you mean to tell me that if he stole Ybarra horses or Ybarra cattle, he'd be hanged, but because he *only* tried to kill me, he'll just go to jail?" she demanded indignantly. "Do you call that justice?"

"No. I call it law made by ranchers."

"Well, I want justice! I don't want Ramon Sandoval to sit in jail for a few years, then get out! I don't want him to breathe air!"

He didn't blame her. He'd killed men for a whole lot less than Ramon Sandoval had done to her. But after she'd been gone for so many years, she'd be the outsider, Alessandro Sandoval the one with political influence. Even if a jury voted for hanging, he suspected Governor Davis wouldn't let it happen. The senior Sandoval would find a way to get to him.

When he said nothing, she realized he'd spoken the truth. "Well," she said finally, "if he cannot be hanged, then I want him to rot in some hell-pit until he dies. Or better yet, drag him out into the desert when the temperature is over one hundred degrees and let him try to walk out with no water. And I'd like to be standing there with a gun just in case he makes it."

"And I thought you hated violence," he murmured sardonically.

"This isn't violence—it's justice," she snapped back.

"Do you want me to kill him for you?"

He said it softly, so softly she wasn't quite sure she'd heard him right. For a moment she stared into those cold blue eyes, and the fury gradually ebbed from her body. "No. I couldn't ask such as thing." She sighed heavily. "And I couldn't really kill him either. Then I'd be as guilty as he is. No, by the time I get home, Ramon will probably have escaped to Mexico, anyway."

"It won't make any difference if he does—it wouldn't be the first time I've crossed the Rio Grande."

"Do you really think the Mexicans will let a Texan bring a Sandoval back to stand trial?"

He smiled faintly. "I don't usually ask 'em."

She stared across the tipi, seeing Ramon as he'd driven off, leaving her alone. "I guess I don't seem very grateful for what you've done for me, do I?" she said. "You saved my life, and here I am carping at you."

"I thought that was just your usual manner."

"Well, I am grateful. And I mean to pay you for your trouble when I get to Ybarra-Ross."

"Don't." He heaved himself up, towering over her. "I don't want your money, Amanda."

"It doesn't have to be money. I mean—"

"I don't want a job either," he cut in shortly. "Right now, I've got something to attend to, but I'll be back later."

He'd turned his back to leave, but she didn't want him to go. "Wait—"

"What?"

"I don't want to stay here." She wet dry lips, then said low, "Please, I don't want to stay here."

"I know, but it can't be helped."

"She doesn't like me—Nahdehwah doesn't like me—and I'm afraid of her."

"She hasn't hurt you yet, has she?"

Inexplicable, unreasonable tears burned her eyes, and she brushed at them with the back of her hand. As furious with herself as she was with him, she flung angry words after him. "All right—go off and leave me alone with your crazy medicine woman!"

He spun around at that, and his jaw hardened. "That was unworthy of you. Thanks to Nahdehwah, you are a damned sight better off than when I found you," he reminded her evenly.

"But I cannot understand her, and she cannot understand me!" She bit her lip to still its trembling. "Please, I'm telling you I'm afraid of her!"

"If she were going to harm you, she'd have done it before now."

"She doesn't even like me! Half the time she sits

there watching me as though she'd like to cut my nose off! That's what they do with female captives, isn't it?"

"You aren't a captive. For what it's worth, I told her you are my wife." Before she could rip up at him, he added defensively, "It was easier to explain. Besides, I didn't want to be bothered with anyone wanting to buy you. This way, you're more or less family."

While she digested that, he ducked outside, leaving her alone with the old woman. She sat there, transfixed for a moment, then she struggled to stand on her sore feet, and tottered after him. A momentary dizziness washed over her, and she had to stop.

"Wait!" she called out. When he didn't turn back, she caught at a cottonwood branch and held on. "I'm sorry!" she managed to shout. "I can't help it if I'm afraid!"

He was going to make a fool of himself, he knew it. But when he turned around, she was leaning against the tree as though she'd fall if she turned loose. Cursing under his breath, he went back to get her.

"All right," he told her, circling her waist with his arm. She clung to him until the world ceased spinning. His other arm came up, embracing her. "You're a damned fool and a nuisance, you know that, don't you?" he whispered. He could feel her body tremble, and he was afraid she was going to cry. His hand stroked her dirty, tangled hair. "Don't."

Nahdehwah had followed her out. Without a word, she handed Clay the clothes Amanda had worn into the Indian camp, then she turned and walked back to her tipi. He looked down, seeing that she'd washed them, and he knew she wanted the calico dress returned.

"Come on," he said, taking Amanda's hand.

Embarrassed by her outburst, she hung back. "Where are we going?" she dared to ask.

"You'll see."

He walked slowly enough for her to keep up. This time, as they passed along the line of tipis, no one stared at her. Finally, he stopped before two women

who were cooking over an outdoor fire. One rose and
went in, then a big Indian came out, smiling broadly.
He and McAlester spoke briefly, then the Indian nodded and turned to address both women. They regarded
Amanda sullenly for a moment, then one went back to
stirring the contents of the pot, while the other disappeared. The big Indian gestured for Clay and Amanda
to come inside.

The tipi interior was larger than Nahdehwah's, and
the smokehole flap was opened wider to let in light and
air. An evil-looking assortment of bone and steel tools
hung from the walls, while several piles of buffalo
robes were arranged around the empty firepit. The Indian patted one of them and said something. McAlester
looked it over appreciatively and nodded.

"What did he say?" she hissed under her breath.

"Two Owls is offering us his best bed," Clay answered. "Smile, or he'll think you don't like it."

"Oh, but—" Seeing that the fierce-looking Indian
was regarding her curiously, she bit back intemperate
words and forced what she hoped was a passable
smile. He grinned.

She grasped McAlester's arm. "You aren't going to
leave me alone with them, are you?" she whispered.
When he didn't answer, she demanded, "You aren't—
tell me you aren't."

"No," he lied.

And then the full import of what Two Owls had
done came home to her. "I can't sleep with you," she
choked out, mortified. "I just can't."

"You didn't want to stay with Nahdehwah, remember?" he gibed.

"But—"

"If it stays hot tonight, he probably won't mind if
we sleep outside."

"I think I'd rather."

"All right, but let's get two things straight right
now—you hold your tongue, and I won't presume anything improper."

But even as he made the promise, the image of her hair falling over his bare skin came to mind so vividly that he could feel the silk of it touching him. And no amount of denial was going to make it go away. By bringing her to Two Owls's lodge before he was ready to leave, he was jumping from the frying pan into the fire, and he knew it.

In the course of the day, Amanda learned that Two Owls was Kiowa, not Comanche, and that Walks With Sunshade, his Comanche wife, and Little Doe, his Kiowa one, whose mien was one of perpetual pout, did not get along. There had been a daughter born to Little Doe, Clay discovered and passed on to Amanda, but the child had died from "ghost sickness." It was why they'd chosen to live in Ketanah's camp—they had no confidence in the Kiowa medicine man who'd treated the little girl, and they believed if Nahdehwah had been there, their child would have survived.

To Amanda, Little Doe's behavior looked more like jealousy than grief, and noting the younger wife's swollen belly, she could almost sense the other woman's despair. But both of them were united in one thing—neither wanted to welcome Nahakoah's woman into Two Owls's tipi. If McAlester and the big Kiowa hadn't been there, Amanda had not the least doubt that the two wives would have joined forces to do her bodily harm.

As it was, Little Doe watched her, her dark eyes malevolent. And whenever she thought no one was looking, she jabbed her unwanted guest with a red-hot stick from the fire. Hearing Amanda cry out in surprise, Walks With Sunshade loudly scolded her rival, and the older woman answered insolently.

Two Owls came outside to mediate the quarrel between his wives, and once Walks With Sunshade explained what happened, he jerked Little Doe behind the tipi, where he shouted at her, while the Comanche wife sat listening, smugly satisfied. When they came back, the Kiowa woman was obviously subdued. It had been, Amanda reflected, much like the proverbial trip to the woodpile.

Not that Walks With Sunshade was any better. Several times, she'd come over and lifted Amanda's tangled auburn hair as though she admired it, but when no one was looking, she pulled it hard enough to bring tears to the white girl's eyes. The last time she did it, Amanda reached out and pinched her, holding on, staring her down, until the Indian woman let go. Through it all, Clay McAlester and Two Owls seemed oblivious to what was going on.

The final straw came when both men left her alone with the feuding wives. Little Doe sidled up with a steaming pot and "accidentally" dumped boiling stew on Amanda's borrowed calico dress, then taunted her. That was the final straw. Forgetting years of convent school and proper Boston upbringing, Amanda caught her tormentor by the knees, bringing her down. The stew spilled, burning Little Doe's arm, then ran in thick rivulets over the hard-packed earth.

Little Doe was remarkably agile, and she came up ready to fight. Her gravy-streaked hands grasped Amanda's hair, pulling it. Unable to get loose, Amanda sank her teeth into the woman's burned arm and bit hard. Little Doe screamed, bringing Two Owls at a dead run, but when he saw what was happening, he made no move to intervene. As the Kiowa woman fought and struggled, Amanda's teeth locked in her flesh, and her arms wrapped around Little Doe's body, imprisoning her in a bearlike embrace. Despite the taste of dirt, sweat, stew and blood, she held on.

Walks With Sunshade circled them, holding a large metal spoon like a weapon, darting in to strike a blow every now and then, usually hitting her husband's other wife. And all the while, she kept up a steady, high-pitched shrieking. A group of squaws drawn by the commotion shouted encouragement at Little Doe, as though they watched some sort of contest. A few men and several children joined them.

Returning from the spring, Clay heard the noise and saw the crowd. Pushing his way through them, he caught Amanda from behind. "Whoa now! What the devil . . . ?" But she wasn't about to let Little Doe loose. He saw the blood trickle down the screaming Kiowa woman's arm. "What the hell is going on here?" he demanded, looking to Two Owls.

The Indian grunted, then shook his head, indicating he didn't want Nahakoah to stop them. "Your woman can fight," he said. "Let her take care of herself."

Trying to get away, Little Doe scratched and pummeled the white girl to no avail, until finally she managed to grab the neck of Amanda's dress, pulling it up over her head, exposing her pale legs. For answer, Amanda's hands caught Little Doe's hair, pulling out a good handful of it. The Indian woman turned loose and fell wailing to the ground.

"Had enough?' Amanda gasped.

Looking around at the now subdued crowd, Amanda realized the enormity of what she'd done. Little Doe staggered up, still clutching her head with one hand, her bleeding arm with the other. Two Owls spoke sharply to her, then pushed her roughly into the tipi, where she could be heard railing and ranting. As he turned back to her, Amanda's stomach knotted, but the big Indian was grinning. He came over and patted her shoulder, apparently congratulating her.

McAlester looked at the stew and blood on her dress, then went inside. Exhausted, Amanda sank to her knees, panting, fighting an urge to weep. Her face inscrutable, Walks With Sunshade came up and began silently wiping what she could of the the mess off the calico cloth. The other women filed past, some pausing to speak a word or two before going. It was probably just as well that Amanda couldn't understand them, she thought, but at least they were no longer belligerent.

Feeling ashamed and humiliated, she knelt there, wondering what McAlester was going to do. When he came out, he had the clothes Nahdehwah had washed in his hand. Leaning down, he reached to pull her up, then supported her for a moment with his arm. She closed her eyes to hide from him.

"Come on. I see you can walk now," was all he said.

Releasing her, he began walking away. Glancing nervously toward the Indians, Amanda followed. So tired she was shaking, she couldn't keep up with him. Finally, just before he reached the spring, she caught at a tree limb and held on, panting. He turned back.

"You're mad at me, aren't you?" she managed to choke out. "You don't know what she did to me."

He stood there, looking at her, one corner of his mouth lifted in a lopsided smile, his blue eyes perceptibly warm. "I'm not mad," he said softly. "I'm damned proud of you."

"Every time you weren't looking, that Indian witch tried to hurt me." Then she realized what he'd said. "You mean you don't *mind*?" she asked incredulously.

"No."

She stared. "I don't think I'll ever understand you," she decided finally.

"You did what you had to do."

She'd been prepared for his anger, not his admiration. And rather than relief, she felt almost betrayed by his manner. "Much you would know about it," she snapped, accusing him. "You said you wouldn't leave me alone with them—you promised you wouldn't! Where were you, anyway?"

"I didn't know you wanted to take a bath with me. Next time, I'll keep it in mind."

"Oh—now, that's too much!"

"You can't have it both ways, Amanda."

He walked back to where she still held onto the tree branch. Reaching for her free hand, he pressed a hard cake into it. She looked down, seeing what appeared to be lye soap. When she raised her eyes, she realized his hair clung wetly to his shoulders, spotting his clean white shirt. The oddly detached thought that he'd shaved crossed her mind.

"Well, you might have told me, in any event," she muttered, looking away.

"I'd say you took care of yourself."

"I'm lucky they didn't decide to kill me. What would you have done then?"

"Two Owls wouldn't let it happen. As it is, Little Doe has disgraced herself and him, so you probably won't see much of her again. While it is acceptable to taunt and threaten a captive, it is forbidden to harm any who comes as a guest."

"I wouldn't put anything past them," she muttered.

"Look—do you want a bath or not?"

"Here? In broad daylight?" She glanced down at the soap in her hand. "You're serious, aren't you?"

"The water's a little cold, but it's a whole lot cleaner than the Pecos." When she said nothing, he held out the shirt and drawers she'd worn into the camp. "Nahdehwah got most of the dirt out."

"I can't take a bath here."

"If you hurry, nobody'll see you. I'll stand guard," he promised.

"You'll be here."

"I'll turn my back. Go on in, and I'll sit over there," he said, pointing toward a clump of cottonwoods. Seeing that she hesitated, he sighed. "As I told you before, you haven't got anything I haven't seen anywhere else, but I don't aim to look. So you might as well wash the stink and grease off before you try to eat. I don't know about you, but I feel a damned sight better clean." As a gesture of good faith, he walked toward the trees, then dropped down to sit under them, facing away from her.

She reached up, feeling her dirty, matted hair; then she rubbed her face. Nahdehwah's black grease came off on the back of her hand, and she knew she had to be an awful sight. She edged closer to the spring-fed pool, then looked over her shoulder. He was still sitting there, his back to her.

"How deep is it?" she called out.

"I wouldn't wade too far in," he answered without moving. "And I wouldn't stay too long."

The spring was sheltered by a rock wall that rose above it and tangled cottonwoods on either side, leaving only the path they'd walked between. Casting one last nervous glance backward, she quickly pulled off Nahdehwah's dress, eyed the crystal-clear water, and stepped in gingerly.

The clarity made the depth deceptive, and she plunged in all the way to her breasts before her feet touched bottom. The water was unbelievably cold. "Whooo!" she gasped in shock.

But she was in, and there was no turning back now. Before she could lose her nerve, she ducked her head underwater, then came up. Grasping the chunk of soap, she rubbed it over her hair, savoring the strong, clean smell, then quickly went over her face, arms, and body before tossing the soap onto the grass, Shivering almost uncontrollably from the cold, she bent her knees and went under again. Her hair swirled out in the clear water, then she came up, smoothing it back from her face, squeezing it out.

Clay leaned forward, clasping his knees, trying not to think of the naked woman in the water. He had too much to do, and not enough time to do it. In fact, if he meant to intercept Sanchez-Torres, he was going to have to leave, and the sooner he did it, the better. All hell was going to break loose when Amanda found out, but with any luck, he wouldn't be there to see it. He'd just have to creep out without waking her in the morning.

He didn't want to think about that either. Resolutely, he went over everything he knew about Sanchez-Torres, playing a mental game, trying to outguess him. And for once he wished he had Hap with him. Unless he managed an ambush, it was going to be hell taking the Comancheros alone. Maybe he was just spooked, or maybe he was getting old, but he'd never felt mortal before. At twenty-eight, he was already older than any active ranger except Hap. The legendary Rip Ford had said it once—rangering was for young fools too green to be afraid.

Not that he could say he was afraid. No, he'd spent too many years with the Comanches for that, and he prided himself in having the fatalism expected of a warrior. It wasn't when—it was how a man died that counted. He'd always sort of expected he wouldn't see the other side of thirty, and somehow that hadn't mattered. Aside from Hap, he didn't have anybody to mourn him.

"Aiyeeeeee!"

He sprang to his feet at the sound of her scream, his gun drawn. Ahead of him in the path stood a Comanche, buck-naked except for his breechclout. The man looked from Clay to Amanda, then back again.

As Amanda watched, McAlester put away his revolver and pointed his hand, apparently a friendly gesture. The Indian smiled, and for what seemed an interminable time to her, they talked. She stood there, her arms crossed over her bare breasts, her whole body shaking, her teeth chattering from the cold water. Finally, unable to stand it any longer, she said loudly, "If you d-don't m-mind, I'd like t-to g-get out."

He swung around, utterly unprepared for the effect she had on him. As his gaze moved from her face to her wet shoulders, he felt his mouth go dry. His thoughts must have been written on his face, because she reddened and crossed her arms more tightly. But it didn't matter. His mind already ran wild.

The Indian, who'd come for water, walked closer, knelt, and cupped his hands, dipping them, then drank. When he finished, he wiped his hands on the breechclout, said something Clay didn't even hear, and disappeared.

"S-some g-guard you are," Amanda muttered, shivering.

"I'll get your clothes," Clay said hoarsely, turning away. Picking them up, he tossed them closer, then retreated.

She didn't even have a towel for drying. She glanced at McAlester's back, then up the path, satisfying herself that no one was looking, before she darted from the water and scooped up the shirt and drawers. Freezing despite the hot air, she quickly dived into the shirt and pulled it over her head. It clung to her wet body as she jerked it downward, nearly covering her thighs.

Thinking she'd had enough time, he turned around as she was buttoning the neck placket. Where the water spotted the cloth, it was semitransparent, showing the dark outline of her cold-hardened nipples. His breath caught in his chest.

"Sorry," he mumbled, retreating back to the cottonwoods. "Just tell me when you're ready."

But the damage was already done. If he lived to be a hundred, he'd never forget seeing her like that. But even as desire rose within him, reason whispered, reminding him that she was Big John Ross's daughter, an heiress far above his touch. He leaned against a tree and counted slowly, silently to one hundred, giving her time to get into her drawers.

Self-conscious now, Amanda fanned the shirt, trying to dry it, then tugged at the legs of the drawers, loosening them. She was barely covered, and her teeth still chattered, but at least she was clean. Bending forward, she squeezed more water from her hair, then straightened, tossing it back over her shoulder.

"I g-guess I'm r-ready," she said, trying to comb the tangled mass with her fingers.

He turned around slowly, not trusting himself to speak. She was biting her lip, eyeing him hesitantly. She forced a tentative smile.

"Not m-much of a fashion plate, am I?"

"No."

He was looking at her oddly, unnerving her. "Yes, well ... I uh ... expect we ought to get back," she managed.

"Yes."

But he didn't move. She walked the path toward him, acutely aware of his eyes on her.

"Is s-something the m-matter?"

"Yes."

Her hand crept self-consciously to her wet hair. "What?"

"It doesn't matter. Come on—I'll get you a comb."

With that he turned and started back toward the camp. She stared after him, then hurried to catch up. When she glanced at him, his face was closed, devoid of emotion. But she'd already seen the heat in his eyes, and it had been enough to make her heart pause.

Sitting on a buffalo robe dragged outside, Amanda picked at her supper, feeling extremely ill at ease with her Comanche hosts. She couldn't eat after having watched Walks With Sunshade toss the slow-moving turtle alive into the fire. The poor creature must have tried a dozen or more times to get out before it finally died. And although another pot of stew had appeared from nowhere, the roasted turtle and a large, bloody hunk of meat provided the bulk of the meal.

Beside her, Clay McAlester sat cross-legged on the grass, eating with apparent relish. He looked over at her nearly full bark bowl.

"What's the matter?" he asked between mouthfuls.

"I can't eat this—I just can't."

"It could use a little salt, but it's not bad."

She shuddered. "The way she cooked the turtle was the most barbaric thing I've ever seen."

"No worse than wringing a chicken's neck and watching it run around the yard without its head. Or hearing a hog squeal when its throat gets cut."

"At least the chicken's dead before it's cooked. And thankfully I've never seen a pig butchered."

"All right," he said, sighing. "Try to eat the stew."

"How do I know she didn't scrape it off the ground?"

"She didn't."

"Do you have any idea what's in it?"

Turning to the Comanche woman, he murmured, "This is good—what did you use to make it?"

Walks With Sunshade beamed, then ticked off the ingredients on her fingers. Corn, mesquite beans, yeps, honey, buffalo marrow, a lizard, and two rabbits.

Clay translated for Amanda, "It's rabbit."

"And it took a hand and a half to say that?" she responded incredulously.

"The rest are spices," he lied. "Go on—try it. It tastes more or less like chicken. And if you don't eat, you'll hurt her feelings. If you don't want to chew it, just swallow it whole."

She glanced up, seeing that the woman watched her. "All right," she muttered. Pulling the small piece of meat off with her teeth, she pushed it back in her mouth with her tongue, and gulped. Whatever it really was, it tasted sweet and greasy.

"I'm not really very hungry," she decided. "And it does *not* taste like chicken."

He speared a chunk of undercooked meat from his tin plate and held it out on the end of his knife. "This is pretty good."

"What is it—raw dog? Mole? Toad?"

"Comanches don't eat dog meat." Seeing that she remained unconvinced, he exhaled audibly. "Okay—it's horse meat, and it won't kill you. I've eaten a lot of it."

Two Owls looked across at her still full bowl, then spoke to Clay, who nodded, then answered. "What did he say?" she asked suspiciously.

"He says you will grow skinny like an old buffalo cow. But I told him the heat puts you off your food."

The Kiowa addressed Walks With Sunshade, and she rose to disappear into the tipi. When she came out, she carried a tallow-coated parfleche and a jagged bone knife. Squatting down beside Amanda, she slit through the grease shell with the blade, took out several flat, thin strips of dried meat, and gave them to the white girl.

"He told her to give you something you'll eat," Clay said low. "If you turn up your nose at the jerky, you're on your own. Just don't come crying to me when you're hungry."

"I'm not trying to be rude," she whispered back.

"Well, you're doing a damned good job of it."

"At least tell her I said thank you."

Walks With Sunshade handed Amanda's nearly untouched bowl to Two Owls, who attacked the turtle meat with enthusiasm. As Amanda chewed her jerky, Clay poured something into his tin cup and passed it to her. Thinking it water, she tried to wash her food down with it. It burned her throat and hit her stomach like fire.

"Arghhhh—what is it?" she demanded, choking.

"Mescal. After a while it grows on you."

"It'd have to." Looking to where the Comanche woman watched her, Amanda lowered her voice. "What happened to Little Doe?"

"She's in the other tipi."

"What other tipi?"

"They have a smaller one in back, and to protect Two Owls's power, his wives stay there when they have their bleeding times. Otherwise it is believed they'll contaminate him. In Little Doe's case, she's there now because she shamed him today."

Seeing that he'd embarrassed her with his frankness, he handed her the cup. "Here—drink up and forget what happened with her. If you don't get a smile on your face, pretty soon Two Owls is going to wonder why I don't divorce you."

"You didn't have to tell them I was your wife," she muttered. "You could have said I was your Anglo sister."

"Once they reach physical maturity, brothers and sisters stay away from each other in Comanche camps. A sister can be killed for failing to observe avoidance."

"Which proves these people are savages."

"You don't stay grateful for long, do you?" he shot back. "You know, you've got a damned short memory. A couple of days ago, you were half dead—now, thanks to one of these people, you're almost back to your old tart-tongued, shrewish self."

He just didn't understand that she was still afraid of them. For all she knew, her mother's scalp could be hanging from a lance or pole in this very camp. And she did not doubt that if he weren't there, these same Indians would be more than ready to kill her. But he *was* there. She sighed, then tried to make amends.

"I don't try to be tart-tongued—sometimes it just happens. But for what it's worth, I haven't forgotten I owe you my life. I'll never forget that."

"I told you—I don't want your gratitude," he retorted. "Save that for Nahdehwah."

She looked up and saw that Walks With Sunshade still watched her. She managed to smile, then bit off another piece of jerky. "This is good," she reassured the woman. Beside her, Clay McAlester apparently translated her words, for Walks With Sunshade nodded, then went back to eating.

This time, when Amanda drank, she took a smaller swallow, followed by another, and another. By the time she finished what was left in his cup, she was finding it tolerable. Compared to the Pecos River water or the warm *pulke,* it was almost good.

Clay tried to appear attentive when Two Owls began recounting his role in the Mexican raid, but his thoughts kept straying to the woman beside him. For all that he was vexed with her, he was also acutely aware of her. Even now, if he closed his eyes, he'd relive the peyote vision—or the sight of her standing in the water, her hands crossed over her wet breasts.

What he needed to do was put miles, not feet, between him and her. And the sooner the better, before he said or did something he might regret. It wasn't like she was a Comanche girl, and he could offer a few horses for her, then bed her.

No, she was the closest thing Texas had to an aristocrat, and more than likely, she'd end up marrying a rancher as rich as she was and having half a dozen children, who'd grow up to be the senators and governors and ranchers of the next generation. If she remembered him at all, she might tell her grandchildren about a half-wild Texas Ranger fool enough to take her to a Comanche camp.

But right now she was too close, haunting his waking thoughts. He could scarce look at her without wondering how it would feel to have her warm flesh pressed against his, her dark red hair enveloping him in its silk, enticing him with the scent of wild Texas roses. And that flight of fancy made his heart pound and his blood race.

He reached for his tin cup and found it empty. Walks With Sunshade refilled it quickly, and he drank deeply before setting it down. All he had to do was get through the night, he told himself, and then he'd leave at dawn. All he had to do was lie beside Amanda one night without touching her. He picked up the cup and drained it, then held it out for more.

From the other end of the camp there came again the beat of drums. He listened to them, his pulse matching the primitive rhythm. He guessed that some proud parents celebrated a boy's first successful raid by holding a giveaway dance.

Feeling the mellowing effect of the potent mescal, Amanda closed her eyes and listened to the drums. It was as though she were in another world, one far removed from Patrick Donnelly and Boston. One far removed from Ybarra-Ross. One where Clay McAlester stood between her and a whole Comanche village.

She didn't even notice when Walks With Sunshade collected the food bowls, then lit Two Owls's pipe with a live coal from the fire. It wasn't until the Comanche woman touched her shoulder, gesturing that they should leave the men alone, that Amanda roused. Two Owls spoke up, shaking his head, and the woman returned to her place by the fire.

"He's going to let you stay," Clay murmured. "I hope you know that's an honor."

"That's kind of him, but as long I'm here, I'm not going anywhere without you. In fact, I'm not letting you out of my sight until I get to Ybarra-Ross. You hear that, Mr. McAlester?" she asked, her voice slightly slurred. "Everywhere you go, I go. Everywhere."

"I usually take a nature walk before I turn in." In the dark, he couldn't see her face, but he was fairly certain she blushed. "I suppose you could turn your back."

"You know, somebody ought to teach you how to act around women," she complained. "There are some things unfit for polite discourse."

He stared absently into the fire for a moment, then sipped his drink. "I'm not usually around any."

"Somehow I'd rather guessed that."

"About all that's out here are border brothels, and there's something about those places that take all the softness out of a woman."

"I expect it's the men, don't you?" she murmured.

He looked at her then. She was hugging her knees, resting her chin on them, while the firelight danced in her dark eyes. She had to be the prettiest woman he'd ever seen. And whether she was way above his touch or not, he was now too far gone with mescal to think about that. He felt wild, reckless, and willing to dare.

"Nahakoah?"

Jerked back by the sound of Two Owls's voice, Clay blinked and tried to remember what the Indian had been saying. Then he saw that he was being offered the pipe. He took a deep drag, then exhaled the smoke, and passed the pipe back. The tobacco sent another surge through his veins. When he looked again, Amanda was sipping from his cup. Again Two Owls intruded, saying, "I had fourteen winters before my mother honored me for counting coup up north against a small party of Cheyenne. My brother and I crept into their camps while they slept, and we took their food sacks, leaving them to eat their horses. It was cold, and the wind blew ice I can still feel in my bones. But those Cheyenne warriors had to choose between walking and starving."

"That was worthy of honor," Clay murmured.

"And you, Nahakoah, how did you count your first coup?"

Resigning himself, Clay told of stealing four horses from a corral while a wary farmer sat by his front door, rifle in hand, oblivious to his loss. Buffalo Horn himself had reported Stands Alone's coup to the band, and Sees the Sun had held the dance for her son, inviting nearly everyone in the village, passing out not only the horses he'd stolen, but probably fifty more.

Abruptly, Two Owls heaved himself to his feet. "They dance for Looks Too Old tonight. That boy has but twelve winters, yet he cut loose a team without waking the owner." His broad face broke into a wide grin. "You know that man was one sore-footed fellow by the time he got anywhere. And without his oxen, he had to leave his wagon." He sobered abruptly. "The parents of Looks Too Old would be pleased if Stands Alone and his woman came to dance, and I'd like to go also. His grandmother was Kiowa," he added.

"I don't—" Clay looked again at Amanda. If he danced with her, he'd have to touch her. Yet if he touched her, he'd want a whole lot more than dancing. And only God could know where that would lead him. His pulse raced, forcing liquid heat through his veins. His mouth was almost too dry for speech. "All right." Somehow he managed to struggle to his feet. Leaning over, he reached a hand to her. "Come on," he said, "we're going to a dance."

She blinked. "A dance," she repeated blankly.

"You'll like it."

Her hands crept to where his shirt was buttoned over her breasts. "But I can't go like this surely . . . I mean—"

"You could go in a whole lot less," he assured her. "It's like a fort social, only not nearly so fancy. There aren't any Louise Baxters here."

"Thank heavens for that at least." She let him pull her up, but she hung back. "This isn't some sort of scalp dance, is it?"

"No, and they won't roast anyone over the fire," he promised her.

Grinning broadly, Two Owls said something to Clay. Walks With Sunshade giggled. "Are you sure they want me to go?" Amanda asked suspiciously.

"Word of a Texas Ranger."

"What did they say?"

"They want to see you dance."

"Oh, I couldn't—I don't know the steps."

"There aren't any. You just keep time to the drums." Her fingers where they curved over his nearly burned him, and yet he didn't want to release them. "When we get there, you'll see what I mean."

Led by Two Owls and Walks With Sunshade, they made their way almost the length of the camp to a place where the area was cleared. As they drew closer, the drumbeat grew more intense, its ancient, primitive rhythm quickening the pulse within his body. His hand tightened on Amanda's, but she didn't seem to notice. If anything, she held on nervously.

She saw the drummers, their faces made eerie by the orange and red flames of center fire. The shadowy figures of Comanche men and women circled, chanting and stamping, writhing and whirling, while a man with a bone-handled rawhide whip ran around, urging them on. Amanda stared, transfixed by the sight, until the man beckoned to her.

"What's he doing?" she whispered.

"That's the *pianehepai-i*—the big whip. He directs the dancing. If he orders you to join in, you have to do it. Otherwise, he can beat you."

"What are those things lying on the ground?"

"They're part of the game. Those who watch can dart between dancers and pick up gift sticks. Everyone who gets one is rewarded with something of value—usually a horse—by the boy's parents. That way, half the camp comes, and the boy gets recognized for his first big coup."

"Oh."

"It's about cunning and nerve. The more danger, the more honorable the coup, so it is considered more worthy to outwit the enemy in an obvious way than to kill him. To steal a horse beneath a man's nose is harder than shooting him from a safe distance for it. I once knew a boy who counted coup by taking a rifle from beneath a saddle while a soldier slept on it."

"And then he killed the soldier, I suppose."

"No. That would have been too easy. He left him unharmed."

"For every one they let live, they kill dozens more, and you cannot deny it."

"No." He didn't want her dwelling on that, not now. "Wait here," he said, letting go of her. As she watched curiously, he ducked between the dancers and picked up two painted sticks. Coming back, he showed them to her. "Now let's hope there's a gray horse for Nahdehwah," he murmured as he shoved them into his pocket.

"Why a gray one?"

"A gray horse brings good luck."

The big whip began prancing and dancing around Clay, then tapped him on the shoulder with the bone handle. Calling out "Nahakoah! Nahakoah!" he turned to the others, gesturing for them to take up the refrain. "Nahakoah! Nahakoah! Nahakoah!" a number of them shouted.

"Come on—let's go." Clay caught Amanda's hand again, pulling her into the circle of dancers. As the chant grew, he put his hands on her waist. She looked around helplessly, then tried to imitate the others by holding his waist also. The five men pounded the skin-covered drums, increasing the beat, while those in the circle whirled and stomped with abandon.

At first, Amanda was extremely self-conscious, then she realized McAlester was right—there wasn't much of anything that could be called a dance step. And the combination of heat, mescal, and drumbeat loosened her reserve. Trying to keep up with him, she copied what he did, stumbling a few times until she got the hang of it. Other dancers stopped to watch, clapping in rhythm, chanting sing-song, but she was beyond hearing them. There was too much warmth, too much strength in his hands. And as his eyes met hers, a primal excitement coursed through her, heating her body. Her heart pounded, imitating the heady beat of the drums.

Suddenly the whip master darted out, tapping Clay again, and the music stopped abruptly. A boy ran up with a gourd dipper, offering it to him. Clay drained it, then wiped his mouth with the back of his hand.

"This won't take long," he promised.

"Where are you going?"

Before he could answer, he was pushed into the open center of the circle. Someone else brought another dipper to her, and she discovered it was more mescal. Thirsty and breathless, she gulped it down, then stood there, her eyes fixed on McAlester as he cleared his throat, then began speaking words she couldn't understand. Several times he turned to a youth she supposed was the boy being honored. And when he finished, there was a collective shout of approval.

At that, the big whip went on to tap a man who sat just outside the circle. The fellow protested, indicating that he had a lame leg, but to no avail. His wife helped him stand, and the pair took their places among the dancers. The drummers began again.

"What was that all about?" Amanda asked when Clay returned to her.

"Before the night is over, every man here will recount his first coup." He hesitated for a moment, then asked, "How about another try at it?"

Whether it was the look in his eyes or the mescal she'd drunk didn't matter. His hand touched hers, and she was keenly aware of how warm, how vital he was.

Not trusting herself to speak, she nodded. As he put
her hands on his waist, she shivered not from cold, but
from the heat passing between them. And all the while
there was the wild, unbridled beat of the drums.

They danced into the night, scarce aware when others crept away, some to tipis, some to lie together in
the trees, others in the tall grass. As the music paused
for a latecomer to be dragged into the circle to speak,
Clay stepped back. He stood there, his chest heaving,
his breath coming in gasps. His hands were still on
Amanda's waist, steadying her. He looked into her
face, seeing her hair clinging damply to her temples,
her dark eyes shining in the moonlight. And from
somewhere in his mind came whispered words, telling
him she was his destiny.

When he finally dropped his hands, she brushed
her hair back with her fingertips. "I . . . uh . . . well,
that was something, wasn't it?" she managed self-
consciously.

"Yes."

He didn't want to stay there. He wanted to be alone
with her. His eyes searched the crowd for Two Owls.
The tall Kiowa saw him and began pushing his way
through those who still wanted to listen.

Standing beside him, Amanda stole a glance at him.
His long blond hair framed his chiseled face, his blue
eyes were pale with reflected moonlight, and his shirt
clung wetly to his heaving chest. He wasn't a pretty,
petulant boy like Ramon Sandoval, nor did he possess
the brash confidence of Patrick Donnelly, but he was
without doubt the most fascinating man she'd ever laid
eyes on. And she wasn't ready for the night to end yet.

"You dance well, Nahakoah," Two Owls said.

Clay held out the two gift sticks. "Pick out a gray
horse for Nahdehwah if you can. The other one you
can have for keeping my woman safe while I am
gone."

"It is not necessary—no one will harm her when she
is in my tipi."

"I want you to have it."

The Indian regarded him gravely for a moment, then said only, "I will choose for you."

"Good."

Despite a faint summer breeze, the air was still warm. Clay looked up, seeing a clear, cloudless sky, one filled with what seemed to be a hundred white-hot stars. As Two Owls returned to the crowd, Clay began walking, and a silent Amanda fell in beside him, following the path toward the spring. He was so aware of her, so tautly strung he was afraid to speak. When he dared to look at her, her face was averted, her thoughts hidden from him.

He ought to be exhausted, but he was more exhilarated than he'd been in years. As they approached the springs, it was so quiet now that he could hear his own heartbeat and the sound of water rushing over rocks. He stopped. His fingers touched hers, and her breath caught audibly, but she did not pull away.

"Amanda—" The word was somewhere between a whisper and a croak. "God, but you're beautiful—you know that, don't you?" he asked huskily.

There was no mistaking the desire in his voice. She knew she ought to turn back while she could, and yet as his hands slid up her arms, her pulse pounded, reverberating in her ears, drowning out reason. All that mattered was that he was going to kiss her, and that she wanted him to do it.

Her eyes were large and luminous in the darkness, then they closed as his arm tightened around her shoulders, holding her. His other hand lifted her chin. "So beautiful," he whispered thickly.

As his head bent nearer, she could feel the soft warmth of his breath against her cheek. A shiver of anticipation raced through her. In that moment it was as though they were the only people in the world, as though time itself paused. His lips met hers with surprising gentleness, touching, tentatively tasting. She hesitated, uncertain of what to do, then she slid her arms around his waist, returning his embrace.

It was all the encouragement he needed. She was soft, yielding, and so close he could feel the swell of her breasts pressed against his chest, her heartbeat through his shirt. And he forgot who she was and what she stood for. Tonight she was the woman of his vision, and that was all that mattered. His mouth hardened against hers, and his tongue sought the hot, inner recesses of her mouth, demanding more.

Despite the shock of it, she liked the feel of what he did to her. Her hands caught at his shoulders, clasping them, holding him lest she lose her balance. His kisses were hot, eager, as intoxicating as the mescal. She felt giddy, almost dizzy with an answering desire. She was shameless, abandoned, and beyond caring.

A couple, whispering and giggling, stumbled past them, and Clay pulled her into the shadows, pressing her against the sheer rock wall a few feet from where it touched the water. He could feel the length of her now, and it wasn't enough. His breathing ragged, he whispered against her ear, "Let me love you, Amanda."

She pressed her lips into the hollow of his neck, tasting his hot, salty skin. His hips rubbed against hers, tantalizing her with his hardness. While some small voice of reason told her what she did was wrong, he eased her into the tall, cool grass, going down with her.

She didn't have much of a notion about it, but she'd heard her aunt's maids whispering enough to know that he shouldn't be lying over her. She rolled from beneath him onto her side, where she faced him. His eyes glittered, almost frightening her with their intensity.

He reached for her, pulling her over him, and somehow that seemed less dangerous, less sinful. "Kiss me," he urged her.

She bent her head, letting her hair fall over his face and shoulders, then touched her lips to his, parting them to give him access to her mouth. She felt a sense of power as his hands moved over her back, downward to trace fire over her hips. His mouth left hers to trail eager kisses along her jaw to her ear, then to nuzzle the soft, sensitive hollow of her neck. She arched her head, savoring the exquisite feel of his mouth.

Her hair was like silk where it brushed against his skin, just as it had been in his vision of her. His hand worked the shirt loose and slid under the hem to touch her bare skin, then moved down over her rib cage to the swell of her breast, cupping it in his callused palm. Something very like a sob escaped her when his thumb found her nipple. It hardened like a knob.

"Please," she whispered in anguish. "No . . ."

"It's all right," he reassured her.

Sliding down beneath her, he pushed up her shirt and rubbed his face against her breasts. His tongue teased the hardened nipple, drawing it into his mouth. He couldn't see her face, but he could feel the intensity of the shudder that passed through her. Her hot skin turned to gooseflesh beneath his fingers.

It was as though her whole being was centered where he touched. And no matter what happened, she didn't want him to stop, not now. His hands moved again to her back, then slipped beneath the waistband of her drawers, easing them down. One hand went under her, dipping between her legs, finding the wetness there. His fingers probed, then withdrew when she stiffened. His mouth left her breasts, returning to possess hers eagerly now.

His desire raged like a fever, and he could not wait. He fumbled with his pants, freeing himself. He thrust his tongue between her teeth, grasped her hips with his hands, and thrust upward. As she felt him breach the soft, wet thatch, she panicked and tried to pull away. He threw his leg behind hers, catching it, and rolled over her, pinning her beneath him. As her legs splayed, he guided himself inside. Her flesh resisted momentarily, tore, then closed around him.

Her eyes flew open, and there was a wild, frantic look in them. "Hold me," he rasped.

She was searing, sundered, and shocked to the very core. He began to move, tentatively at first, then with deliberate rhythm, stroking her, filling her, renewing her desire. Conscious will ended, replaced by overwhelming need. Her slack legs tautened, then wrapped around his, and her hips rocked and bucked beneath him, desperately straining for more and more of him. Her breath came in great, gulping gasps.

Mindless, aware only of the blood pounding through his body, of the near agony of impending release, he rode her hard, scarce hearing when she cried out. He was almost there. Ecstasy came in pulsing waves. Satiated, he collapsed over her, his body hugging hers.

As the heat ebbed slowly from her body, she realized what she'd done. Where there had been desire, now she felt only acute shame and a need to hide. Still pinned beneath him, his body still within hers, she was afraid to move, to open her eyes. She'd never be able to look at him again, she was sure of that.

He could feel himself shrink within her, yet he was loath to leave her. It had been too good, too complete. He looked down, his face nearly touching hers, and he saw her swallow. He reached to smooth her tangled hair back from her face, to touch her cheeks with the back of his hand. They were wet, and he knew she cried. The exhilaration he'd felt deserted him.

He rolled off her and lay there, at a loss for anything to say to her. Finally, unable to stand it any longer, he sucked in his breath, then let it out slowly.

"Amanda . . . don't . . ."

She didn't answer. Instead she lay there, listening to the steady beat of Comanche drums, wishing she'd never danced to them, wishing she'd never drunk any mescal. But it was too late now, and nothing would ever be the same. She'd given herself to Clay McAlester like a common harlot. And she couldn't even truthfully say she'd been seduced.

"I suppose I ought to say I'm sorry, but it'd be a damned lie," he told her.

"Don't." She swallowed again. "Please don't."

She was making him feel like the lowest creature on earth. It was the damned civilized rules he was supposed to live by, and he knew it. A gentleman did not take advantage of a lady, no matter what she'd had to drink. If he did, he was expected to pay the price.

"Look . . . I'll marry you, if that's what you want."

Now she really wanted to bawl her eyes out. "No," she managed painfully. "No. It wouldn't work out— you're not the sort of man I'd want for a husband. And I don't think I'd make you a very good wife."

Turning away from him, she sat up and pulled the borrowed shirt down, covering her breasts. Her drawers were another matter. She stood and yanked them up at the same time. A warm trickle ran down her inner thigh. Not knowing what else to do, she walked to the spring pool, and waded in. As the cold water closed around her, she told herself she'd been utterly foolish, that she couldn't even blame him for taking what she'd so freely offered. She'd behaved like a complete trollop, and she knew it. The only things that made her any better than those girls in border bordellos were that she was John Ross's daughter and she owned the Ybarra.

He sat there, feeling at a loss to comfort her. It was done, and there wasn't any way to change that. Now, if he were a gentleman, he'd tell her that her wet clothes were transparent. But he wasn't.

He heaved his body up and peeled his shirt off. Going to the other side of the pool, he knelt and washed his face, his arms, and chest, letting the cold water sober him. When he was done, he walked to stand over her.

He held out his shirt. "I'd put this on before we go back if I were you."

She looked down, seeing the dark outline of her nipples beneath the wet cloth. Still not daring to meet his eyes, she climbed out and took the shirt. Turning her back, she took off his wet shirt, wrung it out, and put on the other one. Without a word to him, she started back toward the village.

He followed her, making no effort to catch up. He was still going to have to spend what was left of the night beside her, but in the morning he'd be going. Maybe by the time he came back for her, she could at least look at him, even if he wasn't the sort of fellow she could marry. Maybe by then he wouldn't feel so much the fool himself.

Something startled her, and Amanda roused. Already the rosy light of dawn cast an aura of unreality over the silent village. Her head ached, and her body was stiff, almost sore as she stretched her legs. And then she remembered. Shame flooded over her. Very gingerly, she turned her head to look at McAlester, and her stomach knotted.

He wasn't there. Fully awake now, she sat up. Her heart pounding, she looked around. The saddle that had been between them was gone, as was his bedroll. Her gaze sought reassurance in the cottonwood thicket where his horse and mule had been tied. They weren't there either. But hanging from a low-lying limb, something fluttered in the early morning breeze.

Panicked, she scrambled to her feet and ran to look at it. It was the dress she'd been wearing when Ramon Sandoval abandoned her. And on the ground below, her petticoat lay neatly folded with a weighted paper on it. Her breath caught painfully in her chest.

In the dim light she read the note aloud once, then silently again.

Amanda, by the time you read this, I expect to be well down the trail. As soon as my job is done, I'll be back. Until then, I've made arrangements for Two Owls to look after you, and he has promised me that both of his wives will treat you well. Nahdehwah did what she could for the clothes I found in the desert. If you get the chance, I hope you'll thank her for it. As for last

night, don't be hard on yourself. The fault lies in the
mescal and me, not you. I still think you are very
much a lady.

He'd signed it simply "Clay McAlester." No sincerely, no yours truly, only his name.

She stood, rooted to the ground, her heart sinking.
He was gone—he'd left her alone and defenseless in
the Comanche camp. He'd used her and left her. Her
fingers crushed the paper, then let it fall to the ground.
Despite the awful headache, she felt numb all over.

Then her mind began to race. Maybe he hadn't left
yet. Maybe he was somewhere within the camp, waiting to eat before he left. Maybe he still filled his canteens at the spring. She grabbed her dress and petticoat
and ran toward Two Owls's tipi.

A sleepy Little Doe already had a fire going, and a
slab of animal ribs hung from an iron fork braced over
it. When Amanda came up to her, she was stirring
cracked corn into a pot of water.

Forgetting their fight, Amanda demanded breath-
lessly, "Where's McAlester? Where is he?"

The woman looked up blankly, then said something
in Comanche. She hadn't understood.

She had to think. "Nahakoah? Where Nahakoah?"

The Kiowa woman nodded, then went back to her
porridge—or whatever it was. Amanda moved around
to face her. "Nahakoah? Where?" she shouted.

Walks With Sunshade came out yawning and addressed the older wife. Little Doe answered something,
then shrugged. The Comanche touched Amanda's arm,
then pointed toward the spring path. At least she'd understood.

"Thank you." Ducking away, Amanda raced for the
water, heedless of the curious stares of half a dozen Indians.

But the man wading in the water was Two Owls, not
Clay McAlester. When he saw her, he came out and
covered himself with his breechclout. She backed

away, afraid, but when he spoke, his tone was friendly, his hands outstretched, palm up.

She whirled and fled, running as fast as her legs could carry her. Sticking her head into the medicine woman's lodge, she cried, "Where's McAlester? Where's Nahakoah?"

The old woman looked up and answered in quick, punctuated Comanche. The only word of it Amanda understood was Nahakoah. "Yes, yes," she said eagerly, repeating something like what Nahdehwah had said. As the old woman frowned, she tried again, followed by "Where is he?" Getting no answer, she asked more loudly, "Where is he?"

Laying aside her medicine bone and four green sticks, Nahdehwah rose awkwardly, then padded outside on large bare feet. Amanda followed, thinking the old woman meant to show her where he'd gone, but instead Nahdehwah raised her hands, offering some sort of prayer to the rising sun.

Amanda caught her arm, shaking it. "He's left me—he's left me here! I've got to find him! Can you not understand either? I've got to find him!"

"Shhhhh."

Tears were streaming down her face, but Amanda didn't care. "Please—you've got to help me," she pleaded. "Where is Nahakoah?"

The black, birdlike eyes fixed on Amanda's. "Nahakoah—he go," she finally answered.

"Where?"

This time the old woman responded in a spate of Comanche words. It was no use—whatever she was saying, Amanda couldn't understand it.

"But I don't belong here! Surely you can understand that, can't you?"

It was still no use.

"Nahakoah—he come."

"When?"

A short, ugly Comanche came to the flap of another tipi, peering cautiously at Amanda. If she didn't calm down, she was going to waken the entire village. She had to get hold of herself before they all came to stare at her. Nahdehwah reached out to grasp her shoulder.

"You come," she ordered.

Twisting free, Amanda turned and caught sight of McAlester. He was leading his saddled pony and the mule, and by the looks of it, he'd packed for a long trip. Instant relief washed over her. He hadn't actually left yet—there was still time to catch him. But, not seeing her, he swung up into the saddle, adjusted the sheath holding the Henry, and nudged the horse with his knees, turning it.

She broke into a dead run, shouting, "Wait! Wait up! You cannot leave me here! Listen to me!" She ran so hard that she felt as though her lungs would burst. "I'll see you hanged for this!" she panted. "*Damn you,* Clay McAlester! You have no right to do this!"

Clay groaned inwardly when he heard her. The last thing he'd wanted was a scene, and now there seemed to be no way of avoiding one. He gave the paint mare her head, thinking he could outdistance Amanda, that she'd give up when she saw she couldn't catch him.

Two Owls blocked her path, trying to stop her, but she dodged beneath his grasp. Indians were pouring out of tipis as though they thought they were under attack, then stood watching the running white girl curiously. The Kiowa lunged for her, catching her this time, shouting at her in Comanche.

"No! He cannot leave me—he cannot!" Tears were streaming down Amanda's face, but she didn't care. "I'm a white woman! I don't belong here!"

She took a breath, and Two Owls thought she'd come to her senses. As he relaxed his grip, she broke loose again. She could still see McAlester. Her bare feet pounded the hard ground and her elbows swung wildly as she ran so desperately she had no air left with which to shout at him.

Looking over his shoulder, Clay saw she still followed him, and he cursed under his breath. He kicked the paint's flank, and the little mare trotted. When he looked back again, Amanda had passed the last tipi and she was still running. She stumbled once, then got to her feet again and kept coming. Damn her! She was going to make them think she was crazed, and Two Owls wouldn't want her in his tipi.

He reined in angrily and waited. Tripping over a rock, she fell again, picked herself up, and stubbornly pursued him. She'd slowed, but still she came. He knew he ought to go on, to leave her, but he couldn't. Not now that she'd made a fool of herself in front of half the camp.

She caught up, lunged for his leg, and held onto it, looking up at him, too exhausted to stand alone, too out of breath to speak. He fought the urge to kick her.

"What the hell do you think you're doing?" he demanded furiously.

Her head pounded. Dizzy, she closed her eyes for a moment to steady herself, then opened them. "You . . . you . . . cannot go without me," she gasped. "You . . . you cannot."

Knowing that everyone watched them, he clenched his teeth and tried to hold his temper. "Amanda," he managed tightly, "turn loose of my leg."

"No." She shook her head. "Don't you dare leave me," she choked out. "Don't . . . you . . . dare!"

"You are making a spectacle of yourself."

"I don't care!"

"Don't be a little fool!" he retorted. "You're a whole lot safer here than with me."

"I'd sooner steal a horse and try to get back to Fort Stockton by myself."

"You can't."

"You can't just leave me here!"

As angry as he was with her, he was not proof against the tears that stained her upturned face. Leaning from his saddle, he reached to grasp her hand. "Swing up," he ordered brusquely.

She felt a surge of relief. Bracing her foot against

his, she let him pull her up, and throwing modesty to the wind, she slid her bare leg over the paint mare's shoulder. But to her horror, he turned back toward the Indian camp.

"No!"

He didn't answer.

She licked dry lips. "Please ... I don't want to stay ... I'm afraid of these people." Desperate, she grasped for some means to persuade him. "I ..." Seeing that Two Owls's tipi was ahead, she tried to swallow back the awful lump in her throat. He didn't care, and nothing she could say was going to make any difference to him. "I'll do anything you ask—anything!" she cried.

The horse stopped, and she felt the shift of McAlester's weight as he swung down from his saddle. There was no help anywhere, and she knew it. Taking a deep breath, she decided there was no use crying or making a greater fool of herself. When his hands touched her waist to help her down, she pulled herself together and leaned into his arms.

Without so much as another look at her, he conferred with the big Kiowa, while Little Doe and Walks With Sunshade regarded her somberly. Two Owls barked out something, and his older wife disappeared behind his tipi. Resigned, Amanda took a step toward Walks With Sunshade. The woman put up both hands and backed away, shaking her head.

"Now you've done it," Clay muttered. "She thinks you are possessed by a bad spirit."

"Oh, for—"

"Don't look at her," he ordered. "They've already sent for Nahdehwah."

The gathering crowd parted as the old medicine woman waddled through, and everyone watched silently while she circled the Kiowa's tipi three times, stopping each time at the entrance to look skyward and call out. Raising what appeared to be a buffalo tail she moved it back and forth in front of the flap. The fourth

time, she went inside, then came back out, trailing the
tail on the ground behind her. When she saw Amanda,
she held up two eagle feathers and approached her,
chanting something. Twice she circled, waving the
feathers.

Nahdehwah was conducting the Comanche equiva-
lent of an exorcism. Amanda's disbelief must have
shown on her face, because Clay McAlester nodded.
"Yeah—you've made a laughingstock of me."

"Right now I don't care."

Little Doe came back leading an Indian pony. The
silent woman threw a bright-patterned Mexican blanket
onto its back, followed by a wood and deerhorn saddle,
then she stood there, her eyes averted, waiting while
McAlester went to one of the packs on his mule. He
drew out his old revolver from one of his packs,
weighed it in his hand, then held it out to her. Digging
into a pocket on his black frock coat, he pulled out a
small leather bag and pressed it into Little Doe's hand.
She opened it, pouring a small powder horn and a
dozen balls into her palm, then she smiled and nodded.

When McAlester turned back to Amanda, his expression was grim. "You'd better mount up," he said
tersely. "And if you fall behind, you're on your own."

"I can't ride on—" As his expression darkened, she
bit back her words and nodded. "I'll manage," she decided hastily. Moving to the brown pony, she patted its
neck reassuringly, then stepped into a hide stirrup and
swung her leg over. The animal moved skittishly, but
Little Doe jerked the braided rawhide reins, pulling it
up short.

While McAlester mounted, Two Owls took the reins
from his wife, and as the ranger nudged his paint into
a walk, the Kiowa followed him on foot, leading
Amanda's pony. It was a slow, silent procession passing back through the camp, and this time not even the
children wanted to look at her.

At the last tipi the ranger stopped, and the Kiowa
started to tie the reins to the mule, but McAlester

shook his head. His face impassive, Two Owls silently handed them to Amanda, then turned back toward the uneven row of tipis.

"I hope you thanked him for me," she said finally.

"After that little fit you showed him, he'd have known it for a lie."

McAlester clicked his reins and the paint horse moved on slowly, sedately, until they were almost out of the Indians' sight. Amanda's horse jerked its head and reared, nearly unseating her. She struggled with the reins, shouting at the animal. Exasperated, McAlester turned back, leaned from his saddle, and yanked the reins from her hands. He tied them to the mule.

"I could have learned to handle him," Amanda muttered. "He caught me by surprise, that's all."

"He doesn't understand English."

"There's not much about 'whoa' to understand, is there?" she snapped.

Instead of answering her, he mumbled Comanche words under his breath, obviously cursing either her or the horse—or both. But it didn't matter, she told herself. At least she'd managed to get out of the Indian camp with her hair and her nose still attached, and that had to be worth something.

At the crest of the small hill McAlester dug his moccasins into his horse's flank, and the animal broke into a hard, bone-jarring trot. Behind him, Amanda bounced against the wooden saddle so hard that her neck, back, and bottom hurt. But hell would freeze before she complained.

Looking back, he could see her holding onto the carved pommel, her body jostling like a sack of meal. But she'd wanted to come so damned bad that she'd made a fool of him, so he was all out of sympathy for her. By nightfall, she wasn't going to be able to sit or stand.

She clenched her teeth, but they still clattered against each other. Surely to God he was hurting himself as much as her. Finally, unable to endure any more, she decided hell must be freezing. She called out to him, "S-stop th-this!"

He reined in and turned in his saddle. "Want to go back?" he taunted.

"Of course I don't! But I gallop a lot better than I trot, and I'll be hanged if I'm going any farther like this!"

"I can take care of that," he shot back. "In fact, right now I don't think I'd mind hanging you."

"You had no right to leave me there!" she shouted furiously. "What kind of man are you, anyway? You were going to abandon me!"

"Can't you read?" he gibed. "I wrote I was coming back for you."

"When? In two days? Two weeks? Two months? Or next year?" she demanded. "For all I know, your friend Two Owls might expect something from me—they share wives, you know."

"Between brothers."

"For all I knew, he counted you as a brother."

Instead of answering that, he kicked the paint, and the mare settled back into the hard trot. This time, she gritted her teeth and hung on, swearing if he could stand it, she would manage.

It seemed as though they went for miles before he stopped again. When she was nearly too tired to care, he finally dismounted and walked to reach for her.

"Don't touch me," she gritted out. Pushing him away, she managed to slide from the wooden saddle and reach the ground. She swayed unsteadily on legs too sore to hold her. "Just now, I neither want or need your help. You've shown me what you think of me already. If I had any illusions before, they flew out the window when you left me."

"Suit yourself." Untying one of his canteens, he unscrewed the lid and drank. Wiping his mouth with his sleeve, he looked at her, making no move to offer her any of the water. "Going to be a long day," he observed shortly.

The sun wasn't high in the sky, and it was already so hot that it looked like steam rose in waves from the ground. She licked parched lips, her eyes on the canteen. Apparently, he wasn't going to offer her any as long as he remained angry with her. She was going to have to eat a big slice of humble pie, or it was going to be a long, thirsty journey.

"Look," she said, sighing, "I'm sorry for making a spectacle of myself before your Indian friends." He didn't even acknowledge that he heard her. "And I know you could have left me to die, and no matter what else has happened between us, I'll always be grateful that you didn't."

"Don't."

"Don't what? Mr. McAlester, I am trying to apologize to you! Isn't that what you want?"

"No."

"All right," she said tiredly. "I can't go on like this. What do you want me to say?"

He swung around, his blue eyes cold. "Why say anything? I'm not the sort of man you'd want to be around—remember? I just rank a hair above a Comanche to you."

"I didn't say that. I said you weren't the sort of man I'd want to marry. There is a difference, you know."

"Is there?"

"You can't call saying, 'I'll marry you, if that's what you want,' much of an offer, either. What was I supposed to say to that?"

"Nothing."

"All right," she said, exasperated. "May I please have a drink of water?"

He held out the canteen.

"Thank you." As she sipped from it, she looked over the rim at him. There was nothing in his manner or his expression to remind of her of the man who'd lain so eagerly with her in the grass. She handed the water container back. "Thank you," she said again.

He regarded her soberly. "I just hope to hell you don't get us both killed."

"Doing what?"

"You're going to have to stay out of my way. When the shooting starts, you're on your own. I can't look out for you and do my job."

"Why can't you just pretend I've got a price on my head and take me home to Ybarra-Ross?"

"You're too damned self-centered—you know that, don't you?"

"Because I didn't want to live like a Comanche savage?" she asked incredulously.

"I'd have come back for you—you knew that."

"What if you got killed? Then where would I have been? Answer that, will you?" When he didn't respond, she persisted. "Well?"

"Where will you be if I get killed now?"

"I don't know. You won't even tell me where we're going," she retorted crossly.

"Suppose I tell you I don't exactly know. I'm thinking of going northeast to the Llano Estacado, then down toward Big Spring, where I hope to find Quanah Parker." He gestured to what looked like a high mesa. "We're going up there."

She stared. *"What?"*

"Yeah. It's a pretty rugged trip, even for me. See that mountain with all the boulders? We've got to cross it, and then there's an arroyo that's barely wide enough in places for a wagon. It's a pretty good place for an ambush, but it's just about the only way we've got to follow the old war trail up to the Llano Estacado."

"You're lying, aren't you? You're just trying to frighten me."

"You'll wish I were. It's flat and grassy enough in places to lull you into thinking that's all there is up there—until you find yourself on the edge of a canyon so steep-walled and deep that you'll swear there's no way but straight down. There's a lot of those before we get to where we're going."

"It doesn't make sense—why are you doing this?"

"A man named Sanchez-Torres is bringing a gun shipment across from New Mexico, and there's a whole lot of routes he and his Comancheros could take before they reach the gap, but after that they have to cross the Llano to reach Quanah's camp. I figure even if Quanah's going down to the Big Spring, Sanchez-Torres will come this way."

"You're serious, aren't you?"

"Uh-huh. And the trick is going to be getting there before the Comancheros—I want to be between them and Quanah." He took another drink, then screwed the lid on the canteen. "If I don't make it, there'll be hell to pay on every farm and ranch between here and the Rio Grande. Before Mackenzie and his buffalo soldiers can mobilize, the Comanche, the Kiowa, and the Cheyenne are going to be all over Texas. All they need are the guns."

"But you're just one man," she protested. "You cannot be expected to stop them—not alone."

"Oh, but I've got you with me," he reminded her. "Not that I'm fool enough to believe that makes two of us."

As the full import of the situation sank in, she regarded him soberly for a long moment. "I won't get in your way," she promised. "And for what it's worth, I'll do what I can to help you."

He tied the canteen onto his saddle and remounted. As he swung his leg over, he said tersely, "You already *are* in the way. Come on—I'd like to get another twenty miles up the trail before it gets too hot to ride."

It was already too hot, but she forbore saying it. She caught the horn pommel and pulled her aching body up. "Just tell me we aren't going to trot—that's all I ask," she muttered.

"It's too hard on the horses. We'll have to take it slowly for a while."

"How far is it to the Llano?"

"Depends. Without you, maybe a day. With you, maybe two days, maybe more."

She eyed the limestone-rimmed ledge around the mesa skeptically. "Well," she muttered, "it ought to be cooler up there."

"Maybe. Maybe not."

He withdrew behind a shield of silence again. Yet as he rode beside her, his thoughts were on her, not Sanchez-Torres or the Comancheros. Before, it had been the damned vision that plagued him. Now it was her. Long after he'd made the pallet outside, long after he'd put his saddle between his body and hers, he'd lain awake, reliving how it had felt to possess her. He wasn't even sure he'd actually slept at all.

All he knew for certain was that she was going to keep making a fool out of him. Hell, she'd shown she could do it. She was in his thoughts and his dreams, and now she was going to be with him in the flesh, night and day. The safety of distance he'd intended to put between them was gone. Just like that.

But he had no illusions now—no matter what had happened between them, no matter how it had come about, she'd made it abundantly clear afterward that he wasn't her destiny. No, rather than lying awhile in his arms, she'd plunged into the water to wash the taint of him off her. He even knew her coming with him now really had little to do with him—it was that she was more afraid of a band of Comanches than she was of him.

To Amanda his silence was becoming intolerable. "This really doesn't have much to do with me, does it? You're angry about something more than my coming with you, aren't you?" she decided.

"Hap Walker gave me that gun."

For a moment she was at a loss. "What gun?" Then it dawned on her. "The one you gave Little Doe?"

"Yes."

"But you traded it for the horse. I didn't have anything to do with that—I could have ridden your mule."

"No. I got the horse at the giveaway dance. It was the saddle I traded for. And you saw what Hannibal's like—he doesn't tolerate much handling." He looked away. "No, the gun was all I had to trade."

"Look," she offered, "when we get back to Fort Stockton, I'll purchase another one just like it for you."

"No." He took a deep breath, then settled his shoulders. "I reckon a man oughtn't to hang onto things he doesn't need. I've got two brand-new Colt .45s, and I don't even have to fool with balls and powder anymore. But in the last fourteen years that old Navy Colt stood between me and eternity more times than I can count. It had the best sight I ever used."

"I'm sorry. If I could, I'd buy it back for you."

When he turned back, his expression was sober rather than angry. "You know, you are a damned nuisance, don't you? Back in Boston, it might be enough to be pretty, but out here a woman's got to pull her own weight or she doesn't survive. And it takes a whole lot more than money to pull that weight. Frankly, I don't know what the hell I'm going to do with you when the shooting starts."

"If I'm so utterly useless, why did you bother to stop and help me in the first place?"

"I didn't say you were exactly useless. If things were different, I—" He caught himself before he said something stupid. "Well, I guess I'm just going to have to make the best of it, that's all. What can't be helped, can't be helped."

"You know, if you really wanted to stop the Comanches from raiding, you'd lead the cavalry to them. Then all of this would be over, wouldn't it?" she observed reasonably.

"I can't do it."

"Why?"

"I can try to save them from themselves, but I can't betray them."

"Eventually the army is going to get them, anyway—you know that, don't you? You could spare everybody a lot of agony—even them."

"An army doesn't know the land as I do—a cavalry troop can ride for days and never catch sight of a Comanche or a Comanchero. They've tried before, but they don't think like Indians. And there's not a cavalryman alive who wants to go where we may have to go."

"You make it sound so inviting," she murmured wryly.

"No. It's a job."

"For thirty-three dollars a month."

"For thirty-three dollars a month. The way I look at it, somebody's got to do it, and it might as well be me. I don't have anybody but Hap who'd give a damn if I got myself killed, and he'd get over it."

She could see there was no moving him, so she might as well resign herself. Maybe if they were lucky, they'd encounter the Comancheros he was looking for before they reached Quanah Parker. Not that that was really anything to be desired either.

"Uh . . . how many others do you expect to come with this Sanchez-Torres?" she found herself asking.

"I don't know—maybe a dozen, maybe less, maybe more. But when the shooting starts—and it will—you keep out of the line of fire. I wouldn't want to be dragging your body back to Stockton in this heat—you savvy?"

"I'm not an idiot, Mr. McAlester."

"You're green, Amanda—a real greenhorn."

"That's only your opinion of me," she shot back.

He wasn't being fair to her, and he knew it. She'd already shown him she had the grit and will to survive against nearly overwhelming odds. But he was too out of charity with her for costing him his old gun, not to mention the loss of face he'd suffered in Ketanah's village, to relent just yet.

Personally, she thought he probably considered any-

one unwilling or unable to live as he did almost too
weak to live. Well, she wasn't, and she was going to
prove it to him. Someway or somehow she was going
to prove it to him. Redoubling her effort to keep up,
she resigned herself to a long, miserable day.

They'd picked their way over at least twenty of the most harrowing miles she'd ever traveled, she was sure of that, and she was thirsty, hungry, unbearably hot, and almost exhausted. Clay McAlester, on the other hand, seemed impervious to any human weakness. She cast a surreptitious glance his way, but his face was impassive, revealing nothing. Surely to God, behind that set face of his, he had to be as miserable as she was.

She wanted to ask for water, but she'd made up her mind that she could hold out as long as he did. She leaned forward to wipe her sweaty face with the hem of the shirt. It had to be the hottest day she'd spent on earth. She looked at him again, seeing the sweat that soaked his back. Her eyes traveled upward, taking in the trickle of moisture from his shaded forehead, the wetness above his mouth. He had a decidedly masculine, well-featured face, with a straight nose, chiseled chin, and solid jaw. So much so that he made Patrick Donnelly seem almost effeminate in comparison. No, there was no denying that Clay McAlester was a handsome man.

She closed her eyes momentarily, remembering the feel of his body against hers, the strength of his arms holding her, the heat of his breath against her ear, and she was almost weak from the memory. And she knew it had been more than too much mescal. It had been her own desire that had led her astray. That and the heady, powerful beat of those drums.

Resolutely, she returned her attention to the present. If the heat didn't break somehow, and if she didn't get a drink soon, she was going to faint. She was already more than a little dizzy from loss of water. Above her, the sun was merciless, almost burning through her clothes, while under her, the Indian pony sweated heavily, soaking her legs through her drawers. She looked up, wishing that somehow it could rain, but there wasn't a cloud in the whole white-hot sky. She bit her dry, cracked lip and told herself she could wait a little longer—not much, but a little longer.

Just as she was going to give in and ask, he finally stopped. "I don't know about you," he said, swinging out of his saddle, "but I've got to stretch my legs."

The relief she felt was nearly overwhelming, but she tried not to show it. "Yes," she responded simply.

"Thirsty?"

"A little," she lied. If he'd have given her the canteen, she'd have drained it on the spot.

He eyed her oddly, but said nothing.

While she dismounted, he picked his way around scattered boulders and walked into a clump of cedar trees. She stood there, fanning herself with the tail of his shirt, trying to create enough of a breeze to dry her wet face. This couldn't be Texas—it had to be hell, she reflected wearily.

"Your turn," he said when he came out. "I'll get the canteen while you take care of your business."

"All right."

He waited until she was nearly even with the trees before warning her, "Look where you walk—and if anything buzzes, you can bet your life it's not a bee. Try to stay away from the rocks."

"Thank you for that comforting thought, Mr. McAlester," she said under her breath.

She walked carefully, keeping her eyes on the ground until she reached the wet spot he'd left in the dirt. Casting a nervous glance over her shoulder, she pulled her drawers down and squatted. Pulling up a sparse clump of dead grass, she made quick use of it, then hastened back to where he waited.

"At least you're prompt, and that's something," he said when she emerged. He took another swig from his canteen, then passed it to her. "Drink up—you've sweat a lot."

She could almost hear her aunt tell her, "Ladies don't sweat, dearest—they *perspire*." But the niceties of Boston had no meaning to him, she was sure. She wiped the mouth of the canteen on his shirt and drank greedily from it.

"Thank you," she said, handing it back. As he walked toward the mule, she blurted out, "How much farther do we have to go today? I mean, surely it's been more than any twenty miles, hasn't it?"

He swung around, taking in the damp wisps of hair clinging to her temples and forehead, and he felt anew a heat that had nothing to do with the weather. He forced himself to look away.

"Well," he said, scarce recognizing his own voice, "I was thinking of staying here until sundown. I didn't get much sleep last night, so I'm about as tired as you are."

She could feel her face burn. "Yes . . . well, neither did I," she managed.

He'd not meant to bring it up, but now it hung between them like a gaping chasm. If he were going to share his days and nights with her, he was going to have to get past that. "It was the mescal, I expect," he said finally. "We both had too much of it."

"And the drums."

"And the drums. There's something about a Comanche drum that puts fire in the blood."

"Yes."

So she'd felt it also. He sucked in his breath, then let it out slowly. "Look—I'll try my damnedest to keep my distance, if that's what you want. All you've got to do is say it."

She couldn't look at him. "I think it would be wise,

don't you?" she answered, her voice scarce above a whisper.

It wasn't what he wanted to hear, and he knew it. "You're the keeper of the gate, not me." He turned his back to her and began unloading his packs. When he finished, he felt sure enough of himself to look at her.

She was lifting her long hair up, trying to cool her wet neck. As she leaned back slightly, her breasts strained against his buttoned shirt. His mouth went dry, and his pulse pounded in his temples.

"Don't do that," he said harshly.

"What?" Startled, she let her hair fall.

"Nothing." He took another breath. "Look—I'm a man. You can't say you don't want my attentions if you're going to do that."

"I beg your pardon?"

"Keep your arms down, will you?"

"Oh, now that's too much! Surely you don't think . . . you don't really believe that I deliberately . . . that I . . . ?"

It was a situation he couldn't win, he could see that. "No, of course not," he said wearily. "I guess I'm just going to have to learn to look the other way."

"I can't help what goes on in your mind, Mr. McAlester."

"I told you—the name's Clay—Clayton McAlester, if you want the whole of it."

She'd been using the mister as a means of distance. "All right—if it offends you—"

"It does." He felt at a distinct disadvantage just now. "I guess I'll get out the food," he decided aloud. "You can make a tent to suit you."

"There's a tent?"

"No, but you can use the blanket off my bedroll. Just hang it on something to make some shade." He opened the parfleche Walks With Sunshade had given him. "It's too hot to make a fire, so you'll have to be satisfied with jerky—unless you want some mesquite pudding."

"I'll take the jerky."

"Want any *pulke*?" As she eyed him balefully, he offered, "Before we leave tonight, I'll make you some coffee."

She could still remember the awful taste of his strong coffee coming up. "I'd rather have water, if there's enough. I'm not much for coffee either."

"Help yourself to the canteen. Tonight you can cook up something before we leave. You can cook, can't you?"

"A little, but it was always on Aunt Kate's modern range." Afraid he'd think her useless, she hastened to add, "I guess I can try using an open fire."

"Ever make stew?"

"No."

"Boil any hardtack?"

"No."

"Roast any wild game?"

"No."

The corners of his mouth quivered as he fought a smile. "All right—maybe it'd be a whole lot easier if I asked what you can make."

"Pea beans in molasses."

"Pea beans in molasses," he repeated. "What else?"

"Pies and tarts, when cherries are in season."

"Yeah—well, that sort of lets you out as a cook," he observed wryly. "I'm all out of molasses—not to mention pea beans and cherries."

She took his smile as making fun of her. "I wasn't expected to cook, Mr. McAlester," she retorted defensively. "Aunt Kate employed a woman named Sally Parks to do that."

"I don't like the mister—remember?"

"Clay, then. Anyway, it wasn't part of my upbringing. Aunt Kate always assumed I would marry well, so the emphasis was on planning the meal rather than cooking it."

There it was—another reminder that she was too good, too rich for him. Rather than respond, he divided up the jerky and handed her her share. "Chew it slowly, drink a little water with it, and it'll fill you up."

"Thank you."

He dropped to sit cross-legged and opened a smaller container. Taking out a beat-up spoon, he scooped something up with it. She watched as he took a bite.

"What's that?"

"Mesquite pudding."

Considering that she hadn't eaten all day, the jerky looked woefully inadequate. "What's it taste like?" she asked curiously.

"Sweet. Comanches make it by mashing mesquite beans and bone marrow together with a little tallow."

"Oh."

He held out the container. "Here—try it. It'll surprise you."

"It'd have to."

"Go on," he urged her. He dipped some more and carried the spoon to her mouth as though she were a child. "If you don't like it, spit it out."

She hesitated, but her hunger won. She nibbled the end of the spoon, getting the smallest amount possible. It wasn't anything comparable to what anybody would called pudding, but it wasn't as bad as she'd feared. She nodded.

"Like it?"

"Well, I wouldn't want to eat it every day," she murmured diplomatically. "But it does taste sweet, doesn't it?"

"That's the mesquite beans."

"Do you eat like this all the time?"

"Mostly. Sometimes when I get to San Antone, I get a good shave, dress up, and buy a meal or two at one of the hotels. A man gets tired of his own cooking."

"But not a haircut? You never get a haircut?"

"Only enough to see out." His mouth twisted into the semblance of another smile. "Hap's always riding me about that." He looked off for a moment, then settled his shoulders. "I guess it comes from living too

many years with Comanches. A man's hair is his
pride—he spends hours combing and greasing it to
make it shine. It's sort of a disgrace to have it cut off."

"But you aren't a Comanche, Clay."

"I don't know what I am. I guess I just kind of pick
and choose what I want from both sides."

"And you feel you don't fit in either," she murmured
sympathetically.

"Maybe. I never quit wanting to go back, anyway—
not even when I was in Chicago."

"You were in Chicago?" she asked incredulously.
"When?"

"Uh-huh. I lived there for almost four years while
my Aunt Jane tried to civilize me. That was before I
came back to fight Yankees with Hap."

"What was she like—your Aunt Jane, I mean?"

"I don't know." The image of Jane McAlester stood
before his eyes. "I guess you'd call her determined."

"That's all—determined?"

He shrugged. "She was a strong-willed, religious
woman, hell-bent on saving my soul, but she had a
good heart to go with all that determination."

She smiled in spite of herself. "You must have been
quite a challenge."

"Yeah, I guess you could say that. When I look
back, I think she must've been a saint to try it. She
took in a long-haired, wild-eyed kid, who could barely
speak English, with the notion that if she tried hard
enough, she could make a gentleman out of him. Hell,
it took her half a year to get me to sleep in a bed instead of under it."

"I feel almost sorry for her," she murmured. "She
must have considered you rather daunting."

"You don't know the half of it. Here she was, this
little spinster woman, saddled with a boy who'd been
down a Comanche war trail. I was used to eating raw
meat with my hands back then, and she was making
me eat these dainty little meals off her grandmother's
china, telling me to how to use silverware." His mouth

twisted wryly. "Yeah, you could say I was a challenge, all right."

"But she had to have done something right."

"How's that?"

"Well, you speak English, and you can read and write."

"She was determined about that, too," he admitted. "Hired me a tutor with money she didn't really have. He was this old fellow who'd been an actor before he found God, so I learned to read some of the damnedest things. But it worked, I guess. Every now and then, I try to throw some of those big words he taught me into my reports, just to get Hap going." His smile broadened into an outright grin. "Last month, it was circuitous that got him. Yeah, I guess I owe Aunt Jane a lot."

"I'd say so." She hesitated, then blurted out, "Do you ever see her?"

"Not since the war. I was pretty rough on her, but we finally got to understanding one another. She even cried when I left, and I still write her when I'm out on the trail. A man's got a lot of time to think then." Straightening his shoulders, he turned to her. "Turnabout's fair, you know. How'd you get from the Ybarra to Boston?"

"I went there for two reasons—to get a proper Catholic education, and to escape seeing Mama with Gregorio Sandoval. She married him when I was eleven, and I couldn't understand how she could do that after Papa died. At first, I hated her for it."

"But then you weren't walking in her moccasins, were you?"

"No." She sighed audibly. "No, I wasn't. Now I regret that I left her, because Ramon said she and Gregorio weren't happy, and if I'd stayed, she'd at least have had me. Now I've been gone so long that I feel out of place in the land where I was born. I don't remember Texas being like this."

"That'll pass once you've been back awhile."

"Will it?"

"Sure. At least it did for me, and I didn't have a place like the Ybarra to come back to."

She looked up, meeting his eyes. "I really don't know much about cattle, Clay. Actually, I don't know *anything* about running a ranch."

It surprised him that she'd admit it. "Who's running the place now?"

"Alessandro Sandoval—Ramon's father. And somehow I can't see him wishing to stay after I send his son to jail."

"You'll have to hire a foreman. Get someone who's worked at Ybarra—or on another ranch."

"I don't suppose you'd be interested?" As soon as the words were out, she couldn't believe she'd said them. "That is . . . well, I've got to find somebody, and I don't know anybody out here," she finished lamely.

The offer hung there for a moment before he shook his head. "No, it wouldn't work out for you. I'm not the kind of man who can stay in one place and settle down, Amanda. The day I quit moving is the day I die."

She felt like a fool again. "I guess I didn't say it right. I wasn't suggesting anything more than hiring you to help for a little while—until I know who I can trust."

"You might ask Hap—he's always wanted to be a dirt farmer somewhere. Maybe for a place like the Ybarra, he might raise his sights a mite higher and go into ranching."

"I don't know."

"At least you'd know he was honest. He's about thirty-six or seven by now, if that's not too old for you."

"Well, I wasn't intending to marry him," she retorted. "I was speaking of running my ranch. If I wanted a husband, I'd have stayed in Boston."

"I suppose you had men lined up at the door," he murmured, taking another bite of the pudding.

"No—only one. Aunt Kate had her heart set on him, so no one else got near the door to our house."

"Was he rich?"

"Patrick Donnelly? Well, he wasn't anything like King Midas, but he came from a fairly well-to-do, politically connected family, and he wanted a proper wife. He expects to be governor of Massachusetts at the very least, you see."

"A man of ambition."

"Exceedingly so."

"And you came with the moneybags. Damned convenient for him, I'd say."

"It was more than that. I think he believed he loved me."

He felt an unreasonable stab of jealousy. "But you weren't interested in him?" he asked casually.

"Lord, no. If he were truthful with himself, he'd admit that his first love is himself—followed by politics. If I married him, the best I could come in would be third. A rather lowering thought for a woman, don't you think?"

"Yeah. From what I saw in Chicago, a respectable woman expects a man's heart and soul along with his money."

"You were rather young to discover that then, weren't you?"

He picked up his knife, balanced it in his hand, then drove the blade into the ground before he answered. "I was old enough to know I didn't have much of either."

"Money, heart, or soul?"

"Any of 'em—all of 'em." He shrugged and reached to retrieve the knife. "Hap calls me a loner."

"Everyone needs someone, Clay."

Instead of responding, he poured a little *pulke* into his tin cup and drank it, washing the last of the pudding down. Squinting up at the sun, he estimated by its position that it must be about two o'clock. He reached into his pocket and took out his watch.

As he flicked open the cover, she asked, "What time is it?"

"Five after two. You'd better put up that tent, if you plan on getting any sleep." When she didn't move, he regarded her lazily. "I figure you've got to be good for something."

"Nothing you'd appreciate. I'm afraid my education leaned toward music, drawing, and reading classical literature rather than anything truly useful."

"You can sing?"

"And play the piano. You?"

"Can't carry a tune in a bucket, but I can beat out a war dance on drums." He leaned forward, then heaved his body up. "Well, I see I'm going to have a fix my own place to sleep. Whatever happened to 'I'll do anything you ask'?"

She colored uncomfortably. "That was to get out of Two Owls's tipi."

"Even if you had to share my blanket?" It just sort of slipped out before he knew it. "I'm sorry—I shouldn't have said that."

"No, you shouldn't have." Rather than look up at him, she focused on a mesquite-dotted, distant hill. "If it had come to that . . . ," she said, her voice trailing off. As her face went hot, she caught herself. "But I'm not ever going to drink any more mescal with you."

"Me neither." He leaned over, reaching a hand to her. "Come on—if we don't sleep now, we won't cover any ground tonight."

She let him pull her up, then she dropped her hand self-consciously. While she watched, he unsaddled both horses and let them drift off toward where Hannibal already pulled at clumps of grass. He returned carrying his bedroll.

"The saddle blankets are too soaked to be any good, so all we've got is this," he observed, shaking out the roll.

Surveying a small stand of scrub oak, he chose his place, then moved to drape a worn army blanket be-

tween branches. In the shade it formed, he spread out
the rest of his bedding. It was then she realized that she
was going to have to lie beside him. And after what
had happened between them, she wasn't sure she
wanted to do that. Not now that she was out of the Comanche camp.

He dragged his saddle over and placed it at one end
of the bedding. "It'll be a little crowded," he told her.
When she made no move at all, he thought he knew the
reason. "Look—I've got two blankets on the ground. If
you want, you can roll up in one, and I'll take the
other. But whatever you decide, there's only so much
shade I can get from the one I've got strung up here."
With that, he lay down, and using the saddle for his
head, he turned on his side, facing away from her.
"You shared my blanket last night," he reminded her.

"Last night I was drunk."

"Suit yourself."

She hesitated, then took another look at the scorch-
ing sun before making up her mind. Walking to the
other side of the spread-out blankets, she eased down
to her knees. Seeing that his eyes were already closed,
she carefully stretched out beside him. He didn't move.

"Want half my saddle?" he asked.

"No—I'll use my arm."

It wasn't all that much cooler in the shade, but at
least she was out of the sun. She lay there, staring up
at a hole in the army blanket, waiting for him to go to
sleep. But he was too close, so much so that she could
feel the heat from his body—and the steam from his
sweat-soaked shirt. There was a distinct masculinity to
it.

She was lying there, taut as a bowstring, and the ten-
sion between them was almost palpable. "What's the
matter now?" he asked, rolling onto his back.

"I'm too hot."

"I'd tell you to take off the shirt and sleep in your
chemise and drawers, but you'd take it wrong."

"Yes."

Sighing, he sat up, leaned forward, and clasped his hands around his knees. "This isn't going to work, is it?" he said finally.

"No."

He exhaled heavily. "Then I guess we might as well ride. I can't sleep either."

The prospect of doing that was even more daunting than that of sharing the closeness of the shade with him. As hot as it was, she reached behind her and pulled her blanket over her head and shoulders.

"I'll manage somehow," she muttered.

"Amanda, you're a hard woman to please—you know that, don't you? You don't even try to make it easy on a man." When she said nothing, he took a deep breath, then went on, "I'm not asking for gratitude—I don't want it. But you wanted to come so damned bad that it looks like you could pull your load."

"I don't belong here," she said tiredly. "It would be like your coming to Boston."

"Or going to Chicago. Do you think I belonged there? Do you think I wanted to be captured? I was a little kid, for God's sake! And do you know what's the first thing I remember about it?"

"Your parents dying?"

"No—mercifully, I can't remember that. But I do remember that the first night out they gave me bloody milk from the udder of a cow they'd slaughtered, and I couldn't drink it. Then they tried to force me to eat the raw liver, but it wouldn't go down. But you know something? It took me about a day and a half to get over it, and when they killed one of the horses, I was ready to fight for the raw meat. And by that time, it tasted damned good."

"How awful for you," she managed, lifting the blanket off her head.

"It's what you get used to. But I'm talking about more than food, Amanda—I'm talking about survival. And it wasn't easy, I can tell you. Remember that fight you had with Little Doe? Well, it's a hundred times

worse for a boy brought into a camp. The women beat
and threaten him with knives, the boys fight him, and
the men watch to see if he survives. If he does, they
keep him. If not, well, he wasn't worthy of being a Comanche."

"So they kill him? How very civilized of them."

"Usually."

"And yet you love them."

"I came to love the life. Was it dirty? Yes. Was the
food godawful? Yes. Did I like having fleas and lice?
No. But once I was adopted, I learned what it is to be
free, Amanda. Really free. I rode the length of Texas
with the wind in my face. I learned how to defend myself against nearly anything you can imagine. They
taught me to be a man."

"You don't have to tell me this."

"I want to. You look at them and see the dirt and
filth. You look at me, and see the same thing. Well, just
because you don't like what you see, I'm not going to
be ashamed of what I am."

"They're murderers and thieves, Clay—they killed
my mother."

"Maybe. But they have a different set of rules for
living. Before your mother's people came here, the
land was theirs. And just because those who would
take it from them had guns didn't make it right.
They've watched your people and the Texans kill off
the very lifeline of the Comanche, Amanda. It used to
be that one herd of buffalo could cover thirty miles,
and now they are nearly gone. Wasted for greed—pure
greed."

"They tortured my stepfather to death, and they
killed Mama. Doesn't that mean anything to you?"

"It was their land."

"Not anymore."

"Unlike other tribes, the Comanche have never
signed any treaties with the whites. They don't believe
any one band has the right to make deals for the others."

"If you believe this so strongly, why are you a Texas Ranger?" she countered. "Why don't you just go back to them?"

"I've been gone too long. I don't belong there anymore. I guess it's like you said—I don't seem to belong anywhere anymore."

She could almost feel his sense of loss, and it surprised her. "I'm sorry, Clay," she said softly. There was an awkward pause, then she dared to ask, "When you were with them, did you kill for them?"

"I was one of them, Amanda."

"But you were just a boy."

"The first time I followed the war trail, I came home with two scalps—one belonged to a scared old man, the other to his son."

"Mother of God."

"It's a warrior society, Amanda. A boy learns to ride and shoot almost as soon as he learns to walk. His ultimate purpose is to make war, and to be damned good at it. A good Comanche brave gives no quarter, nor does he expect to get any." When she didn't say anything, he looked down at her. "Hell, I don't know why I'm telling you all this. I don't usually talk much about it."

"No, I'm glad you did," she assured him.

She had to be lying, he was sure of that. It was impossible for a woman like Amanda Ross to understand the things he'd done or the reasons for any of it. He lay back down, cradling his neck with interlaced fingers, looking up at the worn blanket. All he'd probably done was send her opinion of him even lower.

"I guess you've decided to share the blanket," he said finally.

"Yes."

"Then you'd better get some sleep. In another four or five hours at the most, you'll have to get up. And the trail gets a whole lot rougher."

"It couldn't possibly."

"Quanah hides out in those canyons. I hope to God

you aren't afraid of heights, because you'll be looking into holes that you'll swear go clear to hell. And we'll be going down them in the dark."

"I'll manage somehow."

Her flesh was cooking beneath the wool blanket she'd wrapped around her. She threw it off her shoulders and sat up. Modesty was one thing, suffering quite another. Turning her back to him, she unbuttoned the shirt and pulled it off, baring her arms. The hot, dry air felt almost cool on her damp skin. She adjusted the shoulders of her chemise, straightened her drawers, then lay down again.

"Just don't say anything," she muttered.

He didn't. As she turned her back again and rested her head on the crook of her arm, he closed his eyes, praying that the peyote vision wouldn't come to him again. But he knew it would.

She lay very still, trying to ignore the man behind her, but she couldn't. She found herself listening to him breathe, and she wondered what he was thinking, if he felt as taut as she did. He was a strange, complicated man, more so than anyone she'd ever known. She'd seen his violence, felt his gentleness, and known his passion, but she didn't understand him. Nobody, not even Clay McAlester, could really want to be that alone.

She came awake slowly to the smells of smoke, coffee, and food. Stretching and yawning, she rolled over and opened her eyes. McAlester was turning something on a makeshift spit.

She yawned again. "If you'd awakened me, I'd have tried to help," she murmured.

He turned his head, and he was actually smiling. "A herd of buffalo thundering by couldn't have done the job. You were unconscious."

She sat up and pushed her hair off her face. "What's that?"

"Supper by McAlester."

"I meant the meat."

"Prairie chicken."

"You went hunting?"

"You might say that." He turned the spit over, then stood up, wiping his hands on his buckskin pants. "I've got some yeps roasting in the coals."

"Yeps?"

"Indian potatoes."

She eyed the fire curiously. "Are they anything like real potatoes?"

"Well, they're dug out of the ground, but that's about as close as they come. They're pretty good."

"I hope so."

"They are."

He walked over to his packs and picked up a flat-bottomed pan. Coming back, he handed it to her. "Here—pour yourself some water and wash up. I left the soap out for you." When she hesitated, he added, "Just pull down the blanket on one side and use it for a curtain."

"Thanks."

He reached into a pocket and drew out a comb. "You'll be needing this, too."

She looked down at her chemise. "I . . . uh, I think I'd like to wear my dress."

"It's over there with the soap. I kinda figured you might want it."

"I just wish I could wash the rest of my clothes."

"We might find water come morning."

Digesting that encouraging bit of information, she picked up the pan, the canteen, the soap, and her dress, then ducked behind the blanket. Yanking the bottom of it, she managed to pull it within a foot of the ground. Satisfied she was out of view, she poured about an inch and a half of water into the pan, then peeled out of her clothes. There was no doubt about it—they were rank.

Using the soap itself like a rag, she went over her entire body. Before she rinsed the rest of her, she cupped her hands and splashed her face, making sure that the precious water went back into the pan. It felt unbelievably good. She hesitated a moment, then picked up her discarded drawers and put them into the pan, where they soaked up most of the water. Working the soap over them, she washed them thoroughly, wrung them out, and tossed the scummy water. Refilling the pan with another inch or so from the canteen, she rinsed the drawers as best she could. Then she used them for a cloth, wiping the soap off of her.

The dress was wrinkled but clean. She pulled it over her head and straightened it against her damp body. Without the bustle pad and the starched petticoats, the skirt just sort of hung around her legs. He'd saved the jacket bodice, but not the waist beneath it, so when she finished buttoning up, there was a deep cleavage showing, and try as she might, she couldn't quite get it covered.

"Do you have a handkerchief?" she called out to McAlester.

"No."

"A piece of cloth?"

"Just the one I use for washing the pots."

"Can I have it?"

Yeah."

He could see the skirt beneath the blanket, so he knew she was dressed. He picked up the cloth and walked around to give it to her. "Here," he said. A flush crept up her face as his gaze dropped to her breasts. "Yeah—well, you'd better use it there," was all he could think of to say.

"I am." She snatched the square of cloth and turned around to arrange it beneath her jacket. "Well, I guess it's better than nothing," she decided.

"Good. Let's eat, so we can get on the trail."

She tossed the rinse water, then followed him, combing the tangles from her hair. She felt a whole lot cleaner and cooler now, but she was extremely hungry.

"If you don't want to get your dress dirty, you might want to sit on a blanket or one of the saddles."

"Do you need any help?"

"You're a little late for that." He removed the green-stick spit and pulled off the chunks of meat with his fingers onto a flat tin pan. "Hope you don't mind, but we're going to have to share the plate—I don't carry much extra around with me." Using the spit, he jabbed among the ashes, then pulled out the yeps, deftly dropping them next to the meat. "Want coffee?" he asked, looking up.

"No . . . uh, thanks."

As she sank down onto the blanket she'd slept on, he handed her the plate and a knife. "I was going to boil some hardtack, but I didn't have room on the fire."

"Not knowing what hardtack is, I'm sure I won't miss it," she murmured.

"Flour and water biscuits," he answered. "You

might as well go ahead and get started while I get my coffee. I figure we'll be leaving in about half an hour."

She studied the evil-looking knife, then the food. She was beyond caviling now, she decided as she speared a chunk of the meat. She bit off a piece and began to chew. It was sweet and smoky, but tough.

"How is it?" he asked, coming back.

"Good—but it must have been quite an old hen."

"Probably. Tried the yeps yet?"

"No. I'm still chewing on the meat." She swallowed, then reached for the canteen. After taking a swig of water to wash it the rest of the way down, she observed. "It's got some kind of sauce on it, doesn't it?"

"Honey. That and mesquite in the fire give it the flavor."

"Well, it's got a good taste to it." She stabbed at one of the blackened balls in the plate, then held it up dubiously. "How do I get the ashes off this?"

"Blow them off—or eat 'em."

"Yes, of course. Silly me—why didn't I think of that?" she murmured wryly.

"Probably because they don't have yeps in Boston."

"Probably." She carried it to her mouth and nibbled on it. It didn't have much taste, or if it did, it was obscured by the ashes.

"Like 'em?"

"I can't tell." Afraid of hurting his feelings, she relented. "Actually, they're not bad. Aren't you having any?"

"When you give me back my knife. I told you—I travel light."

"I'll say." Before she gave it up, she used it to get another piece of the meat. "How come you took this off the bone?" she asked.

"It cooks faster."

Once he began eating, he was all business. It wasn't until he'd washed down the last of the meat that he spoke again. He looked over the rim of the cup.

"Sure you don't want any coffee?"

"Positively."

"It's not as strong as the last time."

"Does that mean it hasn't eaten the cup?"

"Something like that." He leaned back, resting his shoulders against his saddle, regarding her lazily. "Anybody ever tell you you're funny?"

"Odd or amusing?"

"Both."

She considered for a moment before answering. "Well, Mr. Donnelly disparaged my 'propensity for levity,' as he called it. But certainly nobody called me odd to my face."

"Then it's probably a good thing that you didn't marry him," Clay decided. "There's not enough humor in this world as it is."

"That's odd—coming from you, I mean. You don't even smile very often, and when you do, it can't be seen in your eyes at all. Ramon said you had killer eyes."

"He's probably right. Hap calls 'em dead eyes."

"You could change that, you know."

"A man can do damned near anything if he puts his mind to it, I suppose."

"But he has to want to."

"I've never wanted to. A cold eye and a steady hand win every time. Puts the fear of God in every man I face." He drained the last of his coffee, then spit out the grounds that had escaped the straining cloth. "Time to go," he announced, rising. "Need to make a visit to the trees while I pack up?"

The hateful flush crept into her cheeks again. "Yes."

His hand grasped hers, pulling her up. For an instant she was but inches from him, and the clean scent of lye soap was nearly as heady as perfume. She heard the sharp intake of his breath, and time stood still for a moment. There wasn't a single fiber of her being that wasn't acutely conscious of him. She didn't move, afraid he was going to kiss her again, even more afraid he wouldn't.

He released her, breaking the spell. "I've got to water the animals and saddle up," he muttered, turning away.

Telling herself she ought to be grateful that he hadn't presumed, she walked toward the trees. It didn't take her long, and she wasn't inclined to tarry very far from him. At the sound of a coyote's lonely howl, she almost ran back.

Then she saw the skin, its pattern bold and striking, its string of rattles still attached. She stared at it for a moment, realizing she'd been bamboozled. Chagrined, she was determined not to let him think he'd gotten by with it entirely. He was tightening a cinch as she marched up to him.

"Why didn't you tell me it was rattlesnake?" she demanded. "Why did you have to lie to me?"

He straightened up. "Would you have eaten it if you'd known?"

"No—of course not."

"There's your answer." He walked around the Indian pony, making sure the cinch held. "It's all ready for you," he announced.

"You know I'm never going to trust you again, don't you?"

"I probably won't lose much sleep over it."

"What are we going to eat tomorrow?" she asked tartly. "Scorpions? Rats?"

"Whatever crosses my path. Otherwise, there's always buffalo jerky." He collected the empty water pan from beneath Hannibal's nose, ducking a nip. "Next time, I'll leave you in the quicksand," he warned the mule.

It didn't take him long to finish breaking camp. He had it all down to the point where it actually looked easy. Despite her irritation with him, she couldn't help admiring his efficiency.

"Do you do this all the time?"

"No—just when I stop to sleep." This time, when he turned around, he was actually smiling. "Need a boost up?"

She had the word no on her lips, then changed her mind. "Yes," she decided. Then she remembered. "Just a minute—I've got to go back for my ... for something."

"If you're looking for your drawers, I tied 'em on top of Hannibal's packs. I figured they'd dry better there." He cupped his hands for her to step on, then waited until she braced her hand on his arm before he threw her up. "What would your Mr. Donnelly think now?" he wondered as she settled into the seat.

"Well, if he saw me, he wouldn't be offering a wedding ring, I'm sure of that. I must look like a trollop."

"No. None that I ever met, anyway."

His hand was resting on the deerhorn pommel of her saddle, his face upturned toward hers. The glint in his blue eyes was anything but ice. She felt her breath catch, her body go hot. She dropped her gaze to his hand. It was strong, masculine. She had to close her eyes to hide before he saw what he could do to her. He leaned close enough to brush against her leg, then straightened to put the reins across her palm. His fingers closed hers over them.

He could see her swallow, and he could feel the heat of her hand in his. He looked up, seeing her flushed face, the dark, almost black fringe of lashes above her cheek, the rich auburn hair that curled thickly against her neck. His eyes moved lower, taking in the rounded swell of her breasts beneath the piece of dingy cloth. There was no doubt about it—if he had the time and she the inclination, he'd be riding a different saddle tonight. But neither circumstance existed. Reluctantly, he released her fingers, then ran his hand down the Indian pony's neck.

"Guess I'd better mount up," he said, his voice almost thick.

"How far do we have to go?" she managed to ask him.

"Until I come across a sign, one way or the other."

"How are you going to see it at night?"

"With these killer eyes." He put his foot in the stirrup and swung his leg over, then eased his body back until it fit his saddle. "They haven't failed me yet," he assured her.

"Don't you have any weaknesses at all?"

"Not many," he replied. "I can't afford them."

"You're a strange man, McAlester."

He shrugged and nudged the paint mare with his knee. As the animal moved, he caught the mule's lead rope. "Is that as in odd or funny?"

"Both," she answered. "Sometimes I actually like you—but not always," she hastened to add.

But part of him wanted more than that. "I thought we had an understanding—I thought you wanted me to keep my distance."

"You haven't done a very good job of it."

"Have you?" he countered.

"No."

"Then I guess we're about even."

His horse moved out in front, leaving her to fall in behind the pack mule. She considered catching up and riding abreast with him, then decided against it. If she didn't keep her distance, she was going to give herself a whole lot of grief. It was one thing to be fascinated by a dangerous man like Clay McAlester, quite another to lie in his arms. A truly strong man, her mother said, didn't make a good husband because he never really needed anyone, and he never settled down. That had been her argument for marrying Gregorio Sandoval—he was handsome and courtly, but never strong. Clayton Michael McAlester, on the other hand, wasn't courtly at all. He was just strong.

She caught herself, jolted by her own thoughts. It

didn't make any difference to her—it couldn't. A man like McAlester, even if she'd have him—which she wouldn't—would never settle down. He'd already told her so.

It was almost two days before he found what he was looking for. "Somebody's ridden this way lately," he told her.

"How do you know?"

"I can see the signs. Look at how the grass is bent here. By nightfall it'll be standing up again, so that tells me we're not far behind them."

She looked to where he knelt over a clump of grass, seeing nothing. "Indians?" she asked uneasily.

"No."

"You mean there are more than two foolhardy Anglos out here?"

"Mexicans."

"How can you tell?"

"The way the hooves are shod."

"I don't believe this."

"You don't have to."

He stood up, frowning, then walked to where Hannibal chewed determinedly on a sparse clump of grass. Loosening one of the packs, he took out the all-purpose pan and poured water into one of the canteens. The mule drank it dry. Repeating the process, he offered some to his paint mare and the Indian pony.

"I could use a drink myself," she said.

As he handed the nearly empty canteen to her, he told her to go slow with it. Wild China Pond, the place where he'd expected to find water was dry. Flat Rock Ponds probably were also. And it was a long way to the Mustang Ponds. That left only a small canyon stream at the bottom of one hell of a hole in between here and the mustangs.

"Do you really know where we are?"

"Uh-huh. Over there's New Mexico—and this way's the Llano Estacado," he added, pointing eastward. "Back there are the Castle Mountains."

She sipped the tepid water, holding it in her mouth before swallowing it. Handing the canteen back, she dared to ask, "How much farther are we going today?"

"Until we catch up to them."

"You think it's the Comancheros?"

"Well, if it is, there's no sign of a wagon. On the other hand, Comanches don't have much use for any other kind of Mexican, and unless I've missed my guess, these tracks are headed straight for Quanah."

"Why would they do that if they haven't brought anything to sell?"

He shrugged. "They may just be going to set up a meeting for the actual trade. I still think it's probably going to happen somewhere around Big Spring. The way I see it, Quanah's offering either stolen horses or cattle—maybe both—and while he can hole up in the Llano with them, the wagons can't come in. So he'll have to take them someplace where there's both water and access to a wagon trail before he can trade them."

"But why Big Spring? Why not go back across the Pecos?"

"Too risky. It'd be too hard to take a herd the way we came—it's too narrow at Castle Gap. And if they try to go around, there's at least a sixty-five-mile stretch where there's nothing to drink. So I figure they'll be wanting to start out from a place like Big Spring."

"What are you going to do if you find Quanah Parker first?" she asked uneasily.

He didn't answer. He'd mulled that over in his mind himself and reached the conclusion he would have to lie. If he got caught at it, Quanah wasn't likely to forgive him. And if that happened, he'd be a traitor, and being one of The People wouldn't save him.

"I'm pretty attached to my hair, you know," she said finally.

"I'm not worried," he lied. He stowed the pan in the packs, then swung back into the saddle. "Come on—the longer we linger, the closer they get to Quanah."

Resigned, she looked across the broad, high plain and she shuddered at what she saw. On the horizon big black birds circled the sky, waiting for something to die.

"Do you see that?" she asked McAlester.

"Yeah—buzzards."

"Maybe that's your Mexicans. Maybe the Comanches found them. Maybe they weren't Comancheros."

"No. If I had to guess, I'd say something's dying of thirst. Sometimes when I've come this way, I've seen bones and carcasses strung out for miles, and not all of them were animals. But I wouldn't worry about it—we've still got a water paunch."

"All the canteens are empty?"

"Almost." He looked across at her. "Sorry you came?"

"No. At least you speak English."

He'd give her one thing—once she got through that first day, she'd kept up with few complaints. Last night, when he'd fixed supper, she hadn't even asked what it was. He found that rather ironic—the first time she didn't want to know, he'd fixed a stew of jackrabbit, wild onion, beans, and yep that she would have eaten anyway.

She was also a lot stronger than he'd expected, and she seemed determined to carry her own weight. While he'd cooked yesterday morning, she'd fixed up the day's shelter, and when they woke, she'd gathered firewood for him, both without being asked. When he'd cleaned his new Colts, she'd watered the animals. It was as though she were trying to show him that she was neither useless nor helpless.

They'd lingered too long over his stew, getting a late start on the night, but he wouldn't have traded the time for a hundred miles on the trail. After supper, they'd sat there, roasting hackberry balls over the fire, comparing Chicago to Boston. It had been, oddly enough, one of the best times of his life. Until he'd clasped her hand to help her up. Then it had taken every ounce of will he had to quell his desire for her.

No, if he had any complaints of her, the problem lay within him, not her. She was in most of his waking thoughts and all of his dreams now, and nothing he did seemed to change that. One glance, one touch, and there it was—aching within him. And the worst of it was that at times like those, he could almost believe it possible to possess her again.

He'd always been a man in total control of himself—cold, calculating, disciplined to the point that he believed he could endure anything. Except the nearness of Amanda Ross. He could cross the broiling desert, climb the mountain, swim the river, and survive the worst norther nature threw at him. But he couldn't shake the hold she had on his mind and body. He was, he reflected wearily, as consumed by desire as a lovesick youth after his first time with a girl.

"Is something the matter?" Amanda asked him.

"Huh? No, why would you think that?" he managed to answer.

"You aren't saying anything."

"Sometimes when I'm on the trail I go for days without saying anything," he said defensively. "I'm still trying to track the sign."

"But you weren't looking at anything," she reminded him.

"How would you know?"

"I was watching you."

"I'm just tired, that's all."

"I expect that's because you never sleep."

"I sleep enough."

"When?"

"When you sleep."

He reined in and leaned across to pull his telescope from the ropes that secured it atop his packs. Adjusting it, he trained it on the buzzards, then the ground. A horse lay there, its ribs quivering. It was still saddled.

"What is it?" she asked.

"Somebody's mount. It looks like I was right, and they ran out of water. Here—look for yourself."

She held the glass up and squinted, adjusting it until she spied when he'd seen. "It's alive."

"Not for long."

"They just abandoned the poor creature," she said indignantly. "How could anyone do that?"

"What would you have them do—die with it?"

"Would you just leave it like that?" she countered.

"No. I'd have to kill it." He took the telescope back and looked again. "He left a good saddle behind. Come on—I want a look at it," he added, spurring the paint.

It turned out to be farther than she'd expected, and it took a good quarter of an hour to reach the dying horse. The animal's eyes were wide open, bulging, its breathing labored. Clay dismounted and drew a gun.

"Turn your head," he told Amanda.

"You aren't—?" She couldn't even bring herself to say it.

"Yes."

"Please don't."

"It's too late to save it."

He walked closer, taking in the elaborate silver conchos that trimmed the hand-tooled saddle, and his heart beat a little faster. It was Mexican. He raised his hand, pointing the Colt's barrel at the blaze on the horse's head.

"Don't!" she cried out.

"Turn your head, I said!"

He squeezed the trigger. When he turned around, Amanda was crying. "Look—I'm sorry, but it had to be done." He holstered the gun. "We ought to catch up to the owner pretty soon," he observed. "Two of 'em are riding double, and judging by this, they're short on water."

"There's just two?"

"No. Four. But there's only three horses now." He shaded his eyes and looked toward what still appeared to be flat plain. "I don't know why they didn't shoot the animal themselves," he added.

"I don't see any canyon," she protested.

"You won't until you're about ready to fall into it." Turning his attention back to the dead horse, he knelt down and unbuckled a saddlebag. "Well, look at this," he murmured, whistling low.

"What is it?"

"A letter from Sanchez-Torres to somebody named Emilio." He scanned the Spanish words quickly, then reread them. "It looks like Emilio's supposed to tell Quanah there's nine wagons coming. Hap was right— it's one hell of a shipment. No wonder they raided all the way to Durango. Sanchez-Torres wants three thousand horses for it."

"How bad is it?"

"A whole lot of rifles and a Gatling gun. Not to mention enough ammunition to blow up a stockade. I'd say if Quanah gets this, he'll have enough to arm his Quahadis as well as many Kiowas and Cheyenne as want to take to the war trail with him." He read further before looking up. "Well, Hap said there was a Texan involved, and it looks like he was right."

It took a moment for it to sink in. "How on earth could anyone want to unleash an Indian war on his own people? Clay, it doesn't make sense."

"Yeah, it does." Without waiting to explain, he mounted the paint mare. "Come on—there's not much time."

It wasn't until he'd ridden a couple of miles that he spoke again. "You ever hear of Sam McKittrick?" he asked abruptly.

"I don't think so. Why?"

"I'm going to put a noose around his neck. McKittrick's got a spread not too far from the Ybarra. It's not half as big as yours, but Sam's got big plans for it."

"I don't understand."

"McKittrick's behind Sanchez-Torres. He wants the Comanches to come down and clean out his neighbors. He wants them driven off the land and out of business. He knows the army's going to come in and punish the Indians when it's all over."

"And I suppose that by the time that happens, he's bought up cheap land and owns half of West Texas— that's it, isn't it?"

"Kinda looks that way, doesn't it?"

"Yes." She took a deep breath, then exhaled. "But he won't get Ybarra-Ross. We've got walls as high as a fort's."

"An Indian war can sure as hell isolate you."

She fell silent as the full import of what he was saying sank in. With hostile Indians raiding at will, ranch hands would be reluctant to ride herd on Ybarra cattle, and there was no way of telling how many animals she'd lose. Big John always said he had two things worth as much as gold in the bank—his land and his cattle.

"When do you think Quanah Parker means to start this?" she asked finally.

"He's got to have guns first."

"But he's not going to get them."

"Not if I have anything to do with it." He straightened in his saddle. "But the going gets a whole lot rougher from here. From here on, we're going to have to ride during the day."

It didn't take long to realize he meant the terrain. He'd been right about that also. From a seemingly flat, wide-open space, the ground suddenly dropped as though it had been ripped open by an angry god, and she was staring over the brink into a chasm several hundred feet straight down. The walls looked to be solid rock.

"My word!" she gasped. "We aren't going down into that, I hope."

"Yeah." He looked down into the canyon at the small ribbon of water slicing through it. "Hard to imagine that a stream can do that," he murmured.

She was dizzy just looking into the abyss. "I—" She caught herself before she told him she couldn't do it. "I don't see how," she finished lamely.

"There's a path."

"Where?"

"Right down the side. It starts over there—just past where you see that rock ledge."

"Oh." She swallowed nervously. "Have any horses fallen going down?"

"Probably. Want to ride Hannibal?"

"You told me he's temperamental."

"He is, but there's nothing more sure-footed than a mule." He could see she was hesitant, but he was in a hurry. "I'll go first, leading you down. Now—do you want Hannibal or the pony you're already on?"

Vaguely remembering being dunked in the Pecos by the mule, she didn't take long to make up her mind. "The pony."

"Good. I wasn't wanting to shift the packs anyway." He reached to take the reins from her nearly nerveless fingers, then he nudged Sarah with his knee, turning her toward the ledge.

As they began the steep descent, Amanda made the mistake of looking at the canyon floor. It was a long way down. She froze, unable to move.

"I—I can't . . . I just can't," she whispered.

"Close your eyes, and I'll get you down."

"I'm afraid of high places."

"Pretty soon you'll be in a low one."

"You're not frightened at all, are you?"

"No, but I grew up out here."

He knew the longer he waited, the more she'd panic, so he gave Sarah her head, and the mare moved slowly, picking her way along the narrow one-sided path.

When he looked back over his shoulder, Amanda's eyes were closed, her lips moving silently, and he was pretty sure she prayed.

"We'll be at the bottom in no time," he assured her.

"That's what I'm afraid of," she responded tersely. "I'd rather get there whole."

"You will."

It seemed as though her whole life passed before her eyes, as though it took an age, and all she could feel was the slow, stolid walk of the Indian pony plodding downward. She was leaning at a steep pitch, almost over the deerhorn pommel. She grasped the saddlehorn with both hands and held on so tightly that her knuckles hurt.

After about the twentieth Hail Mary, she dared to ask, "Are we nearly there?"

"Almost," he lied.

She opened one eye and wished she hadn't. While the horse hugged the rock wall, there was nothing but air on the other side. She started over, saying the rosary from the beginning, this time whispering it, reassuring herself with her own prayers. Her hands, where they held the saddlehorn, were so wet she was afraid she'd lose her grip.

"Another hundred feet," he told her.

"I don't want to hear it unless we are there."

"All right, I won't say anything more."

She lasted about five minutes. "Where are we now?"

"Fifty feet—do you want me to count them out for you?"

"Yes."

"Forty feet ... thirty-five ... thirty ... twenty ... fifteen ..."

She exhaled, visibly relieved. "I'm all right now," she decided, opening her eyes. This time, she looked up. "I can't believe we started from there."

"There are bigger holes than this around."

"But we don't have to go through them?" she asked hopefully.

"No." He got out his telescope again and looked down the narrow canyon. "We're not far behind our friend Emilio."

"Do you see them?"

"No, but I can smell the smoke of a campfire."

That was too much for her. "God must have given you different equipment if you can smell that."

The corners of his mouth twitched as he turned around. "I reckon he did."

Heat flooded her face. "I was speaking of noses," she said stiffly.

He sobered almost immediately. "It's going to get pretty rough here shortly. I don't think they're much farther than that rock bend ahead, and for all I know they may have heard us coming down. Before we stumble into an ambush, I'm going to leave you on this side of the bend. If it's clear, I'll come back for you. Otherwise, you're going to hear gunfire."

"Yes."

"If you hear shots, and I'm not back right away, you hightail it the other way. There's another trail going up to the rim about two or three miles behind you, and it'll be easier going because you don't have to look down."

"And do what?" she demanded incredulously. "I don't even know where I am."

"If you ride straight north, you're headed toward the leased lands. If you ride south, you're headed for Stockton. It's about four or five days from here."

"I'm not going anywhere."

"Whatever you do, if I don't come back, don't come after me—savvy?" He reached for his shotgun and handed it to her. "It's double-loaded with a charge of number four shot in each barrel. Each trigger fires one load."

"Why are you telling me this?"

"I'm leaving it with you. If you get in trouble, you don't have to have much aim—it'll scatter anything

within a hundred and fifty feet. All you have to remember is not to fire both loads at once."

She could see he was serious. "All right. But you
don't really think anything's going to go wrong, do
you?" she asked anxiously. "I mean, I don't want to be
stranded out here with nothing but Comanches and Comancheros."

"You asked to come."

"I know, but—"

"Amanda, I don't have time for this."

"I'm coming with you."

He gave her a look of long-suffering. "I don't know
what the hell you think you can do."

"Neither do I, but I'm not staying behind. There's no
way on earth I'm going back up there alone."

"Damn."

"There's no need to curse, is there?"

"I could say a whole lot more than that right now,"
he muttered. He looked up the trail, then to the rocky
curve ahead. "How well can you climb?"

"I told you I'm not going back alone."

"You've made that clear—I was looking at that
ledge over there," he said, pointing. "Think you could
climb up to it?"

"Not decently—but yes. At least it looks like I could
find something to hang onto. Why?"

"If you are determined to stay, I guess you might as
well cover me."

She looked at the shotgun. "With this?"

"If you have to use it, it'll do the most damage.
Come on—I'll go up there with you. I'll take a look at
what I'm getting myself into."

"Maybe they won't be there."

"You better hope to God they are. I'd rather take
them out here than risk letting 'em get to Quanah." He
swung out of his saddle and came to stand beside her.
"Are you game to try?" he asked, taking the shotgun
back from her, setting it carefully on the ground.

"Yes."

He reached up for her, and as she leaned out of the Indian saddle, her face was but inches from his. "You know, Amanda Mary Ross," he said softly, "you're one hell of a woman, whether you want to be or not."

She slid the length of him until her feet were on the ground. Before she had time to close her eyes, she felt the warm caress of his breath against her cheek, the surprising gentleness of his lips against hers. His arms closed around her, holding her close, and for some odd reason, she was so overwhelmed she wanted to cry. Her hands came up to clasp his shoulders as she returned his kiss. For a long moment she savored the strength of his embrace, then it was over.

He set her back from him. "You make a man afraid to die," he said, dropping his hands. "You make him want to live."

"You aren't going to die—you cannot."

"I don't plan to, Amanda, but in my business it happens." He searched her face almost hungrily. "Would it make any difference to you, I wonder?"

His gaze was so intense she had to look away. "Yes," she whispered. "Yes, it would."

He sucked in his breath, holding it for a moment, then he exhaled heavily. "Come on—there's no time right now," he said. Leaning down, he picked up the shotgun and started toward the curve ahead.

The floor of the canyon narrowed, obstructed by huge boulders piled like stairs to the low-hanging ledge above them. "Go on," he urged her, "I'm right behind to catch you if you lose your footing."

It was easier than she expected. Though her hands and feet slipped and slid into crevices between the rocks, she managed to scramble all the way up without actually falling. When she reached the ledge, she discovered it had enough of an overhang above it to put her in heavy shadows. She turned back to take the shotgun so McAlester could join her.

"Well, now—would you look at that?" he said under

his breath. "I think we've found Emilio and his friends."

She followed his gaze and saw three men gathered around a small cooking fire beside the stream. While one turned a spit, the other two shared a bottle of something. Two horses were hobbled nearby.

"There's only three men down there," she whispered. "I thought you said there were four."

"There were. And one horse is missing."

"Where do you think he is—the other man, I mean?"

He'd hoped to get all of them, but he was too late. "Unless I miss my guess, I'd say he's gone visiting. Damn, but I hate to see that."

"Why would just one go?"

"I don't know. I didn't think Quanah would be this far north with a herd to feed and water. I still don't."

She could see that he was angry with himself, and she sought to mollify him. "Maybe the other one's gone hunting for food—it doesn't look like they've got much to eat."

"Maybe—but I don't think so."

"What are you going to do now?"

"Take my chances. But I need you to look out for me while I go down."

"Don't you think you ought to wait?"

"No."

He hesitated, then reached to brush her hair back from her forehead. For the first time in his life, he felt a responsibility to live. If he didn't, if he made a mistake, she'd be at the mercy of Comancheros—or worse.

"Well, that's it, I think," he told her. "Don't make a move unless you have to—unless you see I'm in trouble."

Biting her lip, she nodded. But as he started to leave her, she blurted out, "Wait!"

He turned back. "What?"

Feeling utterly self-conscious now, she couldn't meet his gaze. "I guess I'm just afraid."

"For me or for you?"

"Both."

"Hey—" He lifted her chin with his knuckle. "I do this all the time."

She nodded.

"God, Amanda—" He got no further. His arms closed around her, holding her against his chest. "You didn't ask for this, did you?"

"No," came the muffled reply.

"As soon as this is over—as soon as I get Sanchez-Torrez and McKittrick, I'm taking you to the Ybarra," he whispered against the crown of her hair. "I'm going to be there to see the look on Sandoval's face when he finds out you survived."

"I hope so."

"I am."

With that, he released her. "Hold the fort for me, will you?" he said.

She watched as he went back down the way they'd come up, and then he was out of sight. Reluctantly, she picked up the shotgun and waited.

It seemed like forever before she saw him again, this time on the other side of the bend. He was on foot, close to the rock wall, then he stepped into the open, his revolver drawn.

"Emilio!" he called out.

The three men scattered, and one came up shooting. Two shots nicked rock, and the sound reverberated down the canyon. Amanda froze as Clay McAlester returned fire. There was a cry, and the Mexican doubled over. The other two reached the horses. He caught one in the back, and the fellow fell. Desperate, the last Comanchero tried to make a stand, using his horse for a shield. Clay crouched low, waiting until the man raised up to shoot, then he got off the first round. The fellow's head jerked back as the bullet struck, then his body slipped noiselessly to the ground.

The sudden silence had a finality to it. While Amanda looked on, too horrified to move, McAlester turned the first Mexican over and went through his pockets. Finding nothing, he walked over to the other body. As he knelt, he froze, and the hairs on his neck stiffened.

She saw what he heard—coming down the canyon were half a dozen painted Indians and the missing Comanchero. One of the Indians stood in his stirrups and raised a rifle.

"Look out!" she screamed.

The warrior looked up as she pulled both triggers. The blast was deafening, and the world went black. She fell back, oblivious to everything but the pain in her shoulder. Below, four wounded Indians fled, leaving two dead behind. The last Comanchero writhed on the ground, clutching his stomach, dying.

Not knowing for sure if there was a larger band nearby, Clay didn't waste any time. As the smoke cleared, he ran up the rocks to Amanda. She was lying on her back, her expression dazed, the shotgun beside her.

He dropped to his knees and pulled her up, cradling her against his chest. She blinked blankly.

"Are you all right?"

"My . . . my shoulder," she mumbled.

He felt over it carefully. "It's not broken," he assured her. "That was one hell of a shot you got off."

"Was it?"

His arms tightened around her. "You bet it was."

"I'm glad," she murmured, turning her head into his shoulder. "It hurt . . . I didn't expect that." Then she sobered with the realization of what she'd done. "I killed some of them, didn't I?"

"You damned near got all of 'em—two dead, four wounded."

She closed her eyes momentarily. "May God forgive me," she whispered, swallowing. "I never thought I could do such a thing, and now I've done it twice." She looked up, searching his face. "I don't know how you can do this all the time."

"Yeah—well," He took a deep breath, then exhaled it. "For what it's worth, it isn't something a man gets used to, Amanda, but I've had to face the fact that some people just don't deserve to live. When I keep that in mind, it makes what I do a little easier." He reached down with one hand and picked up the shotgun. Still holding her against him, he looked at it. "Well, no wonder—good God, woman, you fired both barrels! You're damned lucky it didn't blow up on you."

"I thought the Comanches were going to kill you," she said simply. "I don't remember pulling both triggers."

"They weren't Comanche, so apparently we haven't stumbled onto Quanah Parker yet. But it tells me that something's about to happen. If I'm right, these were Cheyenne on their way to join him."

"How do you know they weren't Kiowa or Apache?"

"The Apache are bitter enemies of the Comanche, and they wouldn't come into the Comancheria, even in summer. These weren't dressed like Kiowa, so that means they're Cheyenne."

"Clay . . ." She hesitated.

"What?"

"I didn't believe in this—not in the beginning, anyway—but I want you to know I do now. I'd like to think maybe I could help."

"You already have."

But she wasn't finished. "Ybarra-Ross can stand, I know that, but a lot of the others cannot. I don't want to have the only ranch in West Texas. I don't want to have nightmares about what happens to my neighbors."

She seemed so right in his arms, so very right, almost as though she'd been made for him. He looked down, nearly overwhelmed by the tenderness he felt for her. He bent his head and rubbed his cheek against the softness of her hair. "You scared the hell out of me, Amanda," he whispered.

But there was no time. By now, more Cheyennes could be mounting up to come after them. He shifted her off his knee and stood up. "Can you ride, do you think?"

She nodded. "It's just my shoulder."

"It's pretty bruised up." He reached for her other arm and helped her to stand. "Come on—we've got to get out of here. There's no telling who'll be coming back. We might be heading for Big Spring with five hundred Indians on our tails."

"Let's hope not, because it's going to be slow going back up that trail."

"We're riding up-canyon first, just in case we have to make a stand."

Carrying the shotgun, he went down first, ready to catch her if she lost her balance, but she didn't. As he boosted her up into the Indian saddle, he realized how much she'd surprised him. Every day since he'd found her half dead in the desert, she'd surprised him. In spite of everything, she was still doing her best to survive.

He still had his hand on her knee. "Is something the matter?" she asked him.

"No. I was just thinking we must be about even-up now."

"In what?"

"Everything." He dropped his hand and took a deep breath. Moving to his paint mare, he stepped into the stirrup and swung his leg over the saddle. Grasping the reins and Hannibal's lead rope, he turned his horse toward the steep trail up. "Let's get going—we can talk later."

As she fell in behind him, nothing, not even the awful ache in her shoulder, could dampen the exhilaration she felt. She'd not only saved his life, but she'd proven to him that she could pull her own weight, that she wasn't merely useless and in his way.

They'd gone north a few miles toward the Leased Lands, then doubled back, hoping to elude the Cheyenne, and still he couldn't shake the feeling they were being followed. When they finally dared to stop, it was to make a quick, cold camp and wash down a few slices of jerky with water. And instead of sleeping in the heat of the day, Clay stood watch while Amanda napped little more than an hour, and then they were on the road again.

"You still think they're looking for us?" she asked as he took out his telescope.

"Yeah." Just below the crest of a small hill, he reined in and dismounted. "Wait here a minute. I'm going to take a quick look around."

As she watched he walked almost to the top, then dropped to crawl on his stomach as he disappeared from sight. She looked about nervously, thinking the whole place seemed too empty, too quiet. He came back, his face sober.

"I want you to see something."

"What?"

"You'll see," he answered, reaching for her. She slid the length of him, then stood uncertainly until he took her hand. "Stay low to the ground, and don't do anything to draw attention," he advised her.

She didn't need to be told twice. She was on her knees before he was. Her heart pounding loudly in her ears, she crept to the crest of the hill, then looked downward, seeing nothing.

"Over there," he whispered, handing her the telescope.

She didn't need it. As she followed his direction, a hollow pit formed in her stomach, and she couldn't speak. Silhouetted against the horizon, a long, single column of mounted warriors moved slowly, deliberately toward the southeast. There were too many of them to count. She lifted the glass to her eye and focused it, seeking out the leader.

He sat tall, erect, and proud in his saddle. But it was his face that drew her attention—his hawk-nosed visage was set, cruel, his eyes black and unfathomable. Despite the heat, he wore a feathered war bonnet, its tails trailing almost to his stirrups.

Beside her, Clay drew in his breath, then let it out. "There's a real majesty to them," he murmured. "You can't look at them and not see it."

"I'll say."

"There's no question about it now—they're Southern Cheyenne," he declared flatly.

"How many do you think there are?" she whispered.

"Close to two hundred."

"What are we going to do now?"

"Follow them for a few miles." He edged closer to her and took back his glass. Looking through it again, he studied the Cheyenne soberly for a moment. "I'd a whole lot rather follow them than have it the other way around."

"It's a war party, isn't it?"

"Not yet—I don't see any paint, but it's a war chief leading them. I'd say they want to discuss things with Quanah, and if the Comanches come up with enough guns and ammunition, they're ready to join in with the Comanches and Kiowas. Otherwise, they'll probably go back to Kansas." He laid the telescope aside. "At least they aren't tracking *us*."

"Yes, that *is* something, isn't it?"

"Must've lost 'em when we went north. I guess

when it came to a choice between us and a meeting with Quanah, Quanah won."

"What a shame," she murmured wryly. "So, what do we do now?"

He was lying on his side, his head propped up by one elbow, regarding her lazily. A slow smile warmed his blue eyes. "Oh, a man's always got plenty of ideas."

The thought that he might kiss her again sent a shiver of anticipation through her. "I expect you do," she agreed softly.

He was tempted, but he wasn't fool enough to believe she really mean to encourage him. Or that she wouldn't be sorry later, and he didn't want a repeat of what had happened at the spring pool. With an effort, he forced his gaze from her face.

"No, I shouldn't have said that." Reluctantly, he rolled to sit up, then stood. "Come on—we'd better go."

"We'll just catch up to them." she protested.

"Now that I know where they're headed, we'll follow for a while. Later, we'll go west and try to intercept Sanchez-Torres."

Disappointed, she struggled to rise, then smoothed her full skirt with her hands. He was already halfway to the horses before she caught up to him. When she fell in beside him, he was silent and seemingly preoccupied.

"You were going to kiss me, weren't you?" she dared to ask him. Even as she said it, she could feel the blood rise, burning her cheeks.

He kept his eyes focused on the ground. "No," he lied. "Why'd you think that?"

"I don't know—the way you were looking at me, I guess."

As he stepped into the stirrup and swung his leg over the saddle, he looked into her hot, flushed face. "You aren't saying you wanted me to, are you?" he asked soberly.

She shook her head, lying also, "No, of course not."

He wasn't entirely fooled, but he wasn't sure either. "Look—you can't blow hot and cold, Amanda. It's got to be one way or the other—you know that, don't you?"

"Yes."

"I'm not civilized enough to want to play parlor games with words, either."

"No, you're not," she agreed readily. "You're what Papa would have called downright untamed."

"Untamed," he repeated, digesting it. "Yeah, I guess that pretty well says it."

"Yes."

"When I grew up with the Comanches, it was the girls who started everything, which kind of makes sense, when you think about it. I mean, it's up to the woman to keep the barn closed, if that's what she wants." He cast a quick side-glance her way. "The rest of the women I've known have all been cantina harlots, so I've always known where I stood with them—two dollars got me a roll in the clover."

"Clay—"

"I believe in speaking plain, Amanda."

"Yes, but I don't think—"

"So," he cut in, "what would you have done if I had kissed you?"

"I don't know . . . no, that's not true," she admitted. "I guess I would have kissed you back."

He had to close his eyes to quell the desire that raced through his body. No, before she came to him again, he wanted her to think about it. He didn't believe he could stand it if she cried afterward.

She felt utterly, completely humiliated by his silence. As hot tears stung her eyes, she demanded, "Well, aren't you going to say anything?"

"What do you want me to say?"

"Something . . . anything. That you think me a fool . . . that I'm no better than those women in the cantinas . . . I don't know."

"You're not like those women."

"But I'm a fool, aren't I?"

"No." He exhaled audibly. "No, if anybody's a fool around here, it's me. If I didn't think you'd be sorry tomorrow, I'd be rolling in that grass with you right now." He caught Hannibal's lead rope and looped it over his saddlehorn. His mouth twisted as he looked at her again. "Don't offer a man a bite of bread when he's starving for the whole loaf."

"All right—what do you *want* me to say?" she demanded.

"Amanda, I'm not going to put any words in your mouth so you can blame me later."

She pushed back her hair from her hot face and neck. Turning her back to him, she walked to her horse. "All I wanted was for you to hold me and tell me we aren't going to be killed by Indians," she said over her shoulder.

He ought to leave it at that, but no matter what he'd just said, he was still foolhardy enough to push her further. He waited until she'd pulled herself into the wood-and-horn saddle.

"Don't give me any brass-faced lies," he told her, guiding Sarah toward the summit of the hill. Behind him Hannibal jerked on the lead rope, then reluctantly followed.

"I just wish—"

He cut her off abruptly. "Be careful what you wish for—you might get it, you know, and then where would you be? Hell, I'm less than half-civilized—untamed—you said that yourself."

"It wasn't like I was wanting to marry you!" She fairly flung the words at him. "I just said I would have kissed you back, that's all."

She fell in behind the mule, keeping her distance from Clay. He pulled up and half turned in his saddle. "If you want a fellow to peck on your cheek, go back to Boston to that fellow who's got money and political ambitions."

"I don't want a peck on my cheek! And I don't want Patrick Donnelly either!"

"Don't shout—the sound carries," he warned her. But as he said it, he almost smiled. "All right, I'll bite the bait. Just what do you want?"

"I don't know—to be held—to be told we're going to get out of this alive—"

"That's it?" he asked bluntly.

"Look—do I have to have a reason for everything?" she answered wearily.

"No, but if I live to be a hundred, I'll never understand you without a few of them. Come on—let's get a safe distance from those Cheyenne, then we can talk all you want." With that, he dug his moccasin heels into the little mare, and she moved forward again. "I'd like to get far enough away to make a campfire."

By the time they reached the crest of the hill, the long line of Indians on the horizon had disappeared. But what she felt wasn't relief—it was chagrin. It wasn't fair of McAlester to push her like that, not when she really didn't understand what she felt. She kicked her pony's flank with her bare heel and caught up to him.

"You know you started this, don't you? Just what sort of ideas were *you* having back there?"

"The usual ones."

"The usual ones? What kind of answer is that supposed to be?"

"Prudent."

She sucked in her breath, then let it out, blowing wet strands of hair off her forehead. "And you don't understand *me*."

"No."

He was silent for so long she thought that was the end of it. But as they cut west rather than go over a rock-strewn hill, he exhaled heavily.

"I guess maybe that's what appealed to me when I lived among the Comanche. All brutality toward whites aside, they have pretty straightforward ways of doing things. A man doesn't have to guess where he stands. No—" He lifted his hand as she opened her mouth. "No, hear me out. If you were a Comanche girl, and if you wanted me, all you'd have to do is crawl under my tipi hides, and nobody would think anything about it. And if I wanted to make something permanent out of it, I'd just take a few stolen horses, and I'd leave them in front of your tipi. If you or someone in your family didn't come out and get them, I'd know exactly where I stood, and I'd leave you alone."

"And if I took them?"

"Your family would gather up your clothes, your cooking pots, a few knives, and some buffalo robes and send you out with them. We'd load Hannibal up and be on our way."

"That's it? No words—nothing?" she asked incredulously.

"No. But to my way of thinking, it's a lot more civilized than the way whites go about it. You don't have two people sitting in a parlor with the door open, trying to make polite conversation that covers nothing for six months, followed by lengthy betrothal, where nothing more than a chaste brush on the cheek is proper. Then, just because a priest or parson has said a few words, it's suddenly all right for them to do damned near anything with the strangers they've married. Tell me that's civilized, will you?"

"It's a rite that goes back thousands of years."

"I expect if someone wanted to study the subject, he'd find out that the Comanche way goes back a whole lot further. And whether you admit it or not, it's a damned sight more civilized way to do it."

"They have more than one wife, Clay—surely you don't think that's civilized, do you?"

"No, but it's practical. Look at the life. There's a hell of a lot of work for one woman to do. And most wives are related to each other, usually as sisters. It actually works out pretty well."

"I saw what happened between Little Doe and Walks With Sunshade," she said sarcastically.

"They weren't sisters, and they weren't even from the same tribe. But if you had to put up and take down the tipi, butcher meat, tan hides, make clothing, carry firewood and water, and cook, you might have a whole different opinion about having a second or even a third wife to help you. Given the hardness of the life, most Comanche women have only a couple of children. A lot of the women and children die early."

"So they steal other people's children. They kill settlers and travelers and steal their children. Somewhere along your Comanche war trail, your own parents died. They didn't get to see you grow up, Clay. They were murdered so an Indian woman could call you her son, so you could be Nahakoah instead of Clayton McAlester."

"Sees the Sun—her name was Ekatonah. And whatever could be said of her, I never saw her hurt anyone. Not once after I came into her tipi was I whipped or scolded. If she wanted me to behave, she just let me know I was disappointing her. And it was pretty much the same way with the other boys I knew."

"I don't care how civilized their home life is. I know they killed my stepfather horribly, and God alone knows what they did to my mother before she died. If I knew what she suffered at Comanche hands, the burden would probably be too great to bear."

"It's war, Amanda."

"War is too civilized a word for what they do. War is where soldiers meet on a battlefield, where the course of a nation is determined."

"Tell that to the Jayhawkers who raided, murdered, and burned people out of their homes in Missouri. Or tell it to men like Quantrill, or like Bloody Bill Anderson, who took soldiers off a passenger train and murdered them in cold blood. War, for whatever reason man chooses to fight, by its very name is barbaric."

"But you fought in the War of Rebellion," she reminded him.

"I fought in the Civil War."

"On the wrong side."

"Now that depends on who you ask, doesn't it?" Clay gazed up at the high sun and shook his head. "How in the devil did we get from Comanche weddings to this?"

"One thing led to another, I guess."

He twisted in his saddle to see her. "Yeah."

The way he said it, she knew they weren't speaking of Indians or war anymore. Her heart seemed to pause beneath her breastbone. She passed her tongue over her dry lips and said nothing.

He squinted again at bright sky. "Yeah, I guess it did," he said, his voice low, husky. "It's kind of hard to forget that, isn't it?"

"Yes. Very. So—how do we go about forgetting?" she asked, looking away.

Despite everything that had happened between them since he'd met her in the stagecoach station, she was still enough of a puzzle to him that he didn't want to make a fool of himself again. No, if she wanted him, she was going to have to toss the dice first.

"Well, I'm a long way from having any extra horses," he said with a lightness he didn't feel. "So I guess we just let it ride."

She felt dissatisfied, as though she'd been led along, then pulled up short. She was the rich rancher's daughter, the girl who'd listened to the nuns teach piety along with poetry and everything else, and he was the more than half-savage ranger who could kill seemingly without compunction. She was fascinated by him, that was all, and when she got home, he'd move on. Men like Clay McAlester didn't settle down—no, they just moved on.

"Yes, I think that would be wise," she said finally. "Once we get finished with this, I'm going to have my hands full running the ranch."

He hunched forward in his saddle and turned the mare with his knees. He ought to feel relieved, but he didn't. Yet his rational mind told him that even if he could lie with her again, he wouldn't be able to keep her. Not once she got back to the Ybarra. Then she'd be the rich girl again, and he'd only be a thirty-three-dollar-a-month Texas Ranger.

They were camped in a steep, V-shaped draw, where Clay had collected enough dead mesquite limbs to provide them an arbor cover from the main trail. He'd washed up and was gutting a rabbit while she took the soap and pan to the other side of his little brush arbor for her daily ablution. Left alone with his thoughts, he finished cleaning the animal, then spitted it and hung it over the fire. To make matters simple, he tossed several yeps into the coals.

Time was running out, and he knew it. The war drums were beating, summoning any who would join Quanah, and all that held the Comanche, Kiowa, and Cheyenne alliance back was the lack of enough guns and ammunition. Yet.

He hadn't mentioned it to Amanda, but there'd been something else about the Cheyennes they followed that disturbed him. He'd thought he saw a couple of Kiowa-Apaches and some Arapahos with them. If that was the case, Quanah was forming an alliance so big that the whole southern plain was going to erupt like a powder keg. Texas, the leased Oklahoma Territory Indian lands, and Kansas were all going to bleed before Mackenzie could stop them. But the army would get even—after hundreds, maybe a thousand whites died, the army would get even.

"Ayeeeeeeh!"

Amanda's shrill scream broke through his reverie like a war lance. His neck prickled, and drawing his gun, he crashed through the brush. He already had the

Colt cocked when he saw her. She was backed up against the dirt wall, her eyes on one of the biggest rattlers he'd ever seen. It was coiled, its tail buzzing, ready to strike.

"Don't move!" he shouted as he pulled the trigger.

The snake came apart, its head flying, while its body turned like a rope, writhing in a loop, then sinking to lie less than a foot from her. She slumped, and for a moment, he thought the head had struck her.

"Are you all right?" he demanded, kneeling over her.

Her arms came up to clasp his shoulders, and she shook all over as she buried her head in his chest. He dropped the gun and drew her onto his lap. Wrapping one arm around her, he looked her over.

"Did it hit you?"

"No," came the muffled reply.

"Well, it was a big one," he said, feeling enormous relief. "I'd say he had at least six or seven buttons on him."

She shuddered against him. "Just hold me, Clay," she choked out. "Just hold me."

"Hey, it's all right," he said softly. "It's dead." She was warm and soft in his arms, and she smelled of soap. He looked down and, lifting her chin with his free hand, he could see the fright in her eyes. "God, Amanda, what else can happen to you?" he muttered more to himself than to her.

"I'm afraid to find out," she whispered, swallowing.

Her clothes were where she'd dropped them, and all that was between his hand and her flesh was her chemise. It wasn't enough. He sucked in his breath, holding it, trying to master the desire that threatened to overwhelm him.

"Amanda . . . I . . . ." His voice was hoarse, raspy.

It was as though there was nothing in the world but the man who held her. Her own pulse quickened, and her breath caught almost painfully in her chest. She knew if she pushed him away, that would be all there was to it, and yet she couldn't deny herself any more than she could deny him. Her arms tightened, pulling him closer, as her mouth eagerly sought his.

At the first caress of her breath, the first touch of her lips against his, he was lost. As the heat rose between his body and hers, he forgot everything beyond the woman in his arms, everything beyond the hunger he felt for her.

Her lips parted, giving him access, and his tongue plunged into the hot recesses of her mouth, tasting, taking her breath away. There was no gentleness in his kiss, only an intense, overpowering need, and she responded with eager abandon, forgetting everything but her own desire.

His pulse raced, pounding hot blood through his veins, and the roar of it drowned out all conscience, all resolve. He wanted all of her again, and he wanted her now. But there were too many rocks there to lay her down. He tore his lips away to whisper thickly, "Come on—it's cooler in the arbor."

Grasping her hand, he pulled her up with him, embracing her again, pressing his body into hers. His free hand slid eagerly down her back, cupping her hip, holding it against his. She twined her arms around his neck, pulling his head down for another kiss. And everything that had gone before, even that night by the spring, was child's play compared to the urgency he felt now.

"Come on."

His hot breath against her ear sent shivers down her spine. He released her to take her hand again, pulling her after him, and they stumbled eagerly beneath the mesquite shade, dropping to their knees into the softness of blanket-covered grass. Kneeling in front of her, he fumbled with his clothes, loosening them. With one last look into dark eyes made almost black by passion, he tipped her backward and followed her down.

Her hands slid beneath his shirt, her fingers digging into the hot, damp skin of his back as he lay over her, tracing kisses from her lips to her ear to the soft hollow of her throat. She moaned low, arching her body beneath his, thrusting her breasts against his chest. His head moved lower, nuzzling the crevice, then his mouth found a nipple through the soft lawn. It hardened under his tongue. She gasped as he began to suck, then her hands twined in his hair, pressing him to her breast.

His hand slid lower, smoothing the soft cotton, then grasped the chemise, working it upward over her hip, baring her smooth, fevered thighs. He left her breast to return to her mouth, possessing it again. She twisted beneath him as his hand found the softness between her legs, then gave a whimpering moan as his finger stroked the wetness there. Her thighs closed around his hand, and her breath quickened.

He parted her legs with his knee and guided himself inside. This time, there was no resistance, no hesitation. A low, guttural moan began in her throat, then rose to a cry as he began to move within her. As she twisted and rocked beneath him, he rode her, straining in the hot, wet depths. Her fingernails dug into his back, urging him on, while she arched and gasped.

It was as though every sensation was tuned to the feel of his body within hers. She writhed and twisted, trying to reach some distant nirvana, until she felt it. Her animal cries rose as wave after undulating wave of ecstasy flooded through her. He couldn't wait—he was drowning in her. His hands caught her bucking hips as he thrust deeper, then exploded. Somewhere in the distance, he heard himself cry out, and it was over. Her belly quivered under his as he floated back to earth. It was as though he'd died, and this was the peace afterward. He lay there, catching his breath, loath to leave her.

When he looked down, her eyes were still closed, her forehead damp with her sweat. "You must be the next thing to heaven," he whispered.

Still feeling the incredible power of physical union,

she managed to nod. "That was something, wasn't it?" she murmured.

"The best." Afraid she was going to be sorry again, he reluctantly separated from her and rolled to sit up, his back to her. "That's the way I always thought it ought to be, you know." When she didn't say anything more, he felt a momentary loss. "Amanda . . . ?"

"What?"

He sucked in his breath, then exhaled completely. "Just don't expect me to forget it, because I can't. I haven't thought of much else since we were in Ketanah's camp."

She thought he was trying to apologize, that he regretted what had happened, but she knew it had been as much her fault as his. "I guess I just threw myself at you, didn't I?" she managed painfully.

"No." He half turned to look at her. "You're sorry, aren't you?"

She knew she ought to be—she was probably going to rot in hell for it, but she didn't want to lie to him. "No," she said simply. "No." Her nose wrinkled. "Something's burning—Clay, I smell something burning."

"Oh, hell," he muttered, stumbling up. "It's supper." Stuffing his shirttail back into his pants, he quickly fastened them, then started for his campfire. "You'd better wash up again, and I'll see what I can do to save the food. If worst comes to worst, there's always that rattler."

"For you. Me—I've grown downright fond of jerky."

"Liar."

His spit had burned through, dumping the rabbit into the fire. Taking his knife and what was left of the spit, he pulled it out and surveyed the damage, deciding that he could salvage most of it. He'd just wash off the ashes and cut off the charred part, that was all.

"You're in luck—we can still eat it," he told her.

She sat in the shade of the arbor, watching him,

thinking how different he was from any other man she'd known. He was handsome, strong, tough, resourceful, and utterly fearless, and she'd come to believe he could do anything if he put his mind to it. She found herself actually wondering what Big John would have thought of him, if he would have raised hell at the notion of his daughter in Clay McAlester's arms.

As he knelt over the fire, she stood up and walked slowly back to where she'd left the wash pan, passing the dead rattlesnake. With the brush shelter shielding her, she leaned down and wrung out the rag, then began wiping the sweat and dust from her body. She rinsed it out and lifted her chemise to wash where he'd been.

She closed her eyes for a moment, remembering the feel of him, and she was weak all over again. She knew she was a fool and a shameless sinner, no better than those cantina harlots he talked about, she berated herself, but the feeling was still there. Only now it was stronger than ever. Now she knew what she wanted.

She found her discarded dress and pulled it over her head, then tossed the water and carried the pan back. When he looked up, she was almost afraid to meet his gaze. But he was smiling—not smugly—just smiling, and that encouraged her.

"It's pretty good—I've already had a taste of it," he announced, dumping pieces of rabbit onto the tin plate. Taking the pan, he rinsed it out, then wiped it with a cloth. Pouring more water from a canteen into it, he added some coffee, then set the pan in the fire. "I'm trying not to make it too strong for you," he explained.

"That's all right—I don't want any."

"You ought to try things—there's no telling what you might learn to like." Poking around the outer coals, he speared the Indian potatoes and blew the ashes off them before dropping them onto the plate also.

"More yeps?" she asked, raising one eyebrow.

"Afraid so. You don't like them either?"

"They're all right, but I'm beginning to yearn for fried chicken, mashed potatoes, and some real cream gravy—not to mention one of Sally's cherry pies."

"Someday I'll buy you the best dinner in San Antone," he promised. "There's a hotel there that has buffalo steaks two inches thick, and outstanding *frijoles*—" He caught himself almost sheepishly. "Guess that's not as good as fried chicken, is it?"

"No."

At least she returned his smile. "You're a hard woman to please, Amanda—you know that, don't you?" he teased her.

"Not always." As the words came out, she reddened visibly. "I mean—"

"Hey, you don't have to say anything," he said quickly.

There was an awkward silence for a moment, then she reached for the plate. "Which yep is mine?" she asked.

"Take your pick." He squinted up at the sky for a moment. "Well, would you look at that?" he murmured, whistling low.

She looked up nervously, expecting to see Indians. "At what?"

"Clouds."

There were a few cottony fluffs along the horizon. "That doesn't look like enough to make it rain," she observed between bites.

"Maybe—maybe not—but they ought to make it cooler to sleep." He speared a yep and bit a piece off it. "I figure we'll have to hit the trail a little earlier tonight, probably about four or five. Otherwise, we're never going to intercept Sanchez-Torres."

"How far ahead do you think the Cheyenne are now?"

"Not far—a few miles at most. We ought to be tailing pretty close by morning."

"How comforting," she murmured dryly.

"As long as we stay behind them, we'll be all right. How's the rabbit?"

"Pretty good actually—maybe a little dry in places, but better than anything else I've eaten out here."

He pulled off a piece and chewed on it. Leaning back, he studied her, thinking she was truly the prettiest woman he'd ever seen. And less than half an hour ago, she'd lain beneath him willingly. The mere thought of it set his pulse pounding, renewing his desire.

She looked up nervously, then pushed her hair back from her face. "I know—I'm quite a fright."

"No," he said softly, "fright is about the last word I'd use to describe you. I was thinking you're beautiful."

She could feel the telltale blood rush into her cheeks, burning them, and she had to drop her gaze. "I can't be," she mumbled. "Not now."

"No, you are." He continued to regard her lazily, a faint smile on his face. "I was wondering what you could see in a savage like me."

"Well, I don't . . ." She drew a deep breath, stalling, then exhaled. "I was going to say it was because you saved my life," she said finally, "but that's only part of it." When he didn't say anything, she groped for words. "I admire you—truly I do. There aren't ten men in this country who can do what you do, and—"

"Or would want to," he cut in.

"You're so very strong, Clay—so very unafraid."

"Not always."

"But you are. You go out alone, fighting not only these Comancheros, but even the weather, the lack of water, the isolation . . . and . . . and you are so very self-sufficient. You aren't afraid to do what you want to do." The warmth in his blue eyes was unnerving her, making it difficult for her to explain what she wasn't sure she understood herself. "You've overcome so much," she finished lamely.

"No," he said abruptly. "I'm mean, brutal, and un-

couth, Amanda. A killer. Untamed, I think you said.
And as long as I live, there's always going to be part
of me that doesn't want to be civilized, that doesn't
want to live like anybody else."

He was telling her that he wasn't for her, and it
wasn't as though she didn't already know that, yet
there was something within her that wanted to deny it.
Maybe it was that she'd given him her body, that because she had, she had to make herself believe there'd
been a reason.

Her chin came up. "All right, then—you are a savage with positively no redeeming qualities at all.
There—is that what you want to hear?"

"I want to hear the truth."

"I've tried to tell you—to the best of my ability, I've
tried to tell you. Do you *want* people to recoil when
they see you, when they hear your name?"

"I don't care what people think—I'm asking you."

"What do you want me to tell you? That I—?"
She'd nearly said she liked his touch, but she couldn't
quite get it out. "Isn't it enough that I've come to like
you?"

"I guess it'll have to be." He pushed the nearly
empty plate toward her and heaved himself to his feet.
"I've got to take a walk, so you go ahead and finish
up."

As he left her, she had the uneasy feeling that she'd
somehow angered him. He hadn't even poured himself any of his awful coffee. Telling herself she'd been
as honest as she dared, she finished the food, then
took the pan of boiling coffee off the fire. Using a
canteen, she poured water sparingly and wiped the
plate clean. Scooping dirt with her hands, she did as
he'd taught her, snuffing out the fire, covering it to
cut down on the smoke. She dusted her hands on her
skirt.

When she rose, there was no sign of him. She felt a
momentary panic, but the horses and mule were still
there. Besides, he was no Ramon. Whatever could be

said of him, he was a hundred times the man Ramon Sandoval would ever be. Or Patrick Donnelly. Or anyone else she knew, for that matter.

He walked aimlessly above the draw, trying to collect his thoughts before he made a complete fool of himself. He was twenty-eight, almost twenty-nine years old, and he was caught in the throes of his first grand passion like some kid. He hadn't meant it to happen—he'd never meant it to happen. He'd tried to keep it in his mind that she wasn't meant for him, that she was too far above him, that she had too much money, too much breeding to look twice at him. And just because she was alone, at his mercy, he had no right to expect anything of her.

But she'd given herself to him. Not once, but twice. The first time it had been the drums and the mescal. The second she'd been afraid. And even if it happened again, he had no illusions that he could keep her, that once she got back among her own kind she would still want him around. He wasn't the sort of man who could fit in, who could be at ease among her kind of people. It had always been them and him. Until now.

She was a woman who'd make any man proud. She could have a rich man, a powerful man, any man she chose. The likelihood that she'd pick him over any of them was ludicrous, impossible. And if he didn't want to get burned badly, he was going to have to stay away from the fire. He was going to have to get her back to the Ybarra safe and sound, then go on living his life without her. He'd made it alone more than half of his twenty-eight years, and one woman oughtn't to be able to change that.

Well, he felt a little better. Having decided she wasn't for him, he felt a bittersweet relief. He had a job to do, and he was going to do it, and nothing, not even Amanda Ross, was going to stop him.

She was sitting cross-legged in front of the arbor, writing on his pad of paper. As he approached from the side, he was taken again by her fine profile, by the soft halo of auburn hair glinting in the sun. She was so pretty that he almost ached at the sight of her. No, he'd been lying to himself all along, and now he knew it. Above all others, she was the one he wanted.

He backed away, then went up the draw to where he'd tethered the horses and mule. He considered all three for a long moment, then loosened Sarah, the best little Indian pony of his memory, and led her to where Amanda sat. As she looked up curiously, he dropped the rope, then walked off, giving her the space to decide.

At first, she regarded the paint mare uncertainly, then she looked to where Clay stood, his back to her. And suddenly she thought she understood. There was an awful moment of decision, one where it seemed as though her entire life hung in the balance. He wasn't looking at her. He wasn't encouraging her at all. He was just standing there, his body as still as if he'd been turned to stone.

She struggled to stand on legs that seemed almost numb, then reached to take the rope. She wasn't entirely sure what she was supposed to do with it, but in that moment, she knew what she wanted. Turning the mare around, she led it behind the arbor.

Her heart pounding in her chest, her palms damp against the skirt of her dress, she called out, "I don't have any cooking pots or buffalo robes—and I won't skin anything!"

He turned around at that and walked slowly, deliberately back to her. It seemed as though he filled the whole draw, obscuring everything but him. It wasn't until he enveloped her in his arms that she dared to breathe. His blue eyes blurred before hers, and just before his lips touched hers, he murmured softly, "I was beginning to think you were going to turn me down."

She clung giddily to him, giving up her mouth to his, caught in the heady renewal of his passion. For now, there was nothing in the world beyond what he would do to her. Yet even as she felt the eager response of her body to his, she couldn't help wishing a priest had said the proper words.

Crawling cautiously between rocks, Clay expected to find he'd caught up to the Cheyennes they trailed. Instead he was looking down on the largest Indian encampment he'd ever seen. As he adjusted his spyglass, he figured there must be five hundred tipis belonging to Comanches, Kiowas, Kiowa-Apaches, Cheyennes, and a few Arapahoes. At the far end of the camp sentries guarded a huge herd of horses. He'd hit paydirt in a big way. He'd found Quanah.

He lay on his belly, taking it all in, trying to figure out whether he ought to ride in brazenly or get the hell out of there. If it hadn't been for Amanda, he probably would have gone in, shared a pipe in the smoke lodge, and listened for word of Sanchez-Torres. But now he didn't want to risk it. Instead, he scrambled back down the sheltered side of the hill to where Amanda waited with Hannibal and the two ponies.

"You were gone a long time," she said.

"Yeah. Come on—let's go," he decided, mounting the mule.

"We aren't going to make camp?"

"Not here. There's probably a thousand Indians over there."

"What?" Her mouth formed the words "a thousand" silently as they sank in. "Surely not," she said weakly.

"Well, I didn't stick around to count them, but I'd say it's a decent guess. And by the looks of the place, they're still coming in, so I think we'd better ride."

"Yes, of course." She nudged the paint mare up beside him. "Do you think they saw you?"

"I hope not."

"What kind of answer is that?" she asked anxiously. "You're supposed to say they didn't."

"All right—I don't think they did."

"Could you say that with conviction?"

"I just did."

She wasn't exactly persuaded, but she was willing to hope. "So we're going to get help, aren't we?"

"We're heading due west—the way I figure it, Sanchez-Torres will be making a beeline straight across to Big Spring. Now all we've got to do is stop him before he gets here."

She regarded him with troubled eyes. "There's just two of us, Clay. We might get caught between them with nowhere to go."

"I know. For what it's worth, it scares the hell out of me, too."

"A thousand," she repeated, still digesting the enormity of the number. "The Comancheros can't be bringing guns for all of them."

"No. The Quahadis have their women and children with them, and so do some of the others. So I expect Sanchez-Torres will bring a whole wagon train across—guns, ammunition, pots, pans, cloth, sugar— you name it. But if Two Owls can be believed, and I think he can, he's got a war wagon."

"A what?"

"A wagon-mounted Gatling gun," he explained soberly.

"Mother of God," she gasped. "And just what do you think you're going to do about that?"

"Take it out."

Unconvinced, she reasoned, "There's got to be some way to notify the army. Surely it's more their business than yours. I mean—Clay, it's going to take an army to stop them."

She was afraid, and he understood. He didn't want

to die now either. But it was a good two days' ride to
an army post, and sending out a cavalry troop wasn't
going to help. They'd be so far outnumbered it'd be a
massacre. Finally, he answered her.

"There isn't time to put enough cavalry into the
field. Besides, I'm not fighting Comanches or any of
their allies. All I'm going to do is stop the wagons."

"I don't see how you're going to avoid the Indians,"
she countered. "Tell me how you're going to do that."

"I'll cross that bridge when I have to."

"And then what?" she persisted.

"It all depends on what I get into." He knew it
wasn't a satisfactory answer, but it was the truth.
"Look—if worst comes to worst, if it looks like we're
going to be caught out, then we'll just turn back and
throw ourselves on Quanah's hospitality. He won't turn
me away."

"Even if he learns what you've been doing?"

"Even if he learns what we've been doing," he responded patiently. "The *Nermernuh* don't kill *Nermernuh.*"

"I'm not one of them," she muttered. "I'd just feel
better if there were more of us and less of them."

They rode in silence for some time before she spoke
up again. "We aren't going to make camp today," she
decided.

"Not for a while, anyway. Tired?"

"Yes."

"If it looks safe, we'll find a place about noon. Otherwise, I'd just as soon press on."

"You don't have any human weaknesses," she observed dryly.

He regarded her lazily for a moment, then his mouth
curved into a full smile. "You ought to know better
than that."

"Don't you ever get tired?"

"All the time. Look, if you have to, we'll stop for a
few minutes, but then we've got to keep going." When

she didn't respond, he relented. "You're hungry, aren't you?"

"Yes. Very."

Untying the leather sack from his pommel, he leaned to hand it to her. "There's some pemmican in here."

She loosened the drawstring and looked inside. "What is it?"

"The Indian's answer to army rations—dried meat pounded with fruit. That's beef and wild cherries and pinon nuts, which is pretty good. Go on—try it," he urged her. "I made it a couple of weeks ago."

She took a piece and nibbled at it. "Not bad," she decided, surprised. "You've been hoarding this, haven't you?"

"I keep it for when there's nothing else."

"Well, it's a great deal better than hackberry balls and yeps, anyway. And it's —" She stiffened suddenly, and her words died on her lips.

He'd heard it, too—the report of gunfire. He listened intently for several seconds, trying to place the sound. "I'd say somebody's in trouble—real trouble. You'd better stay here while I take a look."

"Oh, no, you don't—you're not leaving me out here alone," she declared stoutly.

"Amanda—"

"Well, you're not."

Rather than argue, he dug his spurs into the mule and took off westward, leaving her to follow him. He just hoped that there wasn't anybody else out there who'd heard the shots. He sure as hell didn't want to be caught between Comanches and Comancheros, not on Hannibal. The mule spooked too easily.

Foam flecks flew back, spotting his buckskin pants, as the animal stretched into a full gallop. As he gained the top of a rock-strewn hill, Clay reined in and reached for his spyglass, sweeping the horizon with it. A sick knot formed in the pit of his stomach as he recognized Hap Walker and a young ranger named Rios.

Besieged by Mexicans, Hap lay behind a boulder

while Rios reloaded, both unaware that they were about to be overrun from a limestone ledge above them. And Clay was too far away to get off a good shot. As Amanda caught up, he handed her the Whitney. "Here—take this and use it if you have to." Before she could ask any questions, he used his reins like a quirt, and the tired mule fought back, rearing.

"Damn you, Hannibal!" he shouted, pulling it up short, then turning it in a circle. He dug his spurs in, and this time the animal shot forward at a dead run.

As he rode hell for leather, he unsheathed the rifle and fired it, hoping to draw the Mexicans' attention. One of the men on the ledge drew a bead on him and pulled the trigger, warning the two rangers. Rios ducked back beneath the ledge, where he crouched, waiting for his chance. As a sombrero tilted over the edge, he fired and missed. Hap Walker crawled further under the rock overhang.

Now all eyes were on Clay. The Mexicans below the rangers scrambled down the hill toward their mounts. Rios fired his Henry rifle, getting one, who pitched forward, then rolled to the bottom, where he lay screaming for help. Two of his compadres got behind their horses, using them for cover. Above, a Mexican leaned over to shoot at Hap, and as the bullet ricocheted off the boulder, Rios stood and squeezed off a shot. The impact knocked the fellow backward.

The men behind the horses targeted Clay, popping up to fire, then ducking back down. As Amanda watched, heart in throat, he went over Hannibal's side, dropping from sight. Thinking he'd been hit, she kicked the paint mare frantically, and tried to get to him. Then she saw him fire his rifle from beneath Hannibal's neck. One of the Mexicans' horses squealed and reared as the bullet hit. The animal took off, then dropped to its knees, mortally wounded. Clay's next shot got its master.

Two Mexicans left on the ledge retreated out of Rios's range, then turned their guns on Clay. He returned fire from under Hannibal's belly, missing. Amanda looked up, saw the ledge, then wheeled the paint pony as though she fled. Behind the hill, she dismounted and crept upward, shotgun in hand.

The remaining Mexican below had had enough. He swung up into his saddle and tried to make a run for it. Clay shot at him, but the bullet went wide. Now he had to pursue—he couldn't risk letting anyone get to the Comancheros before him.

Rios stood up then, and Hap Walker barely shouted "Watch out!" before one of the Mexicans on the ledge shot the ranger. Holding his shoulder, Rios stumbled back, calling out, "I'm hit!"

Thinking they'd got both rangers, the two men on the ledge turned to come back down the hill. Amanda cocked one hammer carefully, waiting for her chance. Bracing the shotgun against her shoulder, she held her breath. One of the Mexicans saw her and raised his pistol as she pulled the trigger. The roar shattered her ears, and the kick sent her staggering. As the first man fell, the other fired. A piece of rock flew up. She cocked the other hammer, closed her eyes, and squeezed. She heard the explosion, then the silence was deafening. When she dared to look, both men lay motionless and blood was everywhere. One was utterly unrecognizable.

Shaking uncontrollably, she sank to her knees, covered her face, and wept. It was there that Rios found her. Still holding his shoulder, he leaned over and picked up the shotgun.

"Where did you come from?" he demanded.

"I don't know—I'm just with McAlester," she answered. "Who are you?"

"Romero Rios." He smiled, flashing a nice set of white teeth. "Texas Ranger."

"Amanda Ross—Miss Ross." She saw the blood between his fingers. "You're hurt."

"Not bad." He looked at the dead men, then back to her. "You did this?"

"Yes." She wiped her wet face with the back of her hand, then stood up. "Where's McAlester?"

"He was going after the last one." He looked her over, then reached to take her elbow. "Come on—I've got to get back to Hap. They got him pretty bad—shattered his leg, I think." As they started down the hill, he turned sideways to help her. "Watch out for loose rocks."

"You don't know how glad I am to see you," she told him gratefully.

"The surprise is mine, I guess. It's hard to imagine a woman being with Clay—real hard. Usually they kind of stay away from him."

"Well, it's a long story—a very long story," she said wearily. "We were—are—looking for Comancheros."

He was looking at her oddly, as though he didn't quite believe her. She sighed, then tried to explain as briefly as possible. "He didn't really have much choice, Mr. Rios. It was a matter of leaving me to die in the desert or taking me with him. Please—I'm too tired to even think. We broke camp at sundown last night, and I've been riding ever since."

"I can believe that," he murmured wryly. "We rode together a couple of times, and I almost didn't survive. When we found a trail, he didn't eat, he didn't sleep, and we covered more than two hundred miles on one canteen of water. Damned if I know how he did it. I thought I was going to shrivel up and die. But," he added, "we got what we went after."

She heard two shots in the distance, then silence, and she wanted to cry all over again. "I just hope he doesn't get himself killed," she said finally.

"Clay always comes back."

"I hope so—I sincerely hope so."

"He will. He's not like the rest of us."

When they reached Hap Walker, the ranger captain's eyes were closed, his teeth gritted in pain. Around the blood-soaked tear in his pants, his leg was already swelling. She bent over him, feeling the leg, trying not to think of McAlester.

"Do you think the bone is broken?" she asked.

He opened his eyes, then forced a smile when he saw her. "If it didn't hurt like hell, I'd think I'd gone to heaven," he murmured.

"Can you move it?"

"Yeah."

But when he tried, she could see where the bullet had smashed through his thigh, taking bits of bone with it. It was going to be awhile before Hap Walker walked again, if ever. She looked up at Rios.

"Do you have any water?"

"Water be damned," Hap muttered. "Get the whiskey."

"I'm just going to wash the wound."

"Use whiskey."

"What?"

"Burn it out."

"With whiskey?"

"Yeah. But give me a shot of it first."

In the end she compromised. After cutting away the bloody cloth with his knife, she gave him a drink from the flask Rios found in his saddlebags, then washed the wound first with water, clearing the debris from it. After some hesitation, she poured a little of the spirits over it.

"What we need is something to splint it with. And then there's the problem of getting him down from here," she told Rios.

"We'd better wait for Clay."

"What about your shoulder?"

"I am all right."

"Nonsense. You're losing blood, Mr. Rios."

He raised his arm, wincing. "Nothing's broken," he assured her. "I've been hurt worse."

"It needs to be cleaned and staunched."

"You don't want to end up like Nate Hill," Hap reminded him. "They can't cut off your shoulder."

Rios shrugged. Reaching with his good arm, he tried to pull off his coat, but couldn't. Moving behind him, Amanda peeled his shirt and coat down from his neck, then eased them off the shoulder. Picking up the canteen, she started to pour from it, then changed her mind. There was more whiskey than water.

"Have you got a handkerchief?"

"Yes."

Rios took a wadded piece of cloth from his coat pocket and handed it to her. She soaked it liberally from Hap Walker's flask, then pressed it over the flesh wound. Pulling his coat and shirt back up, she buttoned them, holding the flimsy pad in place. When she was done, she stood up and flexed aching shoulders. There was still no sign of McAlester.

"You've got gentle hands, ma'am," Hap Walker murmured. He tried to twist his head to look downward. "Clay—"

"He'll be back," she answered, trying to sound as confident as Rios.

"Yeah," he said, lying back. "He's got more lives than a cat." Seemingly reassured, he closed his eyes again.

It seemed as though they waited an eternity, none of them speaking again. Finally, Rios walked back around the hill for another look at the men she'd killed. She sat there, her arms holding her knees, her eyes on the horizon, until she saw him. He was still riding the mule, but he was leading a horse, and a man's body dangled over its fancy Mexican saddle. Tears of relief streamed down her face.

The exhausted mule walked slowly, taking its time, but that was all right now. Clay was back, and he was whole. At the bottom of the hill he dismounted slowly, then turned to cut the ropes holding the body. Amanda slipped and slid down the rocky hillside to greet him.

"You're all right," she said foolishly.

"Yeah."

"I was scared to death, Clay—scared to death."

His arms closed around her, and she stood there, her arms around his waist, her head buried in his chest. He held her, savoring the feel of her body against his. When he looked over her shoulder, Romero Rios was watching them. Reluctantly, he set her back.

"Hap all right?"

"He's got a broken leg. We're going to have to carry him down somehow." She hesitated, then blurted out, "Were these your Comancheros?"

"Uh-huh. Sanchez-Torrez hired 'em to herd the horses back. So before we leave here, we're going to have to do something with the bodies, cover them up somehow so the buzzards won't give everything away. I'd like for him to think they made it to Quanah's camp."

"Mr. Rios is hurt, too."

"Bad?"

"Well, I don't think he can dig any graves."

"Damn." Looking up at the cloudless sky, he shaded his eyes. "In this heat the buzzards will be here before nightfall. All right, then," he decided, "we'll just have to press on, but first I've got to see Hap."

"Well, it's about time you reared your ugly head," Walker said when Clay reached him. "I was beginning to think you'd got lost." He tried to pull himself up into a sitting position, but the pain in his leg nearly took his breath away. "Hand me the damned whiskey, will you?"

"You're half drunk, Hap."

"And I aim to get all the way there." He took a long pull on the flask, then closed his eyes as the fire rolled down to his gut. "I shouldn't have let 'em get me," he muttered. "I got careless."

"No."

Walker opened his eyes again, this time to look at Amanda. "I know I'm not dreamin', so there's got to be an explanation for why she's here. Last time I knew she was leaving with Sandoval."

"He abandoned her half a day's ride north of the

Overland Road, Hap. By the time I found her, she was in a bad way. I knew I couldn't afford the time to go back to Stockton, so I took her to Ketanah's camp up by Castle Rock for a few days, that's all."

"You took her to a damned Comanche camp?"

"Yeah. Anyway, I got an earful about Sanchez-Torres, so I came down here to cut him off." He paused, then added, "There's probably a thousand Indians waiting for him between here and Big Spring."

"Hell, there ain't that many Comanches," Hap protested.

"Every Indian not on the reservation from the Rio Grande to Kansas is coming to join Quanah."

"And me with lead in m' leg," the older man muttered. "Well, I guess Texas is going to burn like hell, no two ways about it." He turned his head toward Rios. "What do you think, Romero—can you ride to Fort Griffin?"

"Yes."

"Tell 'em to get word to General Augur he's got to put Mackenzie into the field."

Clay shook his head. "Mackenzie can't get here, Hap."

"He can damned well try. Besides, I'm not going to have the army say we didn't tell 'em."

"I'm going to take the wagons out—I can do it."

"How?"

"I'll find a way."

The older man's eyes met Clay's for a long moment, then he looked away. "I don't want to lose you, boy."

"Yeah, well, I don't kill easy—remember?"

"One of these days your luck's going to run out."

Clay shrugged. "One of these days everybody's luck's going to run out." He looked to Rios. "While you're over in Shackleford County, you'd better get a warrant for the arrest of Ramon Sandoval—and one for Sam McKittrick, while you're at it."

"McKittrick!" Hap choked out. "For what?"

"He's in thick with Sanchez-Torres. Looks like he's bankrolling him."

"Well, I'll be a son of a—" The older man stopped midsentence and held his breath while he fought the searing pain. "All I can say is you'd damned well better be able to prove it, or we'll both be out of a job."

"I've got a letter here somewhere that ought to do for a start." Clay fumbled in his coat pocket, then tossed the folded paper to Rios. "Here—show that to a judge."

"What am I suppposed to say about Sandoval?" the younger ranger wanted to know. "How do you want him charged?"

"With the attempted murder of Amanda Ross." Turning back to Hap Walker, Clay told him, "You lie low until I get back, then we'll splint that leg and get you down from here. Here—" He unholstered one of the new Colts and handed it over, then unbuckled one of the cartridge belts. "That ought to hold you."

"Thanks."

"Got enough whiskey?"

"I don't know why you'd ask—you never carry any," the older man responded testily.

"No, but I've got some peyote."

"I'd rather bite on a stick," Hap muttered.

"You're a contrary old cuss—you know that, don't you?"

Amanda stood there, wishing the captain could somehow dissuade him, knowing he couldn't. And she couldn't just sit and wait, terrified he wasn't coming back. She swallowed, trying to down the lump rising in her throat. "Please . . ." As he turned to her, she knew nothing she could say would keep him there. "I'd like to go with you," she said finally.

"Damn it, boy—you'd be out of your mind!" Walker exploded.

"You'll be safer here looking after Hap."

"Please—I cannot stand the wait, the not knowing."

She passed her tongue over dry lips. "I think I've earned that much at least."

"Don't let her, son."

But Clay was looking at her as though he and she were the only two people on earth. She met his gaze steadily until he actually smiled.

"Yeah," he said softly, "yeah, I reckon you have."

"There they are."

She followed his gaze across the mesquite-dotted plain and counted nine canvas-covered wagons lumbering slowly behind teams of obviously tired oxen. Nearly a dozen armed guards with rifles lying across their saddles rode beside the wagons.

"They look like they're prepared for trouble," she murmured.

"Yeah." He took out his spyglass for a closer view, training it on the lead wagon. "There's old Sanchez-Torres himself. This is one trade he's not trusting to anybody else." He handed the glass to her. "He's the one on the right."

She put it to her eye and moved it around until she saw the old man. He was squat, dark, and fat, but otherwise unremarkable. As she watched him, he was talking to a companion, sharing a laugh. She lowered the glass.

"He doesn't appear very dangerous, does he? He looks like someone's grandfather."

"If you'd ever seen what he's done, you'd change your mind. When I was with the State Police, I buried what was left of a man he thought had betrayed him." He considered the lowering sun for a moment, then straightened in his saddle. "We've got a while to wait. I don't figure on going in until they're settled in for the night."

"What if they catch you?"

"Then I'm not coming out alive. In that case, you

hightail it back to Hap. Broken leg or not, he'll get you to Griffin."

"You make it sound so matter-of-fact."

"It is. I either win or I lose." He looked at her, and his mouth twisted. "I don't plan on losing, Amanda."

"No, of course not."

"Come on—let's go make a cold camp and eat."

"All right." She wanted to cry out that it might be his last day on earth, that he had no right to act as though it made no difference whether he lived or died, but instead she was letting him get away with it. "All right," she repeated.

He didn't say anything more for a long time, and when he did, it seemed to have nothing to do with what he faced. "Hap's a good man," he said finally. "He wants to settle down." When she didn't respond, he continued, adding, "He'd make a woman a good husband. He's sown all his wild oats, and he's old enough to know what he wants. He's the kind of man who could sit in church every Sunday, the kind who could teach his kids to be as honest and decent as he is."

"Why are you telling me this? I barely know the man."

"You could do a lot worse."

It dawned on her what he was doing then. He didn't have any brother, and in his misguided Comanche logic, he was expecting Hap Walker to take care of her. Her already taut nerves couldn't bear it.

"I'm not a squaw you can pass around," she snapped. "I'll pick my own husband, thank you."

"There's a kindness in him, and he likes you," he went on, unperturbed.

"I don't want to hear this—do you hear me? I don't want to hear this!"

"He'll go after Sandoval for you."

"Of all the thick-headed—"

"I'm just pointing out a few things to consider."

"Well, don't. You aren't going to die—remember?"

He'd bungled the matter, and he knew it. "Nothing's forever, Amanda. Not me. Not you. Not Hap. No one."

"Do we have to talk about this?" she asked wearily.

"No." Abruptly, his expression lightened. "I don't want to talk about it either. I want to find a place where we can just sit awhile and you can tell me again all about Boston."

"Boston?"

"Yeah. I've never been there." His mouth curved into a boyish smile that made her heart ache. "I figure we'll eat and you'll paint me some word pictures. I want to know what you were like when you were growing up."

It didn't make any sense, but she was willing to humor him. "I see," she managed. "Well, there isn't all that much to tell, but—"

"Not here. When we stop."

"All right."

He chose a limestone escarpment overlooking the flat expanse of a sun-baked valley cut eons ago by some forgotten stream. After watering and tethering the animals out of sight, he carried a canteen and parfleche to where Amanda waited. Dropping down beside her, he broke the tallow seal with his knife and began slicing the dried meat, dividing it between them. He pushed a container of honey toward her.

"Don't tell me you don't like this, or I'll know you're lying."

"I like it, but I'm not very hungry."

He stared across the flat land toward a small rise of hills made purple by the lowering sun. "When I come back, there's going to be all hell breaking loose behind me. I figure we might not be eating again until midday tomorrow."

"It's not that far back to Captain Walker."

"No, but if we're followed, we'll have to lose 'em first, and that'll mean doubling back for Hap. So you'd better eat while you've got the chance."

"All right."

Somehow she managed to get most of her food
down. It was he who didn't eat. Instead, he sat there,
his eyes distant, seemingly focused on those hills, his
body leaning forward, his arms clasping his knees. She
watched the straight, even profile of his face, wondering what occupied his thoughts. Finally, she could
stand it no longer.

"You're worried, aren't you?" she asked.

"No. I was just thinking how red the sun is going
down. Blood red, Ekatonah would have called it."

"What was she like?"

"A mother. She fussed over me a lot, and she worried that she'd lose me when I went down the war
trail." He eased his shoulders, settling them, then
added, "She lost her own son in a raid the year before
Sansoneah brought me home to her. In her grief she
wanted to love me."

"Then you were lucky to have her."

"And him. He was strong, disciplined—yeah, disciplined is how I'd describe him. Once when there was
almost no water, when his tongue was black from
thirst, he killed a Crow Warrior who tried to take the
last few drops so I could have them. Not him. Not
Ekatonah. Me. When we staggered into camp, he had
to be carried to the spring, and because he couldn't
swallow, they soaked his body in the water."

She couldn't think of anything to say, so she let him
ramble on, listening as he spoke of Indians she'd never
know, of a life she would never understand. She heard
of bowhunting antelope, of stampeding buffalo over
gorges, of journeying from northern Texas to far below
the Rio Grande.

Abruptly, he stopped, then shook his head. "I don't
belong here, Amanda—I'm like that wasteland out
there, with The People on one side, the whites on the
other, and nothing in between."

"You don't have to make a choice, Clay. You can go
somewhere else until it's over," she said quietly.

"No. I'm not the civilized fellow you want me to be,

Amanda. There's always going to be part of me that wants to be free. I learned that in Chicago."

"You were a boy—you didn't give yourself a chance. You were living with someone who didn't understand you."

"I never stopped dreaming of this, Amanda." He turned to her, his expression sober. "What did you dream of when you were in Boston?"

"I don't know. Oh, that's not entirely true, I suppose. When I first got there, I used to go to this church near our house, and I'd light a candle for Papa. But it wasn't for his soul, as Aunt Kate thought—I was praying for God to send him back. It took me nearly a year to admit to myself that such miracles didn't happen anymore. I'd read about Jesus raising Lazarus, you see, and I didn't see why he couldn't bring back Papa."

"So you lost your faith."

"No. I came to accept that God may or may not give us what we ask."

"A good lesson."

"I suppose so."

"You were going to tell me about Boston," he recalled.

"What do you want to know about it?"

"Anything you want to tell me. What you liked to do there. What you hated. What it was like growing up rich there."

"That's a tall order, Clay."

He stretched out across from her and propped his chin with his elbow, watching her. "Start anywhere you want."

"Well, I went to St. Agnes school, where we wore black cotton dresses, black cotton stockings, and starched white smocks over them. Every day we wore the same ugly things. Then one day as we were filing into Mass, I heard one of the altar boys whisper, 'There goes Mama and all the little penguins,' and I started to laugh, and I couldn't stop. Afterward, I had to listen to the priest scold me for unseemly levity, then Sister Mary Margaret sent a note home to Aunt Kate."

"If that's the worst thing you ever did, I expect God's already forgiven you."

"No, it's not the worst."

Afraid she was going to tell him she regretted sinning with him, he persisted, "Tell me something more about Boston."

"It's a big city. If you go there, you can see the church where the lanterns signaled to Paul Revere. And you can see his house, though where he put all those children is a mystery to me."

"What else?"

"About Boston or me?"

"You."

"I excelled in literature and mathematics, but did poorly in needlework—I don't know what you want me to say."

"Anything. I like the sound of your voice," he murmured.

"I sing soprano."

"Know any lullabies?"

"What? You mean like 'Lullaby and Goodnight'?"

"Yeah."

"No." He was so close that she could feel the warmth of his body, and she knew if he touched her, she'd want everything he could do to her, and she knew also it wasn't the time nor the place, not with so much at stake. "No, I don't sing softly enough."

"That's about all I remember from my mother. A lullaby. That and she smelled of roses—or at least I think she did. It might have been someone else with the roses."

"They're my favorite flower. I like the big red ones best, but I'd take any of them."

He reached out, touching her arm lightly with his fingertips, tracing along the sleeve of her dress. An involuntary shudder went through her. She sat very still, afraid to move lest her composure shatter like an eggshell. The back of his hand brushed across her breast, and her nipple tautened.

"Amanda," he whispered.

"What?" The word came out like a sob.

"I don't think I've ever wanted anything as much as I want you now."

"There isn't time."

"Shhhh." His fingers touched her lips, silencing her. "I just have to go in while it's dark—and the night's only begun," he said softly.

Knowing there might never be another time for them, she allowed him to pull her down beside him. As his mouth sought hers, she twined her arms around his neck, pressing her body against his. And when he left her lips to trace hot, eager kisses along her jaw to her ear, she whispered, "Just love me tonight, Clay—just hold me tonight."

This time there was no furtive coupling, no furious passion. Only the bittersweet tenderness of a night that might be their last. He caressed and explored, heightened every sensation, taking and giving full measure, until she clung to him, gasping and sobbing, as he came within her. And when it was over, he lay back, holding her, watching the stars light the sky.

She must've fallen asleep like that, for it seemed far too soon when he nudged her. She sat up groggily, then came fully awake with the realization that he was dressed, that he had his gunbelt on. When she turned away, she could see the twinkle of lanterns below. She felt him press something into her hand.

"Give me three-quarters of an hour," he said, his voice low. "If you haven't heard anything, and if I'm not back by then, take Sarah and ride back to Hap."

"I don't—" She looked down, seeing the white face of a watch. "But—"

"No, listen to me. I figure it'll take me ten or fifteen minutes to get down there on foot, ten or fifteen minutes to look around, and maybe that much to get back."

"What are you going to do?"

"It depends on how they've got everything arranged. Right now, I'm just going to take a look around."

"If they catch you—"

"If they catch me, don't come down—you hear that? Don't come down."

"Yes, but—"

"I'm leaving the shotgun with you. If you see me hightailing it up here with some Comancheros behind me, don't hesitate to use it. I've got it loaded up for you, and here's more shells." His hand closed over hers for a moment. "And if it looks like they're going to capture you, you might want to save a shot for yourself. Otherwise, they'll sell you right along with the guns."

She held on. "Don't go—please. There's got to be some other way—there's got to."

He lifted her chin with his free hand. "Whatever you do, don't come down. Go over the back and out that way." Leaning, he brushed his lips against hers, then drew back. "I don't have any regrets, Amanda—not now."

Before she could stop him, he was going. In the darkness she could hear rocks slide, a mumbled curse, then silence. She couldn't even tell if he got all the way to the bottom safely. Crossing herself, she whispered a prayer, then picked up the shotgun and found herself a place to sit.

In other circumstances she could have discovered beauty in the small yellow balls of light, but not now. Now they represented an alien enemy, something so vile that the struggle was literally between good and evil. And Clay McAlester, heathen, savage, and anything else people called him, on this night at least, was the only man standing between an uneasy peace and an outright bloodbath.

He'd skinned his hand when he lost his footing, but otherwise he'd made it down all right. He stood for a moment, taking stock of the wagons. Sanchez-Torres hadn't bothered bunching them defensively, which was going to make everything more difficult. Now he was going to have to figure out which ones he had to hit.

Most of the camp was quiet as he approached, but somewhere someone, probably one of the guards, played a mouth harp. Another man shouted at him, telling him to pipe down, and an argument ensued. Moving toward the far end, Clay walked carefully, his moccasins silently scuffing the dirt. Twice when he heard noises, he stopped, once to check again that he'd brought the powder, the oiled rags, and the ramrod he'd broken into five pieces. They were all in his coat pocket.

Just before he reached the shadows, a guard stepped out, took a long drag on a cigarillo, then tossed the butt. Clay froze, his hand on his Bowie knife. If the fellow moved any closer, he was going to have to cut his throat. He couldn't risk anything else. The Mexican looked straight at him, then walked on down the line of wagons. He must've been more than half blind, Clay decided.

Another man came out, spoke to the first one, waved him on, then walked a few feet to relieve himself in the dirt. Clay crouched low, ready to take him, but he moved on also. The mouth harp stopped.

He gained the shelter of a wagon and crawled underneath. Feeling along the boards with his hand, he was able to thrust his fingers inside. He touched the heavy, solid sacks, and guessed he'd found flour. Dropping flat onto his belly, he edged his way past the wagon tongue, crawled several feet in the open, then went under the next one. This time, he felt something wooden and solid, which could either be boxes of guns or ammunition. And he had to know which.

Someone walked past, but didn't stop. As Clay watched, he climbed into a wagon at the other end. A woman giggled, and he knew there probably weren't any guns in that one. He pulled himself up for a better look and felt inside for the boxes. They were long.

As he was groping along the second wagon tongue,

he came face-to-face with a lean, rangy dog. The animal bared its fangs and growled low. If ever he needed wolf medicine, it was now. Rather than cower, he stood up, staring the dog in the eye. It couldn't have been for more than a few seconds, but it seemed like an eternity. The growl faded to a whimper, and the animal turned and hiked off, its tail down between its hind legs.

The third wagon held what he'd been looking for—barrels. He felt along the staves, then drew back his hand, smelling his fingers. Gunpowder. Paydirt. A grim satisfaction took hold. Old Sanchez-Torres might be one wily Comanchero, but this time he'd been downright stupid. He'd put his gunpowder in the middle of his line. And that was one hell of a mistake. Clay backed away.

"Que dow!" somebody called out.

He'd been spotted, and he was on foot. The guard he'd seen earlier grabbed for him, and Clay dropped his rifle while coming up with the Bowie knife. There was a low, guttural sound, then a *whoosh* as the Comanchero fell to the ground. But he'd got him too late. Two others were running toward him.

Never make a stand if you can't hold it, Sansoneah once told him. He scooped up his rifle, ducked between two wagons, grabbed a horse, and swung up by its mane. Now it was do or die. They knew he was there, and they'd be sure to track him. Only right now they didn't know whether he was one man or ten, and he was going to make damned sure they didn't find out.

He kicked the horse and turned it, galloping the length of the wagons, coming up the other side, whooping a Comanche war cry, as men ducked for cover. At the end he dropped from the animal, hit it on the rump, and sent it back. A dozen shots hit, killing it. Now they were all shouting at one another.

Clay knelt, took out the oiled rag, the powderhorn, and a piece of ramrod. Sprinkling the powder on the rag, he used the ramrod to push it up the rifle barrel.

Just as they saw him, he fired at the third wagon. The shot split the air, then the rag flamed as the rod hit a keg of gunpowder. The first explosion shattered the wagon, then spread to the other kegs, lighting the night sky with one fireball after another.

Reloading, Clay fired again, this time into the next wagon. It caught on fire, but didn't explode, telling him it was trade goods. While those Comancheros still standing tried to move wagons away from the conflagration, Clay's third shot got the ammunition. The shells started going off, igniting a chain reaction. Debris from the gunpowder kegs rained down, and flames began engulfing the canvas covers on all the remaining wagons.

With the screams of men and the popping of bullets filling the night air behind him, Clay started walking back to Amanda. He ought to feel exultation or something very like it, but he didn't. It wasn't lost on him that it had been Sansoneah who'd taught him to make fire like that. And now he'd used it to destroy that last hope of The People. As he crossed that ancient plain, the bridge was burning behind him. The drums would never call him again. He could never dream of going back again, and for that he felt an acute sadness.

At the bottom of the layered limestone hill he turned back for one last look. Flames licked the bare canvas supports, making them stand out like iron ribs above collapsed, burning wagons. If his Aunt Jane had been here, she'd have said it looked like Armageddon.

When she'd seen the fireballs shoot into the air, Amanda had panicked, certain no one could have survived the inferno. For a long moment she'd sat there, too stunned to move. And then the tears came, pouring from her eyes, the sobs racking her soul. She cried so hard she couldn't see as she stumbled toward the horses. Somehow she managed to get into Sarah's saddle and make it to the base of the escarpment. She forced herself to look toward the fire, and her heart nearly stopped.

Silhouetted against the fiery sky, Clay McAlester walked almost slowly, his head bowed, his rifle in his hand. He stopped, turned back for a few seconds, then came on. He'd made it out. Somehow he was walking out of hell unscathed.

She nudged the horse out the shadows. "Are you all right?" she managed to ask.

He looked up and nodded. "Yeah. Let's get Hap and head for Fort Griffin. As soon as I tie up a few things there, I'll take you to the Ybarra."

Acutely conscious of the man beside her, Amanda smoothed the dress she'd reluctantly borrowed from Louise Baxter over her knees. She was going home, she told herself, and that was all that mattered. No, that wasn't true. More than anything she wanted to marry Clay McAlester. But something was wrong between them now, and she was at a loss to understand what.

Maybe it was that Hap Walker and Romero Rios were with them. Maybe the reason Clay hadn't touched her since that night he'd blown up the Comanchero wagons was because he didn't want them to think badly of her. She racked her brain, trying to come up with an answer, but she was afraid she grasped at straws. For whatever reason, the intense intimacy they'd shared on the trail was gone. And the closer they'd gotten to Ybarra-Ross, the harder it was to conceal the hurt she felt.

Oh, sometimes she recognized desire in his eyes, but his manner now was guarded, almost distant, as though he were trying to forget what had happened between them, as though none of it mattered. But it did to her, and fool that she was, she desperately wanted him to tell her he loved her. And then she wanted him to tell the world he loved her—in church. Instead, he was turning away.

It began when they'd stopped first at Fort Griffin, where they'd bought the wagon, and continued later at Stockton, where Louise had smothered her with insin-

cerity. At both places Clay had behaved with an almost
ludicrous propriety, as though he wanted to protect her
reputation. It had been she who shamelessly sought
him out at the Comanche Springs, and then before he
could even kiss her, Romero Rios had come looking
for him. She, who'd prided herself on being sensible,
had cried herself to sleep that night.

She cast a sidewise glance at him, taking in the
handsome profile, the set of his shoulders, and she had
to close her eyes to hide the longing that washed over
her. Surely, he had to feel it also. Surely, now that they
were home, he would love her again.

Beside her, Clay kept his eyes on the narrow, rutted
lane leading to the house. Since midafternoon the day
before, they'd been on her land. Her land. Despite
what he'd told Hap earlier, he'd never really thought
all that much about the Ybarra. Now it was overwhelming him, making him all too aware of how little
he had to offer her.

He knew she thought she wanted him now, but he
was almost equally sure that once she was among her
own kind again, she'd come to regret everything that
had happened between them. She'd been dependent on
him before, but that was over. Then she'd been in his
world; now she was returning to hers, and he knew he
was going to lose her. Sooner or later he was going to
lose her. She had the money, the ranch, the big house,
the good breeding. And before long she was going to
figure out that she didn't need a half-wild ranger.

That was already eating at his soul. At night he lay
awake, burning for want of her, yearning to hold her,
telling himself he hadn't had the right when he'd taken
her, that he didn't have the right now. No, he could
spare both of them a lot of pain if he just got out of her
life. Then she could find someone of her own kind,
someone who'd fit in at the Ybarra.

He looked up, seeing the tile-capped walls surround-
ing a big, sprawling house that seemed to rise from nowhere, like an Atlantis in the desert. It was an adobe

palace that made his aunt's neat, lace-curtained house in Chicago seem paltry and insignificant.

He straightened up on the hard, wood seat, stretching the tired muscles in his back and shoulders. No, he thought he'd prepared himself—but he'd never expected anything like this. For the difference between them, she might as well have been royalty. Even if she'd marry him, it would be like the queen of England choosing a footman for consort.

"Mighty big place, the Ybarra," Hap observed, breaking into Clay's thoughts.

"Yeah."

"A man could get lost in it."

"Yeah." Clay sucked in his breath, then let it out slowly. "I'd say so."

Hap turned his attention to Amanda. "This about the way you remember it?"

"Yes, but it seems like Mama ought to be there waiting for me. Instead, it's going to be Alessandro Sandoval—and Ramon."

Hap leaned forward. "I reckon you got a little surprise for Ramon—it ought to make for an interesting family reunion."

"I hope so." She fidgeted with a lace-edged handkerchief, twisting it around her finger. "I want to see his face when you put the handcuffs on him," she admitted. "It'll be almost worth everything I've been through. I want to see his face when he realizes I've survived."

"When it dawns on 'em they're going to jail, they get a funny look to 'em, don't they, Clay?"

"Usually when they see him, they just go for their guns," Rios pointed out. "I don't think it's jail crossing their minds. It's survival."

"Yeah, I reckon that's right," Walker conceded. "Maybe you ought to make the arrest, Romero."

"Sandoval's mine, Hap." The faint, wry smile twisted Clay's mouth. "I want to enjoy that look."

"You're going to kill him," Rios decided dispassionately.

"Maybe. If he goes for his gun."

Walker was more cautious. "There's no telling what you're going to run into. His old man may want a say in it, and you don't know but what there's a dozen more that'll stand with him. They ain't seen Miss Ross in years, and Sandoval probably hired 'em." He shifted his weight on the hard seat, moving his leg. "Damn," he muttered. "I know one thing—I ain't going to be much use to you."

"You should have had the doctor at Fort Griffin look at that leg," Clay said.

"Why? Not much anybody can do about it—bullet's out, splint's on—takes time to heal, that's all. I just appreciate having a place to stay while I'm laid up." He moved again, wincing. "Be kind of good to be out of the saddle for a while. I was beginning to grow to it."

"You are welcome to stay as long as you want," Amanda was quick to assure him.

"Mighty kind of you—might be taking you up on that."

Somehow the notion that Hap was going to be there did nothing to improve Clay's mood. If anything, it made him more tense. "I don't know why you didn't want to stay at Griffin or Stockton," he muttered. "You've got no business being out on that leg at your age."

"At my age?" Hap fairly howled.

"Yeah."

"You got some sort of burr under your tail, son?"

"Maybe."

"Danged if I know what ails you, but you're turning downright mean on me," the older man complained. "You've not said ten straight pleasant words since you blew up Sanchez-Torres. You know what I think? I think it's eating on you. You got some notion you betrayed the whole Comanche nation, don't you?"

"I'm tired, that's all."

But Hap wasn't buying it. "It ain't you putting them on the reservation—it's them. If they wasn't thieving, murdering—"

"I said it wasn't that," Clay muttered defensively.

"Then I'd like to know what it is. You're a hero, son, and looking at you, a man'd think you lost the damned war."

Before Clay could respond, Romero Rios spoke up. "You notice anything odd, Miss Ross?" he asked suddenly.

"Yes." Her eyes scanned the wall again before she answered, "The place looks deserted."

"You tell anybody you were coming?" Hap wanted to know.

"No. I was hoping to surprise Ramon."

They were almost to the tall, iron-spiked gate when a man stepped out into the wagon's path. He waved his arms, signaling for them to stop. Amanda stood up.

"I'm Amanda Ross, and this is my home," she declared crisply. "Please inform Alessandro Sandoval I have arrived."

He didn't move.

"I said I was Amanda Ross," she repeated more loudly.

He still didn't move—not until he heard McAlester cock the shotgun. Then he stepped aside.

"Answer the lady," Clay ordered coldly.

"Señor Sandoval is not here."

"What about his son?"

The man shrugged. "They are both gone."

"Where?"

"They don't tell me."

Hap Walker leaned forward to address the fellow. "Son, you're talking to the law, and I'm holding a warrant for the arrest of Ramon Sandoval. Now, unless you want Mr. McAlester to blast you into the next life, you'd better get to talking—real fast."

The man darted a quick look at Clay, then back to Hap. "They don't tell me anything." But as the shotgun leveled on his chest, he licked his lips, then blurted out, "They quarrel, the old man and the boy."

"Yeah?"

"Ramon left two days ago."

"And?" Clay prompted.

"Alessandro left yesterday."

"For where?"

"They don't tell me." He looked down at the two barrels, then wavered. "Sandro took five men with him, and he was in a hurry. Somebody said he went after Ramon, that Ramon was in trouble and was going to Mexico."

"Damn," Hap muttered under his breath.

"Two days ago—Ramon left two days ago?" Amanda demanded. "But they couldn't have known I was coming—they couldn't have."

The fellow nodded. "Diego was supposed to go up to Oklahoma to sell beef to the reservations, but he came back, saying he had something to tell Sandro, that it couldn't wait. That was when Sandro and the boy quarreled."

"Who's Diego?"

"Diego Vergara," Amanda answered. "He negotiates government contracts for the ranch. Mama mentioned him in her letters."

"Where's Vergara now?" Clay asked impatiently.

"In the house."

"I suppose Vergara went through Griffin on his way to Oklahoma," Hap said, shaking his head.

"Yeah." Clay lowered the shotgun. "It'd make sense to go that way."

Hap exhaled heavily. "Well, I guess he could've heard about the warrant."

"It kinda looks that way, doesn't it?"

"I went to the judge, Hap," Rios spoke up. "I didn't tell anybody else."

"Son of a prominent man wanted for attempted murder—might have been too much for him to keep under his hat," Hap guessed. He looked to Clay.

"Looks like you may be on your way to Mexico. Unofficially, you understand. You'll have to drag him back across the Rio Grande before you can arrest him."

Still stunned that Ramon had apparently eluded justice, Amanda felt empty, cheated. "Don't you think we ought to speak with Mr. Vergara first?" she said finally. "He'll know what he told Alessandro."

"With two days' start, Ramon Sandoval could be anywhere in Mexico by the time you cross the border," Rios pointed out.

"Might as well rest a day or so before you go," Hap observed laconically. "It's a long ride down there."

"No." Clay flicked the reins over the team of horses. "I don't want to give him time to disappear."

It was as though she were in a bad dream, one that wasn't going to end. Ramon had escaped, and Clay couldn't wait to leave her. She wanted to cry out, to ask why they didn't send someone else, why they couldn't send Rios. But she didn't want to make a bigger fool of herself than she already had.

"You're at least staying tonight, aren't you?" she heard herself ask him. "You can't drive a wagon all day, then ride all night."

"He can," Rios murmured behind her. "Believe me, he can."

"Well, he ain't—not this time, anyway, because I'm asking him to take you along, Romero. When he brings Sandoval back, I want him in the saddle, not over it—savvy?"

"No," Clay responded tersely. "I work alone."

"Then I'm ordering you to take him. The Mexicans'll tell him things they won't tell a gringo. You let him go into those cantinas alone first, then you go in later. Don't let 'em guess you even know him."

"I know my business."

"And there's none better at it," Hap agreed. "But this is going to call for some finesse—that's one of your highfalutin words, ain't it? You go in there with guns blasting, and you'll play hell getting Sandoval back to the border."

Clay's jaw worked, but he didn't say anything. The way he saw it, Hap was saddling him with Romero Rios, giving himself a free shot at courting Amanda. There was no question he was smitten with her—only a blind man couldn't see it. And it didn't help that Clay knew Hap was a better man for her. Hap wanted to settle down, and while he wasn't rich like the Rosses or the Ybarras, he came from good pioneer stock. She could pretty much tame him without a lot of trouble.

Amanda closed her eyes and clenched the board seat so hard her fingers hurt. One night was all she had left with him. One night to make him want to come back to her.

She stared at her reflection in the mirror, scarce believing the transformation herself. Her mother's green silk gown clung to her shoulders, dipping just low enough in front to reveal the slightest crevice between ivory breasts. Juana, her mother's maid, had painstakingly tugged out every snarl, then twisted Amanda's hair into a crown of auburn curls, securing them with pearl-headed pins, then covering the whole with a mantilla of sheer black lace.

If she had to, she was going to throw herself at Clay McAlester and dare him to turn her away. The way she looked at it, she didn't have anything but her pride left to lose. And if he didn't come back, she wouldn't have that.

She sat there, eyeing her mother's assortment of perfume bottles, remembering the beautiful woman she used to watch dabbing the rich, exotic scents behind her ears, in the hollow of her throat. Impulsively, she reached for one of them and unstoppered it with shaking hands. It smelled of roses—fresh, fragrant, heady roses—deep, lush, red roses. She touched the stopper behind both ears, then drew it along her jawline, down her neck to where her mother's pearls encircled her throat. Dipping it again, she added a touch between her breasts for good measure.

She was as ready as she was ever going to be. She settled her shoulders, then rose from the brocade chair. Taking one last look at her image in the mirror, she twitched the full silk skirt over her petticoats, straightened the mantilla where it touched her shoulders, then exhaled fully. As she walked toward the door, the silk shimmered beneath the lights of the iron chandelier.

The center courtyard was bathed in the rosy hue of the setting sun, its only sounds those of water trickling over moss-covered rocks in the fountain and her footsteps echoing across the paving stones. Any other time she would have stopped to drink in the beauty of the place, but not now. She was too intent on making Clay McAlester want her.

They were waiting for her—Clay, Romero, Hap, and Diego Vergara, who'd dressed like a Spanish grandee for the occasion. As he turned around and saw her, he smiled. Her gaze took in Walker, who'd slicked back his hair and donned a black coat over gray trousers. Rios appeared lean, almost elegant, in what had to be a borrowed suit. McAlester, on the other hand, seemed totally out of place in his buckskin leggings, worn moccasins, black frock coat, and clean white shirt. The only difference between now and when she'd first laid eyes on him at the stage station was that he was unarmed. He still looked half-wild, dangerous.

"Good evening, gentlemen," she said with a calm she did not feel.

There was a stunned pause, then Romero Rios found his voice. "You are truly beautiful," he said, bowing with courtly formality over her hand.

"Thank you."

"Señorita, you remind me of your lovely mother," Vergara murmured appreciatively.

"Pretty as a picture," Hap added.

But she was watching Clay, waiting. He sucked in

his breath, then let it out slowly, fighting the ache he felt for her. He had to look away.

"Yeah," was all he trusted himself to say.

"Danged if I know what ails you, son," Hap grumbled. "You've been out in the desert so long you've plumb baked that head."

"I'm all right."

Acutely disappointed, Amanda tried not to show it. "Yes, well—shall we go in to supper, sirs?" she asked, reaching for Diego Vergara's arm.

As Clay watched the Spaniard lead her into the dining room, he felt almost relieved. She was with her own kind now, he told himself. She didn't need him anymore. By the time he got back from Mexico, she'd know it, too.

Romero sidled up to him, whispering, "Want me to get Vergara out of the way for you?"

"No."

"I kinda thought she was yours."

"A woman like that doesn't look twice at a man like me—not for long, anyway," Clay murmured evasively.

Dinner proved to be a long, tedious affair, marked by stilted, almost strained conversation. As she looked down the long, polished oak table, she hardly noted the admiring glances cast her way. All she knew was that the dress, the pearls, the perfume were all for naught. She could have been naked for all that he seemed to care.

And when the interminable meal ended at last, the men withdrew to smoke their nasty cheroots, leaving her alone with half a bottle of imported red wine. She sat at the table for a long time, too defeated to get up and leave. Finally, she refilled her chased silver goblet and drank deeply, trying to buoy her sagging spirits, sinking them further.

She'd been there, and he'd used her, that was all. No, she couldn't accept that, she argued within herself. All she had to do was close her eyes and relive that last night on the hill overlooking Sanchez-Torres's wagons.

He'd thought he might die then, that he might not come back to her, and there'd a sweetness, a tenderness in his touch. No, he'd loved her then. She knew it.

"You are finished, señorita?" a kitchen boy inquired politely.

"Huh? Oh, yes, I guess I am," she managed. Having nothing else to do, she rose and reached for the wine bottle. "Tell Juana I am ready to retire."

But once she was back in her mother's richly decorated bedchamber, the green gown neatly hung away, her hair brushed out until it streamed like dark red silk over her white cotton nightgown, she couldn't stand the intense, aching loneliness she still felt. She downed two more glasses of wine, then pushed the empty bottle away.

The English clock ticked loudly, marking the seconds of her life. Resolutely, she walked to the massive carved oak bed and crawled between the crisp, snowy sheets Juana had turned back for her. Lying back on the bank of pillows, she closed her eyes. A long time ago she'd been conceived in this bed, taking life from two very different people—the strong, iron-willed John Ross; the beautiful, delicate, sheltered Isabella Ybarra. As different as night and day, yet they'd loved passionately.

She heard the men come down the corridor one by one, the heavy oak doors open and close, then nothing but the clock counting the hour. Tomorrow he would be going, perhaps leaving her forever, and she had not the means to stop him. She lay there, waiting, listening, wanting, struggling with her pride.

The great, sprawling house was silent now. Unable to stand the emptiness she felt, she crept from her bed and let herself out. Huge, yellowing wax candles impaled on spikes cast tall, smoky shadows on whitewashed walls. She counted the doors, then stood outside the last one, hesitating, afraid to go in, more afraid to go back. Emboldened by too much wine, she reached for the black lever, lifting it. The heavy door swung inward, creaking on iron hinges.

She held her breath, listening for the sound of his breathing, hearing the beat of her own heart. She had nothing more to lose, she told herself, stiffening her resolve. In the darkness she moved to the bed, feeling for the edge of it. He snored softly, telling her he slept. She lifted the sheets and cotton coverlet, then lay down beside him, pressing her body against his back.

Hap Walker came awake with a start. "What the devil—?"

Aware she'd made a terrible mistake, Amanda tried to roll away, but the ranger captain's hand gripped her arm, holding her. He struggled to sit up, peering into the darkness.

"Let me go!" she cried out.

Instead, he leaned across her to feel for his pants. Retrieving a match, he lit it with his fingernail, then held the flame in front of her face. There was no mistaking the shock in his eyes when he recognized her.

"Miss Ross!"

"I must've been sleepwalking," she mumbled, too mortified now to look at him. "Please, I'll go."

"You're looking for Clay."

It was a statement, not a question.

"Yes," she whispered.

Hap turned her arm loose and sat back against the pillows, regarding her soberly. "He didn't want to sleep inside," he said finally. "Told me to take his room because the bed was bigger—said it'd give me a better place for my leg."

"I'm sorry." She slid off the bed and backed away.

He waited until she had her hand on the door. "I don't know what's gotten into him," he offered.

"No." She wrenched the handle, opening it.

"Wish it was me you were looking for," he said behind her.

She escaped then, walking as fast as her bare feet would carry her. Completely, utterly humiliated, she stopped at the end of the corridor, where she leaned her head against the wall, fighting back tears. She'd never be able to look Walker in the eyes again, she was sure of that.

She stood there for a moment, collecting herself, wavering between hunting for Clay or going back to her room. No, she couldn't let him leave before she saw him one last time. He could love her, he could hate her, but he wasn't going to turn her way until she made him tell her where she stood.

The night air was warm, the smell of her mother's roses and bougainvillea mingled seductively as she crossed the courtyard, then let herself out the other side of the house. Above, a hundred stars dotted the midnight sky.

He'd unrolled his bedroll beneath a spreading oak, but he wasn't asleep. He was sitting propped up against the tree trunk, staring into the darkness, when she found him. Knowing he had to see her, she licked dry lips nervously, then walked to stand in front of him. He didn't look up. Instead, he broke off the stick he'd been chewing and threw it away.

He knew if he let himself touch her, he'd be lost. Instead, he willed himself to sit as though he'd turned to stone, saying nothing. But it was as though every inch of his body ached for her. He held his breath.

"Well, aren't you going to say anything?" she asked finally.

"No."

"What have I done to turn you away from me?" she cried.

"Nothing."

"Clay, I love you! I wouldn't have—"

"Don't," he cut in curtly. With an effort he heaved himself up to stand. "I just think it's better if I go, that's all."

"All?" Her voice rose shrilly. "All? What about the horse you gave me? What about those nights, those—"

"Stop it," he said harshly. "It was a mistake, and I'm sorry for it."

"Sorry! How can you be sorry for loving someone?" She sniffed back tears. "Didn't any of it mean anything to you? Was it just a convenience to you? Answer me, Clay, answer me!"

"I can't do it, Amanda. I was a fool to think I could."

"I don't understand—make me understand!"

He hadn't wanted it to end like this. He hadn't wanted it to end at all. He exhaled heavily, then nodded. "I can't live like this—I've got to be free. I'm not a rancher, Amanda."

"You don't have to be!" She took a deep breath again, trying to calm herself. "I don't care what you are, Clay."

"But you will."

He was so cool, so self-contained that she couldn't break through the facade to the man beneath. "I see," she managed, stepping back from him. "All right, then." Wiping her wet face with the back of her hand, she swallowed the awful lump in her throat. "Just tell me one thing—it's all I'm going to ask of you—did you ever love me? Did I ever mean anything to you?"

"That's two." He stared unseeing into the darkness, then nodded. "Yeah. You meant a lot to me."

"I see," she said, sighing. "Well, I suppose that's something, isn't it?"

"Yes."

"Were you even going to tell me good-bye?"

"No. I figured you'd be better off if I didn't."

"Well, I wouldn't have."

"You'll marry some nice fellow—somebody who'll want what you want—and you'll forget all about me."

"No. I guess I'm different from you."

He nodded. "You are. You come from a whole different world. Just look around you, and you can see it."

"You know I was beginning to believe all that stuff about Indian honor. I don't now, you know."

"I'm sorry."

It took all she had to hold out her hand. "Then I guess it's good-bye and Godspeed, isn't it?"

He didn't touch her. "Yes."

"Just to wrap everything up neatly for you, I suppose I should give you an Indian divorce," she decided. "You can take your damned horse."

"I've still got Hannibal."

"No. I don't want anything around to remind me of you, Clay. Do you hear that? I don't want anything around to remind me of you."

Gathering the hem of her long nightgown, she turned and ran back into the house. And once back in her bed, she drew herself into a ball and began shaking convulsively. Her breath came in great sobs, and the tears poured forth until there were no more. She felt sick all the way to her soul. Finally, when she exhausted herself, she rolled onto her side, where she stuffed her knuckles into her mouth to fight back the sobs.

Calmer now, she tried to think. She didn't even belong here anymore. In fact, she hated the Ybarra now. And once she found someone to run it for her, she was going back to Boston. She was going to put half a continent between her and Clay McAlester and hope it was enough.

It had been three weeks since Clay left her—three of the longest weeks of Amanda's life. And now she was faced with a new dilemma, one that almost made her bitterness complete. She couldn't even go back to her Aunt Kate's house now, and she couldn't stay at Ybarra-Ross either. Before long everyone was going to know her for the sinner she was.

There was going to be a child—Clay McAlester's child. When the realization first hit her, she'd actually thought of telling him. But she didn't want him like that—she didn't want him to marry her out of some obligation. And she wasn't at all sure he would, anyway. No, he was the last person on earth she wanted to know about it. She was just going to have to make her plans herself and live with them.

Maybe later, when she felt it move, it would mean something to her. But right now, she still felt empty, almost devoid of any emotion. For a moment she let her imagination stray, wondering if it would look like him. Somehow she didn't think she could bear that. She didn't want to have to look into the child's face and be reminded every day of what a total fool he'd made of her.

"You're mighty quiet tonight," Hap chided her.

"Am I?" She forced a smile, then closed the book she wasn't reading. "I'm sorry."

"No need to be. I reckon you've got a lot on your mind."

"Yes."

"He'll get Sandoval, one way or the other. It just takes more time when he's got to cross the Rio Grande."

"He's not coming back here," she said simply.

"If I were a betting man, I wouldn't put any money on that."

"Yes—well, he told me to my face he wasn't."

"A man says a lot of things he doesn't mean to a woman," Hap observed. "He's like a big fish—it just takes patience to bring him in."

"I'm not a fisherman, Captain. And I don't care anymore."

"God's truth?"

"God's truth."

All too aware that he was watching her closely, she shifted uncomfortably in her chair, then leaned to place the book on a table. Standing up, she walked to stare out the deep-set window. He'd never spoken of her crawling into bed with him. In fact, there was nothing in his manner to indicate he even remembered it. But she knew it had to be there, somewhere beneath the surface, waiting to ambush her.

"If I was to believe that, I'd start hoping," he said finally.

For a moment she didn't follow him. "Believe what?" she asked, turning around.

"That you aren't pining for Clay."

"Pining isn't the word I'd choose, Captain," she murmured dryly. "Right now I'd just like to kill him."

To him, it seemed as though every one of his thirty-eight years mocked him, telling him he was too old for her, that she'd laugh at him if he asked her. "I guess he's got to be as old as me to want to settle down," he said cautiously.

"I don't want to talk about Clay McAlester."

"Well, I was sort of talking about me." He looked up. "I figure I'm about done rangerin', what with the leg and all." He was going to bungle everything, and he knew it, but he had to try. "I got a little money put aside—four thousand dollars—and I was fixing to buy myself a place, maybe run a few cattle on it. Nothing like the Ybarra, of course."

"Clay said you wanted to be a farmer."

"If the leg don't heal better, I won't be pushing any plows. And," he added significantly, "I thought we weren't talking about him."

"We aren't."

"Good. Glad to get that behind me." He'd got himself cornered now, and he was going to play hell getting out of it. "What I was wanting to say is that I admire you—have since that day at Stockton when Nate Hill died. Oh, I know it's pretty damned presumptuous to even think it, but I figure a man's got to put his mouth where his thoughts are if he's ever going to get what he wants."

It dawned on her where he was going. "Captain Walker," she asked incredulously, "is this a proposal?"

He could save face and deny it, but then he'd never know. "Well, I was doing my damnedest to make it one," he allowed sheepishly. "Oh, I know I'm not a young, handsome fellow—that you can do a helluva lot better than a half-lame saddle tramp like me, but if you could bring yourself to take me, I'd try my damnedest to make you happy." Afraid if he stopped, she'd jump in and turn him down, he went on, pointing out, "And I know four thousand dollars ain't much to a lady like yourself, but it's my life savings, and I'd turn it over to you here and now, Amanda. I'll even sign papers saying I don't want your money, that it ought to go to the kids if we're lucky enough to have any." He took a deep breath, then dared to meet her eyes. "That's about it, I guess. Oh, and for what it's worth, I've fancied myself in love with you ever since I laid eyes on you."

"I see." She fought the urge to cry. "And it doesn't make any difference about Clay? It doesn't make any difference that I made a fool of myself the night I crawled into bed with you?"

"No. I was just wishing it was me you were looking for, that's all."

"And you know about everything, don't you?"

"Reckon I can guess, anyway. A man like me'd be proud to have a woman like you, even if he was second choice."

"What if ... what if I can't get over him?" she choked out.

"Oh, I know it ain't going to be easy forgetting him."

"No ... no, it isn't." She sucked in her breath, releasing it slowly, striving for calm. "It'll be harder than you know, Hap."

"I'm willing to make the effort."

The warmth in his eyes cut her like a knife, forcing her to look away. "I'm going to have his child," she admitted baldly.

She could hear his breath catch, and then there was a long, painful silence. "I see," he said.

It was as though the dam holding her tears burst, letting them spill down her cheeks. "Why don't you just tell me I'm no better than those cantina whores?" she cried. "Why don't you tell me I'm so worthless that he threw me away? Go ahead—say it!"

"I've got a lot of love to give, Amanda," he answered quietly. "I've been storing it up a long time." Rising, he hobbled to stand in front of her. "I reckon I can love Clay's kid." His arms enveloped her awkwardly, drawing her against his chest. "When you've been around as long as I have, you'll learn nothing worth having comes easy," he said softly.

"No ... no, it doesn't," she whispered, letting him hold her.

He kissed her then with a surprising gentleness. As his mustache brushed against her lip, she closed her eyes and tried to pretend she felt something. But she didn't. She was too empty, too vacant inside. Except for the baby. And she knew if she married him, she'd be cheating him terribly.

He stepped back, dropping his hands. "I reckon that's my answer, isn't it?"

All she could do was nod.

"I was afraid of that. I guess we're just both fools, huh?"

"Yes. I'm sorry . . . so very sorry, Hap. It would be so wrong of me to let you do it. You'd come to feel cheated someday."

"I can make him marry you, Amanda, if that's what you want."

"No. I don't even want him to know about it."

He digested that, frowning. "All right, then, but what are you going to do if you don't take one of us?"

"I'm going back to Boston."

"Your kinfolk going to accept this?"

"I'm not going to ask them to . . . not for a while, anyway, not until I get used to the notion myself. Maybe not then. I don't know. Right now, I can't look Aunt Kate or Uncle Charles in the face." She shook her head wearily. "I've thought and thought, Hap, and I can't stay here."

"Aren't you afraid of running into 'em?"

"Boston's a big place. No, I'm going to take a room somewhere, and maybe pretend I'm a widow until the baby comes. Then I guess I'll decide where I go from there. Maybe the two of us will go abroad." She looked up at him, and her mouth twisted into a lopsided smile. "I'm rich—remember? I can hide behind my money."

He nodded. "Yeah, I guess you can. Well, just remember if you need a name for your late husband, you can use mine. All you've got to do is call yourself Mrs. Horace Walker." His eyes met hers for a moment, then he grinned. "Ain't any wonder folks call me Hap, is it? I got that from my ma, who always said I was a happy kid. Clay don't even know about the Horace."

"I couldn't use your name."

"Why not? It ain't likely any other female's going to want it."

"Well, I'll keep it in mind."

"Folks'll know you didn't make it up—nobody in his right mind would take the name Horace if he had a choice in it." He hobbled over to where she'd laid her book down. Picking it up, he studied the title. "Shakespeare, huh? You done with it?"

"Yes."

"Reckon I'll take it to bed with me. Be kinda nice to be able to spout some of this back at Clay the next time he starts quoting stuff to me."

As his hand touched the door, she blurted out, "You aren't going to tell him, are you? Promise me you won't."

He stopped. "No. I figure that's up to you."

"Thank you."

As the door closed behind him, she sank to the chair behind her father's big desk. She'd probably been foolish turning him down. There was no question in her mind that he'd have made a good, solid husband. But there'd always be Clay McAlester between them, and that was no way to make a marriage. Besides, if she'd married Hap, Clay would be sure to know about the child. Sooner or later, he'd know. And then it would be like a boil, festering, poisoning all of them. No, she had to get away.

She opened the drawer and took out a pencil. Wetting the nub, she wrote on a blank sheet of paper— Horace Walker; Mrs. Horace Walker. He was right—it had a certain ring of truth to it. And even if he married someone else, there'd be no one in Boston to know it.

He was hot and tired, and dust clung to the sweaty stubble on his face, but he'd finally found Ramon Sandoval. It had been a month of discreet inquiries, and the trail had led them zigzagging across the length and breadth of Mexico, but he and Romero, working separately, then together, had managed to find him. And Alessandro Sandoval was there also.

Now he was ready to move in and take them both if he had to. While Romero snatched a nap on the hard, pebble-strewn ground, Clay sat, his back against a rock, cleaning his shotgun, his mind on Amanda. He'd been thinking about her a lot ever since he left the Ybarra. No, it was more than a lot—she was in his thoughts all the time, haunting his dreams, plaguing his waking hours, tearing at him with every breath he took.

Long before he hit the Rio Grande on his way down, he'd done a lot of thinking, and he knew he'd been a fool to ever believe that he could forget her. And he knew too that he couldn't stand it if she married Hap—or anybody else for that matter. Maybe the realization had come too late, but once he got Sandoval, he was going to ride hell for leather back to her, and he was going to grovel at her feet, if that was what it took to win her back. And if by some act of God's mercy, she was brought to forgive him, he was going to marry her, even if he had to convert to Catholicism to do it. And then he was going to do his damnedest to see that she never regretted loving him.

He might not have John Ross's money or Isabella Ybarra's aristocratic breeding, but he was a hard worker, and if given half a chance, he was determined to make her proud of him.

It had taken him weeks to write the letter of his life to her, but he'd finally posted it in Durango. In it, he'd tried to explain how overwhelmed he'd been by the ranch, how he'd felt she would come to regret trying to take him into her world, how he'd felt there wasn't any place for him there. He'd poured his heart out in that letter, and now he could only hope she'd forgive him. That she'd understand how afraid he'd been of being tamed, of changing his whole way of life for her. That it had been hard giving up his past. Well, he'd written it, and by the time he got back, she'd have it.

When he saw her, he'd look in her face and have his answer. And for the first time in his adult life, he was afraid, not of taking a bullet, not of dying alone, but of losing the only woman he'd ever want for his wife. What was it that Henry IV of France had said? That Paris was worth a Mass. He understood that now. Amanda Ross was worth his freedom.

He flexed tired shoulders, then glanced at Rios. Poor Romero. He was a lot like Amanda in that he didn't like living off the land. But where she'd been pretty game about it, Rios wasn't. From the outset he'd announced he didn't eat raw meat of any kind, nor would he take rattlesnake, no matter how it was cooked. He'd even balked at the armadillo, saying if God had wanted man to eat such things, he wouldn't have given it a coat of armor. Instead, he starved himself between towns, then gorged himself when he hit the cantinas.

He reached over and slapped Romero's rump. The young ranger rolled over and came up with his gun. "Oh, it's you," he mumbled.

"I made some coffee."

Rios glared at him. "I don't want any."

"It'll put hair on your chest."

"The hard way."

"Suit yourself."

Romero passed a weary hand over his face, then yawned. "I could have slept all day." Then he glanced down, seeing the scorpion crawling up his pants leg. He grabbed the pan of coffee and dashed it over his leg, nearly scalding it. The scorpion's tail twitched, then fell into the dirt, where it jerked around in a circle before dying. "At least the stuff's good for something," he muttered. "Maybe you could sell it for poison or weed killer."

"I figured we go down for Sandoval about siesta time," Clay explained, ignoring the barbs.

Romero looked down at the hacienda below. "How many do you figure there are?"

"It doesn't matter."

"Maybe not to you, but I'd like to have an idea."

"They know we're after them, anyway, so the only surprise we've got is the time." Reaching for his spyglass, Clay adjusted it, then trained it on the house. "Yeah, they're there, all right. The fancy boy's Ramon—and if I had to guess, I'd say that's Alessandro standing behind him," he said, handing the glass over.

Rios fanned it over the whole area, counting. "Looks like the two of them and five others that we can see."

"There'll be some in the house."

"That's what I was thinking." Romero exhaled his resignation. "That only makes the odds four or five to one, huh?"

"Easy pickings, as Hap would say it."

"I'm not Hap," the younger man pointed out. "I'm just wondering how we get them out of there without putting the whole country on our tails. If it was up to me, I'd take my Sharps and just shoot 'em from here, then make a run for it."

"It's not—and I want Ramon to know what's happening to him. I want him to know it's because of what he did to Amanda."

"If you want to kill him, I'll tell Hap he drew on you," Rios offered.

"If we get the drop on the old man, the rest of 'em won't put up much of a fight. But to make sure, I want you to tell 'em in Spanish that I don't have any quarrel with them—that all I want are the Sandovals."

"All I can say is I'll be damned glad when I cross the Rio Grande."

"This is your country, remember?"

"Not since '36. I was born in Texas."

"You complain a whole lot more than Amanda Ross."

"I guess I don't love you," Romero countered, lying back down. "Wake me up when you're ready. Until then I don't want to think about it."

Nothing was stirring except for the flies. They were everywhere. That was the thing about flies—if there was anything to eat, they'd find it. Clay swatted one that landed on his arm, then he leaned over to shake Rios.

"Come on—let's go. As near as I can tell from the glass, there aren't many in the house—the Sandovals and a couple of women, I think. The others are in the bunkhouse behind."

"Huh?" Rios passed a hand over his eyes, then squinted up at the sun. "Yeah, I guess it's time," he agreed.

Clay handed him a canteen. "Splash your face—you'll feel better."

"God, but I'm tired."

"Three days and you'll be across the border."

"Five days and you'll be at the Ybarra."

"Uh-huh." Clay picked up the shotgun and started for the paint mare.

"You're going to give up your badge, aren't you?" Romero murmured behind him.

"Yeah. I figure I've had all the luck I'm going to

have, and it's time to move over and let somebody like you have my moccasins."

"What are you going to do if she won't have you?"

Clay hesitated before swinging into the saddle. "I guess I'll cross that bridge when I get there. But first I'm going to get Sandoval."

"Sort of like 'bring me the head of Ramon Sandoval,' eh?"

"He tried to kill her."

Romero had his answer then. There was no way Clay McAlester was going to let the younger Sandoval live long enough to reach Texas. And he didn't blame him, not one bit.

It was the heat of the day, and there was no sign of life as they approached the hacienda where the fugitives had come to hide. A small dust devil whirled across barren ground, then disappeared. In the corral several horses stood clustered against a small adobe building, trying to find what little shade it provided. One raised his head, and his nostrils twitched as he caught the scent of them.

It was a small house for men like the Sandovals, a real comedown from the Ybarra. But that made it easier—once inside there weren't many places anybody could hide. Keeping to the back of the squat adobe building that served as a bunkhouse, they dismounted.

"Cover the door, and shoot the first man who tries to come out," Clay ordered.

"You're going in there alone, *amigo*?"

"I don't see any more of us."

Leaving Romero, Clay moved around the side of the house, keeping close to the wall as he approached a window. When he looked inside, he could see the naked back of a man riding a woman so hard that the bedposts rocked noisily on the hard-packed floor. He'd found Ramon.

He came around the corner, then tried the door. It gave way, creaking inward. He gripped the shotgun and slipped inside. He could still hear Ramon taking his last ride, but now he had to find the father. The soles of his moccasins made no sound as he crossed the main room toward the arched door on the other side. He caught a glimpse of white shoulder, and heard the soft, melodious voice of a woman coaxing the man straining beneath her. Like father, like son, he guessed.

He went back to the younger Sandoval, easing his way to the door. Clay swung around the opening, leveling the shotgun on him. Ramon was too busy to notice. Clay moved closer, jamming the barrel against the younger man's bare back.

"Now you come off real easy," he said softly. "Otherwise, your guts are going to be all over her."

The girl's eyes widened, first in disbelief, then in terror. Panicked, she struggled to crawl out from under Ramon, who seemed to have frozen.

"Get over against the wall," Clay told her. Going to the foot of the bed, he pulled off a dirty sheet, then tossed it toward her. "Cover yourself."

Ramon's mind raced, assessing his chance of getting away. It was as though the ranger read his mind.

"I wouldn't try it," Clay drawled. "You just get down without pulling anything funny, and we'll go get your father together—savvy?"

"Papa!" the younger man cried out. "Papa, they've found us!"

At that, Clay grabbed his hair and slammed his head into the wall. Ramon slumped as he caught him with his free arm. Dragging the junior Sandoval, he came out ready to shoot. But Alessandro, on hearing his son's warning, went out the window, leaving a cowering woman behind. Still holding Ramon, Clay gained the door in time to let one barrel go. Too far away to kill the old man, he nonetheless got him. Blood spattered the sallow skin where the buckshot hit.

Alessandro went down, rolling naked in the dirt, wailing he'd been shot. Grim-faced men watched from the bunkhouse, while Rios kept them covered. His eyes on the doorway, the younger ranger moved to where the old man wept. Leaning down, he pried a revolver from Alessandro Sandoval's hand, then tossed it out of reach.

Clay turned his attention to Ramon. "It's your turn," he said silkily.

"No! It wasn't me!" Ramon cried. "I didn't do it!"

"I brought Amanda Ross back to the Ybarra. Don't tell me you didn't do it—you left her out in the desert to die. She's alive, Ramon—she lived to tell what you did to her." Clay's voice was soft, menacing.

The boy's eyes darted to where Alessandro had managed to sit up in the dirt. "Papa, tell him—tell him it wasn't my idea!"

"Shut up!" the old man shouted at him. "Shut up!"

"Killing's almost too easy for you," Clay went on. "Maybe I ought to just take you out and leave you, huh? How would you like to crawl through rattlesnakes and scorpions. I guess if you got lucky, they might make it quick. Otherwise, you could do what she did—you could walk for miles without water."

"No! It wasn't me, I tell you! I never wanted to do it!"

"You went back once to put a bullet in her."

"I didn't want to do it—he made me do it!" Ramon cried tearfully.

"Shut up!" Alessandro screamed. "Don't be a fool! It's just your word against hers!"

"But I'm not going to let you get to court, Ramon," Clay whispered. "So if you've got anything to tell me, you'd better say it now. There isn't any tomorrow— I've got every one of them in this gun."

"Papa, tell him—tell him it was you who wanted her dead! Please, Papa, please! He's going to kill me!"

"He won't do it—it would be murder!" the old man yelled at him.

"I don't have to leave any witnesses, Ramon."

The younger Sandoval closed his eyes and swallowed. "Please," he choked out, "it wasn't me, I tell you."

"You'll have to do better than that. Your father didn't take Amanda Ross out there. Your father didn't leave her."

"He said I had to do it. He said if she wouldn't marry me, she had to die." Ramon swallowed again. "After the Comanches got Gregorio, Isabella wanted Papa to leave."

"Ramon!"

"Go on."

"We took her out into the desert, just like with Maria. There wasn't anybody to know. And when we went back, the animals had eaten her. There was nothing but bones and a few pieces of her clothing. It was easy to say the Comanches had taken her."

"You sniveling bastard—you worthless idiot," Alessandro fumed. "You should have brought the girl to me. You weren't smart enough to do it right."

"I'm sorry, Papa."

"Sorry! Before it was attempted murder, but you couldn't wait to tell everything," the old man told him contemptuously. "Now you have put a noose around your neck and mine."

Clay and Romero Rios exchanged glances, then Romero went into the bunkhouse, leaving the old man within a few feet of his gun. Clay turned to Ramon.

"Get inside," he ordered curtly.

Even as he said it, he could feel the hairs on the back of his neck stand. Counting silently, he waited until he was sure, then he spun around as Alessandro cocked the revolver. He squeezed the Whitney's other trigger. The full blast ripped a hole the size of a cantaloupe in the old man's chest. A look of stunned incredulity crossed his face as he fell backward.

"Papa! You've killed my father!"

"He threw down on me."

"He didn't have a chance! Papa!" Dodging Clay, Ramon fell on his father's body, sobbing. "Papa, I didn't mean to tell him!" he cried. He looked up at Clay. "You murdered him!"

"If anybody throws down on me, one of us is going to die."

But as he lay over Alessandro's body, Ramon felt the cold steel of his father's pistol under his bare skin. And he knew the ranger had discharged both barrels of his shotgun. He pressed his mouth against Alessandro's unresponsive lips as his fingers found the trigger.

"For you, Papa," he whispered.

He rolled over and came up shooting, his bullet going wide of his mark. He never got the chance to fire another. Clay's Colt .45 blazed, and the impact of the shot as it hit the younger man's heart turned him around. He pitched facedown in the dirt.

Rios came out, gun still in hand. "Me and the boys in there have been talking, and we've sort of agreed that they didn't see anything."

"Oh?"

"Uh-huh. And now that he's not paying them, they'd just as soon move on—if that's all right with you."

"I don't care. I got what I came after."

Clay walked over where the two bodies lay, and as he looked down, he couldn't help remembering what they'd done to Amanda and her mother. He felt a surge of anger that they'd never feel the terror that the two women had felt, that they'd never suffered the terrible thirst, the heat, the relentless sun that had nearly taken Amanda's life. But he could still get even for her. Taking out his Bowie knife from his belt, he grasped Alessandro's hair and ripped it back with the blade. Moving to Ramon Sandoval, he did the same. He wiped the bloody knife on his buckskin leggings, then sheathed it. Coming back, he picked up his shotgun. The Mexicans who'd come out of the building stared at him as he walked by.

Rios looked at the bodies, then back at the Mexicans. "¡Ándle—muy pronto!" he told them. They didn't wait to be dismissed twice. To a man, they made a run for their horses. As the dust kicked up behind them, Rios caught up to Clay. "Why'd you scalp them?" he asked.

"I didn't want either of them going to heaven."

"What?"

"You heard me." Clay swung up into his saddle, then shrugged. "A man can't go into the great beyond without his scalp."

"I don't think they were going anywhere but hell anyway," Rios murmured, stepping into his stirrup. "But who am I to judge?"

"Yeah."

"You'll never get that blood out of those buckskins," he added.

"I reckon I'll be throwing them away, anyway."

And as he clicked the reins, turning the paint mare northward, he felt an immense relief. It was over, all over. Now all he had to do was convince Amanda Ross she still wanted him for a husband. It was a tall order, but somehow, some way, he was going to do it.

Boston: September 17, 1873

It was raining again, she reflected wearily. It had rained every day for almost a week, keeping her inside. She lifted the lace curtain at the window of her room and looked into the street below. It was nearly deserted except for a single horse-drawn cab. She let the curtain drop and returned to her needlework.

By the time the baby made its appearance, it was going to be the best-dressed infant in Boston. But there wasn't much of anything else to do. And she had no one to share her pregnancy with—except Hap Walker.

She moved to a table and picked up his last letter. He and Vergara were getting along fine, he said. Between them they'd managed to land that fat government contract, and they'd be supplying beef to the reservations up in Oklahoma. He was learning the ranching business and liking it. She reread it, getting to the part that had interested her most.

You won't be needing to come back for any trial. Both of the Sandovals were killed trying to escape, then buried somewhere down in Mexico. Before he died, Ramon confessed, implicating his father in the death of your mother. The motive was control of the Ybarra. I know it won't make you feel any better knowing it wasn't the Comanches, but Clay wanted me to tell you. Other than that, you don't have to worry none about the place. Vergara and I are keeping it going until you decide to come back.

There was a sharp rap on her door. Hastily refolding Hap's letter, she went to answer it.

"Mrs. Walker, there's somebody to see you," the boardinghouse maid told her.

"Are you sure? I mean, I don't know who it could be."

"Yes'm. He said Mrs. Walker—Mrs. Horace Walker. That's you, ain't it?"

"Yes. Yes, it is," Amanda said more resolutely. "He didn't give a name, did he?"

"No'm."

Mystified, she hesitated. It couldn't be Kate—Kate didn't even know she was there. "It's a man, you say?"

"Yes'm." The girl bobbed a quick curtsy, then disappeared.

It was probably a mistake. Nobody knew her real identity, and certainly nobody knew Hap Walker. Her hands crept to the pins in her hair, pulling them out. She was a mess, and she knew it. She was letting herself go terribly. She picked up her brush, then glanced in her mirror, and what she saw there almost made her heart stop.

There stood Clay McAlester, hat in hand. His long blond hair was gone, cropped into unruly waves that reminded her of Alexander the Great. There were rainspots on the shoulders of his neat navy blue serge suit. He even wore a tie. Her first instinct was to hide. Then she felt the surge of anger.

"Leave it down," he said softly, closing the door behind him.

He filled the whole room with his presence. She spun around to face him. "What are you doing here?" she demanded furiously. "Hap told you, didn't he?"

"Hap's not even talking to me, to answer your second question. As for the first, I've had a devil of a time hunting you down. It was a whole lot easier finding Sandoval in Mexico than tracking you in Boston."

"Maybe I didn't want to be found."

"I kinda figured that out. Where'd you get the Horace?"

"If you don't go away, I'll be turned out of this place."

"Why didn't you go to the Ryans?"

"You didn't tell Aunt Kate I was here, I hope," she said, alarmed. "You had no right—no right at all! Now she'll wonder—"

"I didn't tell her anything. I acted like you were still at Ybarra—like I was just a friend of yours visiting Boston. They're real nice people."

"Yes, I know."

"Amanda—"

"Just go, please."

He shook his head. "I can't. Not until I've said my piece, anyway."

He was so close now she could reach out and touch him. She closed her eyes to hide from him. "Please."

"I want to marry you, Amanda."

"He said he wouldn't tell you—he promised he wouldn't tell you!"

"I'm damned if I know what you're talking about."

"Why now—why come for me now? You let me throw myself at you when we were at the ranch, and you turned me away! You let me tell you I loved you, and you never said anything! You let me make a fool of myself, Clay McAlester!"

"For what it's worth, I'm sorry."

"Well, sorry doesn't get it! Not now—not after everything else! You threw me at Hap and left! You threw me away, Clay!"

"I know."

"And then you have the gall—the *unmitigated* gall to come here and say you want to marry me?" she demanded incredulously.

"Yes."

"Well, it won't work! I don't know how you found me, or why you even tried, but I'm not falling twice for you—do you hear me? It hurt too much getting over you!" She ducked behind him to open the door. "Now just get out of my life forever!"

"All right—if that's what you want. I just want you to know that I changed my mind before I even got to the Rio Grande. I tried to write you about it, to apologize, but by the time it got to the Ybarra, you were already gone."

"There wasn't much you could have said—not after the way you told me good-bye." She held the door for him. "Now, are you going, or do I have to call for the proprietor to throw you out?"

He was losing, and he knew it. Down to his last card, Hap would say. He reached into his pocket and gambled. "Here—all I'm asking you to do is read this. Then if you want to burn it and pretend there was nothing between us, I suppose I'll be getting what I deserve. But I'm asking you to read it," he said again. "If it changes your mind, you can reach me at the hotel down at the corner—I took a room there for the rest of the week."

"And if it doesn't?"

"Then I guess I'll go back to rangering. Eventually I'll probably go to Austin to read law. But whatever I do, I know one thing, Amanda—I'll always love you." He pressed the folded papers into her hand. "If you don't change your mind, it doesn't make much difference to you what I do anyway, does it?"

"No."

For a moment it looked as if he was going to touch her, as though he wanted to kiss her, but then he dropped his hand. "Yeah—well, as I said, if you want to talk to me about anything that's in there, I'll be down at the corner."

It was as though there was a vacuum, a void when he left. She stood there for a moment, listening to him go down the stairs, then she went inside her rented room and closed the door. He had no right to do this to her, no right at all.

For a moment she considered throwing whatever

he'd given her into the small heat stove, then curiosity got the better of her. She sat down next to the kerosene lamp and unfolded the papers. They formed a letter, a very long letter, written in a neat, even script, the sort a schoolboy would use to please his teacher. The date caught her attention. He'd written it just a few days after he left the Ybarra-Ross.

She read the first few paragraphs skeptically, then was drawn to his words, and as she read, the man she'd thought she knew emerged once again. A proud man, one torn between two peoples, one with no place he could fit in. A man who'd blown up those wagons, yet was devastated by the ultimate consequences. A man who felt it better to lose now than later, all too sure that one day she'd look at him and be sorry. By the time he'd gotten his head straight and decided he had to take the risk, he was tracking Ramon Sandoval, making her step-cousin pay for what he'd done to her.

> I always thought I had to be free to do as I pleased, but there's not much joy in doing something just to prove I can do it. Not since I met you, anyway. If it means waking up next to you the rest of my life, then you can put a ring around my finger and tie me down with it. Providing I can do the same with you. I'm willing to be as domesticated as you want to make me. You can drag me to Mass, and I'll sit with you and the kids, trying to make sense of it.

But above all, in nearly every eloquent word he wrote, there was no mistaking that he loved her. If she didn't take him, he was going back to rangering, he'd just said. That meant he'd already left it. She read further, taking in the part where he didn't want to own the Ybarra-Ross, that he'd just as soon read law and earn his own living. The law was a good place for a rebel, because rebels were always ready to take up a cause, he wrote. But if she wanted him to be a rancher, he'd try it.

She was reading through a mist of tears, almost unable to finish the rest of his letter. But the most important thing of all wasn't in there. Not knowing about the baby, he'd come back to her, not because he felt obligated for anything, but rather because he wanted to. Because he loved her.

And suddenly it didn't make any difference whether it rained or not. She threw on her cloak and ran down the stairs, nearly knocking the disapproving Mrs. Murphy down. Mumbling an apology, she darted out into the cold rain, and ducked her head down against the bitter wind.

The warm air of the lobby blasted her face when the doorman opened the heavy brass door. Breathless, she pushed back her wet, tangled hair, and marched up to the reception desk.

"Mr. McAlester—Mr. Clayton McAlester's room number, please."

Clearly unimpressed, the man looked her up and down before answering, "We don't run that sort of establishment, miss."

"No—no—you don't understand." She sucked in her breath, then exhaled, trying to slow her pounding heart. "I'm Mrs. McAlester," she announced baldly. Her hand crept up to her hair, trying to pat it into place. "He's expecting me, but I'm afraid there was a small accident."

"Indeed?"

"Yes, but I'm all right," she hastened to add. "I was just shook up a bit."

His gaze dropped to her cloak, taking in the tailoring, the soutache braid trim, and he relented. "Room 310, madam. It's up those steps and to the right."

"Thank you."

It was all she could do to walk rather than run up the stairs, and when she reached the top, she hurried down the carpeted hall, counting the doors until she reached 310. She hesitated, almost afraid to knock. She stood there, trying to compose what she wanted to say to him. She wasn't going to tell him about the baby, not yet. She didn't want him to think that weighed in her change of mind. Finally, she gave his door three quick raps. It seemed like an eternity before he answered it. He was in his shirtsleeves. His muddy shoes were just inside.

As the door swung inward, she blurted out, "I read your letter—all of it."

He almost couldn't believe she was standing there. And despite her wet hair, despite her bedraggled appearance, she was in that moment every bit as beautiful as when she'd worn that green dress. He stepped aside to let her pass, then closed the door behind her. His pulse raced as he turned toward her.

"You didn't have to come in the rain," he murmured, smiling crookedly. "I would have still been here tomorrow—and probably a lot longer than I was letting on."

"Yes, well . . ." The warmth in his eyes made it hard to think. "I came to tell you I've changed my mind. There's nothing on this earth I'd rather be than Mrs. Clayton McAlester."

His arms were around her, holding her close. His hand smoothed her wet, tangled hair over her soaked cloak. "I don't deserve this," he murmured against her crown.

"If we had to deserve everything, we'd never have anything," she whispered into his shoulder.

"If you want, you can have a big Catholic wedding at Ybarra, but right now I'd like to find a judge. I don't want to wait for the banns. Then if you'd like, I've got enough money saved to take you someplace nice for a wedding trip."

"Like where?"

He tried to think of a real exotic place, then decided, "How about London? I hear they got all kinds of things over there."

"No, I don't need that, Clay. I'd just as soon camp in the desert. As long as it's not a hundred degrees out, and you don't make me drink your coffee—or eat any rattlesnake. I don't care what you say—it does not taste like chicken."

"You sure you'd want to go back to the desert?"

"Yes."

Reluctantly, he released her and stepped back. "If you don't get out of those wet clothes, you're going to take pneumonia. While you're doing that, I'll go down and register you. And I'll ask the fellow at the desk about the judge."

"Uh . . . if I were you, I wouldn't do that." Her fingers worked the hook on her cloak. "I sort of told him we were married already." The cloak slid to the floor, revealing the plain cotton dress. Her eyes on him, she reached to undo the buttons. "I never thought I'd do this again, Clay." As the dress joined the cloak, she stepped out of it. Her mouth curved seductively. "We can find a judge after while," she said softly.

"You sure do know what's on a man's mind, Mrs. McAlester," he murmured huskily.

"Do I?"

She never got an answer. This time when he took her into his arms, he bent his head to hers. A low sob rose from her throat, then died in the heat of his kiss. His hands moved eagerly over her hips, gathering her chemise, lifting it up to find the hot, smooth skin below.

"Love me, Clay," she whispered. "Love me now."

He lifted her then, taking her to his bed. As she fell back against the featherbed, she was still smiling. Her arms reached out, pulling him down over her, and they were lost in a delicious tangle of arms and legs as they undressed each other. He rolled over, putting her on top. As her legs parted, she received him, then began to move languorously, testing what she could do, savoring the feel of him. His mouth found a nipple, and he began teasing it with his tongue. She threw her head back, giving him better access, and she began to move more deliberately. Her eyes were closed, but there was no mistaking the ecstasy in her face. His hands moved over her back, stroking her bare skin. She twisted her hips, rolling him within her, taking him.

She was panting now, her body demanding more of him. Her head came forward, spilling her hair onto his chest and shoulders, enveloping his face in the auburn silk. She was taking him with her now. His arms closed around her, holding on, while his body rocked in rhythm with hers, straining. And somewhere in the distance he heard his own cries rise in crescendo as he came.

When it was over, she lay there, her head resting on his shoulder. He twisted his head slightly, taking in the soft, white sheets. And he knew she was his destiny. He knew she was forever.

Ybarra-Ross: April 28, 1874

The faint, yellow glow of the kerosene lamp cast his shadow over the bed, making her auburn hair seem almost black where it tumbled over her pillow. In the crook of her arm, the small, down-covered head was barely visible. A lump of pride constricted his throat, nearly overwhelming him.

Reluctantly, he tore himself away and went back to her writing desk, where he opened the latest copy of the *Daily Austin Republican*. Picking up Amanda's sewing scissors, he carefully cut out the small, boxed announcement.

M/M Clayton M. McAlester of the Ybarra-Ross welcomed their first child, a daughter, Katherine Isabella, born April 20, 1874. Mrs. McAlester, the former Amanda Ross, is the daughter of the late John Ross and the late Isabella Ybarra, a descendant of the original land grant family. Mr. McAlester, a former Texas Ranger, reports mother and daughter are doing well. We at the *Republican* wish to offer hearty congratulations to both proud parents.

It was a far cry from what they used to write about him, no doubt about that. He unfolded the letter he'd written his Aunt Jane earlier and placed the clipping inside, knowing she'd want to put it in the family Bible. A wry smile curved his mouth as he pictured her sitting in her straight-backed rocker, her hands clasping that Bible, and he knew she'd be pleased to know he'd been tamed at last. It might even make her overlook the fact that he'd turned Catholic.

Behind him, Amanda stirred, then roused. "What are you doing?" she asked sleepily.

"I just finished a letter," he replied, returning to her. For a long moment, he looked down again, taking in the spill of tangled auburn hair, the swell of full breasts straining against the thin lawn of her nightgown. "God, but you're beautiful," he whispered. "You know that, don't you?"

"No, but I like to hear it."

"Every day of my life," he promised. Turning around, he adjusted the lantern wick until it flickered one last time, then went out. "Every day of my life," he repeated, climbing back into bed. Taking care not to disturb his tiny daughter, he wrapped his arms around his wife and nuzzled her fragrant hair. "I'm the luckiest man in Texas," he murmured. "No—make that the luckiest man alive, Mrs. McAlester."

Here's a peek at another
great romance
coming in July 1995

Simon stared down, openmouthed, into wide, gray eyes which gazed back without comprehension. Without thinking, he placed his hand on her shirtfront, conscious immediately of the curving softness of her breast. To his relief, he felt a heartbeat beneath his fingers, at first febrile and fluttering, but then growing strong and steady. At the same time, the girl began to stir, first blinking up at him like some creature of the wild disturbed in its nest, and then struggling to free herself from his embrace.

"Are you all right?" asked Simon, hastily removing his hand to safer territory.

The girl drew in great, gasping lungfuls of air. "Yuh—yes—I'm fine." She thrust herself to a sitting position, falling immediately back against Simon in a half swoon.

"Gently, now." He laid her carefully upon the ground and hurriedly removed his coat to place beneath her head. In a moment, having caught her breath once more, she sat up again.

"That was an insane thing to do," he said severely.

"It was not!" retorted the girl. "Talavera has taken me over that hedge a hundred times. I don't know what happened this time. He landed a little shorter than I expected, I think." She struggled to her feet and ran to where the horse stood a few feet away, placidly cropping at the lush grass that surrounded them. She examined the animal briefly, running expert hands over head, legs, shoulders, and flanks. "Thank God, you're all right, old fellow." She turned to address Simon. "At any rate, it was all my fault."

"I daresay," replied Simon dryly, collecting his own mount and returning to where she stood. Who the devil was she? he wondered, glancing in unwilling admiration at the lithe curves in evidence beneath the cotton shirt. Short, blond hair, so pale as to be almost silver, cupped her head like a sleek, silken cap, curling about her cheeks in feathery wisps. Her eyes were deep and luminous as mountain pools touched by moonlight, fringed with—white, scraggly lashes that clumped together unevenly.

He drew back suddenly, a horrid suspicion creeping into his mind. "Who—?" he demanded hoarsely. His gaze traveled down over her pink-tipped nose and firm little chin. "My God, you can't be—"

He noted abstractedly the blush that started in the slender "V" of her throat, exposed by the shirt, and flooded upward until her cheeks and then her whole face matched her nose.

Simon stood abruptly. "Well, well," he said unpleasantly. "If it isn't 'my cousin Jane.'"

Jane stared at him for a long moment, and Simon fancied he could see the thoughts scrambling behind those polished pewter eyes. She drew a long breath, and said finally, "Yes." She continued hastily. "I thank you for coming to my rescue, Lord Simon, although it was not really necessary, after all. That is, I suffered no serious damage, and neither did Talavera."

She flashed him a wide, brilliant smile, and turned to remount her horse.

"One moment, if you please, Miss Burch."

Jane hesitated, with one foot in the stirrup then, sighing, she straightened and turned to face him.

"Might one ask," began Simon, in the tone he had often used on recalcitrant ensigns, "what you are doing in—male garments, riding astride an animal that is obviously not a lady's mount?"

The tone, which had reduced many a junior officer to stammering incoherence, had no noticeable effect on Miss Burch. She merely stiffened her shoulders and re-issued the smile.

"I am forced to agree that the shirt and breeches are not acceptable," she said, "but I was not expecting to meet anyone. One cannot ride with any degree of freedom hampered by a skirt, and I do love to gallop."

"So I noticed."

"If it really oversets you," she said with a martyred air, "I promise not to do it anymore. At least," she added ingeniously, "not when you're likely to be about."

"I see. And what about the neighbors?" snapped Simon. "Or the staff, for that matter?"

"Oh, I am careful to remain unobserved by anyone who might be visiting, and as for the staff, they are quite used to my oddities."

"Which brings me to another point."

Jane's heart plummeted into her worn, scuffed boots. She glanced at Lord Simon from beneath her sparse lashes and her heart gave an uncomfortable lurch. His expression was forbidding, to say the least. He looked very different from the impeccable gentleman who had made his appearance in the Selworth drawing room the day before. His mahogany-colored hair, ruffled by wind and exertion, glinted with golden highlights in the early morning sun. He had rolled up his shirt sleeves, and the expanse of tanned forearm, as well as the muscled frame visible beneath the snowy lawn, created a queer, prickly sensation in the bottom of Jane's stomach.

"I beg your pardon?" she asked distractedly.

"We were discussing your oddities. And I must say, Miss Burch, the marked difference between your appearance this morning and that of yesterday seems extremely odd."

Jane turned swiftly and mounted Talavera. Once seated, she faced him straightly.

"Yes," she said in a low voice, "I suppose I do owe you an explanation. It was—"

"But not now," interrupted Simon, swinging into his own saddle. "I want my breakfast. I shall speak with you later in the study."

Incensed at his peremptory tone of voice, the apology she had been about to utter shriveled on her lips. Tossing her head, she spurred her horse into motion. "Clod!" she murmured to Talavera as the wind whipped tears to her eyes. "Idiot! Arrogant boor!"

Some ten minutes later, however, as she guided her mount into the stable yard, her indignation spent, cold reality seeped in to replace her anger. It was an understatement to say that she had not handled the situation well. Dismounting, she chastised herself. She should not have indulged herself by galloping off in a huff. She should have remained to explain—logically and rationally—to Lord Simon why she had chosen to present herself to him in the guise of a middle-aged spinster. She should have . . . Her shoulders slumped. What on earth could she possibly have said to assuage the man's understandable wrath? He must think her either a complete idiot or the worst kind of schemer. Dear God, what if he sent her away? That would mean the ruin of all her grandiose plans for Jessica and Patience.

She trudged despondently into the house. She would just have to try to repair the damage when she met with Lord Simon later. In the meantime, there was breakfast to get through. Perhaps, by the time she had changed from her breeches, he might have departed the dining room.

She spent some time pacing in front of her wardrobe. Deciding to abandon her padding and tack, she chose one of her own gowns and, having completed her ensemble to her satisfaction, she paused before the mirror. After a moment of indecision, she artificially darkened her brows and lashes to their normal color, a shade of charcoal in startling variance to her silver blond hair. She applied a little salve to her raw, reddened nose, but was forced to admit that only time would heal her abused appendage.

As she entered the breakfast room, her hope that Lord Simon would have finished his breakfast was shattered. He sat at his ease among the remains of a repast of sirloin, eggs and ale, reading *The Times*. Feeling remarkably foolish, she snatched toast and coffee from the sideboard and slid into a place at the table as far away from his lordship as possible. She lifted her eyes with great reluctance, to discover that he sat motionless, a forkful of eggs halfway to his mouth, staring as though he had never seen her before. Which, in point of fact, she thought, he hadn't really.

"G-good morning," she said hesitantly, a flood of heat surging over her cheeks. When Winifred entered the room a moment later, Jane sighed with relief.

"Good morning," caroled Winifred hurrying to the sideboard, where she helped herself to a substantial portion of eggs and York ham. "I hope no one has made any plans for the day because I want to get started on rehearsals for the play. I already have Act One, Scene One blocked out in my mind, but—oh, my goodness! Jane! You're not—" She darted a glance at Simon. "That is—you forgot—"

Jane cast an anguished glance at Simon, who said nothing, merely sending a sardonic glance to each of the young women before returning to his paper. Jane cleared her throat.

"Ah," she began. Her usually quick mind, however, had deserted her and she trailed off into a despairing silence. Once more, Winifred spoke, this time, in a voice pregnant with meaning.

"Jane, dear, I wonder if I might have a word with you." She jerked her head toward the corridor.

At this, Jane forced herself to attention.

"I have just come in from outside, Winifred," she said, her voice brittle in her attempt to keep it steady.

A blank, "What?" was Winifred's immediate response.

"Yes," continued Jane, picking up momentum, "I went out for a gallop before breakfast, and I wore the—the clothes I usually wear to go out, er, galloping, and I met Lord Simon out on the greensward."

"Oh?" said Winifred, her expression still uncomprehending. "Oh," she said again. "O-o-oh," she concluded, her eyes now wide with horror. She glanced at Lord Simon, who was still immersed in *The Times,* apparently oblivious. She lifted her brows in agonized query to Jane, who merely closed her eyes and nodded. The newspaper rustled, and both women jumped.

"Ah, good morning, Miss Timburton," said Simon frigidly. "I wonder, would you take it amiss if I were to call you Winifred? It seems so much simpler, considering our present relationship." Winifred nodded in numb acquiescence. "Good. As for the play, I'm afraid you will have to exclude me from your plans. I will, however, wish to speak with you later in the day regarding your future." With a tight smile he laid *The Times* down on the table and moved toward the door. "I shall bid you ladies good day, then." He bent a look of chilly propriety on Jane. "Miss Burch, I shall see you shortly."

Without waiting for an answer, he closed the door firmly behind him. Winifred immediately swung to her cousin. "Jane!" she shrieked. "What happened? Does he Know All?"

"Of course, he knows," replied Jane tiredly. "I all but fell into his lap, wearing my shirt and breeches."

"Well, what are you going to do?" Winifred's voice lowered only minimally.

"What am *I* going to do? I rather thought you might ask what *we* are going to do, since this whole charade was your idea. However"—Jane lifted a hand against Winifred's incipient protest—"I cannot see where this is anything either one of us can do at the present. Lord Simon will, in all probability, send me packing." She paused suddenly, an arrested expression in her eyes. "Unless—"

"Unless what? Unless what, Jane?"

"Unless I can talk him around, of course. I only hope—"

Her words were cut off by the entrance of the Viscount Stedford.

"Ah, ladies. I thought I would be first down, but I . . ." He trailed off uncertainly, staring at Jane, who nodded in a genteel fashion.

"Good morning, my lord," she said demurely. "I trust you slept well."

"Ur," responded the viscount. "Ah. Oh, yes, very well indeed." His eyes still on Jane, he moved unsteadily to the sideboard and paused for a long moment, still gaping, before turning to procure kippers and eggs.

"Well, said Jane, rising, "do pray excuse me. I'm sure Winifred will keep you well entertained during your meal, my lord. Lord Simon expressed his desire to see me as soon as I finished here. There is something he wishes to discuss with me."

"Is there, by God?" asked Marcus faintly. He sat down at the table with rather a thump, and when the door closed behind Jane, he turned to Winifred in bafflement.

"Ah, about your cousin . . ." he began

From *My Cousin Jane*
by Anne Barbour